HARROW THE NINTH

The Locked Tomb Trilogy

Gideon the Ninth
Harrow the Ninth
Alecto the Ninth (forthcoming)

HARROW THE NINTH

TAMSYN MUIR

A TOM DOHERTY ASSOCIATES BOOK

NEW YORK

HARROW THE NINTH

Edited by Carl Engle-Laird

A Tor.com Book
Published by Tom Doherty Associates
120 Broadway
New York, NY 10271

www.tor.com

Tor® is a registered trademark of
Macmillan Publishing Group, LLC.

The Library of Congress Cataloging-in-Publication Data is available upon request.

ISBN 978-1-250-31322-5 (hardcover)
ISBN 978-1-250-31320-1 (ebook)

Our books may be purchased in bulk for promotional, educational, or business use. Please contact your local bookseller or the Macmillan Corporate and Premium Sales Department at 1-800-221-7945, extension 5442, or by email at MacmillanSpecialMarkets@macmillan.com

First Edition: 2020

Printed in the United States of America

0 9 8 7 6 5 4 3 2 1

for Isa Yap,
who understood Harrow too well,
and without whom so much of me would not have happened

and

for pT

◆

DRAMATIS PERSONAE

The Emperor of the Nine Houses
"A.L.", his guardian

Augustine the First
Alfred Quinque, his cavalier
FIRST SAINT TO SERVE THE KING UNDYING

Mercymorn the First
Cristabel Oct, her cavalier
SECOND SAINT TO SERVE THE KING UNDYING

ORTUS the First
Pyrrha Dve, his cavalier
THIRD SAINT TO SERVE THE KING UNDYING

Cassiopeia the First
Nigella Shodash, her cavalier
FOURTH SAINT TO SERVE THE KING UNDYING

Cyrus the First
Valancy Trinit, his cavalier
FIFTH SAINT TO SERVE THE KING UNDYING

~~Ulysses the First~~
~~*Titania Tetra, his cavalier*~~
SIXTH SAINT TO SERVE THE KING UNDYING

~~Cytherea the First~~
~~*Loveday Heptane, her cavalier*~~
SEVENTH SAINT TO SERVE THE KING UNDYING

~~Anastasia the First~~
~~*Samael Novenary, her cavalier*~~

Ianthe the First
~~*Naberius Tern, her cavalier*~~
EIGHTH SAINT TO SERVE THE KING UNDYING

Harrowhark the First
~~██████████████████████~~
NINTH SAINT TO SERVE THE KING UNDYING

One for the Emperor, first of us all;

One for his Lyctors, who answered the call;

One for his Saints, who were chosen of old;

One for his Hands, and the swords that they hold.

Two is for discipline, heedless of trial;

Three for the gleam of a jewel or a smile;

Four for fidelity, facing ahead;

Five for tradition and debts to the dead;

Six for the truth over solace in lies;

Seven for beauty that blossoms and dies;

Eight for salvation no matter the cost;

Nine for the Tomb, and for all that was lost.

HARROW THE NINTH

prologue

THE NIGHT BEFORE THE EMPEROR'S MURDER

YOUR ROOM HAD LONG AGO plunged into near-complete darkness, leaving no distraction from the great rocking *thump—thump—thump* of body after body flinging itself onto the great mass already coating the hull. There was nothing to see—the shutters were down—but you could feel the terrible vibration, hear the groan of chitin on metal, the cataclysmic rending of steel by fungous claw.

It was very cold. A fine shimmer of frost now coated your cheeks, your hair, your eyelashes. In that smothering dark, your breath emerged as wisps of wet grey smoke. Sometimes you screamed a little, which no longer embarrassed you. You understood your body's reaction to the proximity. Screaming was the least of what might happen.

God's voice came very calmly over the comm:

"Ten minutes until breach. We've got half an hour of air-con left . . . after that, you'll be working in the oven. Doors down until the pressure equalizes. Conserve your temp, everyone. Harrow, I'm leaving yours closed as long as possible."

You staggered to your feet, limpid skirts gathered in both hands, and picked your way over to the comm button. Scanning for something damning and intellectual to say, you snapped: "I can take care of myself."

"Harrowhark, we need you in the River, and while you are in the River your necromancy will not work."

"I am a Lyctor, Lord," you heard yourself say. "I am your saint. I am

13

your fingers and gestures. If you wanted a Hand who needed a door to hide behind—even now—then I have misjudged you."

From his far-off sanctum deep within the Mithraeum, you heard him exhale. You imagined him sitting in his patchy, worn-out chair, all alone, worrying his right temple with the thumb he always worried his right temple with. After a brief pause, he said: "Harrow, please don't be in such a hurry to die."

"Do not underestimate me, Teacher," you said. "I have always lived."

You picked your way back through the concentric rings of ground acetabula you had laid, the fine gritty layers of femur, and you stood in the centre and breathed. Deep through the nose, deep out the mouth, just as you had been taught. The frost was already resolving into a fine dew misting your face and the back of your neck, and you were hot inside your robes. You sat down with your legs crossed and your hands laid helplessly in your lap. The basket hilt of the rapier nudged into your hip, like an animal that wanted feeding, and in a sudden fit of temper you considered unbuckling the damn thing and hurling it as hard as you possibly could to the other side of the room; only you worried how pitifully short it would fall. Outside, the hull shuddered as a few hundred more Heralds assembled on its surface. You imagined them crawling over one another, blue in the shadow of the asteroids, yellow in the light of the nearest star.

The doors to your quarters slid open with an antique exhalation of gas levers. But the intruder did not set off the traps of teeth you'd embedded in its frame, nor the gobbets of regenerating bone you had gummed onto the threshold. She stepped over the threshold with her cobwebby skirts rucked high on her thighs, teetering like a dancer. In the darkness her rapier was black, and the bones of her right arm gleamed an oily gold. You closed your eyes to her.

"I could protect you, if you'd only ask me to," said Ianthe the First.

A tepid trickle of sweat ran down your ribs.

"I would rather have my tendons peeled from my body, one by one, and flossed to shreds over my broken bones," you said. "I would rather be flayed alive and wrapped in salt. I would rather have my own digestive acid dripped into my eyes."

"So what I'm hearing is . . . *maybe*," said Ianthe. "Help me out here. Don't be coy."

"Do not pretend to me that you're here for anything other than to look after an investment."

She said, "I came to warn you."

"You came to *warn* me?" Your voice sounded flat and affectless, even to you. "You came to warn me *now*?"

The other Lyctor approached. You did not open your eyes. You were surprised to hear her crunch through your metrical overlay of bone, to kneel without flinching on the grim and powdery carpet beneath her. You would never sense Ianthe's thanergy, but the darkness seemed to give you an immense attunement to her fear. You felt the hairs rise on the back of her forearms; you heard the hammering of her wet and human heart, her scapulae drawing together as she tensed her shoulders. You smelled the reek of sweat and perfume: musk, rose, vetiver.

"Nonagesimus, nobody is coming to save you. Not God. Not Augustine. Nobody." There was no mockery in her voice now, but there was something else: excitement, perhaps, or unease. "You'll be dead within the first half hour. You're a sitting duck. Unless there's something in one of those letters I don't know about, you're out of tricks."

"I have never been murdered before, and I truly don't intend to start now."

"It's *over* for you, Nonagesimus. This is the end of the line."

You were shocked into opening your eyes when you felt the girl opposite cup your chin in her hands—her fingers febrile compared to the chilly shock of her gilded metacarpal—and put her meat thumb at the corner of your jaw. For a moment you assumed that you were hallucinating, but that assumption was startled away by the cool nearness of her, of Ianthe Tridentarius on her knees before you in unmistakable supplication. Her pallid hair fell around her face like a veil, and her stolen eyes looked at you with half-beseeching, half-contemptuous despair: blue eyes with deep splotches of light brown, like agate.

Looking deep into the eyes of the cavalier she murdered, you realised, not for the first time, and not willingly, that Ianthe Tridentarius was beautiful.

"Turn around," she breathed. "Harry, all you have to do is turn around. I know what you've done, and I know how to reverse it, if only you'd ask me to. Just ask; it's that easy. Dying is for suckers. With you and me at full power, we could rip apart this Resurrection Beast and come away unscathed. We could save the galaxy. Save the Emperor. Let them talk back home of Ianthe and Harrowhark—let them *weep* to speak of us. The past is dead, and they're both dead, but you and I are alive.

"What are they? What *are* they, other than one more corpse we're dragging behind us?"

Ianthe's lips were cracked and red. There was naked entreaty on her face. Excitement, then, not unease.

This was, as you understood it dimly, the psychological moment.

"Go fuck yourself," you said.

The Heralds came plopping down onto the hull like rain. Ianthe's face froze back into its white and mocking mask, and she dropped your jaw—untangled her restless fingers and her awful gold-shod bones.

"I didn't think this was the time for dirty talk, but I can roll with it," she said. "Choke me, Daddy."

"Get *out*."

"You always did think obstinacy the cardinal virtue," she remarked, quite apropos of nothing. "I think now, perhaps, you should have died back at Canaan House."

"You should have killed your sister," you said. "Your eyes don't match your face."

Over the comm, the Emperor's voice came, just as calm as before: "Four minutes until impact." And, like a tutor chiding inattentive children: "Make sure you're in place, girls."

Ianthe turned away without violence. She stood and trailed her human fingers over the wall of your quarters—over the cool filigreed archway, over the polished metal panels and inlaid bone—and said, "Well, I tried, and therefore no one should criticize me," before ducking through the arch to the foyer beyond. You heard the door shut behind her. You were left profoundly alone.

The heat rose. The station must have been completely smothered: wrapped in a squirming shroud of thorax and wing, mandible and antenna, the dead couriers of a hungry stellar revenant. Your communicator crackled with static, but there was only silence at the other end. There was silence in the lovely passageways of the Mithraeum, and there was a hot and sweating silence in your soul. When you screamed, you screamed without sound, your throat muscles gulping mutely.

You thought about the flimsy envelope addressed to you that read, *To open in case of your imminent death.*

"They're breaching," said the Emperor. "Forgive me ... and give it hell, children."

Somewhere far off on the station there was a warping crunch of plex and metal. Your knees became jelly, and you would have collapsed to the floor in a spasm had you not been sitting. With your fingers you closed your eyes, and you wrestled yourself into stillness. The darkness got darker and cooler as the first shield of perpetual bone cocooned you—the act of a fool, meaningless, doomed to dissolve the moment you submerged—then the second, then the third, until you were lost in an airless and impregnable nest. Throughout the Mithraeum, five pairs of eyes closed in concert, one of them yours. Unlike theirs, yours would not open again. In half an hour, no matter what Teacher might hope, you would be dead. The Lyctors of the Resurrecting Emperor began their long wade into the River to where the Resurrection Beast squatted—just out of the orbit of the Mithraeum, half-alive, half-dead, a verminous liminal mass—and you waded with them, but your meat you left vulnerably behind.

"*I pray the tomb is shut forever,*" you heard yourself saying aloud, and you could not bring your voice above a choked whisper. "*I pray the rock is never rolled away. I pray that which was buried remains buried, insensate, in perpetual rest with closed eye and stilled brain. I pray it lives* ... O corse of the Locked Tomb," you extemporised wildly. "Beloved dead, hear your handmaiden. I loved you with my whole rotten, contemptible heart—I loved you to the exclusion of aught else—let me live long enough to die at your feet."

Then you went under to make war on Hell.

* * *

Hell spat you back out. Fair enough.

You did not wake up having passed into the thanergetic space that was the sole province of the dead, and the necromantic saints who fought the dead; you woke up in the corridor outside your rooms, on your side and broiling, gasping for air, soaked right through with sweat—your own—and blood—your own; the blade of your rapier leered through your stomach, punctured through from behind. The wound was not a hallucination or a dream: the blood was wet, and the pain was terrible. Your vision was already curling up black at the edges as you tried to close the rent—tried to sew your viscera shut, cauterize the veins, stabilize the organs whimpering into shutdown— but you were far too gone already. Even if you had wanted it, the *imminent death* letter would not be yours to read. All you could do was lie gasping in a pool of your own fluids, too powerful to die quickly, too weak to save yourself. You were only half a Lyctor, and half a Lyctor was worse than not a Lyctor at all.

Outside the plex, the stars were blocked by the skittering, buzzing Heralds of the Resurrection Beast, beating their wings furiously to roast everything inside. From very far away you thought you heard the ring of swords, and you flinched at each bright scream of striking metal. You had loathed that sound from birth.

You prepared to die with the Locked Tomb on your lips. But your idiot dying mouth rounded out three totally different syllables, and they were three syllables you did not even understand.

₱₳Ɽ₵₲₳₵₴

FOURTEEN MONTHS BEFORE THE EMPEROR'S MURDER

In the myriadic year of our Lord—the ten thousandth year of the King Undying, our Resurrector, the full-pitying Prime!—the Reverend Daughter Harrowhark Nonagesimus sat on her mother's sofa and watched her cavalier read. She idly fretted her thumbnail into a decaying brocade skull on the cover, carelessly destroying in a second long years of labour by some devoted anchorite. The mandible unravelled beneath the pad of her thumb.

Her cavalier sat very upright in the study chair. It had not taken anyone of comparable bulk since his father's day, and was now in danger of a final fatal sag. He had tucked his considerable frame tight within its borders as though breaching them might cause Incident; and she knew full well that Ortus hated Incident.

"*No retainers. No attendants, no domestics,*" read Ortus Nigenad, folding the paper with obsequious care. "Then I will wait on you alone, my Lady Harrowhark?"

"Yes," she said, vowing to keep her patience as long as possible.

"No Marshal Crux? No Captain Aiglamene?"

"In fact, *no retainers, no attendants,* and *no domestics,*" said Harrow, losing her patience. "I believe you've cracked the elaborate code. It will be you, the cavalier primary, and me, the Reverend Daughter of the Ninth House. That's all. Which I find . . . suggestive."

Ortus did not seem to find it suggestive. His dark eyes were downcast behind their thick black lashes, the sort Harrowhark had always fancied you might get on some nice domestic mammal, like a

19

hog. He was perennially downcast, and not out of modesty; the faint crow's feet trampling each eye were lines of sadness; the fine creases at his forehead were a careful act of tragedy. She was glad to see that someone—maybe his mother, the mawkish Sister Glaurica—had painted his face as his father had once painted his own, with a solid black jaw to represent the Mouthless Skull. This was not because she had any especial love for the Mouthless Skull, as paint sacrament went. It was merely because any jawéd skull he affected became a wide white skull with depression.

After a moment, he said abruptly: "Lady, I cannot help you become a Lyctor."

She was only surprised that he dared to offer an opinion. "That's as may be."

"You agree with me. Good. I thank you for your mercy, Your Grace. I cannot represent you in a formal duel, not with the sword, nor the short sword, nor the chain. I cannot stand in a row of cavaliers primary and call myself their peer. The falsehood would crush me. I cannot begin to conceive of it. I will not be able to fight for you, my Lady Harrowhark."

"Ortus," she said, "I have known you my entire life. Did you really think I entertained any delusions that you could be mistaken, in the dark, by a dementia-ridden dog raised with no knowledge of bladed objects, for a *swordsman*?"

"Lady, it is only to honour my father that I call myself a cavalier," said Ortus. "It is for my mother's pride and my House's scarcity that I call myself a cavalier. I have none of a cavalier's virtues."

"I am not sure how many times I must relay to you how truly I am aware of that," said Harrowhark, picking a tiny fragment of jet thread from her fingernail. "Given that it has constituted one hundred percent of our exchanges over the years, I can only assume you are coming to some new point, and begin to feel excitement."

Ortus leant forward on the edge of his chair, his restive, long-fingered hands locking together. His hands were big and soft—all of Ortus was big and soft, like a squashy black pillow—and he spread them open, beseeching. She was intrigued, despite herself. This was more than he had heretofore dared.

"Lady," ventured Ortus, voice deepening with timidity, "I would not venture it—but if a cavalier's duty is to hold the sword—if a cavalier's duty is to protect with the sword—if a cavalier's duty is to die by the sword—have you never considered **ORTUS NIGENAD?**"

"What?" said Harrow.

"Lady, it is only to honour my father that I call myself a cavalier," said Ortus. "It is for my mother's pride and my House's scarcity that I call myself a cavalier. I have none of a cavalier's virtues."

"I feel as though we have had this conversation before," said Harrowhark, pressing her thumbs together, testing with risky pleasure how malleable she might make her distal phalange. One misstep, and her nerves might split. It was an old exercise her parents had set her. "Each time, the news that you have not spent your life in acquiring martial virtues comes as a little less of a shock to me. But have a go. Surprise me. My body is ready."

"I wish that our House had produced some swordsman more worthy of our glory days," said Ortus meditatively, who always found enthusiasm for alternate histories where he was not pressed into service or asked to do anything he found difficult. "I wish that our House had not been diminished to '*those who are fit but to hold their blade in the scabbard.*'"

Harrowhark congratulated herself on not pointing out how this lack of production was directly due to three things: his mother, himself, and *The Noniad*, his ongoing verse epic devoted to Matthias Nonius. She had a vile suspicion that the quotation, around which he had somehow contrived to pronounce quotation marks, was from that very same verse epic, which she knew was already on its eighteenth book and showed no signs of slowing down. If anything it seemed to be gaining momentum, like a very boring avalanche. She was composing a rejoinder when she noticed that a serving sister had arrived in her father's library.

Harrow had not noticed her knocking, or her passage in; this wasn't the problem. The problem was that the sister's ashen paint was decorating the lovely dead face of the Body.

Her palms felt wet. In this scenario, either the sister was real and her face was not, or the sister was herself unreal. One couldn't simply gauge all the osseous mass in the room and do a best guess; bones in meat generated so much deceptive soft thalergy, only a fool would try. She flicked her eyes over to Ortus in the faint hope that he would betray her reality one way or another. But his gaze was still levelled at the ground.

"Our House has received good service from '*those who are fit but to hold their blade in the scabbard,*'" said Harrowhark, keeping her voice even. "Which is not a line that scans, just so you know. Nobody will be surprised to find you a laggard."

"It's enneameter. The traditional form. *Those who are fit but to hold their blade in the scabbard—*"

"That's not nine feet of anything."

"*—never to draw it forth for the battle.*"

"You will train with Captain Aiglamene for the next twelve weeks," said Harrowhark, rubbing her fingers back and forth, back and forth, until the pad of her thumb felt very hot. "You will meet the very minimum that is expected of a Ninth House cavalier primary, which is now, fortunately, that you be as broad as you are tall with arms that can carry a weight. But I need . . . significantly more from you . . . than the edge of a sword, Nigenad."

The serving sister shadowed the edge of Harrow's peripheral vision. Ortus had raised his head and did not acknowledge the sister, which complicated things. He looked at Harrow with the faint kind of pity she always suspected he held her in: the pity that marked him as an outsider in his own House, and would mark him as all the more an outsider in the House of his mother's line. She did not know what made Ortus *Ortus*. He was a mystery too boring to solve.

"What more is there?" he asked, a little bitterly.

Harrowhark closed her eyes, which shut out Ortus's tremulous, worried face and the shadow of the Body-faced serving girl that fell over the desk. The shadow told her nothing. Physical evidence was often a trap. She shut out the new and rusty rapier that now creaked in the scabbard at Ortus's hip. She shut out the comforting smell of dust made hot by the whirring heater in the corner of the room, mixing with the just-milled ink in her inkwell. Tannic acid, human salts.

"This isn't how it happens," said the Body.

Which gave Harrow a curious strength.

"I need you to hide my infirmity," said Harrowhark. "You see, I am insane."

ACT ONE

1

NINE MONTHS BEFORE THE EMPEROR'S MURDER

It was in the close of the myriadic year of our Lord—that far-off King of Necromancers, that blessed Resurrector of Saints!—that you picked up your sword. This was your first big mistake.

The sword hated you to touch it. The long hilt burnt your bare hands as though heated to starlike temperatures. The vacuum of space outside yielded no thanergy and generated no thalergy, but it didn't matter. You no longer needed either. You iced your palms over with thick bands of cartilage, and you tried again.

Now the grip seemed cold as death, and it was just as heavy. You lifted, and your elbows locked, and you grasped the pommel to try to steady yourself. You tried a new trick—you slipped a narrow ribbon of bone up from your living metacarpal and eased the fragment gently around the flexor tendon, and you pierced it through the back of your hand. You didn't flinch. It was never your way. From there you unfolded long fingers of bone to grasp the handle, then more, to grasp it again; you lifted it, in a manner of speaking, assisted by a seething, clattering basket of eight phalanx articulates.

So now you could wobble the sword up in an obtuse angle before yourself. You waited. You felt nothing: no understanding, no mastery, no knowledge. You were just a necromancer, and it was just a sword. It fell away from your hands and clattered to the floor, and you folded in half, and you upchucked violently all over the hospital tiles.

There were many uniformed people in that room, but they were used to these antics. Harrowhark the First, ninth saint to serve the Emperor Undying, might throw up as much as she cared to. You were a walking sacrament, even if your early contributions to Lyctorhood seemed to be finding new and different ways to puke. They only intervened if it looked like you might choke to death on your own vomit, a mercy that you always vaguely thought a shame.

* * *

The first time the man you called God had delivered you the sword—in what seemed to you his aspect of the Kindly Prince, intending only gentleness—you'd fallen into a deep stupor from which you had never really risen. Maybe the sword had reified your grief into six feet of steel. You had loathed that thrice-damned blade from sight, which might have been unfair before you knew it loathed you in return.

You kept trying to wield it, all the same. Each touch ended with the contents of your stomach splattered colourfully on the floor. Your days dissolved like ashes in front of a fan—scattered beyond any hope of retrieval—blown back into your face or fluttering upward beyond your grasp. Sometimes you would rise, and you'd take up the blade, as though in expectation of something. Nothing ever happened; you felt nothing except the sword's enormous, empty hate of you, which you knew to be real, even then. You and the sword would seethe in your mutual bitterness and fury, and then you would end up with blistered hands and a floor's worth of vomit.

Details sat at awkward angles to one another. You'd been in this bed some time, wearing clothes that weren't yours. Occasionally ticklish rasps at your ears or forehead would frighten you numb before you realised it was your own hair. Away from Drearburh shears, it grew in a way that was almost debauched. You would cut it yourself and still find irregular little licks of it tucked behind your ears—or maybe you had not cut it at all. Sometimes, in reaching up to it, you would then recall that you had no robe or skeletal mask. Nobody had given you any paint and there wasn't a stick of grease on board the whole ship, though even if there had been it would not have been blessed properly. The first time this happened, in your hot upset and shame, you ripped a sheet to shreds and covered your head with that. This still left most of your forehead nude, discounting the hair. Also, you were wearing a bedsheet. You took the poetic way out and used a black vestal's last-choice gambit: you opened a vein and, trembling neither from pain nor blood loss, daubed blind upon your skin the sacramental skull of the Inglorious Mask.

The uniformed attendants were always busy with things that weren't you. Sometimes you were humbly prevailed upon to sit up and part your ad-hoc veil to struggle through a bowl of clear soup, though those memories were doubtful fragments. It did not seem right that you could ever eat again. Sometimes people would move all around you, and you lay supine on your cot, astonished and shivering before the vista of stars out the window. The thick plex barrier seemed too light and frangible to keep you safe. Beyond it the great black throat of space bared itself to you, which frightened you beyond sense. At these times you fell in and out of sleep, somehow. You had long since ceased to care for human voices, which only talked nonsense: they would murmur their prayers of *Three thousand units— replenish, that's on the provision list—dump that stock, munitions will take it.*

In your old life you might have been curious. But other noises haunted you, quite apart from the ones occurring to your ears. There was a great unmusical straining aboard ship—the sounds of wet drums—which had panicked you before you'd realised, with settling calm, that you were hearing the heave of seven hundred and eight beating hearts. You heard seven hundred and eight brains, thrumming in their cerebral fluid. You knew without checking that three hundred and four of those straining hearts belonged to necromancers; a necromancer's heart myocardium flexed differently to your ears, worked worse, squeezed more feebly. You were sensing the living. Once you worked out what you were hearing, you became aware of everything immediate to you: the dust settling on the gleaming black plaques of the floor; the roiling of your pulmonaries; the soft marrow of your bones sucking up oxygen. Despite all this cacophony, you could not stay awake.

Sometimes you found yourself standing, gorge risen, staring at the great sword left untidy and naked on the floor. You would not remember rising. You would not remember how you had come to be there. Sometimes you would forget who you were, and at recalling yourself, weep like a child.

In these digestions of time the Body would come. She would put her cool, dead hands on your forehead and close your pumping eyelids with her fingertips, so that you could not see the sword nor the people.

This was great honour. This was great mercy. She always came to you now with such easy forbearance, and you were so grateful for it, you were so relieved. The Body's hands were grey with death and they were so soft and familiar on your skin, so much so that you were absolutely sure you could really feel them; that this time around, the dead caress was tangible. And when the Body turned so that you could see her face you were amazed, as ever, by that beauty unblemished by breath.

Then she would draw you back to your bed and direct you to sleep. For the Body you tried to be obedient, for once in your benighted life; it seemed beneath you not to. When the Body appeared time could be relied upon to work as it ought, rather than melting away like chips of ice only to reappear in unexpected places. But at these times your brain kept nagging itself to stay conscious. The fact that the Body had come to you now seemed tremendously important, if only you could stay awake long enough to figure out why.

And your face itched from the dried blood, and all around you the people whispered, *Thousand kilos of osseo—old—keep that, that's the first thing we run out of— No, Sergeant, ditch it; we're behind schedule already.*

* * *

Your world was a white and sterile box. This box was the hospital quarter on board the *Erebos*. The *Erebos* was the Behemoth-class flagship of the Emperor Undying. These facts you held on to like an asphyxiating man to a last lungful of air. You lived in a cool, colourless room of dismantled beds and cartons, and you had for your own a bed and a chair and a sword. They had tried to remove your sword, once—they had tried to take it away on some pretext you could not exactly remember—and you were perturbed in some distant way by that memory, which was red, and wet, and ill defined.

They no longer touched your two-hander. It appeared and reappeared around the room wherever you had dropped it, usually accompanied by the mysterious smell of upchuck. You now slept beside it, like it was your large steel infant. Truth be told you would have been happy hurling the thing straight into the hot heart of Dominicus, as it was loathsome to you and you were convinced it wanted to do you harm; but it was very important that it should not be placed in anyone else's hand.

This didn't stop you from dulling the blade, nicking the polish, and altogether fucking up the edge, as you vaguely knew you were. You knew so little about swords—you had never bothered to ask; you could barely differentiate between them. Some were narrow. Some were broad. Some were big, some were small. This two-handed soldier's sword was huge and aberrant and frankly malicious, and utterly your responsibility—even if you could not touch it without power-heaving.

Sometimes you knelt by your bed and tried to pray. With the Body there, you had nobody to thank and no intercession to request. Your greatest peace you found in that half-asleep, druglike state on the bed, holding your heartbeat low before the cold white stars, sick with a fury you kept forgetting existed and were corrupted by possessing. Around you, people would go back and forth, giving you the widest berth possible, ignoring you so entirely that at one point you were convinced you were dead. With that conviction, you had felt only intense relief.

2

GOD STOOD IN YOUR DOORWAY and said, "You've thrown up again, Harrowhark."

You always tried to thrust yourself back into full consciousness for the Emperor of the Nine Houses, who regularly had the grace to knock on the door and wait for entry to be granted, proving by itself his divinity. He stood now at the threshold with his ever-present flimsy and ever-present tablet; a cluster of uniformed people tailed him, but his monstrous eyes, oil on carbon, were only for you. "You're losing all your muscle," he said, "and you didn't have much to start with."

Your mouth said, with gratifying clarity: "Why does a Lyctor need a sword? Lord, what use can we have of one? I can control bone. I can shape flesh and evoke spirit. I no longer need outside thanergy. Why anything so crude as a *sword*?"

"Nice to hear you're feeling better," he said. "I'm not going to talk philosophy with you, not when you've spent the last three hours venting your gut." (Had you?) "I'm not a monster. Go rinse your teeth. I don't care that you can fill your own cavities, not looking after those things seems wasteful."

Swaying on your feet, you rose from the bed like a ghost from the tomb and went over to the nearby sink, where you parted your shitty veil and resentfully rinsed your teeth with antiplaque. There was an urgent murmuring from the asteroid belt of aggravated Cohort officers, with the Emperor saying, "Yes," then, "No," and "Don't bother with new plating. They'll be using the *Erebos* for transport."

Another officer said, "My gracious lord, the loyal Saint of Joy . . ."

"Has not yet learned to wait," said God. "Hold the comms. I answered three of them just this morning."

"But her order countermands—"

"A Lyctor's order is the order of God and should be carried out with the same grace you would have honoured me with," he said. "Except for right now. Station the last person to graduate Trentham on the stele and tell them to make static noises if she keeps it up."

"Lord?"

"Air blown through the teeth, tongue high, hand flaps up and down over the mouth. Sounds suspect, I know, but she's never caught on when I've done it."

You spat into the sink. In the mirror, you perceived the Body, waiting quietly beside you; she wore a turquoise hospital shift exactly the same as your own, her hair shimmered over with frost, her exquisite mouth a hard and ready line. There was a sword strapped to the Body's back—you met God's gaze in the mirror, and for a moment you were convinced he could see her too, that he beheld you both— but it was a trick of the eye.

"Harrowhark," he said, "I would like you to come with me."

The grave and unslept faces of the officers surrounding him gave a sort of communal wince. One said, very low and very quiet: "Forgive me, Kindly Prince, but let me bring to your awareness that the Admiral of the Dead Sea and the Admiral of the Ceaseless Fleet began their meeting . . . ten minutes ago."

The Emperor said: "No meeting will raise eighteen thousand dead. I need time with Harrowhark the First. Please attend to me in the Old Chamber ten minutes hence."

The attachés drifted apart as though they had suddenly lost fixity, all moving down the corridor at barely less than a run. You were afraid someone might take your sword away from you if you left it; rather than lifting it, you lay down next to where it glowered at you blackly from the bed. You rolled over *onto* its flat steel breadth and bound crisscross straps of dense bone across your back, around the blade, around the hilt. Straining beneath its weight, with nothing but a ripped-up sheet to mask you, pathetic in your turquoise nudity, you found yourself accompanying the Emperor down long black corridors, trying to fix yourself in time and space.

You were basically naked. The sword weighed you down so much that you were affecting a hump. Your Inglorious Mask was a patchwork of flaking osteology. You looked like an imbecile.

God was murmuring to himself: "Please . . . as though any Admiralty meeting ever ended after twenty minutes."

You said, with difficulty: "What is happening to me?"

"You've had a shock," said the Emperor, which was not an answer, actually.

"Does this happen to all new Lyctors?"

"Some of them," he said vaguely, which did not fill you with relief. His tablet started to softly peep, and after a cursory glance he shoved it in his pocket. "How are you feeling right now?"

You had no room for personal feeling right then. You were assaulted by the sensory data from seven hundred and eight pulmonary muscles. Every body on board felt like the awareness of a meal cooking, a good smell, a pillar of something hot and rich. Their thanergy and thalergy rippled in and around each other like a bloom, or like light playing over metal. And there were more: you could hear on the edge of your senses a deeper, sleeping seethe of life and death, a huge body count, but muffled. You felt the dead in some onboard morgue—ten bundles of discrete dead, of thanergy with the rot of thalergy arrested, snap-frozen. The stillness of this thanergy was profound: not even a body in ice was so still.

You realised that the Body had stopped moving, and that the Emperor was waiting quietly for you.

You said, "I'm very tired of this convalescence, Lord."

"If I had it my way it would take months, not weeks," he said. "I would let you come back, bit by bit, until you felt entirely ready to wake up. I can't. I mastered Death, Harrowhark; I wish I'd done the smarter thing and mastered Time. I have to ask you to get ready soon, and so I am going to show you something I hope might . . . trigger your readiness."

You were deeply and gravely relieved by his understanding, by his tact. It kept you awake and alive all throughout your trip down the elevator, even though the elevator took full minutes to sail through the enormity of the *Erebos*. You had never seen anything so fresh and new. You focused on the lovely silver-and-black chasing on the metal boards, the inlaid panels of rainbow colour, the skull above the door that some artistic adept had fashioned into the skull of the First; someone's bones beautifully moulded into that central sign with the eight answering Houses around it. The skull of your House looked plain and silent next to the others. Soft dark hangings obscured the plex and the metal and the antiquated LED gleam of electronics.

Then the doors whispered open to a cavernous, echoing space where an overhead speaker was announcing, "*Our God the Emperor sees fit to grace the second cargo hold,*" and you perceived many people moving away—stray Cohort officers in their white jackets making themselves scarce, bowing quickly, stopping their work to leave their lord in privacy. Their scuttling footsteps sounded like fleeing animals.

You were on a steel-frame balcony overlooking a field of hundreds and hundreds of oblong boxes. Each was a body long and half a body tall, and all were constructed of bone—their lines and ranks so dizzyingly even that it took you a while to comprehend them, as your eyes kept wavering and crossing. The chill breeze of the recyc air ruffled your smock and goose-pimpled your thighs, but the cold kept you conscious, and you wanted to be conscious. The bone of the boxes gleamed less purely white than the amalgam metal and plasticised panels that made up the sides of the hold, and the bone was topped with a soft transparent skin so taut and fine you could see through it, and through it was—

"My promised gift. Your renewed House," said the Emperor.

When he looked at your face, he cautioned you gently: "It's a little under five hundred, and only a third will display necromantic aptitude, and the same for their next generation. They're all between the ages of fifteen and forty, which I thought was easiest."

"Oh my God," you said, forgetting that the deity in question was right there. "The ancient dead. You've committed resurrection."

He said, "No. I haven't truly resurrected anyone in ten thousand years. But at that time . . . I set many aside, for safety . . . and I've often felt bad about just keeping them as insurance. They've been asleep all this myriad, Harrow, and it's frankly a relief to my mind to wake them up. I'll begin the process of bringing them to the surface before they're shipped off to the Ninth."

You unpinned your cloth mask so that you could look with your whole face, only a little ashamed to show it so nakedly to the Emperor. He, after all, had seen it before. A sick hope rose in you like nitrogen bubbles in a diver, and you forgot yourself: "Let me go with them," you said. "Not long. Just enough to introduce them to my House—my seneschal—enough time to tell them—"

"Slow down, Harrowhark," he said. "We must talk, you and I, before you ask me for that. I only wish I had more time to explain."

You took the chilly metal stairs two at a time, feeling your heart ram against serous pericardium, feeling the slim covers of the steps chafing your bare feet. Sharpened by the pain, you wandered between the rows of your silent, sleeping people. You paused over their cradles and stared through the blurry films of skin, with their little radiating burses of veins and cells, at each face in turn. You tried to commit each one to memory, but their features blended together in one amalgam, one sea of strangers newly Ninth. You drifted a little, overawed and dizzy. The Body followed, exactly one half step behind, hand dead calm on the small of your back.

The Emperor kept a respectful distance between himself and his handiwork as you and the Body peered into each casket. Eventually the ranks of bone-and-skin boxes terminated in a clearing of their smaller, more colourful siblings. These were formed of white stone, not osseous matter, and were so freshly carved that the powder of their planing still clung to the sides. They were all of different shapes: some the six-sided funerary box of the deep burial, some the compact hexagon of the ossuary. All were draped in the spectrum of House colours, lacking only black—no empty coffins for your House tonight—except for one plain casket to the side. A little household rose sat atop it, shedding milky blush petals on the stone.

These were the corpses you were aware of before: each a crisp, silent slice of thanergy, without even a flicker of bacterial thalergy pattering over their skins. They were statuesque and incorruptible. The Emperor's doing, maybe. But some of them were aberrant. You stared with calm vacuity at a six-sided container draped with the Second House's scarlet and white, which had no human remains inside. The single casket covered in tissue the gorgeous gold of the Third had no one from the Third in residence. Nor could you locate bodies within either of the plain grey-sheeted hexagons intended for the Sixth, though there were pitiable scraps and remains in one: leavings only, much less than a corpse. Something flickered in your nervous system that was a bit like an emotion, but it struggled and died, much to your relief.

You were aware of the Body standing a little way behind you, quite close beside the Emperor. You said: "How will you explain the missing corpses?"

"Among the dubious privileges of the First House," said God, "is that one is rarely forced to explain."

"The cavaliers—"

"Have joined their Lyctors," he said. "It's not really a lie. It's simply a flattening of an awesome . . . and sacramental . . . truth."

You said nothing. He said, "We went over Canaan House with a fine-tooth comb when we picked you up. We found nobody alive and no more remains, and whatever end came to those we can't account for—if an end has come to them—is a mystery I plan on solving. Until then, I have declared them dead. Call me premature, but I'd rather the Houses weep now, Harrowhark, with room for later rejoicing."

It was the plain, uncovered coffin you stared at, the one with the waxy little rose; you suddenly understood which ancient cancerous corpse was frozen within. Your nervous system tried to process many emotions at once and then shut down entirely. The Body came and turned your face away, but she could not turn back the sudden access of patchwork memory.

The Emperor said gently, "She needs to go home, Harrow."

You did not look. "And will the Seventh House accept her?"

"That was never home," he said. "I am taking Cytherea back to sleep with her brothers and sisters."

You ached. You burnt. The Body's fingernails ran a smooth, cool rill down your hot cheek, and she made you look instead at the bone-and-skin boxes behind you, at the dead who were only sleeping now and had been privy to the oldest miracle you knew. Part of your promise had been fulfilled. You wanted to be relieved, but no longer recalled how that worked, glandularly speaking.

Now you and God stood facing each other. You could study him without shyness: the shining iridescence of his irises, the unyielding black of the cornea and pupil, the long, square, urbane face. God had very deep lines at his forehead and beneath his eyes. His brows were somewhat sorrowful, but the rest of his face was humourous and mobile, plain and normal. The cool white lights of the docking bay picked out all the parts on his shirt that were shiny with wear, and cast the warm browns of his hands and face into an everyday ochre. If you had seen him and not known you would have thought him utterly nondescript; but you could not look at him and not know. Terrible divinity clung to his skin.

"You could resurrect them," you said, without bothering to filter much between thought and speech. "You alone are capable of it. But you won't. Why?"

"For the same reason that I haven't for ten thousand years," he said. "For the same reason that I cannot come back to the Nine Houses. The cost is too great."

You swayed a little. Maybe you fell. The metal grille was beneath your knees, making red sore marks in your flesh, the air through the grate reeking of antistatic pastes. You said into the panels, "Teach me, Lord, how to count that cost."

God helped you up instead. He put his hands beneath your arm-pits in a perfectly normal way and raised you to stand, and clasped your arms clumsily—a quick, awkward squeeze, as though wanting to comfort and not knowing how—before he took his hands away. He said, "Harrow, you won't kneel to me. I won't let you, not until you know exactly what it means when you do it. It hurts me to see you perform obeisance when—if you knew the full story—you might strike me full in the face instead."

You coloured at that, and protested, "My God—"

"And you shouldn't call me God either," he said. "You don't comprehend the word, and I don't want to be God to you yet. You're an invalid, not a disciple. Listen to me. Can you do that? I hate to push you, Harrowhark, but we have so little time."

This was not to be borne. "I still maintain *some* of my faculties, Lord."

"Well, that's all anyone can hope for," he said.

You propped yourself up against the coffin that did not contain Coronabeth Tridentarius, as it was a heavy slab that couldn't be hurt by your leaning on it. The sword was making your back ache. The Kindly Prince watched you try to stand, your shoulders bowing beneath the steel, and then he said: "Harrow, we're still just outside the Dominicus system. Once you're better, we will send the *Erebos* to the Ninth House, and it will deliver what I said to you it would deliver. Then it will go from House to House to give them back their dead— but I won't be on it. You can choose to part ways with me. Or you can come with me as my Hand. In a real sense, it's up to you."

You tried to remember what you had said when you had first woken up aboard the *Erebos;* what you had said when first faced with your Resurrector. But you couldn't. "I chose—"

"In ignorance," he said. "It was no choice. Listen."

He went to half-lean against the bulkhead closest to the plain coffin, put his tablet atop it, and let his hand rest upon the unadorned surface quite close to the little rose. The Emperor said, "Harrowhark, what happens when somebody dies?"

It was a crèche question. You ought to have been able to answer it in the same way other people walked or breathed, which was why you found it difficult. The simplicity seemed a trap. You dug your thumbnail into the top of your thigh until it squelched all the capillaries beneath the skin, and you said: "Apopneumatism. The spirit is forced from their body. The initial thanergy bloom occurs."

"Why?"

"Thalergetic decay causes cellular death," you said carefully, pressing the nail in harder, "which emits thanergy. The massive cell death that follows apopneumatism causes a thanergetic cascade, though the first bloom fades and the thanergy stabilises within thirty to sixty seconds."

"What happens to the soul?"

"In the case of gradual death—senescence, illness . . . certain other forms—transition is automatic and straightforward. The soul is pulled into the River by liminal osmosis. In cases of apopneumatic shock, where death is sudden and violent, the energy burst can be sufficient to countermand osmotic pressure and leave the soul temporarily isolated. Whence we gain the ghost, and the revenant."

"And what has a soul?"

You weren't going to last the distance. The questions were beginning to sound stupid, or sophistic. The Body watched you with careful, filmy eyes. "Anything with a thalergetic complexity significant enough to . . . have a soul. So, humanity."

The Emperor drummed his fingertips atop the plain coffin, and he said, a little whimsically: "*Why have we not an immortal soul? I would give gladly all the hundreds of years that I have to live, to be a human being only for one day.*"

This threw you utterly. "I— Pardon?"

"Harrowhark, *think*," he said, which reminded you very unwelcomely of someone. You gave your thumbnail a better edge, sharpened the dead keratin to a point, and finally drew blood. "What else has an enormously complex mass of thalergy? What's the role of a Cohort necromancer?"

Your brain bowed out disgracefully, but something of the old Harrowhark remained, enough to stand there and ask questions. You were grateful for your impertinent ghost-self to ask: What *was* the role of a Cohort necromancer? Better to ask the purpose of a Cohort swordswoman: to support the necromancer, to provide the death and the thanergy to begin the cycle for necromantic magic to work. Foreign planets were never thanergy planets; they possessed dilute thanergy, of course, but fundamentally they were thalergenic in character. Send a necromancer down there and she would be largely useless. Thanergy really came from—

More to the Body than to him, you said: "A planet's a ball of dust. Its thalergy comes from the accumulation of microbial life. You can't consider it one coherent system."

"Call it a communal soul," said her Emperor. "What's a human being, other than a sack of microbial life? You're a bone adept, aren't you? Flesh magicians are exposed to this idea of a system earlier than in your school." This was kindly, even humourously said, but you still found that you immediately wanted to be tossed out the airlock at the idea that your aptitude made you less than a *flesh magician:* someone whose entire education was in the carnal. Experts in things that were yellow, and wobbled. People who thought there was something really interesting to be found in *meat.*

He mistook your deeply bigoted hate for disbelief, and said: "Just accept the proposition for now that a planet has an enormous single amount of thalergy. If this thalergy is converted, what might happen during that transition?"

"We already know what happens," you said. Your tongue was growing thick in your mouth, and your eyelids were sore and swollen from wanting to close. The first rush of adrenaline had run its course. The Body came and took your wrist in her hand and ringed her fingers around your bones, quite tightly. This let you say: "The Cohort prepares a planet for necromancy every time they have to breach it. Over time, with the introduction of thanergetic decay, the planet converts. Necromancy proceeds as normal afterward. Nothing *happens* . . . plant and animal life both change, of course . . . and eventually the planet flips totally and the population has to be moved, but that's such a long-term process that it takes generations. You can't quantify it as something *happening*."

"Now kill the planet all at once," said her Emperor. "What then?"

You looked at him. The Emperor of the Nine Houses raised his hands, palms up, as though offering a helpless prayer to the roof of the cargo hold. His alien eyes were cool and calm. You knew of only one mass dying-off of planets.

So you said: "You tell me, Lord. You were there for the Resurrection."

"Yes," he said. "And I saw the thalergy convert immediately. The difference between dying of illness and dying from murder. An enormous shock, the immediate expulsion of the soul. And just as when a soul is ripped untimely from a human being, when a soul is so rudely taken from a planet—"

Sweat came to the centres of your palms totally unbidden. A trickle of blood started down your leg, and you stopped it in midflow, dried it to flakes on your skin, and clotted the breach. Such an act took no effort now.

"A revenant," you said.

"Always a revenant," he said. "Every single time, a goddamned revenant. Pardon the pun."

You fancied you could see the Body breathing, her chest rising very slightly, in and out. The Emperor crossed his arms and stared across the cargo hold, his face lit from beneath by electric lighting, the gleam in his eyes black and wet. You caught him moistening his lips with the tip of his tongue.

"We called them Resurrection Beasts," he said.

It took him another moment to continue, and when he did, it was with the air of a man telling a very old story. "When the system died . . . when I was younger, those ten thousand years ago, and I brought us back from that brink—all those revenants scuttled off to the farthest parts of the universe, as the soul runs from its corpse in the blind first fear of transition. I have never seen a planet make another in the same way; I've seen lesser monsters—minor Beasts—but nothing, *nothing*, like that first wave.

"Harrowhark, those revenants move through the universe, inexorably, without pause . . . and they feed on thalergenic planets as they go, like vampires . . . and they won't stop until I and the Nine Houses are dead. They have had me on the run for a myriad, and they're nearly impossible to take down."

This made very little impact on you. It had the dim and nonsensical ring of a fairy story. You said, "The Lyctors have died . . . fighting these things?"

"Fighting them?" said God. "Harrow, I've lost half my Lyctors *distracting* them. They're hideously complex to destroy. The ones we've killed, we killed through luck—they were young, and we were at full power—and then . . . once our numbers thinned out . . . by sheer accident, or by suicide mission."

"How many revenants *are* there?"

You prepared for an astronomical number. The Body raised its eyebrows when the Emperor Undying said, "Three.

"There were nine. We called them by number. Over ten thousand years, we have managed to take out a grand total of five. Number Two fell soon after the Resurrection. Number Eight cost a man's immortal soul, and—I still see that day in my dreams. Number Six died because one of my Hands—Cyrus—drew it into a ultramassive black hole, and Number Six had *better* be dead, because Cyrus won't be coming back."

Before you could do anything—exclaim, or question his mathematics, which did not hold up even on first acquaintance—he did something dreadful. The Emperor of the Nine Houses pushed himself away from the plain coffin with the rose and he stood before you at the Third's, with his monstrous eyes and his ordinary face, and he took both of your hands in his. He patted them gently, as though you were a child whose pet had been squashed in a tragic accident. It would have been preferable for him to rip your ribs from their costal cartilage and waggle them around. It would have been preferable for him to take your throat beneath his hands and snap your neck. There were bright lights in your vision. You were deeply distressed.

"The choice I offered you was always a false one," he said. "I'm sorry. The Resurrection Beasts always know where I am, and wherever I am they turn themselves to me and start moving . . . slowly . . . but never stopping. And they don't turn to me alone, though they focus on me most strongly. They hunt whoever has committed the—indelible sin."

You stared at him. He dropped his hands.

You said, "*Which* indelible sin?"

"The one you committed when you became a Lyctor," said the Emperor.

You heard, dimly, the doors of Drearburh close. You perceived the grind of their mechanism and their indelible *clang,* the echo of their shutting ringing throughout the bottom atrium and upward into the tunnel shaft. Then your memories of it muddied and disappeared, back with the rest of your unsorted collection.

"They will be coming for me," you said, and you said the words only because you thought you ought to make them come true. "If I returned to my House they would follow me there."

He said, "No Lyctor has ever returned home, once we understood the repercussions . . . no Lyctor except one, who knew I would come to intercept her for that very reason."

You looked at her plain coffin again. It was not particularly large; the body it held was not tall or broad, nor imposing, nor grand. You found yourself saying distantly: "And so the intention is to teach me how to fight these things?"

"Not before I teach you how to *run,*" said the Emperor. "It's a rough lesson to learn. It's never complete. But I've been running for ten thousand years . . . so I will be your teacher."

After a moment he laid his hands on your shoulders, and you found yourself looking up into his weird and ordinary face.

"What he is saying," said the Body distinctly, "is that you have to learn that sword."

You looked at her, over his shoulder. The Emperor instinctively followed your gaze, but he could never have seen what you saw: the weals where the chains had passed around the other girl's wrists, neck, ankles. He would not perceive that long hair hanging wetly over her shoulders, that resinous colour that in death might have been brown or might have been gold or might have been anything. He could not have heard the voice—low, husky, musical—or its dry and uncanny echo of other voices you had known: your mother's, Crux's.

He would not know that in truth the Body of the Locked Tomb had not spoken to you since the night you massaged the purple, swollen clots of blood out of the necks of your dead parents, so that their strangulation might not be so obvious. He would not know that you had only walked with her one tranquil year, and trysted with her afterward only in your dreams. He could not possibly know that in your youth her eyes had often been black, like yours were, but that ever since you had writhed in Lyctoral agony her eyes had turned a yellow that made you dizzy to behold: a bronzed, hot, animal yellow, as amber as the inside of an egg.

When you were ten years old, the Body was quiet and rigorous, practical and merciful. At fourteen the Body was tender and serene, and sometimes smiled. When you were sixteen the Body was resolute and impassioned. In all these incarnations, she had preserved her vow of silence. Now the sound of her voice meant the madness had returned to you in full.

"I can't," you said, as carefully as possible. "I can't, beloved. It's gone."

The Emperor said, "Harrow?" but you'd mostly forgotten he was there.

"You are walking down a long passage," said the Body. "You need to turn around."

"I am standing in the dark," you told her. Each of the Body's eyelashes was wet with frost. "I lost it. It's gone. There's nothing there. I must have misapprehended the process. I am half a Lyctor. I am nothing, I am pointless, I am unmanned."

Hands fell heavy on your shoulders. You looked from the face you loved to the face of the Resurrecting King.

"Ortus Nigenad did not die for nothing," he said.

As he spoke, his mouth looked strange. A hot whistle of pain ran down your temporal bone. Your body was numb to grief; perhaps you had felt it once, but you did not feel it anymore. "Ortus Nigenad died thinking it was the only gift he was capable of giving," you said, "and I have wasted it—like—air."

The Resurrecting King took on the expression of a man working out a very difficult and emotionally taxing anagram. He said, "Ortus," again, but the bile was sputtering up into your throat, your mouth, before the Body passed her hand over your eyebrows and the bridge of your nose and you slipped from his imperial grip. You fell almost senseless to the floor.

"Ortus Nigenad," said the Emperor again, almost wondering; but then you knew nothing more, except that you hadn't thrown up on God, which had to count as consolation.

THE REVEREND DAUGHTER Harrowhark Nonag-
esimus ought to have been the 311th Reverend Mother of her line. She
was the eighty-seventh *Nona* of her House; she was the first Harrowhark. She was named for her father, who was named for his mother,
who was named for some unsmiling extramural penitent sworn into
the silent marriage bed of the Locked Tomb. This had been common.
Drearburh had never practiced Resurrection purity. Their only aim
was to keep the necromantic lineage of the tomb-keepers unbroken.
Now all its remnant blood was Harrow; she was the last necromancer, and the last of her line left alive.

Her birth had been expensive. Eighteen years ago, in order to
wrench a final bud from this terminal axil, her mother and father
had slaughtered all the children of their House in order to secure a
necromantic heir. Harrow had been created in that hour of pallor
mortis, while the souls of her peers were fumbling to escape their
bodies, her genesis their ignition of thanergy as they died with a
simultaneity her parents had agonised to calculate. None of this had
been kept from her. It had been explained to Harrow, year after year,
right from the time she knew both when to speak and when to not.
This skill came early to Ninth House infants.

As a child, she was allowed to pull down the coverlet and get into
bed only after she had worked her way through forty-five minutes of
evening prayers, bracketed by her wretched great-aunts Lachrimorta
and Aisamorta. They had been strict with her infant catechism, and
their presence was a strong motivation for Harrow to get her prayers
exactly right and not start over, as they smelled like incense and tooth

decay. She had enunciated clearly—no lisping—devotions of their own devising: *The Tomb I will serve till the end of my days, and then see me buried in two hundred graves . . .* which they'd thought sweetly whimsical, just right for a little girl.

Otherwise, Harrowhark was left completely to her own devices. She would rise well before First Bell and pray in the chapel before they turned on the heating, her fingers much too cold to count her prayer beads, and then she would ensconce herself in one of the libraries with a battery lantern and a blanket and her books. She embarked on her study of necromancy alone: the dead were her mentors and tutors. Harrow had no idea how difficult it was to understand the work of adult necromancers, which meant she did not fear trying to under-stand it. Her development suffered from neither ego nor apprehen-sion. Her parents would sometimes have her recite her theorems of an evening, or make her conjure ulnar bones from a skeleton ground up to powder; or they would have their elderly marshal, Crux, heave some recent corpse over the top tier to squash right to the bottom, and have her fuse the bones back together blind, through the dermis and meat. Then they would open up the body to see how well or badly she had done, but either way their approval was mostly relief. In her genius, they had received the goods that they had so dearly paid for.

Crux told her that her parents had been different, once. This must have been before they committed a little light child massacre. Harrow had been dimly interested in this factoid; she could never recall her parents being anything but exhausted, their joy all spent. Her mother rarely spoke, or if she did, addressed all her remarks to their hulk-ing cavalier, a man who looked as though he would weep if he could only figure out how. Her most vivid memory of her mother was of her hands guiding Harrow's over an inexpertly rendered portion of skull, her fingers encircling the fat baby bracelets of Harrow's wrists, tightening this cuff to indicate correct technique.

Her father had been the more voluble of the two. In the evenings he read to his little family, sometimes sermons and sometimes an-tique family letters. That was another rare memory: the electric light strung up behind her father's chair, her sat on a three-legged stool next to her mother, her father's voice a drone unceasing until a touch from his cavalier indicated that he might stop. Harrow would shrug herself inside her black-hooded church robe and practice moulding tiny motes of bone between her finger and thumb, pressing them into soft fingerprints, mentally chopping her body into two hundred relic pieces.

Then everything changed, abruptly, forever. Harrowhark fell in love.

* * *

"Falling" was not the right term, precisely. It was a long process. She more correctly climbed down into love, picked its locks, opened its gates, and breached its inner chamber.

Her life had been dedicated to the Locked Tomb, and what was interred within had commanded her whole attention since she understood what it was: the comatose corpse that lay in state amid the tatters of the Ninth House. She'd been taught to love the Emperor, who ten thousand years ago had given them all release from a death that none of them had deserved, and to view the Tomb as symbol of his victory and his demise. Her mother and father feared what lay consigned to that locked-up grave. Her tedious great-aunts worshipped it, but in desperation, as though their collective awe might flatter it into sparing God. They had never wanted to open the doors and look upon it. Those doors had opened for the body to be brought in, and they would only open again for the body to come out, in some doom yet to come.

Harrow was forbidden entry in the same way she was forbidden from going up to the top tier of the drillshaft and taking a hammer to the oxygen-sealant machines. It would be the end.

Most of her life was spent in silence; there were many moments when she found living—difficult. Tedious. On the worst days, fatuous. Memory now recalled what had happened very bloodlessly, and the details were unimportant. One very bad day—when it seemed as though everyone hated her, and as though this were a completely correct way to feel—with bloodied fists and a bruised heart, she wrote a note explaining her suicide then went and unlocked the door. Unexpectedly, this did not kill her; and what did not kill her made her curious.

She was much older before she could cross the threshold. It was trapped like all hell. But the traps were Ninth traps, made of bone and grinning skeleton, and she'd been using them herself since she was toddling. In the end, the experience was merely educational. She crossed the cave, which was trapped, and passed the central moat of black water—which was deep, and trapped—and then climbed the island (trapped) to the frozen mausoleum (*ridiculously* trapped), and when she got there—alive—she could look into the open-faced coffin where lay the reason for her existence.

God's victory and death was a girl. Maybe a woman. At the time Harrowhark had not known how to tell, and the gender was only a self-interested guess. The corpse lay packed in ice, wearing a white shift, her hands clasping a frost-rimed sword, and she was beautiful. The formation of her muscles was perfect. Each limb was a carved representation of a perfect limb, each bloodless foot the lifeless and high-arched simulacrum of the perfect foot. Each black and frosted lash lay against the cheeks with perfect still blackness, and her nose—it was the pinnacle of what a nose should be. None of this would have broken Harrow's spirit except that the mouth alone was perfectly imperfect: a little crooked, with a divot in the lower lip as though someone had softly pressed a dent into the bow with the tip of their finger. Harrow, who had been born for the sole privilege of worshipping this corpse, loved it wildly from sight.

So the death of God had been Harrow's death too. She had been careless with her visits. Her parents had . . . found out . . . about what she had done, what manner of sin she had committed, and they reacted just as they might have if she had admitted to smashing up the oxygen-sealant machine with a hammer. Faced with apocalypse, they chose to die by their own hands before another death could claim them. They weren't even angry. It was with a calm and earnest understanding that her mother and father and their cavalier tied five nooses—one for Mother, one for Father, two for Mortus, one for her. Then they hanged themselves with barely a gasp and barely a kick. It would have been better, really, if Harrow had hanged herself up beside them. It would have been best if she had crawled into the tomb beside the woman she loved and let the freezing temperatures take their course.

But Harrowhark—Harrow, who was two hundred dead children; Harrow, who loved something that had not been alive for ten thousand years—Harrowhark Nonagesimus had always so badly wanted to live. She had cost too much to die.

* * *

Love had broken her life into two separate halves: the half before she had fallen, and the half afterward. Afterward, she hated to sit in the apse during chant and listen to a weird, thuddering beat disrupt the prayers of the faithful, a distant striking at the back of her head that she had taken for someone being out of time. She heard doors open and close in distant halls where no doors were opening or closing; her body would become very frightened, and her brain very frustrated. In her agonies she would have to sit right beside her ageing marshal Crux, usually while being spoon-fed; he was insistent that she had to eat. And all the while she would demand, *Is that real?* for half of what she heard. And he could say, *Yes, my lady,* or *No, my lady,* and she might be content.

It killed all her peace. Even in the long dark days she spent wholly alone—in the libraries, or in her laboratory, fingers burnt from handling fatty ashes—she would hear voices just out of her hearing, or see things in her periphery that were not there. It seemed to her that sometimes her hands would grasp her own throat and press up against her windpipe until she saw spots in her vision. She would see dangling ropes; she would forget where she was and wipe out a whole morning's scholarship with false memory.

In that first year after her parents' deaths she often saw the Body, when she was sleeping or when she was waking, and that was relief and frustration both. The Body brought her total peace, but in its presence she lost track of time; she would sit with her hand very close to the dry, dead hand of her obsession, and when she looked up the hours would be eaten away. Or she would check the time and be astonished and discombobulated that it had been only a few minutes. When her pituitary gland kicked in, the Body stopped appearing when she was awake, but the other hallucinations kept on. Harrow was furious that she was doing something so—so *pedestrian* as to pubesce.

But as puberty changed her yet again, with hormones or time or both, she was able to regain some semblance of control over her maggot-eaten mind. She prayed often. Her brain took refuge in rituals. Sometimes she fasted, or ate the same thing for every meal, arranged in a specific pattern on her plate, consumed in the same order, for months on end. She wore her paint far beyond the strictures of any nun, wore it in private, sometimes slept in it. She found the sight of her own unpainted face in the mirror impossibly wearisome, monstrous, and nonsensical, somehow faraway and yet heinously attached to herself. Harrow did not often weep, but at times she sat within the shroud of her cot and rocked back and forth with hard, fast motions, often for hours.

The scholarship grew difficult once she realised belatedly that it was difficult; but that was cured by working harder. She spent sometimes half a month on the same theorem. She moved her mother and father through the House like chess pieces, trying every year to correct their stiff and unnatural gait, sitting them in chapel as her people asked them for guidance she had little idea how to give. But the penitents and devoted of the Locked Tomb were getting old, and she learned that they all wanted to be told the same thing. More often than not she would stand between her parents' corpses at some death bed, watching one more of her penitents rattle their last as she repeated the words of their final service. They died happy. They loved it. She had a real talent. Harrowhark had attended so many deathbeds, and given so many solemn takes about death and duty, that in the end she started to believe them.

The Ninth House elderly became the Ninth House decrepit, and the Ninth House decrepit became the Ninth House dead. Harrowhark was by most of them when they died, except if they had a sudden pulmonary, and even at fourteen she was good enough with a heart arrest to keep them going until she could give them final rites. She'd always disdained flesh magic, but she had a knack for the aorta. Later, when their meat had trickled away, she personally raised their defleshed skeletons to work the mangle or quietly rake the snow-leek fields in the upper reaches of Drearburh. Much of her necromancy had been sharpened by the day-to-day busywork of geriatric death, of the niche and the skull, of sitting with osteoporotic bones and filling up their honeycomb so that the constructs did not end up a confusion of ribcages with their legs powdering off. Her parents knew what they had been about, making a genius out of two hundred dead children: it took a genius simply to keep the House from deliquescing into a pile of bones and pneumonia victims.

But even a genius could only maintain the status quo. The House had never had the tech, nor the understanding, nor the on-duty flesh magicians to work a vat womb. The womb-bearing populace was too old to have babies, barring two of their number, one of whom was herself. Harrow could only thank God that duty had never fallen to her. The only viable source of healthy XY had been located in her House's cavalier primary, a boy seventeen years her elder. Back then she had considered him a walk-around man suit surrounding some quite good calcium carbonate, and she knew he considered her with an awful respect, the same type one might have for a hereditary cancer that one knew was on its way. Thankfully, their marriage would have mingled the Drearburh cavalier and scion lines beyond any hope of repair: Ortus Nigenad was an only child. Harrowhark had her parents quash the idea so enthusiastically that she cracked her father's molar. The only virgin who could possibly be more relieved was Ortus himself.

So the years passed, unshriven, crusting up and drying as they went. Harrowhark watched Crux get older, and older and older, and tried all the tricks in her box to keep him upright—there was terrible plaque in his arteries, and he pretended that he did not notice her scraping them. She knew that when she finally laid her nursemaid in his niche, it would be the death of the only other person invested in her sanity. And if she went mad again, then what? At any point she could have asked for assistance from her sister Houses. At any point she could have asked for Cohort intervention, and they would have been there the next day with foetal care boxes, and volunteer penitents, and loans, and plant samples—and with incontrovertible suggestions that Harrowhark really ought to marry *this* son of the Second, or *this* daughter of the Fifth—and she could have watched coloured banners get strung up next to the black skull of the Black Anchorite. And that would be the end of the Ninth House, even more completely than a hammer to the oxygen-sealant machine.

They needed a resurrection. They needed a miracle. Harrowhark had been studying miracles for years, and then one landed squarely in her lap: the chance to become a Lyctor. The chance to serve the Emperor her God, the chance to become a fist and a gesture, the chance to become an immortal servitor and advocate for Drearburh; to refresh the Ninth House on her terms, with the rock never rolled away and the love of her life and her death quiet and unmolested in her deadly shrine of stone. Another ten thousand years of solitude. Another long and snaking line of Reverend Mothers, Reverend Fathers. Harrow took the unready cavalier from her House, and she snatched the chance with both hands.

But like falling in love the first time, becoming a Lyctor had all gone wrong. Her cavalier had given himself to her with a numb readiness that still burnt her to ash with shame. Even with that readiness, she had committed the indelible sin halfway; she had gathered up the matter of Ortus Nigenad's soul and not been able to choke him all the way down. She was Harrowhark alone in front of the mirror again: a nonsense, a monster, an alien geometry. A loathsome squawk of a person. She was nine, and she'd made a mistake. She was seventeen, and she'd made a mistake. Time had repeated itself. Harrow would be tripping over herself for her whole existence, a frictionless hoop of totally fucking up.

There had been another girl who grew up alongside Harrow—but she had died before Harrow was born.

4

You STILL PRIDED YOURSELF on three things: firstly, bloody-minded composure; secondly, an inhuman intellect for necromancy; thirdly, being very difficult to kill. You were so immune to murder that you had not even been able to inflict the act upon yourself.

When you woke up midway through the first attempt on your life, your mind startled itself out of its thick fug and shook itself awake. There was a soft, all-encompassing warmth pressing over your face that could only have been your pillow, the thin cloth cover damp with your spit and breath. Someone was standing to the right of your cot and holding the pillow down. As you reflexively bucked, one hand moved to put hard pressure on your throat, and your hyoid would have cracked had you not reinforced it with a thick rime of cartilage.

They were a damned fool for not getting atop you. You found your fingers and plucked the thumbnail from your left hand, screaming into that asphyxiating white darkness, and separated your bloody disc of keratin and flesh into a thousand racine fragments, then expanded those into a multitude of jagged, splintering fléchettes. Blind, airless, you swung these stiff and hairy missiles into your assailant like so much shrapnel; you heard them thud into flesh and ping off the wall and bury themselves in steel. Good. Good. The weight on the pillow lightened, and—

* * *

You came to on your bare, bierlike cot all at once, hyperventilating.

The pillow behind your head was perfectly dry. You held your left hand up before your face, before the light, the even white light with its hot tungsten filaments. The thumbnail was whole and even. Too even? Were you wont to chew your fingernails still, that unattractive tic of your girlhood? The great two-hander lay next to you like an undisturbed baby, and across the wall of your quarters—

Nothing. No nail fragments. No scarring on the wall. Just a neat stack of crates. And in a chair dragged close to your bedside—the little chair that usually sat by the door, the one you had only ever seen the Emperor occupy—was Ianthe Tridentarius.

Your gazes met. The other nascent Lyctor—the Third House saint, the Emperor's bones and the Emperor's joints, the Emperor's fists and gestures—was clothed in a beautiful nacreous robe that glimmered all the colours of the rainbow: gauzy, iridescent white stuff that changed violently in the light. The mother-of-pearl made Ianthe's hair a lurid yellow and threw up all the mustard tints of her skin; her face was blotchy, and her eyes were sleepless pits. She looked like shit. You noticed that the eyes were a curious muddle of colours: washed-out purple jostled for space with a milky blue, freckled here and there with a lightish, hazy brown. Ianthe was sitting significantly too near to you, and she had arranged herself in the chair in a strangely lopsided, tilt-shouldered fashion. She also possessed two arms, which was one more than you'd last seen her sporting. None of that particularly bothered you.

What bothered you was that now the Princess of Ida—pale haired, all height and elbows, twilight shadows beneath her eyes—was looking at you with an expression you struggled to remember ever seeing on her face. Ianthe was fond of languid attitudes and postures; she affected a heavy, artificial tedium, or a faint and glittering malice, sometimes even a self-deprecating and idle humourousness; but she looked at you now with a soft and thoroughly uncharacteristic hunger. She smiled down at you with a frank, overfamiliar indulgence that frightened you. Ianthe looked lit from within.

"Good morning, my comrade," she said. "My colleague, my ally. I *do* like your eyes, Harrowhark—like flower petals in a darkened room. And even I can admit that your eyelashes are delicious. Stop wearing that pillowcase any time you like—I've seen your face before, and I know it looks like both of your parents were right-angled triangles. We must work with what we've got, as the flesh magician said to the leper."

Your whole soul flinched. A livid heat rose up your neck. With a titanic struggle, you managed not to shield your face with your hands, to be sure of your bedsheet mask. Lyctoral perception had made you complacent. Ianthe Tridentarius was a black hole where no heart could be sensed beating and no brain could be seen sparking. The brain, you knew grudgingly, existed. The heart was an open question. She looked at your face—saw, most likely, her own death reflected in your expression—and reached inside her robe. The palm of your hand slapped to her forehead with a ringing *thwack*. You could not sense her: she was a locked door in a dark room to you; but with a touch you could feel the orbital bones you might remove from her face.

"Before you do anything I am quick to reassure you that you will regret," said the other Lyctor, who had not moved—who had not recoiled at your palm's promise, except, perhaps, a quick shuttering of those mixed-up eyes—"I have a message for you."

The hand slowly withdrew from the robe. None of this would have been enough, except (the blood howled in your ears; you thought you heard footsteps, but then they slurred into voices, then back into footsteps again) that caught between Ianthe's fingers was a piece of flimsy with the name *Harrowhark* clearly upon it. The name *Harrowhark* was lettered in your hand. Underneath, in smaller lettering, and still your hand: *To be given to Harrowhark immediately upon coherence.*

You looked at the letter. You looked at Ianthe. Even in that short interval, the battlefield of her eyes had changed. From beneath your palm, you could see that one iris was now wholly a washed-out purple, like a fading bruise or a dying flower; the other one was blue and brown commingled. This glittering mess of heterochromatics focused on you, totally calm, utterly sure of itself.

"I wish you'd explained to me what *coherence* meant," she complained. "Did you mean *coherent* as in, *I recognise objects and their names*? Did you mean coherent as in, *I am no longer remotely out to lunch,* which means you're still not eligible? I wasn't going anywhere near you in the first instance of you opening your eyes. Your only settings were *power-vomit* and *murder.*"

"Tell me how you came to have what you are holding," you croaked.

"You put it in my own hands, you skull-faced fruitcake," she said soothingly. "Go on. Take it. It's yours."

You withdrew your hand from her forehead, and you took it. You were desperately afraid that your fingers were shaking, and that you would not know to make them stop. In your lap, under the strong white light of the hospital quarter, you could see no error or artifice in the writing: it was yours, not an exceptional copy. It was written in your blood. When you touched the smooth, plex-rendered surface, you could see in your mind's eye the pen nib, the soft bite of the metal into the inside of your lip.

Unfolding the flimsy and spreading it across your knees was the final gobbet boiling off the skeleton. The letter was written in Ninth House crypt-script; your own cipher, based off that of your parents and developed when you were seven years old. It was unbreakable to anyone who lacked your rosary, Marshal Crux, and a hundred or so years to spare.

You read:

ADDRESSING THE REVEREND LADY HARROWHARK NONAGESIMUS, KNOWN AS THE REVEREND DAUGHTER BY HER OWN DESIRE, NOW HARROWHARK THE FIRST, WRITING AS THE SAME, NOW DEAD.

"I'll give you a moment," said Ianthe, and she stood and crossed over to the window, standing bathed in the light of the nearest star.

* * *

ADDRESSING THE REVEREND LADY HARROWHARK NONAGESIMUS, KNOWN AS THE REVEREND DAUGHTER BY HER OWN DESIRE, NOW HARROWHARK THE FIRST, WRITING AS THE SAME, NOW DEAD.

LETTER #2 OF #24. TO BE READ IMMEDIATELY ON COHERENCE.

Harrowhark—

As I write, it has been forty-eight hours since you became a Lyctor at Canaan House. By the time you read this you will not recall the writing thereof, as the Harrowhark of the writing will be dead and gone. Her resurrection constitutes a fail state and must be avoided at all costs.

This letter cannot answer questions. What I have done I will refer to as the work, and its character is actively harmful for you to know. I will instead provide guidelines on how to live the rest of your life. As your life may hopefully now extend into the myriads, it is of enormous import that you are not tempted to deviate from them. You are the living surety of promises I have made. Break troth with me, and from beyond my destruction I will brand you Tomb heretic, cut off utterly from that which lies on the frozen altar, asleep and dead; removed from the adoration thereof, and any promise of part in her resurrection.

GUIDELINE #1: <u>STAY ALIVE</u>.

You may not end your own life through suicide. You may not end your own life through carelessness. Accidental death must be avoided at all costs and never accepted as an outcome. The work relies upon your continuance.

GUIDELINE #2: YOU CAN <u>NEVER</u> RETURN TO THE NINTH HOUSE.

The way home is closed to you. Do not set foot within the House again. Do not allow yourself to be taken there by force.

GUIDELINE #3: THE SWORD <u>WILL</u> REMAIN ON YOU AT ALL TIMES.

Wipe it down with your arterial blood nightly. Coat the blade in the ash which regrows. Do not cut flesh with the naked blade. Do not cut bone with the naked blade. Even this may not prove

*enough. Treat the sword as your promised death, and act accord-
ing to the first guideline.*

GUIDELINE #4: YOU <u>ARE</u> COMPROMISED.

*You may already suspect this, if you're not as big a fool as I take
you for. I will confirm your access to the Lyctoral well. This battery
is, most likely, the extent of your capability. Make up for your inevitable failings through study. Your understanding of flesh and spirit
magic is execrable, so start there. Do not aim to only build upon what
you already know. It pains me to admit this, but you know piss-all.
I refuse to let you build your house on such shiftless & ureal sand.*

GUIDELINE #5: YOU OWE IANTHE TRIDENTARIUS THE FAVOUR OF THE CHAIN.

*This will be difficult to justify. I will therefore not justify it.
Tridentarius has made what has come to pass possible. I owe her
a debt that you will undoubtedly be paying for the rest of your
life. The agreement <u>does</u> end on your death. The agreement <u>does</u>
extend into the House, but NOT into the Tomb. The agreement is
singular but <u>does</u> take precedence over and above any debt you
have sworn to anyone lesser than the Holy Corpse, over and above
the Emperor of the Nine Houses. In order to avoid philosophical
quandaries she <u>will</u> expect you to re-swear immediately on receipt
of the letter, and any failure to do so undoes the whole business.
Do not be tardy here.*

*It goes without saying that Ianthe will destroy you if she can.
She has helped me ably, but it has cost her nothing and you everything. I have guarded from her full understanding of the work so
that she cannot undo it on a whim or by accident. You are in her
power. I am in no doubt of her misusing it. You yourself never had
power over anyone else but you misused it violently.*

GUIDELINE #6: READ THE OTHER MISSIVES <u>ONLY IF AND WHEN</u> YOU MEET THEIR REQUIREMENTS.

*I have left other instructions in case of new circumstances.
Ianthe holds twenty-four of these letters and will give you twenty-*

two, including this one. They are numbered accordingly. Memorise the requirements and carry the letters on you at all times, ready to act the moment you are required to read them. Follow their instructions without hesitation. I repeat: do not read them otherwise.

To myself: a brief break in guidelines follows, before the last. You will think at this point that I have given you a terrible hand to play the game with. I am not unsympathetic. Nonetheless, understand that I envy you more than I have ever envied anyone, and that I look upon your birth as a blessing. Look upon me as a Harrowhark who was handed the first genuine choice of our lives; the only choice ever given where we had free will to say, No, and free will to say, Yes.

Accept that in this instance I have chosen to say, No.

GUIDELINE #7: EXAMINE IANTHE'S JAW AND TONGUE AFTER YOU READ THIS.

Owing to her Lyctoral status this will require physical touch. Under no circumstances can you let her know you are examining them. Do whatever it takes. If you suspect either jaw or tongue has been replaced, DO NOT SWEAR THE OATH. Instead kill her immediately.

> *In the hope of a future forgiveness,*
> *I remained,*
> **HARROWHARK NONAGESIMUS**

* * *

"Come here," you said, less steadily than you would have liked.

Ianthe—still dreamily doused in starlight—obliged you instantly, still smiling that same secret, conspiratorial smile, like a spider tucked inside a shoe. She arranged herself in the chair by the bed, and you noticed again her favouring the left arm, as though the right was too heavy a burden.

You swung your legs off the hospital cot, and you took the sheeting away from your face, despising your nakedness. Her mismatched eyes widened, just briefly, as you stood before her, considering—the sword was six feet of abandoned steel tangled in the thin blankets, but you thought that for now, a small distance would have to do—and you reached out to cup Ianthe's face in your hands. Your thumbs pressed up against the warm flesh that skinned her ramus and your other fingers butterflied over her cheeks. Your metacarpus nudged up against the body of the mandible. When you tilted her jaw up to you your skin was discoloured against her skin; her skin was discoloured against your skin. There was the faintest suggestion of dried blood beneath your fingernails.

You found your mouth and eyes screwing up, as though against the light, or a sour taste; you could not help it. But the vile course of action was obvious. You leant down and—holy shit—kissed her squarely on the mouth.

This, at least, she hadn't expected—how could she, what the fuck—and her mouth froze against yours, which gave you time to work. Ianthe was a black hole to you, a null, an empty, overradiant space, unreadable; but close physical proximity could echolocate that darkness. It was osteoids your fingers searched for. New bone always gave itself away, its fresh collagen spongy and bright with thalergy. The lining of her cells was in keeping with old bone. When you pressed the tip of your tongue to her tongue she made a small, tight, half-wounded sound—she was probably trying to call for help—but although the lingual muscle was not your area of specialty, you could probe through flesh the signs that her foramen bone was whole, unscarred by a fresh rip of the tongue from the mouth. You were safe.

You withdrew, finally, your mouth from her mouth. Ianthe was left, lips slightly parted, eyebrows raised, her bloodless face untouched by maidenly blushes.

"I pledge myself again to the service of Ianthe Tridentarius, Princess of Ida, daughter of the Third House," you said. "I swear again to honour any previous agreements I made to her. I swear by my mother; by the salt water; by that which lies dead and unbreathing in the Tomb; by the ripped and remade soul of Ortus Nigenad."

"Who?" she said. "Oh, yes—the cavalier."

Ianthe wiped the pad of her thumb over the blanched bow of her lips, then considered her fingers. "Well," she said eventually, "that constitutes some improvement over your sewing my lips shut, like you did the . . . no, pardon me, I agreed *not* to mention incidental detail."

"Wait. You submitted to be made a Sewn Tongue?"

"Ask me no questions and I shall tell you no lies," said the Princess of Ida, wiping her thumb against her bottom lip again, very delicately. "Look, all I shall say is that for a House that trades solely in bone, you own some *enormous* needles. I accept your fealty again, Ninth House, and can only assume that you have now read the agreement."

You sat back down on the bed and placed your hand on the sword, which had the effect it always did: your oesophagus gave a little exhausted shiver, your salivary glands jolted, and the nausea rose up behind your eyeballs. "You have wrung a great deal of blood from what seems to be a very little stone," you said.

"I gave you something you cared about very deeply at the time," she said, idly swinging one leg to perch over one knee. "I don't consider my price all that high . . . and neither did you. What's more, now we are about to embark on what promises to be a truly beautiful friendship, with me the lone fruitful thing in your salted field, et cetera, so I'll thank you to not embark on the *I have been hard done by* act."

Your fingers pressed down hard on the wide breadth of steel. The thundering in your ears was a patchwork of sound and adrenaline, and your heart was sore. "The pledge did not condone disrespect," you said. "I will not suckle at your bootheel." ("Unnecessarily descriptive," said Ianthe.) "I will not suffer insult. I am the Reverend Daughter. I am a Lyctor. I am in your debt . . . but I am not here for your amusement."

"Not in that thing you're not, certainly," said Ianthe, whose lip was curling. "You look like a huge peppermint. Take this—and this."

This—as Ianthe reached suddenly beneath her chair, right arm still strangely flopsome—proved to be a great shiny wadded-up bundle. She tossed it lightly at you—you didn't even try to catch it—and it landed in a lovely pool on the bed. It was a mass of the same thin and frivolous material that currently shrouded Ianthe: a robe in mother-of-pearl colours, all its wrinkles and creases disappearing as you tentatively shook it out. It had a hood. It had deep sleeves. That was all you needed. The colour was not going to become you, but it was hugely preferable to the turquoise shift. You squirmed inside it with unseemly haste. You pulled the hood deep over your head and did not bother to hide your sigh of relief. You were clad from the arms down to the legs, if not modestly; the whole rest of your face was on show.

And this was a neat stack of flimsy envelopes, the same as the first. The Harrowhark who had addressed them had taken the time to write their labels—apart from the numbers—in neat crypt-script. You flicked through them to count, and could not help scanning the requirements. Some of them were plain and stark. *To open in the event of the Emperor's death. To open in the event of Ianthe's death. To open if the Ninth House is in mortal danger.* Some of them were opaque to the point of madness. *To open if your eyes change. If met, to give to Camilla Hect.*

You wondered, mystified, if you had ever known the last name of Camilla the Sixth, a woman you could not recall interacting with at any point.

"I will remain in possession of the last two," said Ianthe, having risen to stand. It was always difficult when she stood: she looked so completely like a shoddy wax cast of some more beautiful sculpture. "I will tell you openly that there's one I get to open in case you die, which is fun."

You flipped through. Your eyes fell on: *To open if you meet Coronabeth Tridentarius.* This was different from the other envelopes in that it was not written in cipher. You were not happy at the idea that Ianthe had spent any time with your code, and thought your past self complacent in the extreme. Ianthe's eyes fell on it too. "You wrote that one in front of me," she said. "I can summarise the contents . . . you are now pledged to me and by extension to Coronabeth, and I tell you for free that one of the riders is that you will never harm a hair on my sister's head."

"Your sister is likely no longer alive," you said, seeing no reason not to say it.

She threw back her pale head and laughed outright. "*Corona!*" she said, when she was done. "My sweet baby Corona is far too stupid to die—she'd walk backward out of the River swearing blind she was going in the right direction. I will tell you when my sister is dead, thank you, Harrowhark—and that day is *not* today."

Your head was swimming. In a way, you were relieved. Part of you was afraid that this was just another complex part of the hallucination; that you would wake up again, and soon, back in a world where you were not part of your own master plan—a plan you resented, as you resented any peremptory order and any attempt to keep things secret from you, but a plan that nonetheless existed. You could follow any blind precept, if the alternative was madness.

"If it is all the same to you, I would like to be alone now," you said. "I have a great deal to think about."

Ianthe said, "How politely expressed!"

She drew her skirts around her and curtseyed to you—a beautiful, thoughtless movement, prismatic breadths clutched in her fingers, and it was somehow also mockery. When she looked up at you, you saw her eyes had changed yet again. They were both that bleached lavender now, but freckled with light brown like a constellation of little pupils.

"Take your time," she said. "I would have thought time was the last thing we had at the moment . . . but who am I to judge the King Undying, the God of the Nine Houses?"

You said, because again you could see no reason not to: "You should have disciplined Tern better, if he's still fighting you this way."

Ianthe considered this. She nudged the confection basket hilt of the rapier at her hip aside, and took out a long knife that, again, ran a hot rill of pain down your temporal bone. It was—though you had never bothered to learn—Tern's main-gauche, his trident knife, a long blade from which two other blades would spring at the press of some hidden mechanism; she flicked that mechanism now, and with a *snickt* they burst out like a firework, two hard points of gleaming steel. She flicked it again, and the blades went *snickt* back into their housing.

She placed her palm before you, outstretched. Without a moment's hesitation, or sign of pain, or even much give, she thrust the knife through the meat of her palm. It must have done enormous damage—to flexor muscles, to the nest of carpal bones—and ruby drops of blood splattered the sleeves of her shimmering robe.

As she withdrew it, the wound knitted together as though it were nothing. She simply withdrew, and the skin closed up—the meat bounded back on itself, elastic—the hole sizzled to a close, leaving her palm whole and unblemished except for a few wet drops of crimson red. These she shook off, and they disappeared into powder. For the first time, when you looked at her, Ianthe gleamed with thanergy as a coal gleamed red with heat.

"Hold out your hand," she commanded.

You did, knowing full well what was to happen—you did it without hesitation, as she had done it without hesitation. Ianthe held your hand gently, by the wrist, considered the angle, and thrust the blade home.

Every fibre in your being bent toward not throwing up. The delicate tendons in your palm snapped under the razor-sharp blade; the steel juddered against a metacarpal—chips went flying into the muscle bed—your blood sprayed promiscuously against your face, a hot, salty thickness of it against your lips, your nose, your right cheek. Your eyes rolled back in your head in an ecstasy of suffering. The world rocked. You saw the Body, pressed against the back wall, her hands clasped together as though in prayer; you looked at the blade sunk deep into your hand and looked at Ianthe, and for a moment understood that she was about to press the mechanism and rend your hand utterly—leave your palm a smoking ruin of gore and muscle, of whiteness of bone—that you were being punished both, perhaps, for the kiss, and for something you could not even recall doing.

She pulled the blade clear. This was also agony. Now you understood the object lesson: there was no sewing-up for you. Your meat was left ripped bare and vulnerable, a gaping, heinous hole in your hand, your skin a pitiful red-and-pink mess of shredded dermis. You grasped the wrist she was also grasping with your free hand; you poured thalergy in with embarrassing torrents, a hot, shameless gush of it, flicking free chips of bone and wending muscle back into muscle.

This took effort and thought. You refilled the blood; grew new shiny spans of skin; left your palm as whole as before, your nerves screaming, shaking with the memory of pain.

"Harrow," said Ianthe gently, "don't fuck with me. I'm not here for your amusement either."

She turned away from you and walked toward the door. Your mouth was dry. You kept trying to rewet it, but you were afraid that it would come out as bile; your head was swimming. You steadied yourself enough to say, "Is your cavalier a forbidden subject, then?"

Her hand stilled at the pad of the autodoor, standing by the hanging that showed the First House picked out in white thread. "Babs?" she said. "I don't care about *Babs* . . . Just don't suggest my sister is dead to me, ever again."

She touched the pad beside the door and crossed the opened threshold. The door closed behind her, leaving you alone. There was blood on your face and the knees of your robes. After a moment you shook them clean as she had done, drying out the blood, rendering it powder. You were weak. You staggered over to the Body, standing so quiet by the wall, and you buried your face in her thighs. The dead cool nearness of her was so close to being real that it rendered itself genuine comfort.

You were close enough to the crates stacked up by the door now to see that they had been placed against the wall hastily, and somewhat ajar. You wobbled to your feet and pushed them down in a domino cascade of clanging plex.

Behind the boxes were hundreds of thick nail fragments, like the broken horns of some weird animal, scattered on the floor and embedded in the wall. Some of them were brown with dried blood. Long, ragged missiles of keratin were, at some points, finger-deep in the panelling. You crawled back to the cot where the Body laid you down on the sheets, placed the heinous sword within your arms, added the letters to this pile, and gave you the go-ahead to fall unconscious.

5

SHE WAS FIRST AWARE OF LIGHT. It poured through the plex windows in lavalike radiance: white and steaming light, making her undershirt stick to her ribs with sweat. In the tiny black confines of the shuttle, the light took up all the space with its irradiating, corneal presence; and Harrowhark cried out as though she were dying from it, and then was tremendously self-conscious and discombobulated.

"Please," a voice was saying. "Please, my Lady Harrowhark. Be—be peaceful. What can I do for you? What must be done?"

Ortus was almost bigger than the light, filling up the black-and-steel spaces of the passenger seats as much as the radiance did. Harrow realised, smarting, that his expression was that of a man who considered her a source of embarrassment. Somewhere down the years, she had come to understand that Ortus Nigenad, that perfect modern Ninth cavalier—perfectly shaved head, perfectly appropriate paint, perfectly grim solemnity, perfect body of two cabinets nailed together, perfect ability to carry six kilos of bone—considered her a slightly sorry object. How sorry an actual object, he could not possibly conceive.

"Am I making the sign?" she managed. "Am I giving you the signal? No? Then I will remind you that anything else is none of your business, and hope I do not have to remind you twice."

He was not sweating as she was, but those lashes were damp from the light. "As you see fit, my lady," he said. His rapier was not belted at his hip. He carried it over his lap, as though it were someone else's baby. Harrow was pleased, dimly, to see that for his main-gauche he carried his pannier, despite Aiglamene cutting up so rough at the idea; that felt appropriate. She had always desired a helpmeet, not a circus performer.

"Where are we?" Harrow added, in another sudden welter of nervousness. "I thought—perhaps—"

"We must be four hundred kilometres above the surface now," he said, mistaking her question. "They are securing our clearance to land. We shall leave orbit soon, I trust."

Harrowhark rose from the placket of House dirt she had been sitting on, which held the merest suggestion of thanergy at this point anyway, and she crossed to where the light was coming in. At the last moment she remembered what she had brought with her and drew a piece of thick voile from within her sacramental vestments. She tied it around her head and pulled up her hood, which still smelled of the salts that Crux had so carefully packed it away with: that herbaceous, acrid, homelike smell, the one that made her eyes smart again with familiarity. Then she looked through the plexiform window.

From space, the House of the First resembled a box of tumbled jewels. Haloed in white, its blues deep and brilliant and oxidised, a planet of water, close enough to the fiery gyre of Dominicus that the water was not allowed to freeze yet nor so close that it burnt away. Insubstantial and ever-shifting ocean, as far as the reddened eye could see. Her smarting eyes fell upon a tiny jumble of squares, ringed around a central greyish smudge.

She turned back to her seat, and found herself saying, restlessly, "At times now I forget . . . I thought I was dreaming, perhaps."

"I find it perfectly normal, my lady," he said. "Perhaps I am right in perceiving that you thought it might surprise me, your being . . . with the infirmity of . . ." When she looked at him, he immediately seemed to find the rattle and thump of the shuttle's mechanisms overpowering, and began a traditional Ortus shutdown. "Your . . . so-called . . . the frailty."

"Nigenad, use your words."

"The insanity," said her companion. Her shoulders relaxed a fraction. He mistook her rising relief for an emotion he ought to have known she never felt. Ortus said, distracted: "The only surprise really being in it expressing *this* way, rather than . . . No, I am not surprised, Lady Harrowhark. Perhaps you may yet have cause to find it useful."

"*Useful.*"

Ortus cleared his throat. *This* engendered many emotions in her— Ortus Nigenad cleared his throat with the import of a sword being slid from a scabbard, or knucklebones jostling in the pocket of a Locked Tomb necromancer—but it was too late, as he was already declaiming:

> "*Then did the dire bone frenzy fall upon Nonius, the*
> *mightiest arm of the Ninth and its bulwark;*
>
> *Spasmed his veins with the death lust; his great heart*
> *roared like a black iron furnace, hungry for*
> *corpses . . ."*

"Ah," said Harrowhark. "Yes. Book Sixteen." And, presently: "I think 'bone frenzy' might be a term open to coarse misinterpretation, personally."

Better death by the drawn sword, and better the death of the knucklebone. There was only one trigger to drive Ortus Nigenad so comprehensively berserk, and she had forgotten that it was not a trigger to use lightly. Ortus primly said he thought that nobody who read the *Noniad* would be the sort of churl who misread a simple and evocative collocation like *bone frenzy;* he went on to suggest that such a person probably didn't even read in the first place, and would be more inclined to trifle with prurient magazines or pamphlets than to bother themselves with a complex epic such as the *Noniad;* he said that he wouldn't want such a person to read his poetry anyway.

"At least now I possess the time to finish it," he added a little moodily, but apparently satisfied with that thought.

This surprised her only in that it was so obviously expressed. She did not voice what she thought: that even if he was right—even if the last thing Harrow wanted was for Ortus to get in the way as she studied the paths of Lyctorhood, to become a finger and a gesture, to take the only divine path that had ever opened for her in order to save her House from a destruction she herself had inflicted—it didn't behove him to *say* as much. She hoped he never finished it. She hoped there was never world enough or time. Harrowhark had always thought Matthias Nonius, legendary cavalier of her House, sounded like an absolute horse's ass.

"Harrowhark," said her cavalier, "I wish to ask you a question."

He did not sound timid now; his mood had shifted to a more typical restrained sadness, though she thought, perhaps, there was something else within it. Harrow took a moment to study his face. Ortus would be a good rest cure, should the homesickness get too acute. He had classical Ninth eyes: a tintless shade very close to true black, sharply ringed around the iris, very like her own.

Ortus said a little restlessly: "What do you think it is like—to be a Lyctor? Do you think it is a central tragedy to them, their great age, their timelessness?"

She was surprised again. "Nigenad, what would be the tragedy in living for a myriad? Ten thousand years to learn everything there is to know—to read everything that has ever been written . . . to study without fear of premature end or reckoning. What is the tragedy of *time*?"

"Time can render one impotent beyond meaning," said Ortus unexpectedly. He made his eyes downcast again, and said: "I would not expect you to—be crushed by the weight of that particular comprehension, Reverend Daughter."

He might as well have said, *You are a baby of seventeen, and I am an adult of thirty-five.* She regretted, not for the first time, not going for broke and taking Aiglamene. Perhaps there *would* have been something in rocking up to the First House with an octogenarian in tow: a sort of wild and confident fuck-you—*Oh, your cavaliers are young? And they fight? How classic! So jejune!*—but that would not have been the wild and confident fuck-you of the Ninth House. The Ninth House character, she was forced to admit, had always been low on wild and confident fucks.

"Nigenad," she said, "I am what I am, and I am seventeen. Yet I assure you that I contain multitudes."

"I am fully aware of that, my lady," said Ortus.

Which was perfectly correct of him to say. But Harrow somehow did not like the way he said it. "They are taking too long to vet us," she said, and stood, and restlessly pulled down the plexiform barrier between them and the empty cockpit. She was about to press her fingers to the communication button, to ask the pilot what the holdup was and how he was to explain it; but she saw something she either had not seen before or that had suddenly appeared, upon one of the padded seats. It was a piece of flimsy. She took it and withdrew into the bleeding light of the passenger hold.

She could feel Ortus's eyes upon her as she turned the piece of flimsy over. It was coloured all over with thin blue ink, scribbled so hard that the termination of each letter pushed holes into the surface, and it read:

THE EGGS YOU GAVE ME ALL DIED AND YOU LIED TO ME

She gave it to her cavalier. The shuttle seemed totally quiet now. No mechanism ground; no pipe gurgled. The light was very still and white and she no longer felt it moving. He scanned over the piece of flimsy, frontward, then flipped it over to scan it backward. He cleared his throat—Harrowhark found herself flinching, and nearly tore herself to pieces for it—and he said:

"It's blank, my lady."

"Fuck," said Harrow.

6

WHEN YOU WOKE, you were already sitting up. Your chin was bowed on your chest so that you had an exciting view of your lap. You were no longer in your bed, and the lower walls and floor were blurring past you in scuffed washes of black stone, bones, and steel.

Your vision swam. It became apparent immediately that you could not move. Your clinical brain rose to the fore as your meat brain shied and ran around and barked like the badly behaved animal it was. Your clinical brain took stock and realised that you were seated in some kind of chair being wheeled down an *Erebos* corridor, and that someone had pinched a high cervical nerve right into your spinal cord—not deforming the bone at all, but manipulating the flesh only—in such a way that you were locked out of your body from the neck down. You could not raise your head. You could blink, and breathe sufficiently, and swallow poorly. Otherwise you were as marble. It was an astonishing act of necromancy. You were righteously indignant, but amazed at the act.

You were still in your beautiful mother-of-pearl robe, head deep in your hood, hearing the thick and papery rustle of twenty-two letters secreted within your clothes. The sword was laid across your lap; a thick, fatty webbing joined the hilt to your forearm, a webbing that you had no memory of creating but was nonetheless your lacework. Perhaps you had woken up at an earlier point to stash the letters down your shift and fix the blade to your arm; you did not recall, but that was not unusual. Sometimes your conscious days were dreamlike ordinances of movement, functions, sounds. Rather than muscle mass within the web, there was a honeycomb of bone stretching out from your forearm through the webbing to the hilt. Nobody was going to get it away from you in a hurry. It was as though you had been picked up bodily, plopped in the chair, and disabled from the neck down. You hoped distantly that your bladder hadn't evacuated.

The chair stopped. There were voices. You concentrated hard on whatever had been done to the back of your neck—visualized your known friend, the odontoid peg that protruded from your other known friend, the cervical vertebra—the bracelets that surrounded the vertebral arteries, the tangle of physeal joints. If it had simply been bonework, you would have been able to identify the mischief immediately, and unfuck accordingly. The voices coalesced—

"—can clear this instantaneously, Saint of Saints, once the Holy Prince has finished giving audience to—"

This came from in front of you.

"The meeting! The *meeting*!!" It was difficult to articulate extra exclamation marks, yet the new voice did so. "Do you think I have time for—for—for the *extra hour* in which three generals and your Resurrector, the God of Dead Kings, try to schedule *another meeting after the first one has done*? Do you think I came here to wait for *three personal assistants, six calendars, and God himself changing his mind nineteen times*??"

This came from behind you, and above. This voice, in all probability, belonged to the person who was pushing your chair.

"Sacred Hand," said another voice, "forgive me. It was his order that she was not to be touched. There were no allowances; there were no riders."

The first voice said, "There was no opposition when I ordered the shuttle. Nor to my preparations."

"The order regarding Harrowhark Nonagesimus was specifically stated by him, Holy Finger, Holy Thumb."

The voice above Harrow said, "And is my order suddenly not God's order? Am I no longer Lyctor of the Great Resurrection, the second saint to serve the King Undying? Have I lost my rank among the

Four—or, now, as I so horribly find, the Three? Am I not the last sister serving in a charnel house of dead sisters, all of whom gave their long and dutiful lives so that your squalling children and their germ-ridden children's children's children could bask in the light of Dominicus?"

The other voice paused. "No," it said. But then it added, and there was a hint of stoic wretchedness: "Most Holy Saint of Joy—forgive me—I still ask you to please wait until the meeting is done."

There was an explosive sigh. "It's all right," the voice said, quite normally. "It's all right, Lieutenant, I understand. You've only met *this* baby and the *other* baby. You've never met a *Lyctor.* You're not to know . . . even if you're in his presence, it's another thing altogether to understand . . ."

The voice trailed off, and the person standing behind your chair crossed over to the person in front of it. You were distantly interested in what happened next, if only because you were not used to being granted a front-row seat. You beheld one normal person before you— the other was a black hole, and now you knew why—and that person had two kidneys. A sudden one-two punch of thalergy emerged from nowhere, as far as your senses were concerned—no, not punches: a stiletto, an unutterably focused dart, a syringe—and each kidney was hosed with angiotensins. A perfect spike. Blood pressure plunged. A body joined the shoes and trouser bottoms in front of you as the officer fainted, and the chair was wheeled around the neat human pile.

The voice behind the chair was muttering:

"Horrid . . . just vile! *Erebos* placements never do have any horse sense . . . told him time and time again to rotate them each decade . . . just a nightmare. My presence ought to have the same effect as a fire alarm . . . I do *not* want to wait . . . I do *not* want a cup of tea. I am not asking for feudal submission; I am asking for *understanding!*"

This blast of volume might have made you jump, had your spine been connected. The chair paused in front of one of the elevator shafts; the dark doors whispered open to the rainbow inlay and the hangings of the lift chamber, and the chair was rolled inside. You were busy flexing the ragged end of your dorsal root—you had assumed it must have been severed, which would have been the simplest thing to do, but you realised all at once that it had been *tied into a knot*. It had been bowed out, twisted, and looped.

The keypad made low, electronic chirrups as somebody pressed down upon it. A mass of fabric whispered past you—you could not feel it on your body, but you felt the air upon your cheek—and then a person knelt in front of your chair. A shining, shimmering billow of pale fabric came into your field of vision, a rainbow-hued whiteness that ran through shades beneath the hot tungsten light, like the reflection of coloured glass on ice, the same stuff that now was draped around you. Then, awfully, your vision was lifted. Someone had pressed a finger lightly beneath your chin, and they were tilting it up so that you could see their face.

You looked at the Lyctor. The Lyctor looked at you.

The face beneath the icy parti-coloured hood was a prim, virginal oval; much in shape and feature like the shape of a saint's face in a portrait, or a death mask. The nose and jaw and forehead were all carven and serene, and therefore had the same indifferent dullness of a well-formed statue. You noticed the colours first, beneath that harsh and unlovely light: that the hair was a dead flower or apricot colour, and that the skin and lips and brows were of a similar hue, so that beneath the nacreous cowl the saint looked like a painting with a very limited palette; and the eyes . . .

You had seen a Lyctor's eyes only once before. Lyctors kept their own faces, but the eyes they stole from someone else. You had been lucky that your own transition was not as startling. This pair of eyes were a slumbrous, sand-tinted hazel with grey-madder clouds within them, like a red hurricane moving over a gaseous mantle, like a storm-ridden planet of red dust. The expression did not match these dreamy and quite beautiful eyes: the expression was paralytically repellent in ways that had nothing to do with your dorsal nerve. It saw right through you, marked what you had done, and let you know that there would be a reckoning. No signs of age touched the corners of those screwed-up, dust-storm eyes, but nonetheless it was a gaze as elderly as Crux's. There was something in the look she gave you—after she read the whole of your features, as though searching—that puzzled you. Then fell the final indignity. She hooked her finger into the seam of your hood and tugged it down to your neck, so that she could look at your whole face without permission, bloodied skull and all.

You flushed until the tips of your ears were red hot. Fear and humiliation formed a bone hook at the back of your superior articular facet; acrimonious rage drove it forward, caught the loop, and withdrew it backward, as though unknitting your nerves. The scythe of pain that swept over the back of your scalp nearly made you sick again, and you would have been if you had not of late become the Saint of Emesis. You squeezed the nerve flat with the muscles around it and wedged the minute hook back into your spinal mass where it belonged. This resulted in a whole-body case of pins and needles so profound that all you could do was thrash like a fish on the end of a line. The finger was withdrawn. The stormy eyes widened, just fractionally. An emotion was playing out over her face that was—not unfamiliar to you—but nonsensical; you discarded it.

"You oughtn't to have done that," she said. "You might have blown out your dorsal nerve and asphyxiated."

She looked at your face and saw what was so nakedly writ there: disbelief that she could perceive what you'd done. "No, I cannot sense you," she said, in answer to your unspoken dismay. "But your body is not a mystery to me. I may know it better than *you* do, you—you Ninth baby." You were fumbling with the hood with clumsy hands, hiding your face. "How old are you?" she asked abruptly. "How old in years?"

You held your flopping idiot's head up, to look at her face again. For some reason—and you never needed a reason; you were very good at producing a reaction to no stimulus whatsoever—you became afraid. It was then that the Body emerged from behind the Lyctor's shoulder, squatting somewhere close to the doors. Her sweet dead face floated a little behind the Lyctor's. She looked at you with her heavy-lidded, yellow-gold eyes, and she said, quite clearly, with the voice of Aiglamene and your mother commingled:

"Lie, Harrow. Now."

"Fifteen," you said immediately, hoping your own meat would not betray you.

She pressed, "Counting from conception, or from birth?"

"Birth."

That emotion played out over the face again, like the ripple of darkness across a briefly disturbed body of water. The whole body clenched and unclenched. It didn't matter that she was a black hole to you, without thanergy or thalergy to speak of; it was just a matter of seeing her shoulders. It was relief. It was unalloyed, full-bore relief.

"Yuck," she said.

The elevator came to a thudding halt. The doors behind the Lyctor opened; she stood, then looked down at you. The relief was gone; the distance remained.

"I have asked the Emperor multiple times why he has allowed himself to sit, exposed, for this long on the edge of the place he must not come back to," she said. "And the reason turns out to be you. Some lost Ninth scrap who never had anything to do with anything . . . a nobody. But he acted so *surprised* . . . I said, *Put an age requirement in the letter!* I said, *Everyone will be pubescent if you don't!* And now we reap what he sowed. *Hiss.*" (For a moment you thought you'd had an aural hallucination, that nobody who had lived ten thousand years— that nobody who had lived—would verbalise the word *hiss*.) "Well, you have three options: you can walk with me now to the shuttle, I can wheel you, or I can drag you. Which do you pick, you half-grown juvenile? I will tell you: the other one walked."

You stood up. It cost you.

"Good," she said, looking at you critically. "You look like a bat stuck in a birthday cake and you need at least two haircuts, but you are— you will be—you were—God's breath, and God's bones."

The Lyctor rearranged your hood a little bit and smoothed out the shoulders of your robe—for this you vowed to one day take her dorsal nerve—then looked at the sword webbed into your arm, bent nearly double beneath its weight and your weariness. Her expression said quite clearly what she thought of it, but she had seen your naked face and perhaps seen something there. Perhaps your plans for her dorsal nerve.

"You're not as pretty as Anastasia" was all she said.

Now the Reverend Daughter followed more like a cavalier of her House than a necromancer of it. You creaked like a pack skeleton beneath the weight of a burden, following in the Lyctor's wake. Thankfully, you no longer felt shame. Pride was swiftly becoming a planet you had travelled to once but no longer remembered in detail. The docking bay she led you into was a hive of activity. A speaker gave a belated *parp* of "Our lady the Saint of Joy is gracing Docking Bay Fourteen," yet this did not seem to encourage everyone to scurry into the gleaming steel-and-bone culverts of the ship, but rather to take whatever they were doing into double time.

Whatever they were doing involved, primarily, a shuttle. It was not large. It was of a size, in fact, with the type that had used to bring the Ninth House lightbulb filaments and vitamin supplements, manned by a single pilot who always looked as though he had gained the job by losing a bet. There were boxes being carried up into it. You were distracted by the beating hearts and muscles straining all around you, weeping lactic acid as they slid and locked containers and crates into position. At the top of the ramp, sitting on an upturned container in a whisper of opaline skirts and distinct peevishness, was Ianthe; her focus was on the back of the shuttle, not on you. She sat within the sea of heaving stacks and bundles like a pillar.

"All right," said the Saint of Joy. "Chop-chop. Get in there and don't move an inch. Don't get in anybody's way. Just go in, and sit, and be good."

The Cohort officers saluted Ianthe as they passed her up and down the ramp. You noticed the ones who reeked of thanergy kiss their thumbs in a gesture you did not recognise. As you dragged your numb idiot body across the bay and staggered up the ramp, you were grateful that nobody did the same for you; you were once again given the wide berth accorded to a Ninth House necromancer.

The inside was as cramped as you'd suspected, and sordidly simple.

What arrested you immediately was the source of Ianthe's fascination and open admiration. Before the back wall of the shuttle, a necromancer of the Cohort squatted; necromantic miasma shone upon her as brightly to you as a torch. There was no fuel here for her to use to commit necromancy. She was in deep space, and she was not a Lyctor. What she *could* do was put the final touches on an exquisite nullification ward—wet and red with her own blood, which was being pumped out from a long syringe. It would have been difficult and arduous work even had she access to her aptitude. The arms of her robes were rolled all the way up to her shoulders so that the cloth would not touch and blur the pattern as she worked; you noted rucked-up House ribbons of pale seafoam green.

Ianthe saw you, and she startled. Before you could be relieved that there existed one Lyctor who might still startle for you, she made room for you on the upturned crate on which she was perched. You did not like to, but you sat primly on the corner proffered, trying to press your knees together to stop your bodies from touching. Today—and how much time had passed?—her eyes were that washed-out blue, with amethyst lights in them.

"You've met our respected elder sister, I see," Ianthe said. "She accused me of being twelve, called me one of *those* animaphiliacs, then told me I wasn't as good looking as someone called Cyrus. It was like being back with Mummy," she added, with a touch of fond nostalgia.

Your palm remembered the knife, and you resisted the chumminess. You said, "Where is the Emperor?"

"I don't know, and nobody will tell me anything," she said, more peevishly. "Everyone has been acting frankly mulish . . . which I suppose I can't blame them for, as I might act the same if I were peremptorily dropped from the Emperor's personal attaché and shipped off to the front . . . but what is the good of being *Ianthe the First,* if I can't even leverage it?"

You hazarded a quick glance to the Cohort necromancer; but the Seventh adept paid you no attention. You noticed that her ward—an expert's work, and an artist's, that of genius married to style—was a very familiar one: it was a ghost ward. You tried to wrench your brain back to the words Ianthe had said, and the order she had put them in. This was difficult, as what you knew about the Cohort and the front could fit into a teaspoon. Even that much knowledge had always annoyed you, but something she'd said had rattled your co-matose hypothalamus.

You said, "That makes no sense. The Imperial Guard doesn't see action."

"Oh, my sweet, you don't know . . . Well, how could you? It's not as though anyone's told you; you were too busy with your binary of throwing up or being murderous. Well, Nonagesimus, they *do* see ac-tion when the Cohort suddenly loses three warships to as many orbital radiation missiles, which is three more warships than we've lost in the past thousand years," said Ianthe. Were it possible for someone to puff more with self-satisfaction, she would be swollen and gouty and dead; but rather than irritated, you found that Ianthe just made you feel tired. "Eighteen thousand dead soldiers *will* grab the attention . . . Corona would love it. She's mad for military funerals."

It was difficult for you to muster empathy. You had nobody at the front, or indeed in the Cohort. The last Ninth House chaplains and construct adepts had, as you recalled, been lost in action five years back. The numbers remained numbers, lacking context. You were more interested in the conversation happening outside the shuttle's docking doors, before the ramp: an unfamiliar voice saying steadily: "Holy Saint, the *Erebos* is his vessel. I speak for every commanding officer aboard when I tell you how reluctantly we would see the end of his eighty years aboard."

"Eighty years!!" was the response, again with that articulated extra exclamation point. It was the result of extreme irascibility: the saint had a high, fluting voice, a young voice for someone who had now accused both you and Ianthe Tridentarius of actionable puberty, and it was piercing now. "Eighty is *shameful*—you knew the writing was on the wall when the call came for more Lyctors. His seat is elsewhere, and there he must return, and should have returned thirty years ago. You're now *Admiral* Sarpedon? Really? It *is* Sarpedon, isn't it?"

"Yes," said the *admiral,* whose title had been suggested by the

Lyctor in the same tone of voice as might be said *Chief Leper.* "And it
has been . . . twenty years since we last met, Most Venerated Saint?"

"Around that," agreed the most venerated saint, whose office had
been enunciated by the admiral with the faintest and most well-bred
suggestion of *motherfucker.* "In any case, you've had him eighty years,
and the Mithraeum has lacked him for a hundred."

"You are invoking throne silence," said Sarpedon. "You are removing him from the Empire."

"I can't very well invoke throne *speech.* We'll be forty billion light
years away."

The admiral said, through a thin rime of ice: "He has expressed, in
no uncertain terms, his close personal interest in this war."

"He can very well maintain a close personal interest in it from forty
billion light years away," said the Saint of Joy, who had just strongly
implied the opposite. Her name was sounding increasingly ironic to
you. "*I* do not blush to remove the Emperor from his enemies. *I* do
not blush ensuring the God of the Nine Houses is not molested by
those who hate him."

"I do not recognise," said Sarpedon, "any such frailty in the God
who became man, nor the man who became God, nor the Necrolord
Prime who may resurrect a galaxy with a gesture."

The Lyctor's voice rose further: "The risen star Dominicus gives
light and life to the Nine Houses, and yet I don't think we should *crash
anything into it*!! You just wore out my *last nerve,* Sarpedon, and I still
remember when there were fewer pips on your shirt, so I would ask
that you not mistake a Lyctor for someone you can—"

There was a shout from the other side of the fourteenth cargo hold.
It was the voice of the God who became man, and the man who became God. He approached the ramp at a swift clip, making a beeline
for the boiling-mad Saint of Joy. Beside you, Ianthe smacked her lips
as though in anticipation of a good meal; a sort of *mlem, mlem, mlem.*

But the Emperor wrapped his arms around his Lyctor as though
she were a precious and runaway child; he pressed her to him,
drawing down the hood and tousling that overripe rose-tinted hair,
heedless of the curtseying, bowing Cohort officers in the wake of

his passage. She froze as though dipped in liquid nitrogen. He said something that you couldn't catch, and then: "Thank you for your work here. You've done well."

The Saint of Joy was ramrod straight and still, as though her feet had been fixed to the docking-bay floor with big steel pins. The Emperor of the Nine Houses turned from her to the admiral, who was half into his own genuflection, pressing a hand to his shoulder and immediately embarking on a low conversation you could only catch in bits: "—no hurry going around the belt. If the wind off Dominicus gives you problems, take the same route back . . . Subluminary speed's fine. After you do your deliveries, stelitic travel will get you out of the supercluster and back to the second arm of the fleet, but you're going to have to go a lot slower than you have the past two weeks . . ."

"Then you do intend to leave us, Lord," said Sarpedon. He had moved so that now you could see him properly; your new hood, unlike good Ninth House furze, was transparent enough to let you see quite clearly, albeit through a stippled violence of rainbow light. You beheld a man of middling age in a sober Cohort uniform, perennial white jacket and scarlet neckerchief. The two pips on his collar were ringed around with mother-of-pearl. If you had not heard his rank, you would not have known what they signified. Necromantic vapour rose off him in roiling waves like sweat, unused and impotent in the vacuum of deep space. "I confess that I had not prepared for it."

"I hate to, Admiral," said God. "The *Erebos* has been my home."

The admiral said, a little stiffly: "We are unworthy of such love."

"I am unworthy of this pitiful goodbye," said the King Undying. "What I planned on telling you, I will tell you now, swifter and more gracelessly. Don't get caught up in the drama of the Cohort command. I know exactly who is behind this terrible blow, and they were fools to show their hand. They have revealed themselves to be as coarse and juvenile and foolish as the act they have just committed. But our retaliation should not be swift. Let them understand the inevitability of the Nine Houses."

"As inexorable as death," said the admiral.

"And as kind," said the Emperor. "You have shown your loyalty to me, Sarpedon, and I have never questioned you. You made the *Erebos* my respite. But—as I imagine you have just been told—" (Did the Saint of Joy writhe at that, or were you imagining it?) "—my station is my seat, and the *Erebos* is needed elsewhere."

"But to go unaccompanied, Lord—with the stele, a transport ship could be out as far as the Hadals in two years."

"Eighteen thousand good soldiers," the Emperor said gently. "Take the *Erebos* to them. And give her a new name—*Seat of the Emperor*."

"My lord—"

The Saint of Joy muttered something beneath her breath. The Emperor did not bat an eyelid. "Yes, I know it's lowly to captain a chair," he said. "But I won't have anyone in the Admiralty forget what she was, and what I hope she will be once more. In any case, the name ought to get you to the head of orbital queues, even if I'm not in residence. I'll miss her like fury, Sarpedon, but she's got thicker plates than anything else in the fleet, and when she's refitted she'll carry two thousand."

"Yet, Lord—"

"As for you, your bones will be hallowed in the Mithraeum, for all that you've done in my service. If I don't see you before then, all I can do is hope you get a chance for retirement."

The Emperor of the Nine Houses reached out to clasp Sarpedon's hand. The Cohort admiral looked as though he were being branded. The Emperor held this grasp, and the admiral's gaze, for a long time; then he turned back to the ramp up the dock, followed—a little reluctantly—by his Hand.

As he drew closer, you could see that he looked as though he had prepared in a hurry; he carried a small bag, hastily packed, slung over his shoulder—the ever-present tablet peeked out of his pocket, along with what seemed to be at least five styluses—and he was dressed simply, as per usual, in a black shirt and trousers. The lack of tint had always pleased you. It was very Ninth, even the collar and the cuffs of his shirt that were scruffy and pilled from too much wearing. But he wore a crown of office that you had not seen before: a wreath of ribbon and pearlescent leaves in his dark hair, rustling prismatically in the windless docking bay. Each leaf was intertwined with a match-sized infant fingerbone. He turned and strode up the ramp toward you, and he said very normally, like you'd never fainted before him in a lather of pre-puke: "Are you all right, Harrowhark?"

"I am perfectly capable, Teacher," you said.

"That's not the same thing."

Ianthe said, with a close approximation of winsomeness: "Put her under my care, Teacher," and you were disgusted to hear God reply, "I will. Keep an eye on her. Now—"

He turned to find the beautiful ward completed on the wall, and the Seventh adept quietly dying on the floor. There was a whorl of blood down her front; at some point she had levered her syringe deep into her subclavian artery. After finishing the final touches on the perfect nightmare spiral, which betrayed no trembling from myocardial trauma, she had sprayed fixative across it, then silently collapsed. She lay with her eyes rigid on the ceiling, hands clasped over the growing stain on the front of her robes, which were turning Second House scarlet with blood.

The Emperor mumbled something that, you would swear on the rock before the Tomb, sounded like *For fuck's sake.* After a moment's consideration, he pressed his hand to his mouth, as though in thought. The bloom that followed blinded you beyond unpicking, or even comprehending.

The stain crumbled to dust. The blood ceased flowing. The Seventh adept's hands clutched clean robes. Her expression changed from glassy-eyed expectation to resignation; she rolled over to kiss the dusty floor of the shuttle. You and Ianthe were left blinking, eyes and noses streaming, as though you had just eaten something slightly too spicy.

"Most Holy Lord," she said, but there was half a question in it.

"Not today, First Lieutenant," said God. "We need necromancers like you now more than ever."

She kissed her fingers at him, a little mechanically—and then to the Saint of Joy, and then to Ianthe, and then, after a pause, to you— half a dozen times, and then curtseyed to the point where she nearly folded herself right in half. She rose and escaped down the ramp, booted footsteps bouncing in her wake, the only sign she had been there the enormous whorl of the ward. The Saint of Joy watched her go with an unreadable expression on her placid portrait of a face.

With two more aboard, you could see how small the shuttle really was. To your left, there was a partitioned area that might have been for bodily functions—or going to the toilet, as everyone else in the known universe would have put it—but otherwise the space was bare. There were no beds. There were no real seats for passengers, except for a few pull-downs at the side. The boxes brought on were quite small; the biggest was a stone square strapped down with lengths of steel rope. Displaced from its fellows, the tiny rosebud gone, it took you a moment to realise that it was a coffin, and another moment to recognise whose.

To your right was a cockpit with empty seating for one pilot, spread with a wide and beautiful wrap of embroidered pearly material— and with a lurch in the back of your brain you saw it wasn't empty at all: the Body had taken up residence on that rainbow shawl, sitting there with her hands prim in her lap and the chain of welts clearly visible. The gorgeous and severe angles of her face were softened as though in recognition, and her lips were a little parted, enough to show her dead black tongue. When you followed her line of sight, she was looking at the entryway, and the Emperor.

The Emperor pressed a button next to the door and the ramp sucked up into the shuttle with a great mechanical *slarp*. Then he turned to his Lyctor and said, in a tone of thinly sprinkled sugar upon infinite salt: "Well, this looks a great deal like forcing my hand."

"Lord, I would never dare—"

"*My* flagship, to *my* admiral, among *my* people. Is the *Erebos* really the best place to publicly gainsay your Emperor, Mercy?"

She rounded on him. The canvas of her portrait face was now scrunched up in passionate fury. You had expected that ten thousand years would be enough to school a face whenever one wanted it schooled; apparently not, or Mercy had never bothered with schooling.

"The only one who forced your hand is coming home with us in a box," she cried out. "And it's *ugly* of you to use my name in front of the infants. We agreed our names were sacred—we let them all be forgotten—"

"Mercymorn," said the Emperor, "you know as well as I do that keeping your name from your rightful sisters is ridiculous. Also, you are trying to start a fight with me to get out of the fight I am trying to have with you, which is a painfully domestic tactic."

"You are nearly in Dominicus's halo—it looks suicidal—"

"You know why I came, and my reasons for waiting are out of—"

"Some would call it madness, or ego, or both—"

"Who's *some* in this instance, and does their name rhyme with *Nercynorn*—"

"It rhymes with *Naugustine*," said the Saint of Joy, with no small amount of hauteur.

The Emperor of the Nine Houses' face suddenly lit up like the sunrise of an inner-circle planet. "Then you and Augustine the First are talking again?"

Mercy threw her hands in the air, milking an invisible and gigantic cow in order to assuage her feelings, and flung herself to sit down on another secured crate. She put her chin in her hands; her rapier clattered beneath her rainbow-white cloak with the movement. "We were *talking*," she said, chilly and measured, "as little as nineteen years ago, if you'd recall. If we talk again now, it doesn't actually signify, being as *speaking* is so different from *talking*. And I am not on speaking terms with—the person you refer to. Nonetheless, your actions moved me to *talk* to that silly man-shaped worm, and *I* came here to take matters into my own hands." Before he could say another word, she said: "Nobody's answering calls on the Mithraeum. Come home, please!"

"But that's—"

"Three of us remain," said the Lyctor simply. "I can't even confirm the third is alive."

"He was keeping tabs on—" began the Emperor, and seemed as though he were about to elucidate those tabs; but he caught sight of you and Ianthe sitting quietly, waiting for this dreadful conversation to end (you) or nakedly desperate for more (Ianthe). He set his little shoulder bag down in what appeared to you, wild with panic, to be the Body's lap. She looked up at him, impassive, and then at the bag, nonplussed. Then he dropped down on his haunches in front of his sullen Lyctor.

What followed was a conversation entirely in shorthand: at one point it was simply conducted in shrugs. He would say a word; she would retort with a totally different word, and the Emperor would grimace or give her sharp rejoinder. On occasion, that sharp rejoinder was simply a quirk of his mouth, and the Lyctor would turn her head, loser of that bout. You were watching two people who had outgrown conversation half a myriad back. It was more a dialogue between arm and elbow; heart and brain, shared via electrical impulse. At no prearranged point, they suddenly returned to normal speech, and God said:

"I was going to wait on the *Erebos* until we had heard definitively whether or not the launch—"

"I don't care if it was them or not," sniffed the Saint of Joy—Mercymorn—whom you now knew possessed *two* utterly inapt names. "They're *remnants.* They can't do anything. Their leader has been gone for nearly twenty years. You've got to prioritise."

"But this is so obviously—"

"I beg you to recall the *stakes,* Lord!!" said the Lyctor.

"The Mithraeum is a destination we can reach by only one means," said God, with the air of a man pulling a final brick out of a wobbling tower. "I cannot yet in good conscience take either of them on that journey."

You were terribly afraid that *either of them* had been a hasty replacement for *Harrowhark.* The elder Lyctor did not assuage your fears when she looked up at him with those unfathomable tempest eyes and said, "If you are that unsure of—*either* of them—then put them down now! They won't thank you for keeping them alive! It's the only test that matters! Thanks!"

The Emperor of the Nine Houses stood up. His Lyctor stood also. Her hand had twitched aside the nacreous folds of her robe to rest on the end of a simple and unpretentious rapier, the mesh nest that formed around the handle unadorned and uncomplicated, no decoration other than a white knob at the very end of the—you didn't know the exact technical word. It was a pommel though. He said: "Prepare to launch. I'll make the call," and you knew that, somehow, Mercy had won the war.

It was with a strange admixture of relief and hard, resentful shame that Mercy stood and leaned over the pilot's chair, flicking switches, avoiding the Body by a hair's breadth. The switches made nice haptic clanks within their plex housings, and more lights came on overhead, bathing you all in an unpleasantly orange glow.

Though there was no change in God's pitch or cadence, his voice had taken on a different cast. It was as though a steel tool had been taken from its housing. He said, "Double-check those boxes. Get them in the straps—make sure that one's nice and tight—Ianthe, there are belt chairs by that window—Harrow, I want that sword out of your hands and fixed to the floor. Use marrow in the bone; I don't want it to crack or bend."

You and Ianthe knelt to fix the containers at his instruction. You reluctantly melted the comb of bone attaching your sword to your straining arm. As an afterthought, you did what you had been told to in the letter from your past self: you iced the whole blade over with a casing of bone, and found the result significantly more pleasing to the eye and brain. You could never castrate its anger, but thus sheathed, the sword—that object of your resentment, and hate, and protective panic—could be dimmed somewhat, like a lampshade dimmed a lamp.

Afterward, you dropped into a pull-down seat next to Ianthe and clicked the safety belt together while your bare feet kept troth with the bone-enamelled sword, and you watched God's final test of metal hasps and cinches on the boxes. He brushed his hand very lightly over the secured stone of the coffin, the very briefest of touches, before stopping in front of the ward that had been applied to the wall. He pressed the tip of his little finger to one of the whorls, very gently, as though afraid to hurt it. The foetal fingerbones and leaves crowning his hair kept swaying in some nonexistent breeze. "Brilliantly executed . . . nearly perfect levels of carbon dioxide in the fixative," he said, taking a stylus from his pocket. "She was much too good to die for it, Mercy."

"I didn't tell her to *die* for it," said Mercymorn snappishly. With a sudden *clunk*, the open door to the shuttle started descending, groaning into place where the ramp had disappeared. It fell into its housing with a *ker-chunk*. "Her going full atria was perfectly over-the-top. The crew on your horrible flagships are always trying to martyr themselves whenever you so much as ask for an orange juice."

"I'm telling Sarpedon to give her a commendation," he said, tapping at his tablet. "That will have to do. It's not exactly an appropriate thank-you for nearly bleeding out."

The communicator at the pilot's chair crackled. The admiral's voice in question said clearly, "My lord, you're cleared to leave. We await your word."

"Loose the clamps," said the Emperor.

"The clamps are set for release," said Admiral Sarpedon. Then he cleared his throat and began what you now thought of as the common prayer: "*Let the King Undying, ransomer of death, scourge of death, vindicator of death, look upon the Nine Houses and hear their thanks—*" and from behind him joined in the tinny voices of the entire docking crew: "*Let the whole of everywhere entrust themselves to him . . .*"

You peered over your shoulder at the porthole. The dimmed interior of Docking Bay Fourteen was lightening: they were opening up some outer airlock, and the shuttle itself was travelling on rails as though to be offered to space like a sacrifice. The velvety blackness of the outside world became naked; cold stars burnt in the distance. The Body came to stand next to you all of a sudden, and you had to school yourself not to reach for the hem of her dirty white shift, the pallid dimpled flesh of her calf. You were leaving, for where you did not know, and you did not know how to feel.

Ianthe kept her eyes downcast, modest and pliant, as though this sickening and poorly acted rôle would convince anyone with a brain. She sat with her rapier belted at her hip beneath her robe, raising bumps beneath the mother-of-pearl cloth, and when you caught her gaze beneath those pallid lashes you could see the hot anticipation in her eyes—one blue, one purple—of someone about to be announced for an award. She was deeply excited. That starry, far-off gaze refocused on you, and she whispered coyly: "Should we hold hands, in girlish solidarity?"

At your expression, she puffed away a strand of colourless hair and remarked, "*You're* the one who investigated my tonsils."

Over the prayer still crackling through the speaker grille, Mercy said, "Releasing in thirty," and the Emperor, "Don't triangulate. We don't want to put them in danger. We'll hold course until the *Erebos* is out of our radius."

He took the lovely rainbow shawl and draped it over the pilot's chair, and Mercymorn daintily sat down upon it, belting herself in. The Body was gone. Little clusters of bone set over the cockpit window tinkled musically with the displaced air. The Emperor stood behind Mercy, one hand on the chair back, himself a light plex jangle of styluses whenever he moved, and he leant down to press down on the comm button. The prayer stopped as though everyone praying had lost the air from their lungs.

"Our enemies have once more raised their hands to those who would be at peace with them," he said. "Again, we are a violated covenant, and again we are struck at with anger, and with fear, by those who cannot reason and those who cannot forgive what we are. You who have served on the *Erebos*—my soldiers and necromancers of the Nine Houses—if you find yourselves on the battlefield, remember that I will make even the dying echo of your heartbeat a sword. I will make the stilled sound on your tongue a roar. I will recall you when you are a ghost in the water, and by that recollection you will be divine. On your death, I will make the very blood in your body arrows and spears.

"Remember that I am the King Undying."

He lifted his hand off the communicator button, cutting short the primal, triumphant howl that had echoed from the docking crew. You were painfully aware of the lamplights of thalergy signifying the

Cohort officers in the dock—ten of them in a cluster a mere forty metres away: too close to be doing anything to aid the shuttle, but praying, maybe. There were more of them, farther away. An orderly line, flushed with blood, pattering with gut flora. They were perhaps working the mechanisms. There were muffled booming sounds as the shuttle clamps were loosed.

The engines behind the blood-daubed wall groaned to life in a huge, dull roar; those thalergy lights fell farther and farther away as you were lowered out the airlock on long struts of plex and steel. Mercy eased a lever upward, nose wrinkling in concentration, and then the thalergy rose away entirely. You dropped through space. The shuttle might as well have been empty for all that you could sense within, except for that single foetal bundle of thanergy lying still inside the coffin. As you looked through the plex window behind you, you saw the *Erebos,* and for the first time you got a sense of the enormity of the flagship: its scintillating, dark, and rainbow-hued steel, like an oil spill; the interlocking skeletons tessellated over the whole boxy structure, so that the vessel seemed an enormous moving ossuary. The iris of light from the fuel ignition hurt your eyes as it sped away.

Artificial gravity meant you were perfectly still and stable, but you still felt ill from the idea that you were drifting and tumbling through space like an abandoned piece of cargo.

God said, "Children, attend."

You hardly needed the invitation. The Emperor was drumming his fingers on the back of the pilot's seat, his curious black-on-black eyes not focused on you. He said, "You are both going to have to listen to me very carefully. The Mithraeum is far away, and our route is not typical. I'm about to teach you the first lesson, and this lesson will be the foundation of the most important lesson you will ever learn as a Lyctor. There will be a time for you to learn through questioning—a time for you to learn through trying and failing—but right now you'll learn by doing exactly what I ask of you. The only other option is your destruction."

This did not give you much pause. You were a daughter of the Locked Tomb. The option of destruction had been your constant companion since you were three years old. Ianthe, whose voice was low with barely suppressed excitement, said: "I thought there might be a stele."

"A stele is eight feet tall, covered in the dead languages by special Fifth adepts, and continually bathed in oxygenated blood," said Mercymorn from the pilot's seat. "The type of thing where, if there is one on board, you say quite soon, 'Oh, look, a stele!'"

"Thank you, elder sister, I so love to be educated," said Ianthe.

"Where we are going there are no obelisks for a stele to hook on to," said the Emperor, whose fingers had ceased drumming on the back of the pilot's seat (after his Lyctor had told her God, repressively, "That's quite annoying, thank you,") and were now restlessly adjusting one shabby shirtsleeve. "I am taking you both through the River."

There must have been no small measure of blank incomprehension on your faces. He said, a little abstracted now: "It's the only way. Faster-than-light travel turned out to be a snare—the way it was originally cracked, anyway. The first method destroyed something to do with time and distance, rendering it unusable for any good purpose . . ."

"I've always thought it should be correctly managed with wormholes," said the Saint of Joy, doing something obtuse with the controls, "or spatial dilation."

God said, "It's in that wheelhouse. We came up with the stele instead, and the obelisk, which are less to do with travel than they are to do with transmission. But there will be times in your future when you will have to move unfettered by needing an obelisk, and even times yet to come when you will fulfil the sacred Lyctoral duty of *setting* obelisks, and that means travel through the River. I like to think of it as descending into a well."

There was a small noise of upset from the pilot's seat. "Teacher," said Mercy, "it is the River. There is a perfectly good water metaphor waiting for you."

"Well, I want the idea of two depths, and I don't want to confuse them with the idea of speed where none—"

"—it's the *River,* which perfectly well lets you say, *Imagine the River—*"

"Mercy, either you don't like my previous, perfectly good river phrasing, or you do. Pick one."

"I will not help you to make *hyperpotamous travel* happen, thank you for the option, my lord," said Mercy.

"In that case, despite *hyperpotamous* being a perfectly good word that both catches the ear and does what it says on the tin, let's deviate," said the Lord of the Nine Houses, who apparently existed within a complex power dynamic. "I'll use Cassiopeia's." ("Oh, no, the *lava*," said Mercy.) "Girls, imagine a rocky planet with a magma core beneath the mantle.

"Travelling overland from point to point might take a year. If you understood your journey and the relative spaces well enough, you could instead drop into the magma, which would carry you to your destination in an hour."

He paused. The inside of the shuttle seemed very silent to you; there was no sound from its internal apparatus, excepting an occasional huge creak from its rudder mechanism. Ianthe's voice broke this mechanical, cold-steel silence by saying, quite carefully for Ianthe: "Teacher, the River is an enormous liminal space formed from spirit magic, populated with ghosts gone mad from hunger."

"The magma metaphor falls apart from here," said Mercy, eyes still on the pilot's switches.

The Emperor responded with perfect gravitas: "Let us imagine the magma is full of unkillable man-eating magma fish. Two problems arise. The first is that beings made of flesh and blood immediately die in magma. The second is our vulnerability to man-eating fish."

Your tolerance for man-eating magma fish would have been tested sorely by anyone who was not God. His divinity earned God, you thought, about sixty more seconds. But then he said, more quietly: "We are about to travel forty billion light years, to where we first ran . . . myself, and my remaining six. One of our number was dead already, and another had been removed from play. We needed somewhere to lick our wounds, somewhere far away from anything we loved, to wait—to disperse—without fear that the eyes turning upon us would plough straight through the Nine Houses as they went. It's a dark and cold and unlovely part of space, and the stars there are old and were nearly dead then. We nuked them with thanergy and now they'll shine forever, but the light is not the same . . . It would take us years to get there if we went from stele to stele. How far away from the system was Number Seven at last reckoning, Mercy?"

"Counting down, five years," said Mercymorn, whose hands had at last stilled on the board of buttons and switches and enamelled bone. "Five years, six months, one week, two days."

"The merest blink of an eye," said the Emperor, beneath his breath. He pushed himself away from the pilot's chair and said, "We worked out a while ago—I say *we*, but I had little to nothing to do with it—that distance is different down there. The River doesn't flow through the time and space we're experiencing right now; the River is—well, it's a current *below* us, as in the magma analogy. Distance in the River doesn't map to distance above. If I drop us into it we can emerge almost immediately across the universe, home. The station, our refuge. We call it the Mithraeum."

He spread his hands wide: ordinary hands, ordinary fingers, ink-smudged nails. "Look at the ward. What is it?"

You were beginning to note the register of his *Teacher* voice. This was familiar ground, untouched by magma. The ward undulated in the shadows a little, which was a trick of the light and the blood. You said, "It's just a ghost ward," and after a second regretted speaking like a provincial bone witch.

Thankfully Ianthe was even more petulant, and a dyed-in-the-wool flesh magician, as she added: "It's not even a *sophisticated* ghost ward. I mean, it's exquisite, impeccable right down to the coagulation. But I was doing those when I was five."

"That ghost repellent will keep our ship from shaking apart," said the Emperor. "That ghost repellent will have every lonesome spirit for kilometres screaming away. For a time."

"One minute, thirty-three seconds," said Mercy.

He said, "Give or take."

The Emperor came to drop on his haunches in front of you and Ianthe, as he had squatted before Mercymorn earlier. It still hurt you in an undefinable way, to see him lowered so: as though he offered a compliance test where you ought to flatten yourself in front of him as low as you could go. The white ring around his pupil was so white. "Your job is simple in the way most very tough things are. I will push us into the River, and I'll push the ship with us. You'll have to keep your minds—I can take your physical bodies, but your souls won't go with them, not without you holding them steady."

"Physical transference past the liminal boundaries," you said, and were surprised by the knowledge coming out of you, as though it weren't your own. "This is deep Fifth spirit magic."

"And I bless the Fifth House and I bless their long memory," said the Emperor. "They only go far enough to tempt lost ghosts to them. They stand on the sidelines and wave around bits of meat and anchoring material. But they don't even approach the shore."

Ianthe sounded much more like her twin sister when she said, wonderingly: "But if applied universally, this would revolutionise the fleet. We could expend no fuel or effort, travelling instantly. We would be truly unstoppable."

Mercy laughed a nasty trill of laughter. "A powerful necromancer at the peak of their game could last ten seconds in the River," said God, pushing himself up to stand. "Soul magic is the great leveller. In the first few seconds their thanergy would all be stripped away . . . then their thalergy, and then their soul. They wouldn't have time for the ghosts to get to them. They cannot, returning to our analogy, live in magma."

"*We* can live in magma," said Mercymorn, then pressed one elbow into the pilot's deck and pressed her head into that elbow, and complained: "Now I'm doing it."

"A Lyctor has a metaphorical sitting temperature of over a thousand degrees," said the Emperor. He had gone to check the boxes again, and the clasps. Space rotated slowly past the windows, inordinately black and dizzying. "We have this incomparably done ward, exquisitely created by an expert who gave her heart's blood for it—it may last for around a minute and a half. I'm hoping for up-ward of a minute forty, with work like that—and we're on our own from there . . . No Lyctor has lasted longer than seven minutes in full physical submersion. And that was a titanic effort on the part of Cassiopeia the First, who was brilliant and sensible and careful—she thought she could bait physical portions of the Resurrection Beast into the current. She was right. It followed her."

You said, "And?"

Mercy said lowly: "It turned out that being sensible and brilliant and careful doesn't keep you from getting ripped to shreds by ten thousand feral ghosts."

Ianthe said, "But the Beast—?"

"Emerged unscathed twenty minutes later," the Emperor said. And: "Life's a bitch."

He looked out the window to the stars, and to the jewelled gleam of a planetoid in the distance, which looked a sooty red from your position. "Unbuckle your belts," he said. You both did so. "Lie down on the floor."

You and Ianthe said as one, your voice a parched whisper, hers low and cool: "Yes, Teacher."

Self-conscious of your limbs, you lay down on the floor. The Kindly Prince said very evenly: "Start slowing your breath. I want it at two per minute. If you need to flush yourself with oxygen, do it now. It has been a long time since I have thought about teaching this trick, and I barely know where to begin."

"You should start with Pyrrha's trial," called out the other Lyctor immediately.

"Right," said the Emperor. Then: "I mean, I was being more or less facetious, Mercy, but yes, I'll probably begin there— Do you both recall the projection trial, back at Canaan House? It would have been in Lab Three."

You recalled the enormous construction of regrowing bone, your hands encased in it so that you could not wrench yourself free, your mind voyaging nauseously into the chamber of another person's brain. God said, "You'll need that skillset now. Your mind and body won't couple automatically in the River. You have to hold them together, and any wrong move will see your consciousness stuck on the outskirts of Dominicus, wondering how the hell to get home. Most of the time you won't even bother taking your body into the waters—it's too dangerous—but for physical travel, we'll need mind and body both."

Your mind was racing, and you cursed yourself, not for the first time, for not continuing your advanced studies into spirit magic. You said, "What happens to a Lyctoral body without a soul?"

God hesitated. "Being separated from your soul won't kill you," he said. "Not immediately. But—"

"But *we'll* kill you," said his saint. "Immediately. A Lyctor's body, empty, with its battery intact but nobody in the driver's seat? Do you know what could take up residence? *Anything* could get inside you—any horrible or evil or lonely thing, any miserable revenant, or worse—and *you*, you Ninth House child, are not remotely qualified to fight an outside predator. You are like a little baby. Listen to this: if we get to the other side and find you've gone and left your soul behind—I will separate your brain from your skull without waiting for you to catch up."

And God said nothing.

"When do we start?" Ianthe's voice was clinical, like she was waiting for a tooth extraction.

"Start?" said Mercymorn. "He began submerging thirty seconds ago."

God said, "Timer?"

"Set at five minutes."

"We need a slower pace. Set it to six."

"Five minutes thirty," said Mercymorn, but God said: "I am not negotiating. Call out the increments once we hit waterline."

The Saint of Joy said, with unexpected obedience: "Done. Be careful, Teacher."

In the depths of space, now the depths of the River, the shuttle was a false gravity cocoon. You did not know which way was up, or down, or in what direction you were going. You were lying on the floor, trying to stop your lungs from expanding too quickly. Slowing your breath was blurring you out. You did not feel at peace, but rather numb and transfixed, heavy eyed, until God said, "Keep conscious," and you stretched out the muscles of your calves until they strained, down to the tendons above the balls of your feet.

You lay on your mummified sword, which skulked sullenly beneath its caulk of bone. You stared at the ceiling. You tilted your head and found Ianthe looking *through* you. She was lying bracketed between her own rapier and her own offhand, and you were close enough for discomfort. Mercy said, "Hoods over your heads. They're translucent for a reason," and the Emperor added, "It's easier when you can perceive light, but not get distracted."

You were not sorry to do this. Your vision softened into a jumble of lights, like looking into a headache or white noise. There were no shapes or shadows. Ianthe faded into a mother-of-pearl lump beside you. It was impossible to tell which visual sparks of colour were due to the cloak, and which were your own shimmers of migraine fright.

Your breath sounded an unlovely peal. Ianthe's sounded like a bellows. You could not hear that of the Emperor of the Nine Houses—maybe you never had—nor that of the elder Lyctor. The shuttle's habitation controls had either been turned off or set low even by Ninth House standards: beneath the thin robes and minty smock, your thighs were pimpled with cold. And nothing happened. No thanergetic flush, no thalergetic wane. You'd never been a spirit adept, and you did not feel now any subtleties of transition; it was very cold. That was all.

You were dead weight in that heavy chill, each breath a ponderous inflation of the lungs, in and out, in and out. You were aware of yourself, of each juncture of energy inside you; you were aware that your feet had blisters, that your throat was stripped by too much upchucking, and that you felt alone in your head. You were embarrassed by your distraction. The physical body had never occurred to you so much in previous meditation. The light from the ceiling above had dulled to a sooty orange glow like that from a lit furnace; you fell into a numb, half-alive, half-dead reverie, your anxiety stifled and calcified, until you heard Ianthe cry out.

You stared through the minute slit where your hood brushed your cheeks. You made no sound, because you were not sure you were seeing what Ianthe was seeing: for your part, you saw the water.

7

THE WATER CAME BUBBLING up through the bolted seams in the floor panels, a filthy, rusty red, with a bloom like sewage upon it. It had already boiled up to the front of the shuttle and was to the top of what you could see of the Emperor's shoes. It seemed unsure of gravity, running this way and that; then it started coming in high-pressure spurts through the sides of the cockpit's front window.

"Thirty seconds," said Mercymorn, whose voice had gone so utterly from petulant to clinical that it seemed the voice of a different woman. "Five minutes thirty remaining."

There was rustling from right next to you. The Emperor said, "Keep flat."

Ianthe said urgently, "Lord, I can see them."

Them? But the Emperor said, "Focus on them. Don't be afraid. Take off your hood if you want to. But think about the details of the shuttle too . . . where you were, where I am, where Mercy is, where Harrowhark is . . . the details of the shuttle are a projected memory and they are not all real, but they will dissolve further as you leave your body behind, and I don't want to lose you."

To the empty reaches of space, or to Mercy? The Lyctor said, "Four minutes, thirty seconds remaining. Ward has an estimated half a minute left."

You were too curious to resist. You wrenched the opaline hood from your face and were startled all the way to your soul. Turbid, filmy water was filling up the shuttle at a rate of knots. The floor had gone entirely, and you were affrighted by its wet and corporeal reality: you were soaked through almost to the ribs by tepid, greasy waves. Ianthe had sat up—she never could follow instructions—but she was staring, glassy-eyed, at some point you could not see, rigid and uncomprehending. You scanned around, but the Body was nowhere to be seen.

It was just water. It soaked the hems of the Emperor's trousers—he sat calmly flicking at his tablet as though it were no inconvenience. You could not quite see the other Lyctor, except her arms, bathed in the glow of the cockpit switches. The water seeped around your neck and started trickling into your ear canals. This did not fill you with the rigid terror it apparently produced in Ianthe: as a child you had been plunged into water by your mother and father, so the sensation was old and familiar, if wretched. The waters swirled and rose. They brushed against your cheeks, and you reflexively held your breath.

"Let that go, Harrow," said God, tapping on the tablet with his stylus. "You don't need to breathe."

You exhaled, trickling it out of your nose and mouth. Your brain panicked briefly as you took a shy lungful of warm, muddy water. The fluid went down your throat in a peculiar and unreal way: it sat there, seething in your craw, peristalsis not coming into play. You filled up with water like a rubber doll dropped into a well. It was with very little joy that you saw this was distressing Ianthe a great deal more than it was you: she had wrapped one arm around herself, leaving the rightmost to trail abandoned in the water, and was shaking in a kind of convulsive spasm of the soul. It was only the memory of the knife and the palm that prevented you from being moved to pity.

God was saying, quite encouragingly: "You're fine, Harrowhark. You're doing very well," which put you in a paranoid panic that you were not, in fact, doing well at all. Something brushed past your ankle, and the water closed over your head. You did not float: you stayed stuck to the bottom like a concrete weight, without buoyancy. Something floated in the water quite close to the pilot's seat where Mercymorn sat. A long skein of abandoned skin, fresh and virgin, as though taken from someone's flank and carded of its flesh and fat. The water in which it floated felt warm against your eyeballs, and smarted a little going up your nose.

From the shifting, refracting ripples within this tide, you beheld the ward upon the wall: it was steaming. Its bottom whorls sizzled and sparked like malfunctioning machinery where they touched the water. Showers of blue sparks pattered into the greasy water like rain.

"The ward has lasted for one minute, forty seconds," said Mercymorn. "One minute forty-one."

God said, "*Two* commendations for the lieutenant."

She called out, "One minute forty-four . . . . One minute forty-five," and in the space between *forty-four* and *forty-five*, the ward exploded. The dried blood came off the wall in flakes of brown confetti. It left behind a burnt, warped indentation as it slithered away to dissolve in the rising current. Next to you, Ianthe arched her spine so acutely that she folded up in the middle, as though she had been electrocuted. The light from the panels limned her in amber; her hood had come loose and her long pale hair floated about her shoulders like a caul. You propped yourself up on your elbows, distracted by something nudging against the plex viewing panel where Mercy sat piloting the shuttle. The star-pocked blackness of space had retreated entirely: the shuttle looked as though it were sinking down into a murky, obscure ocean.

Another nudge. Then something slapped two wet and rotting hands on the plex.

"Ick! Bleff!!" said Mercymorn, quite calmly. "Three minutes remaining."

"I hate this part," said God.

A nude, fish-eaten body thudded down hard atop the plex, leaving a momentary bloom of blood before it bounced off again. Another hit a few seconds later, but this one stayed put; it was a torso with the legs gone and the face eaten away, leaving the shiny skull to bang against the surface. It pressed one hand down, as though beseeching, but was sucked away again into the deep water outside the shuttle. The water inside now sloshed up to the Emperor's shoulders, washing over Mercymorn's hands. She did not bother to take her fingers away from the controls.

Ianthe's face remained slack and unfocused. You rounded your

spine up cautiously and looked around the shuttle, underwater, at the
dissipating blooms of brown and red in the liquid, as though someone
were bleeding out into it. At the back of the shuttle, you thought—you
thought you could perceive a high and keening wail, at the very edge
of your hearing—but neither God, nor the elder Lyctor, and certainly
not Ianthe reacted to it.

The wail was coming from within the shuttle. It had a hard, pained
edge to it, like frustration. You cast around trying to figure out from
where. There was another big wet thump as a fourth body slammed
itself on the plex, and this one managed to hold on, scrabbling grue-
somely; but you focused on the thin cry of violence. You found yourself saying, "Someone's crying, Lord," but he just made a nonsense
sound beneath his breath, a mumbled word that you didn't recognise.

"Two minutes, thirty seconds remaining," said Mercymorn, and
her voice took on a hard edge of caution.

The Emperor said, "They're not as numerous as I'd have expected."

"I do not like this," said his Lyctor.

Your eyes slid back up to the ceiling. The water, oleaginous and
warming, was thick now with the flotsam and jetsam of bits of corpse.
When something bumped your foot, you flinched and grasped a fine
fleck of bone from your tibia, tried to work it through your skin to
ice over your feet. It didn't precisely succeed. Instead of a fine outer
needle of matter, you pulled a wet plug from just above the epiphyseal
line, and your shinbone opened like a flower; your blood and cellular
matter opened up on your rainbow robe and floated upward, and
God turned around, and his face was indistinct in the murk but his
voice was not—

"Oh—" He used a word you did not understand. "Harrowhark,
no theorems!"

"Don't be ridiculous. She can't be using theorems," said Mercy.
"She'd be barely awake and it's totally beyond her at this poi—*John,
stop her, she's using theorems!!*"

The pain did not matter. The shuttle had shivered, somehow,
around you: synaptogenesis had erupted in your braincase, and
your eyes were opening. You were lying in a sea of bodies. They had

bumped up against you before you had realised it, before you could flinch away from their nearness: perhaps the blood conjured them into being, so suddenly were they there. You stood up without thinking, and more bumped gently into your elbows, your arms. They carpeted the bottom of the shuttle. They bobbed in an unseen current low to the ground, lacking the air to drift to the top. Through a thin curtain of your blood you could see the dizzying array of slippery corpses, their faces painted in black and alabaster greys. Dead girls in their teens, their half-exposed bones still caught in the act of fusing at the caps; dead boys still shedding their milk teeth; ungendered infants, mostly skull, their nails like tiny chips of stone. A rubber-bodied toddler with a painted face and very red hair lay dead beside your knee and for some reason it was this that destroyed you, it was this that kindled within you something you had no hope of defending against. You howled in a purity of fright.

The Emperor was wading toward you through this bobbing array of dead. He was saying something you paid no particular attention to: "Harrow, it's not real. Only you can see what you're seeing, and everything inside the shuttle is illusion. It's the River. The River is a predator—the dead are in your brain. It's trying harder with you because you're fundamentally deeper in it than Ianthe. I didn't think you'd be able to go this deep, first time in, but you have. Walk back toward me."

"Two minutes remaining," said Mercy. And: "They are coming for the source of the noise. I stood on the bank and watched Cassiopeia die, Teacher—"

"—do *not* rev that engine, Mercymorn—"

"She led them away from the brain; I was there in projection, and I saw when they seized her legs and arms . . . I was laying stakes for the Beast, and I was there, and I thought to myself, Lord, *But what will we do with your ceramics collection? There is so much of it.*"

You pressed your hands to your face and were startled all over again that you could not close your eyes. When you pressed the lids down, the light changed, and—you recalled this, as though you had done it before—you lost visual complexity. The shuttle was gone, but the water was not, and the bodies were everywhere. You were lost in a deep aperture. Hot bloody blisters bubbled up from your skin, and you were aware of yourself, not as a structure, but as a sickly radiance: one sickly radiance among other sickly radiances, one, two, three, four, five, all around you, one beneath. The distant scream coalesced. You realised it was coming from you.

Your eyes opened. You looked at the blanketing bodies of the dead children of the Ninth House, were aware of yourself as an ova cluster of two hundred pinpricks of light. You were a sigil: you were an intermingled fire. The fluid was sucked from your sinus cavities, and with it your brain, soon disassembled. You were made small. You were a throat, you were an oven. The water was boiling hot and your skin was sloughing off you in reddened, shrinking frills; those pinpricks boiled within you, and the bodies boiled without—you were a hunger without a stomach. You felt the thanergetic pit inside the coffin, the curve of a childlike jaw, the pallid bow of a dead mouth. You did not understand yourself as standing, nor understood yourself as walking, but you were doing both. You were dying in that hot water; whatever wanted your meat suit could have it.

"Harrowhark," said God. "Over here—over here, kid. I daren't touch you. Come toward me. *Toward* me—*Mercy, as you love me, do not push that button.*"

"Thirty seconds," said Mercymorn, and quietly: "Lord, you doom your Houses."

You could see everything. The shuttle was a tawdry nest of fuselage and metal sheeting, wiped over with plex and antifriction gels; breakable, startlingly so. You could see in a multiplicity of directions. You could see the dead blood ward churning beneath the water, the metal where it had etched itself curling and seizing beneath superheated steam. You could see your live blood, rising up in bright red plumes before you, leaving streaks of red on your robe.

Mercy said, "Twenty-five. The shuttle is becoming porous. I'm starting to feel drag."

"*Hold* it."

Something hit the shuttle like a closed fist: it spun from side to side, going nearly all the way around like a top, and you fell off and away from that needle. You fell to your knees on a soft dead pile of children and stared over your shoulder where Ianthe lay propped up on the floor, shrieking shamelessly in fright.

Mercy did not pay attention. "Twenty seconds."

"I'll grab Harrow. Gun it."

"Oh, thank God, finally–what do you mean, *grab*—"

"I'm going to have to touch her. Hit the acceleration."

"Wait, Lord, if she pulls you away—"

"The *throttle*, Mercy, in Cristabel's name!" God roared.

She slammed a lever. Five points of light. Ianthe was staring and insubstantial, shuddering out of her lineation as though vibrating straight out of reality. Everything was borne away into this mad and boiling riptide, and when you followed Ianthe's line of sight, the plex screen of the shuttle was a mass of dead hands, and trailing guts, and water, and blood. From your kneeling point, someone grabbed you from beneath your armpits and dragged you backward; there was a huge and overwhelming sound like some vast machine backfiring, and you kept thinking, *Five?* but then there was nothing left of you.

8

THE TEA WAS OVERWHELMING, and tasted too much. By choice Harrowhark had only ever drunk water. When she had been younger, or ill, the marshal had made her sugar-water with a drop of preserved lemon in it, as a treat; even then she'd had to take her time over each sip. Each bright citric burst had been half pleasure, half pain on her tongue; the sweetness so acute as to almost hurt her teeth. This new hot stuff tasted like a forest fire. It was with seriously burnt taste buds and no saliva in her mouth that she froze when the dire little man said, smiling: "And perhaps the Locked Tomb will favour us with their intercession?"

What seemed like a thousand eyes turned upon her. With a great internal fury, Harrowhark blanked. It was her cavalier who opened his mouth in the vast, corpsified atrium of Canaan House, and began: *"I pray the tomb is shut forever. I pray the rock is never rolled away . . ."*

She did not join him. If one did not begin a prayer in perfect unison, better not to pray belatedly. She listened as Ortus said words she suddenly doubted he even believed, full of a very weary resentment at herself and at people, everywhere. In that rotting hall there were people of all different sizes and postures; apart from the three priests they were all young, or young enough to eyes accustomed to her grey congregation, and they were dressed in a nightmare spectrum of colours and fripperies and materials. Classic constructs stood by dressed in white. She hated it when people dressed constructs; it smacked of whimsy, like making one's hammer wear a hat. They had provided escort into the hall, dropping big handfuls of something green and white for people to gingerly crush beneath their feet as

108

they walked under the cracked marble arches of the First House dock. She had realised with a thrill of frugal, exotic horror that it was plant matter. Some of those assembled had given fleeting, backward-shoulder glances to her, and to Ortus; and she was aware that she was not imposing—was acutely aware that she might be mistaken for younger, was aware of the optics of Ortus, whose bigness and sadness filled rooms she was already minute within—and their gazes held flickers her eyes were too sore to translate. Fine. That was manageable; that was their mistake to make, whole and entire.

O corse of the Locked Tomb, she prayed silently to herself, *the cold death to anyone who looks at me in pity; the heat death to anyone who looks at me in amusement; the quick death to anyone who looks at me in fear.*

As Ortus finished, the priests of the First smiled, just a little, and only with their mouths. It occurred to Harrow that the First and the Ninth were the only two Houses that understood how to wait for a thing that would never happen. Her cavalier rounded off the prayer, dolefully: *"And so hail to the Lord of the Sharpest Edge, and the gossamer thinness of his blade, and the cleanness of his cut."*

"An ancient epithet!" said the ghastly old man that Harrow would come to curse as *Teacher.* He looked near death with excitement. He looked close to capering, which filled Harrowhark with a dry and powdery despair. "A classic, unuttered for years even in this House! How may I bless you for that, Ortus the Ninth?"

"Pray only that my bones be one day interred in the Anastasian monument, where even the ghost of the light does not go," said Ortus, in front of everybody, like an absolute shit. Even in the shadow the heat slapped down on him, and beneath his veil some idiot had painted him with the Skull of the Anchorite Dying, that idiot probably being Ortus. As he wept from the sunshine the alabaster wounds of the Anchorite turned to big runnels of paint. No First priest's blessing could get him inside the Anastasian, the tomb reserved for warriors: Ortus was only likely to die with a heretic's blood still wet on his sword if he found a very slow heretic. "That is the only blessing I desire."

The other priests murmured. "Incredible," said Teacher. "I love it. I bless you that way, twice. Now, won't somebody fetch me the box?"

What followed was a long and incomprehensible parade of cavaliers, starting with Marta the Second. After Teacher called out, "Ortus the Ninth," Ortus went up for his prize and returned to present it to his necromancer, as he ought. He placed within Harrow's gloved hands a ring with a single key laced upon the iron: a singularly dull and uninteresting key, with two teeth and a triangle head. It sat very heavy in the black leather of her palm.

The little man eased himself down upon his stool, from the sides of which no small amount of stuffing was emerging, like a sat-on cream-filled roll. He said comfortably: "Now I will tell you something new, something you are not meant to know: about the First House, and about the research facility.

"The base of Canaan House dates back to before the Resurrection. We first built upward, to get away from the sea; then we built outward, to strive toward beauty . . . This was meant to be the palace of the Kindly Master, where he might work and hold court and live for always, and oversee all the rebuilding that had to be done. For the Resurrection did not resurrect every broken thing, you understand, and nor did it create anything new. There was hard work ahead—fixing, or designing, and it took a great deal of blood and sweat and bone. Yet those were lovely years, happy ones. And that was the time before Lyctors."

He took a sip of his tea, sighed briefly in pleasure, and continued: "They were *disciples*, to begin with. Ten normal human beings of the Resurrection, though half were blessed already with necromantic gifts. But necromancy alone does not confer eternal life. Our Lord, the First Reborn, kept those ten devotees young and alive through his sheer might, but it was a shadow of living . . . They had to stay tucked near the Emperor's feet so as not to strain his powers. They desired to spend their lives in service of him, not the other way around. They realised in the first hundred years how difficult their situation was, even as necromancy spread through the Nine Houses, and even as other disciples joined their number. Some of them took up the sword and became the first cavaliers, in the hope that their strength of arms might prove useful; the adepts honed their master's craft, trying to break the rigors of deep space. And there was so much still to be done, and new necromancers being born, and ruins to reclaim. What a time to be alive."

He sighed again, this time more nostalgically, and then he said: "Necessarily a great research had to begin, into how best to serve alongside our Lord without needing him to confer immortality—this search for what would become Lyctorhood. And it took place *here*."

He pointed downward. Everyone looked at the floor beneath his feet, seeking out the origins of Lyctorhood in a few square inches of rotting carpet. "Below our feet. The laboratories. The original body of the building—a place steeped in the death of ages—the quietude of the last sacrifice . . . that is where Lyctorhood was begun, and that is where Lyctorhood was finished. You will see it. You will see where they threw down their tools and left the building like a palimpsest, unknowing, for you; where they left their blueprints to those who may yet have the strength of body and spirit to walk their path. This place was meant to be a palace, and they have left it as a road in the wilderness."

Someone spoke up—the Fifth woman—and she said, fearlessly and amiably: "Then the path to Lyctorhood is independent research? Gosh! And it isn't even my birthday."

One of the young people sitting close to the Fifth made a sound like an exhausted balloon squeal.

"*Part* of the path is independent research, Lady Abigail," said Teacher, smiling. "The other part, the greater part, is the silence . . . is the care. You are not alone in the facility. In its heart lies the Sleeper, and how long that creature has lain there I do not know; but I do know that they are your greatest threat, for although they lie in sleep . . . in that sleep, they walk."

Here he trailed off. He stared into the middle distance, still grasping his cup of tea, as though seeing visions the assembled scions and cavaliers were not privy to. The pause stumbled execrably, fell down the stairs, and lay in a tangle at the bottom in full view of all listeners, who had to watch it bleed out in embarrassment. One of the grotesquely young pair of the Fourth actually tried to fill it in, and bleated: "There's a—monster in a research laboratory? And we've got to—fight it?"

"No, no!" said Teacher impatiently. "Lord Over the River have mercy! The Sleeper cannot die. I doubt they can be wounded; they certainly cannot be killed. The greatest advantage we have is that the Sleeper sleeps deeply! The *second* threat to your work is if the Sleeper wakes—it has never happened, though I know the Sleeper yearns to escape its incognizant state and pick up where they left off—for if they wake, none of us will live. If the Sleeper meets you on their unconscious peregrinations, your weapon should be stealth; if through unholy means you wake them, there will be no other weapons left. We are reliant on a communal soundlessness. Travel in groups; tread softly; go where *I* durst not go: because I love my life, and I love noise, also."

There was no pause here, just a perfect babel:

"—isn't how it—"

"How much *sound* is—"

"—doesn't make any—"

"—what kind of cack-handed—"

"I do not know the answers to any of these questions," said Teacher calmly. "Only that, already, you are being too loud."

The babel froze, in midair, on everyone's lips. Harrowhark, who had never spoken, and Ortus, who had only sweated, almost audibly, stilled further. In that anechoic atmosphere one could have heard a hair split from someone's scalp and twiddle down to the floor. One could have heard their own heart beating—Harrow did, loud and wet and hot. That silence was absent of anything, except those tiny, helpless noises of living.

"I am making a joke," said the vigorous little priest, whose cheerful admission did not ease the room. "I josh. I kid. I do that. Believe me when I say that you are safe up here. You see, if you are not, then there is nothing to be done, not really. It is only down through the hatch for which you hold the key that you are in peril, and it is a peril you will bring on both yourself and those around you. Keep your swords sharp and your theorems nimble. I can guide you no further; this place has changed beyond my ken. But I wish you luck," he added, and the priest with the long salt-and-pepper plait said, very softly, "I wish you luck," and the tiniest and most wizened priest added in a wheeze, "God grant you luck to carry out your task."

Those gathered were almost too stunned to attend to the constructs who came to get them; eyes that had been bright with excitement, or anticipation, or even in some cases a weird, weary comfort, were now troubled. They were greeted by those limber, reactive skeletons that moved in the manner of kindly in-laws, welcoming strangers to a house they knew was unfamiliar to them but nonetheless wanted to prove comforting. They were led away in twos—barring the Third House trio—and Harrowhark waited next to her cavalier, who was apparently trying his damnedest not to breathe, for a skeleton to cross over to them.

She realised that Ortus was very frightened. This was not unexpected. "Lady, I cannot do this," he breathed. "I cannot protect you in this way. Monsters are beyond me."

"The rock has been rolled," Harrowhark said, and she was relieved by how much she believed it. She was not fearful. She felt dry inside, as though the liquid had all been wrung out. Monsters were never beyond her. There was no abomination she could not give a run for its money in foulness. "You are my cavalier primary. Your job is to stand, to face our foes, and to die when the panniers are empty, but not before."

This did not comfort him, strangely enough. "You need a blade, and someone with the will to wield it," he hissed.

"How strange! I have never needed such a person in the past."

"I would that you had chosen differently."

Harrowhark was unsettled now, and she had been at peace, so she was cruel: "The choice is beyond me *now*, Nigenad—unless you can conjure me the spirit of Matthias Nonius, in which case I'll take on his services if he promises to not speechify."

Their own First House skeleton, ridiculously girdled in that pure white, had come over to make them both a very respectful bow. A thrill of suspicion was growing in Harrowhark regarding the fluidity of its reactions. Its movement was too free, and when she angled her body in its direction it mirrored her in unconscious response, which was beyond *her* and therefore beyond any skeleton-raiser of the Nine Houses. But her cavalier primary did not seem to notice. He had fallen into a reverie of his own devising, and when the construct gestured—*gestured,* who wasted time on ossein instructions for *gesture*—he turned instead to her, his dark eyes earnest, his painted skull deliquescing.

He cleared his throat—

"No," said Harrowhark immediately, but it was too late.

> *"Baleful the black blade struck at the shimmering stuff*
> *of the spectral beast, biting deep in its false flesh;*

> *"Shrieking, it flailed with its claws at the pauldrons and*
> *casque of the Ninth, yet his heart never faltered or*
> *failed him . . .*

"Harrowhark—I don't understand why you chose me."

Harrow said, "There was nobody else."

His mask slipped, and not the mask made of alabaster and black paint. Ortus looked at her with his steady dark gaze, and his heavy face flickered; she realised with electrified astonishment that he was *exasperated.* "You never did possess an imagination," he said, and, obviously upset with himself, his mask reappeared as swiftly as if slapped back on with both hands. He did not know that she was far more interested than angry. But he added in a hurry, "Forgive me, my lady. I am overset and afraid. I do not yet know how to die. The Locked Tomb is far from here, as are its graces, and so I forget myself."

"You do, I agree," said Harrowhark, shortly, and became exasperated herself, though more with herself than him. Ortus could not be blamed for simply being Ortus. "Forget dying, Nigenad, and let's go. It is obviously my fault if I have failed to impress upon you who I am, necromantically. *We* serve the great corpse that lies dead and unwaking, and should not let *our* hearts falter or fail regarding some fiendish somnambulist. In the worst-case scenario you can simply declaim to it, which ought to cure anyone's insomnia."

"You are very humourous," said her cavalier with perfect solemnity. "I understand. I will follow, Lady—and let duty be my pauldrons and casque, and loyalty my sword."

The skeleton construct gestured to them both as they made the initial step to follow, and Harrow was struck when it opened its yellow-molared mouth.

"Is this how it happens?" it said.

9

You could not say with perfect accuracy that you woke up. Having achieved a grotesque mollience and dripped and resolved into a bad-smelling puddle of yourself, you did piece yourself back together again: your eyes opened—you were lying flat on your back—and, slowly, carefully, with great effort of soul, you congealed. A weird, hard wad was present in your lungs, pairing each breath with a hideous trachea whistle. Otherwise you were fine, though dishevelled. Your robes were askew. Your chest was heavy, but not with water, with—the shadow of a memory, or the last remembrance of a dream. For a moment you shivered all over. After your lungs, your eyes were the second thing to connect, and they perceived a room both big and dark, with spatters of quiet yellow light. This light resolved the shadowed angles of a high and vaulted ceiling. You recalled the wetness—you recalled the corpses—but then that recollection slithered away. The only thing you could hold on to was where you had been sat. You would know if all your sensation was removed; you would know if your brain had burnt away. You were the Reverend Daughter, and you had been placed in a pew.

A heavy weight pressed on your hips and legs. You strained to see, chin tucked hard against the top of your chest, and beheld with relief your double-handed sword. Your relationship with it was becoming increasingly complex: you hated its presence, but the world without it would be unimaginable. You smelled blood. You smelled something else more distantly; above the blood hung the crisp, faecal sweetness of a rose. You struggled to sit up: the breath seized in your lungs, and you worried yourself out of a thrusting cough just as a hand touched your shoulder, lightly, in warning. You nearly flinched off your seat.

"Quiet," said Ianthe, beneath her breath.

She was sitting next to you, an incandescent pillar of white, staring straight ahead. The look on her face was typical of her, a recollection; an icy, exhausted tedium, with top notes of intrigued disgust. You were dazed. You hated her to touch you. You glued the sword to the back of the pew with a push, the bone lifting it and muffling the noise, sticking in hot gobs to the genuine wood as you swung your legs over to press your toes to the floor. And you saw where you were, and you were immediately stricken with horror.

You had been laid in a pew halfway down a small, exquisite chapel. Now that you could look, you recognised the tender and yellow light as that which came from hundreds of candles. They lit an interior of shining charcoal-coloured stone, layered with whorls of bone—bone everywhere, bone enough for a hundred Ninth House tomb chapels: the chancel formed of long carved runnels of bone, fretworked into human lace; the black check tiles polished granite beneath your feet, their white counterparts soft worn squares of femur, orange in that lenient candle light; and the seats of wood—wood like you'd first seen in Canaan House, real, brown, glimmering wood, polished to the particular sheen that neither stone nor bone could take. You stared up at a plex cruciform window: cold stars outside, gleaming with a weird and unearthly light. You stared up at skulls: an ossuary of skulls, a multitude of skulls, set into the wall, overlapping in empty-eyed rows, set cheek-by-jowl to await infinity. Thin sheets of metal had been worked over this lovely mass of faceless dead, in shadowed tints: deep red crimsons, smoky amethysts, lightless navy. House colours. House heroes brought here to rest. Slender columns of white tapers bathed those bones in forgiving lights that made them beautiful in the way only bones could be for you; the candles were wrapped in different colours, which made them look like the dressed-up throats of flowers, or rings on long slender fingers. And great clusters of these candles shone down on a central altar, and on the central altar was a body.

You were at a funeral. You knew its bride; you'd killed her.

You sat in a pew in the chapel where had been laid the time-apprehended body of Cytherea the First. In order to survive the gaucherie of your presence, you sent your brain voyaging elsewhere. You tucked your hands deep inside the veil of your nacreous sleeves and slumped so that the snowy rainbow gauze hid your face. Even the vague pressure of the blade at your back caused the gorge to rise up in your chest and your heart to hammer wildly as though trying to construct a barricade, but at least the threat of coyly spewing kept you present and sane; you weren't that far gone. It was only the fourth funeral you had ever been to where you had been responsible for the corpse.

The corpse on the altar was covered in little blush rosebuds, scattered thickly over her, a roseate white like seconds-old bone. They lay in sheaves in her arms; they were tucked in her pallid brown curls and pressed to her feet. On her sweet dead mouth there hovered a rueful frown. Once upon a time you might have fallen to position on the kneeler—soft and supple human leather, buttery, lovely—and thanked the Tomb that you had lived to see the death of a Lyctor, enshrined so, in such a place. You would have pressed your prayer beads to your mouth with one knuckle caught between your lips, the knuckle of your great-grandmother that represented the Rock, and the Universe, and God. Now you considered whether or not you could pass out again.

Before the altar knelt Mercymorn. Her shimmering white robe had fallen down her shoulders, and she was weeping—the sound was not articulated aloud, but her shoulders rocked as though her sobs were an explosion. She ground her molars audibly, so much so that they sounded like walnuts going through a rock polisher. You could not imagine the Saint of Joy weeping with anything other than fury or disappointment.

Next to Mercy knelt God. Next to God knelt somebody new. You could only see the back of the head, and you surmised they were fair-haired. That was all. The stranger was tall, kneeling—taller than the Emperor, and taller than Mercy. They wore the iridescent robe of the

First House, and you could not sense them: another black hole in a triplet of black holes, scooping out the space in front of you.

After a moment, the new figure said in a light, masculine tenor, "I will have a full psychological meltdown if you don't stop that ghastly noise, Mercy."

The Saint of Joy gritted out: "I will kill you if you talk to me right now, you *mean*-souled little *man*."

The God of the Nine Houses said, "Stop it," and they were silent.

The molar-clunching subsided gradually. You wove your fingers together in your deep pearly sleeves and bent your thumbs backward nearly to the point of dislocation. Ianthe looked at you, and when you looked at her in the candlelight—her eyes not betraying her; right now, they might have been blue—you were struck by her exhaustion. She had been dimmed, somehow. Something had been taken from her since you watched her scream on the floor of the shuttle. Her line of sight flicked to the gap at the front of your robe—you shouldered forward to close it—and she quirked her eyebrows in brief, enervated amusement.

You mouthed, *Where are we?* But she did not answer.

After a moment, the Emperor spoke at the corpse, in the smiling cadence of a man giving a talk at a dinner party:

"When they first brought her to Canaan House, I thought there'd been some mistake. You know that I'd been to Rhodes, to see the miracle, but I asked not to see the woman—just so I could be a dis-interested party—and of course once I saw that she *was* necromantic I said yes, she should come to me to be a disciple. She was just shy of thirty then, I recall. And I knew she was sick, but I had no idea how bad it was until Loveday brought her in, looking as though she wanted every one of us beaten to death, and she could hardly walk . . . I went to kiss her hello, and she said: 'Lord, I can't kiss you back. My lipstick's perfect and I refuse to smear it.'"

The strange Lyctor barked out a hollow laugh. They—he?—inclined his head, and you saw him in part-profile for the first time. He *was* very fair, but in a greyish, damp, slicked-back way that showed off the promontories of his skull. Fine, impatient lines were set around his drooping eyes, and quite deeply carved into his mouth. He looked older than your father had looked, when he died. These haughty features were set in a tall, aristocratic face, with an arched and supercilious nose, which nose he was currently staring down at the Emperor with an expression of supreme suffering.

"It wasn't, though. She had it on her teeth."

Mercymorn muttered, but not so quietly that it wasn't audible: "Of course *you'd* notice that, *Augustine*."

But *Augustine* was adding, in a light, cultivated voice: "I remember now . . . Lord! The time flies! . . . That was a damnable business. They sent her to us barely alive, and back then none of us could do anything for her, excepting you. Was she the first gen, or second?"

"Second," said God. "Early second. We were still experimenting with getting the Sixth installation up and running. Some of the Houses were empty."

Mercymorn spoke up: "No. We had it running by then. Because Valancy was with us, and Anastasia."

The Emperor clicked his fingers, as though she had triggered some neuron flash. "Yes, you're right. We were all there to meet her. All sixteen of us—and she acted as though she were at a wedding and was doing a receiving line of tedious cousins . . . I could hardly keep a straight face. When was the last time you saw her?"

This last question was asked a little abruptly. Both Lyctors fell silent for a moment, and then the one they called Augustine said: "Recently. Ten years ago. I told her she was getting to be a bit of a hermit, and she acted as though I was rather stupid . . . but she seemed in good spirits."

Mercymorn said: "Cytherea was good at seeming," to which Augustine just said, a little distantly: "You'd know, I'm sure."

Before this could decompose further, the Emperor pressed: "And you, Mercy?"

You heard the molar-grinding again. Then the Saint of Joy said, colourlessly: "Nearly twenty years ago." And: "She laughed too much."

All three of them fell silent at the altar. The wasted body in front of them would no longer laugh too much, in any case. Augustine said, "Does anyone remember her name—her actual House name? Didn't she have one?"

The Emperor suggested, "Heptane," but Augustine said, "No, you're thinking of Loveday. We've forgotten it! That's unnatural. Who would have ever thought we could forget—a thing like that?"

Mercymorn stood. She tucked her hair behind her ears and away from her deceptively serene oval face, and she crossed primly to the back of the altar. She put her hands behind her back as though afraid to touch anything with them. She looked at Cytherea's dead face with an intensity that was in its own way worse than tenderness. It was as though she were willing something from the corpse; like she could conjure something through sheer force of wanting. "Call her Cytherea Loveday," she said. "That's what she wanted to be called—and I found it unbearable and glutinous then, and I find it unbearable and glutinous now; but that is what she said . . . I never saw her cry except once," she added in a pointless rush. "The day after. When we put together the research. When she became a Lyctor. I said, *There was no alternative*. She said . . ."

At this point, she broke off. Thankfully, she did not glance in your direction. Augustine was staring at the floor, hands crossed demurely in a posture of awkward respect, and the Emperor was looking up at Mercy, but all you could see was the back of his head where mother-of-pearl leaves and baby fingerbones adorned his hair. The candlelight flickered heartlessly over you all.

He asked, "What did she say?"

The other Lyctor said nothing, for a moment. She cleared her throat: "She said, *We had the choice to stop*."

After a second, the Prince Undying sank his head into his hands. A stylus fell out of his pocket and rolled across the sleek black-and-bone tiles. It was the first time that he had seemed at all mortal. Humanity touched him briefly, like a passing shadow.

Then Augustine said, quite irrelevantly: "I wouldn't have called it *glutinous*. She was just lucky that *Cythe-re-a Love-day* trips off the tongue. Now, mine would alliterate in a way I couldn't have abided. Abode?"

"I will say this," said Mercy presently, acting as though Augustine had never said a word. "I *never* mourned for Loveday Heptane. She did one good thing with her life, and she knew it."

"Eulogise her," said the Emperor, through his hands. "For God's sake, eulogise her anyway. Eulogise them both."

Augustine reached over and squeezed the shoulder of the man who became God and the God who became man and yet still invoked himself, apparently; the Lyctor got up with a grunt as though it hurt him and went to stand at the foot of the altar. You saw now that he *was* tall, and not particularly imposing, but—there was something removed from real life in the lineaments of his face, as though he had once looked at something terrible and it had lodged in his cheeks and forehead. He twitched open his First House cloak and stuck his thumbs in the belt loops of his elegant trousers—his white robe floated around his shoulders like an overjacket, filmy and beautiful—and he cleared his throat.

"Cytherea was gorgeous," he said simply. "Ten thousand years, and I never heard her say an unkind word except when it was very funny. She loved us unguardedly, all of us, which showed both her patience and her enormous capacity . . . She was a worthy Lyctor and a beloved Hand—and Loveday gave her to us, so I suppose God bless Loveday."

Mercymorn pressed her hand down close to the small fat blush roses. She had to draw herself together quite tightly. Her voice was light and a trifle strange when she said, "She could be a dreadful little fool. But she was generally an endearing dreadful little fool, and her death was beneath her."

She slowly turned those dreamy hurricane eyes on the pews, which meant she turned them on you and Ianthe, and she started. She said, "The infants are awake."

The Kindly Prince craned his head over his shoulder and saw that you, the infants, were awake. He stood and, horror upon horrors, came down the aisle to you; he looked you both over, as though he were glad to see you, as though he were glad to see Ianthe, some nameless softening in his face and in those white-ringed, primordial eyes. He reached out for your hands. You could not refuse him, and in any case had no choice of doing so; your body reacted long before your mind did, and the meat of your meat and the flesh of your flesh belonged to God. And so, with your hand in his left and Ianthe's in his right—Ianthe had arranged herself so that she had given him her left hand, rather than her less-favoured right—he said, "Welcome home. Come closer—we're just saying goodbye . . . we're used to saying goodbye."

Both you and Ianthe were led like sacrifices to the bier, to kneel where the other Lyctors had on the black-and-cream tiles. Mercymorn did not deign to look at you, but the strange Lyctor they had both called *Augustine* did. He looked down his long nose at you both, and he remarked: "Well, which one of the kiddies did her in?"

The Emperor said sharply, "That doesn't matter."

"It's not like I hold it against 'em—I couldn't. Believe me, if she went she *chose* to go. Well, I'd hate to guess . . . Two of them! What a funny old world," he added bracingly.

The Lyctor came away from Cytherea's bud-covered feet and dropped to crouch in the transept before Ianthe. He said, "My name is Augustine the First, the Saint of Patience, Lyctor of the Great Resurrection, first finger on the hand that serves the King Undying—and your eldest brother, for my sins. Who are you, my doves?"

Ianthe said, lifelessly: "I am Ianthe Tridentarius, Princess of Ida," and you said in the same automatic way, "I am Harrowhark Nonagesimus, the Reverend Daughter."

Augustine laughed in a glassy and elegant way that had no relationship with mirth. He reached over and shook both your hands—you were befuddled; you had always considered a handshake the action of a misfit—and he said, "Not any more. Your obedient servant, Ianthe the First—you're the one who ascended first, didn't you? So you're counted as the eighth saint? Your obedient servant, Harrowhark the First—*ninth* saint, then, looking at you I can tell that's appropriate. Your allegiance is to one House now, and one House only. Behind you is your eldest sister."

"We've met," said Mercy impatiently. "Can we not do this *right at this moment*?"

"I imagine she didn't have the grace to introduce herself, so I must:

Mercymorn the First, the Saint of Joy, would you believe. She is a Lyc-tor of the Great Resurrection, the second finger on those two hands so outspread, that pray to the Kindly Prince. And she is all your sisters now—the one in front of you being, alas, completely dead—and I am the last of your brothers, excepting . . ."

He trailed off, as though expecting God to fill in, which God did not. He finished with, "Teacher, d'you think he knows about the missile strikes?"

"He's never been particularly interested in the day-to-day," said the Emperor.

"But he *is* interested in you-know-what, and I'm just thinking, if he's heard, and maybe put two and two together . . ."

God said, "He had a mission. The Saint of Duty reflects his name."

"Right, right," said Augustine. "Unlike *Joy* and *Patience*. Quite right. Just—coming back here, and not seeing him—it gave me the heebie-jeebies, to be perfectly honest with you. I can't quite shake the feeling that something's wrong."

"Can we get back to this blasted funeral," said Mercy. "Sitting through six of these is worse than dying myself. I will let you know now that the plan for *my* funeral is in my top drawer, and I've got it down to a minute-by-minute framework, and it's only twenty-four minutes, and it's just lovely."

"I can only imagine," said her brother Lyctor fervently.

This excruciation was cut short when the doors at the back of the chapel banged open. Everyone alive swung around in a hurry, and in walked the next terrible part of your life.

It was a man. The missing Lyctor—as empty to you as all assembled, more still even than the frozen corpse of Cytherea the First. Unlike the other Lyctors, all of whom skewed hungry, soft men and women of the necromancer build, his frame carried nothing but muscle. He was sinew over bone. He was a walking tendon. He had a raw, stretched look to him like an idiot's construct, bones that had been slippered in meaty fibrils to keep them moving. A metabolized, contracted stria-tion, without fat, the only curve a hollow tautness from rib to stomach.

The Emperor's face cleared. "Well timed," he said with naked relief.

The stranger wore the Lyctoral robe of office slung over his shoulders rather than enveloping him, and it was a shabby thing with a ragged hem that did not look very well cared for. He strode down the centre aisle too swiftly for you to see his eyes. In that brief glimpse you beheld a blunt brown face, skin too close to the skull, all shabby defeated features with its lineaments more temporalis muscle than anything else. His skull was a bumpy, knobbled, close-capped thing, hair shaven nearly to the bone. This hair gleamed a dull and unappealing russet, like a vague and bloody shadow on his head.

The Emperor had risen to stand with his arms open in offered embrace. The muscle man walked into it briefly—enough to let God press one hand familiarly to his back, enough for him to clasp God round the shoulders—then pulled roughly away and directed his gaze to the figure lying bookended by Mercy and Augustine.

"She's dead?" said the stranger. When the Emperor nodded, he closed his eyes, very briefly. Then he opened them and said bluntly: "So are we. Number Seven's at the rim."

At this statement Augustine suddenly leant heavily against the altar. He looked as though he might fall over, like a drunk. Mercy's lips turned to snow. They became an exaggerated painting of tragedy: a lithograph of the moment before shirts were rent and hair was torn and blood rain pattered over the scene.

The Emperor had turned his terrible eyes on the stranger, and they looked like dead planets in the pitch of space, and the white ring was like dying. He was no longer human. He was immortal again.

"It can't move that fast," he said. "It never has. You must have seen a Herald, or a pseudo-Beast. Look, don't scare the children. Come into my quarters and let's talk this out, all three of you."

The new arrival was immovable.

"It's Number Seven," said the stranger. "Run, or fight?"

Mercy said, "But we reckoned it at five years, just a year ago."

"It caught up with us," said the stranger. "The brain is already in the River. If we drop through the waters we'll run into it no matter what direction we go. The corpus will be here in just under ten months, and it will be full of Heralds. Run, or fight?"

"We need to think about—"

"No thinking," said the stranger, cutting Augustine off without hesitation. "Run? Two of us take the Emperor and hike to the nearest stele. The one left stays as a distraction, then leads it away. Or fight: we all make a stand. John, I am your servant. Tell me to stay and die, and I'll stay."

You recalled that name from the shuttle, but had ignored it at the time. There was a ghastly moment now when you realised that he had looked at the Resurrecting Prince when he said *John;* that God had responded to so banal and cursory a word as *John;* and that he was looking at the rope-made man with something closer to despair than you had ever seen in him.

"We'll fight," he said. "We made the choice years ago to increase our numbers and fight these things. Five years, ten months . . . in the end, perhaps it is the same."

"Stay?" said the stranger.

"Yes," said God. "Stay, I do think." And, lowly: "Thank you for making it home, Ortus the First."

Something pooled inside your ears, culminating in a hot and intense dripping down your earlobes. You touched it and your fingers came away wet; it was blood. Ianthe was staring at you through a fine curtain of achromatic hair, the whitened curve of her lips a tight and careful line. You silently crumpled up in the transept and hit your head quite hard on the tiles before you were rendered senseless. Under the circumstances it took people quite a long time to notice.

10

"*Then Nonius spake full wroth; thunder'd his voice as the black sea roars on the tomb-gate of Algol,*

"*Blazing his eyes with the fell light thrown from the Emperor's corpse-fires; answer he gave, and he told them—*"

"Stop," said Harrowhark, from behind.

This did not go down well with the audience. The steel-panelled, split-floor library of Canaan House was perhaps one of the strangest rooms within it: it was the only room above the facility that evoked the same blunt sense of utilitarian workspace. It was like entering a modern chamber only to find an ancient artefact in the centre. The panelled floors were spread over haphazardly with old and hairy rugs, and the shelves were plain laminated metal. When Ortus declaimed, his voice rang through the place like the Secundarius Bell, except significantly more embarrassing.

"No, no, Reverend Daughter," protested the curly-haired moron from the Fifth House, the one whose clothes could have provided the Ninth with material resources for a decade. "Please. Nonius is about to give the rebels what-for. I *never* got what-for in school. Fifth poetry is very much *I come from climes of sulphur gas/I shine in plasma sheet/Er-hem-er-hem-er-hem, surpass/My spot a crimson feat,* and by then I was always comatose. One little stanza of what-for, I beg of you."

Harrowhark knew from experience that no what-for was in the offing. Matthias Nonius never did battle in *The Noniad (Matthias hight*

Nonius his Deeds and Accomplishments) without a *significant* amount of talking first. He generally spent at least fifty lines destroying his opponents in speech before he began to destroy them physically, wading through the giblets of the immoral for another two hundred or so. This part was no exception. It was hardly to be borne that Ortus would launch into *The Noniad* in company; she had been subjected to so much of it herself because she *knew* he hoped that one day she would be deeply moved by it, release him from the duty of cavalier primary, and make him a Ninth bone skald. The idea that he would give a public reading ought to have been a whipping offence.

Now he stood, wide and black and shadowy among all the brushed-steel shelving. The necromancer and the cavalier of the Fifth sat at a table spread wide with books, and fragments of delicate loose-leaf paper safely slipped into plex covers, and browned-out flimsy, and pens. The necromancer looked entertained, and the cavalier looked beside himself. The necromancer, the woman who had been so delighted with the idea of independent research, a grown woman with a very even smile, did not put Harrowhark in any good humour. Even she had heard of Abigail Pent.

"Lady," said Ortus, and, sorrowfully: "Forgive me. Nonius has heroic standing among the priests and anchorites of our House," he added to the others. "Perhaps I do him wrong by making poesy of the sacred mysteries."

"I never realised that Nonius had passed into cult worship," said Pent.

"He has not," said Harrowhark shortly, and then was forced to admit: "Or, at least, the idea is passé."

"Heroes are passé, you see," explained Ortus with heavy sadness.

She did not murder him. It was a very near thing. Sir Magnus Quinn, that perambulating white-toothed smile, intervened quickly: "Have you made use of this space yet, Reverend Daughter? We prefer it for the moment to the idea of going downstairs. We're taking up the biggest table, I am afraid—my wife found an annotated copy of *The New Necromancer*—my only contribution was that in the gentleman's restroom, I found what is almost certainly an ancient theoretical epigram. That is how we got Ortus the Ninth onto the subject."

"An *epigram*?"

He hesitated. Pent said mildly, "Magnus is being amusing. It reads as a dialogue between magicians from the schools of flesh, spirit, and bone magic, the punchline being: *Yes, but my bone expands when I touch it,* which at least proves that joke is as old as the Nine Houses themselves." Before Harrowhark could take this prompt to make a hasty exit, the necromancer of the Fifth said without transition: "Are you interested in Lyctoral materials?"

This was an introduction, or a probe, or something different altogether. Scrutiny into the Ninth's affairs might be deflected. She was more intrigued by the idea of an introduction.

"If you are asking whether or not we have any within my House," said Harrow slowly, "I will not answer that question."

"What a shame! I understand," said Pent, who did not appear to be discomfited by refusals, or by the sacramental paint. "It was more to gauge your interest though. This library is *stuffed.* The books, now, the books are interesting—but the Lyctoral traces—*phwoar.*"

Abigail Pent had not seemed the type of woman to articulate *phwoar.* She said it very boyishly. On any other day Harrowhark would have been pushed beyond measure hearing *phwoar* after bone-related jokes and made her exit. But she was aware that priggishness was not a virtue. She was also aware that winnowing the secrets of Canaan House was going to take more than the skeletons she could construct and the diary she was documenting. She was very tired. She was being offered something. Wary of offering herself in return, she took it.

Harrow crossed around the table to see what was spread out in front of the adept of the Fifth. It was a curious assortment of the high and the low—a warped automatic pen with a thin inner cylinder of ink and a plex casing, rather more antiquated than one with an ink cartridge; reassembled scraps everywhere, like someone cleaning confetti up in an overly orderly fashion after a parade. A strand of hair. An open book with black ink still clear in the corner: *This is nonsense.*

"The books come from a later period, so I gather," said Abigail. "The notes are priceless."

She had reassembled a torn half page of flimsy that read:

> After that cut into cubes, fry in the butter or oil, turn it occasionally until it is crispy. Cut up the pickle so there are no big chunks and mix it into the pan before taking off the heat.
> M told us yesterday that Nigella "eats like a child," so I

Harrowhark said, "This proves by itself that antiquity does not give an object automatic value."

"I disagree. With this," said Abigail smilingly, "some blood—positive identification—perhaps a few more examples—I will be able to call the writer's ghost."

Then she added again, "*Phwoar.*"

"She can, you know," said Magnus, reading disbelief in Harrow's carefully schooled expression. In fact, she was cursing inwardly; she felt cold and thoughtful. "Though I *have*, er, asked her not to."

"You would need something for it to feast on," said Harrowhark, and not to Magnus.

"Yes."

"A ghost that old—the feeding—"

"It would be unprecedented," said Pent. She was talking a little bit too much, too fast. "I mean, there's the issue of whether the Lyctor in question is even *dead.* That's the first thing to consider. As a speaker to the dead, I really am at my best when people are not alive . . . If they *are* in the River, whatever the depth, I can only hope that a handful of minor relics and the new blood of my beating heart will tempt them to the surface. Nobody has ever tempted a Lyctor before. I am not even certain where they *go.* Do Lyctors enter the River? Do Lyctors pass as we pass? I don't know where they wait. I don't know how to direct them. But I would so love to try."

Harrowhark waited, her thumbs pressed together within her sleeves.

From the half a step behind her, Ortus said: "Your indefatigability in the face of ancient death becomes you."

"Stop flirting with my wife," said Magnus. (Harrowhark had forgotten that he was Abigail's husband, and found the concept of making eyes at one's cavalier too revolting to bear.) When he caught sight of Ortus's expression over Harrow's shoulder, which Harrow could only imagine, he said hastily: "Joke! A joke. Wouldn't suggest it of you, Ninth."

"I would like to give you something," said Abigail Pent.

This was to Harrowhark. She watched as the capable hands—strong, for a necromancer's, beautifully formed and with very even nails—took a bit of folded paper from the table. She passed it to her Ninth colleague as though it did not hurt her to give away such precious material. She was smiling, very slightly.

"Scholarship is best made as a communal effort," she said. "If you can tell me anything of interest about that paper, I'd be very grateful for it. If you could tell me anything tedious, I'd still be thankful. Bone adepts do have such a notorious eye for detail."

Harrowhark Nonagesimus was of the Ninth House; if it had been her in possession of Abigail Pent's resources, she would have kept them all to herself. On dying she would have put them all in a chest and buried them to keep them from the greedy eyes of other scholars for another thousand years. She took the gift with gloved fingers, turned it around in her hands—it was just paper; it had the thanergy of paper, and unlike flimsy, she would be able to feel the seethe of bacteria eating away at it if she pressed it to her bare skin.

"I am—obliged to you, Fifth House," she said.

Magnus was saying: "Ortus. What *does* happen to Nonius, after he faces the ensorcelled swordsmen? I assume they fight?"

Harrowhark was surprised at how immediately she could answer in her cavalier's stead: "He cuts down seven men in about as many lines. Then the leader of the swordsmen approaches, carrying two swords. *I* would have assumed there was a swift rate of decay in the efficacy of additional swords. The others part to let Nonius and him fight. Nonius wins easily, though he takes eight pages to do so. The remaining onlookers he kills, rather more cursorily, as it only takes around four lines."

She was surprised to find Magnus looking at her, and not at Ortus; was unsettled by the press of his mouth, of his good-natured and rather foolish expression, of his curly well-brushed hair and slightly wanting chin. She was mostly unsettled by his eyes, which were of a colour suddenly hard to define, and whose focus was on her entire.

"Is this really how it happens?" he said.

"Pardon?" said Harrowhark.

"I say, Reverend Daughter, is it an ancestral Locked Tomb tradition for your spirit energy to be so diverse?" Abigail asked brightly. "I've counted up to one hundred and fifty signatures contributing to you, and there's more—they're stamps rather than complete revenants, of course, which means their spirits were manipulated to leave marks on you in some way, which is fascinating if it means . . ."

It took long years of self-discipline not to kill the woman then and there; or at least make the attempt. Against any other ghost-caller, their wards so exquisite and so fatally slow, Harrowhark had no doubt that a single decisive strike would do the job. Abigail Pent introduced doubt. It was that doubt that made her turn and flee—a tactical retreat, as she kept telling herself; Ortus broke into a trot to catch up with her, the rapier clanking at his side. She caught their voices, because she had very good hearing for low, hushed voices of any type. Magnus was saying, "Dear, you didn't have to . . ." and Abigail, mildly: "It's just curious, considering . . ." and nothing more.

She left the gas-levered autodoors of the library—which were, as far as Harrow could tell, the only autodoors that existed outside of the deep LED-lit basement with its metal grilles and groaning air conditioners—and stalked down the corridor as quickly as possible. It was hard not to admit that she was badly shaken; and she said lowly: "We now avoid Pent and Quinn at all costs. For the sake of the Ninth House, and of the sanctity of the Locked Tomb. Do you understand me?"

"Yes, my Lady Harrowhark," said Ortus.

"If I believe they pose a threat, or that they intend us direct harm—frankly, on any minor excuse—I *will* invoke Tomb retribution. I'll kill Pent where she stands if I need to, and you will swear that there was no sin of unjustified House war, no matter the circumstances."

Only a pause. "Yes, my Lady Harrowhark," said Ortus.

This calm agreement made her all the more furious. She did not examine why. "And it ought to be *Non-i-us* as three syllables, or *Non-yus* as two," Harrow added, taking bloody satisfaction in cruelty. "Not whichever you happen to feel like at the time. It's amateurish."

Her cavalier stopped immediately, like a beast of burden shying before a jump. He said, "Yes, my Lady Harrowhark. I am flattered by your attention to my craft. It's consciously archaic. Emphasising my commitment to spoken performance."

"For God's sake, Ortus, please stop sounding as though I'm about to whip you. I am taking care of our affairs, despite your ignorance."

"Let me not be unpleasing to my lady," he said. "Let the unseeing eye of the Locked Tomb gaze down upon me, and see me guard her with the unmoving aegis of a cavalier's love. But I will not modulate my tone for you."

She rounded on him. Harrowhark knew that she was being unfair; she knew that she was being petulant—had been scared into it, and could not soothe herself, and was using any means fair and foul to try to do so now. But when she was scared, she was a child again, and she was more afraid of being a child again than anything else in her life. Almost.

"I have every right to correct you. We are at the gates of the Tomb, even now," she said. "I carry it with me, and its rules hold clear."

"Let us never leave it," said Ortus. "My lady, I follow your every order . . . I will accept your chidings gratefully. I will watch you slay whomsoever you feel the need to slay, and I will sponge the blood from your brow . . . but when I lay me down to sleep, I am a fully grown man who is allowed to feel *precisely* what I want, about anything I want. There has never been a rule against doing so, and that has always been my deep and unyielding relief with regard to you—to my lady mother—to Captain Aiglamene. Your final will be done, my lady."

Then he bowed to her—the very correct bow of a Ninth House tomb swordsman; his paint a perfect, if sad and melting, skull, his attitude sombre, his face the blankness of the grave. And just when his Lady might feel the pain of any reflective empathy for him, he saved her by establishing his position as the biggest source of passive aggression her House had ever produced. "I might *also* note that synizesis is characteristic of some of our finest examples of early Ninth prosody. I'm certain your studies have kept you from the full breadth of the classics."

Harrowhark looked at him, chose to make that look her final word, and then drew him into an alcove. The alcove was shallow, but he provided good cover. Her fingers shook a very little, so she withdrew them into her sleeves, so it might not be too obvious. She took the innocuous piece of paper that Abigail Pent had given her to examine, and she unfolded it.

When she saw what was inside her eyes seemed to strobe; the streaked red writing almost hovered above the page, the letters crowding and cramping themselves together as she read—

> THE EGGS YOU GAVE ME ALL DIED AND YOU LIED TO ME SO I DID THE IMPLANTATION MYSELF YOU SELF-SERVING ZOMBIE AND YOU STILL SENT HIM AFTER ME AND I WOULD HAVE HAD HIM IF I HADN'T BEEN COMPROMISED AND HE TOOK PITY ON ME! HE TOOK PITY ON ME! HE SAW ME AND HE TOOK PITY ON ME AND FOR THAT I'LL MAKE YOU BOTH SUFFER UNTIL YOU NO LONGER UNDERSTAND THE MEANING OF THAT GODDAMNED WORD

They were totally alone. Harrowhark nonetheless made her fingers very still, and made the sign she had taught to Ortus—the one that asked the question, *What am I seeing?* He instantly took the paper from her shivering fingers and scanned it.

"*If you come to my room, I will make you the potato dish you liked,*" he read aloud, with gravity. And: "How must we understand *potato*?"

"As your closest vegetable relative," said Harrowhark, who'd never seen one in real life.

"You *are* a ready wit," her cavalier said, with no apparent rancour and every sign of appreciation. "I have always admired your facility for repartee, my lady. Oftentimes someone will say something to me, and later I will think up the perfect riposte—so perfect the hearer could not help but wilt, and be ashamed that they had set themselves up to receive it—but by that point it is often hours after the fact and I am lying in my bed. And in any case, I hate conflict, all kinds."

Harrowhark rounded on him.

"The Tomb have mercy, Nigenad, you should be ashamed to advertise as much," she snarled, and did not even understand her incandescence. "A cavalier's life is conflict. She is a warrior, not a human-sized sponge. If only duels took the form of competitive passive-aggression, I'd probably be a Lyctor already. And you have the temerity to call yourself a son of Drearburh? Don't answer that; I know you barely have the temerity to call yourself anything at all. For the love of God, Ortus, I need a cavalier with *backbone*."

"You always did," said Ortus. "And I am glad, I think, that I never became that cavalier."

Hours after the fact, when she was lying in her bed, Harrow's brain let the response roll up to the surface: *What the hell do you mean by that?* Which was not a comeback.

11

Someone took you to bed—at the time you had no idea whose bed, or where, or how; you did not wake up for it. Later that night, or perhaps early that morning, you were found by the Lord your God in the little chapel.

You were leaning over the corpse, your arms stretched high above your head, clutched around the hilt. Your two-handed sword was thrust through Cytherea's breast for the second time. The rosebuds were scattered and stained with drops of old, sour blood. You could never recall how you got there.

That was how you passed your first night in the Mithraeum, apparently.

ACT TWO

12

SIX MONTHS BEFORE THE EMPEROR'S MURDER

ON LAST COUNT YOU'D killed twelve planets, but you still found that first quick slice to the jugular the hardest. You felt your own breath wet on your face in your crinkly hazard suit; worn to keep the dust off; needless, at least for the moment. You judged the angle. You hesitated.

Your unwilling tutor mistook your hesitation for anticipation, sitting opposite you in her own rustling orange suit, the triple light of the three-star sunset dyeing her face orange through the soft plex stuff of the hood. A light hail of sand and dust particles pattered over the fabric and went *plinkety, plinkety, plink.*

"Don't bother waiting for the timer, Harrowhark," she said, muffled behind layers of amalgam plastic and thermal fibre. She was already sitting in the posture of submergence: knees high, back a soft curve, hands light over the fronts of the shins. "I'm confident you don't need a timer anymore, and it'll drop to flash-freezing out here in half an hour, so hurry up—it won't be *me* they'll be emptying out of the dustpan for the funeral."

Mercy added this with no small relish. Your brain said: *Fuck you for choosing this particular climate, you bursting organ, you wretched, self-regarding hypochondriac and half-fermented corpse with the nails still on,* but your mouth said, "Necessarily, eldest sister."

Mercymorn watched as you extracted your sword. Not the rapier that hung from your hip, which God had asked you to wear and which you wore as a sop to his extreme optimism; the great sword that you carried on your back. Your exoskeleton came into play here: the plates you wore in long overlapping scales running from back to ribs to elbow to forearm, the rudimentary apodemes that helped you heave a blade far too heavy for your body. Not for you the light ripple of muscle that now showed on Ianthe's back and shoulders, especially if she was wet with sweat: for you the socket, the bone, the external ridge.

All the Saint of Joy said was, "*I* never needed the dramatics, but go on, and try not to do anything tectonic."

As you had never done anything tectonic in the past, it was with an edge of resentful fury that you lifted the hilt high above your head. You drove the point of the bone-sheathed blade into the talc—obviously you never wanted it to have an edge of any kind, ever again—and using the sword as your focus, drove a killing lance of thanergy right into the planet's heart.

The planet did not quake, or howl, or freeze, or writhe, skewered on your necromancy's tines. You began the cascade outward, as you had been taught. A wide thanergetic scythe sheared out into the mantle, deeper into the minute thalergy of the rock, into the solid stone's buried recollections of the day its ball of dust was formed. So much more difficult, on a planet of this character; that was why Mercymorn had chosen it, along with the hope that you would end up an ice corpse. The thanergy reaction had to be carefully wrought. Here the soul of the planet was in the striations of its sand and minerals: a soft woven network of miniature creatures, of bacteria, of thin, stretched-out skeins of life. You had not even understood what to look for, the first time. Now you felt it as you felt the sand scouring the outside of your suit.

You fell to a sitting position, and adopted the same posture as Mercymorn: feet flat on the sand as the wind howled, your spine a soft C-curve; this way when it was over you wouldn't have a serious backache. You pressed your haz-shod shoe tips to the upright blade of the sword, and you felt the planet become aware that it was dying.

The cascade was perfect. Your cascades always were. The thanergy scoured through the soul like a lit taper touched to flimsy. The living flush of this rocky outcrop began to die in dizzying, concentric rings: flipping, the thanergy feeding on the thalergy as locusts fed on wheat. As the soul tore away, an extra thanergetic bloom fanned the fire of what you had already done. You were satisfied with the precision of your strike: you did not sit around anxiously, as you had done the first half a dozen times, but you closed your eyes, and you waded into the River even as the ghost of the planetoid started to rock itself free.

Teacher had described the bone or flesh magician's transition to the River as like a sculptor being given a bowl of water and told, *Build a statue*, whereas the spirit magician was a swimmer given a block of marble and told, *Do a lap.* You loved God like a king, and you loved God like the promise of redemption, and you loved God like you weren't even sure what, you had loved so seldom. But you hated his analogies with the depth and breadth of your soul.

Sculptor or swimmer, *letting go* proved more difficult than anything else. Part of you was always dimly frightened of it. Your fellow necrosaint-in-training now bragged that she could do it near-instantaneously: like closing her eyes, she always said. You had never found it natural. Your mind you dug out of your meat, and you drove it downward—always downward, somehow—and pushed with your awareness until you felt underfoot the dagger-sharp rocks of that grey and unimaginable shore beneath that grey and featureless sky. Then a step into that icy water, and another, until you were waist-deep and might open your eyes. You could see where the planet's soul was thrashing. The ghosts had parted as though promptly combed away from that turbulent whirlpool churning. A Minor Beast. No Resurrection Beast, of course: this newborn ghast would need a thousand years of malign intent to become anything close to a true Beast. Or so you were told. You'd still never seen a true Beast. The great two-handed sword was in your hands, now light as forgiveness. You hauled yourself up to stand upon the face of the churning grey waters, and, wet through with filthy, bloodied spume, you began to walk toward the maelstrom.

You knew without venturing a look over your shoulder that Mercymorn the First stood on the shore, watching critically, the hem of her pearlescent Canaanite robes wet through. She was probably making faces at the growing stain. In the River her hurricane eyes were scouring, widening curlicues of ruddy grey, excruciating to look upon. You were glad that Mercy would see your facility with the spirit, a skill you were killing yourself trying to perfect. Nonetheless, you were also glad she was not close enough to distract you as you approached the jerking, squirming soul: a nightmarish mess of the organic and the inorganic, all of it a false mirage of spirit-stuff. It was a mass of bloody, crumbling rock faces; it was a hexapod with hairy insect legs, bristling with clay-covered spines. It was primarily grey, but a gory, slimy, sandy grey, organically seething yet still somehow stonelike. And it made a break for it.

Mercymorn hollered from the shore, her voice a muffled shout in the wind and the creak of the grinding waves: "*It's getting away!!*"

You sheathed the sword and dived. Better to stay alongside the creature than to deal with importunate ghosts. The surface of the water parted for you, murky and oily—smelling like blood, and tasting like effluent. You opened the back of your wrist and worked needles of bone from your distals, and from them you formed a cluster of long, ragged harpoons. You told the pain that it was not truly pain, not truly your wrist, not truly your bones, only your mind's excellent approximation thereof. You tied your perceived tendons into sinewy ropes. You raised the first harpoon. You judged. You threw.

The first harpoon bounced off the trembling mess of mineral and muscle, though not before it dislodged crumbling clumps of crystal viscera. The second stuck fast. The third popped its way through some gritty, corneal mass and was left floating in the water in a cloud of boiling, dusty fat. The fourth and fifth found their targets. You skidded and bumped behind the planet's soul as it screamed and took off. As it dragged you through the River, the water rocketed up your mind's sinuses and scoured the backs of your mind's tonsils, and so your mind vomited gouts of water as it was bumped along in a single indignity behind the proto-Beast. You tugged yourself along on the slippery ropes of your own muscle and collagen, and from the shattered remnants of your javelins you raised construct after construct. You let your javelin clatter alongside one hip and climbed alongside your skeleton crew until you had mounted the ghost entirely, clutching handfuls of false stones that tore the soft flesh of your palms, holding on to carapaceous insect tarsus, holding on to gobs of aggregate and flesh.

Your constructs climbed over themselves, over the pseudo-Beast—it thrashed a few back into the water, but the rest climbed on steadily, untouched by fear—and, panting, you hauled yourself up after them. To your hand you transferred the javelin, ringed around your forearm by your seeping rope of tendon, and in the other you raised your two-handed sword. This might have been cool if it wasn't faintly ridiculous. The Beast started to roll, an infant animal ghost that knew nothing but to flounder in its predator's jaws: you drove your sword into its spirit as you had driven your sword into its mantle, as the water closed over you again in a maddening rush of filthy, tainted waves.

You thought: *I'll end it.* The skeletons—you had made their legs sharpened stakes, driven them into anything soft and jammed and glued them on to anything hard—were tilling up the damned thing with their fleshless hands. You turfed up boiling rock and flesh with your javelin, trying to scrape away the surface, trying to uncover the brain. It was too young and weak to have made a skull. Gathering up your hate, your fear, and your serenity, you thrust your javelin down the moment you perceived a wrinkle of hemisphere, straight through the lobes, and you made the spike a wheel, and you cleaved in half that which was already dead.

Less than sixty seconds later you were curled up on the surface of the planetoid, half-dead with cold, trying to flush your extremities and dilate your blood vessels. Wading out of the River had never been a problem for you; you were always happy to go. The night-stricken planet had not reacted overmuch—you prided yourself on being the knife that cut silently—but the sandstorm had died as though arrested in midair. Particles that had been whipped miles up into the atmosphere were pattering down like rain. It grew exceedingly dark as the suns set in unison, and Mercy had clipped a little light to her ever-present clipboard as she wrote, which created a tiny corona of her pen, and the clipboard, and the softly falling sand.

A shaft of light fell on the dead beauty of the Body. She was always there, when you made the cut. She was always there to welcome you home from the abattoir. She thoroughly screwed up your peripheral vision: at times you panicked and speared her through, and she would only look at you with an unreadable, lifeless expression.

"One fewer for Number Seven to eat on the way in," said the Saint of Joy. "Eight minutes thirty-four," she added, because Mercy always lied when one thought she wasn't going to, and never lied when one assumed she would, and mixed it up every so often to unbalance everyone further. "Not *really* good enough, Harrowhark."

You swallowed down large quantities of icy saliva in the cold, in the dark. Within your helmet, frigid strands of hair had glued themselves to the back of your neck with sweat: you were going to need another haircut. You could not keep the querulous note out of your voice when you said, "That's two minutes off my previous time, eldest sister."

"Yes," said the Lyctor, and you could imagine her focus behind the dark plex of her haz mask as she carefully drew another line on the graph she was plotting. "You've been improving rapidly. But you could take it down in *four* minutes, infant, and it would still be not really good enough."

Your tongue slurred in your mouth: "Because these are so different from the real Resurrection Beast?"

"No," said the Saint of Joy, and her voice took on the gossamer thinness of a razor blade, poisoned by being perfectly reasonable. "You could take it down in two. You could take it down in one. But what it boils down to, baby sister, is that you've got hypothermia and *I* don't!"

All the way back to the Mithraeum, in the tiny shuttle, you brooded on that. So many ways you had tried to contravene the inescapable fact that, when you went into the River, your necromancy on the meat side fell apart. Mercy never had to ask the unkind elements for her namesake, but *you* were unutterably vulnerable, no matter what you tried. Constructs crumbled, even ones you'd made of permanent ash.

Your wards faltered. Your theorems failed. Bone you had manipulated would hold shape so long as you removed all artificial stimulation, but it took tedious trial and error to discover how to make your exoskeleton inert so that upon reawakening you would not find yourself weighed down by dissolved collagen. When your brain travelled back to your flesh, your arts would all spring neatly into being as though a valve had been turned to let them flow once more; but until then . . .

This was the secret of the Lyctoral process. When a normal Lyctor's soul went to the River, the dead, blank energy that had once been their cavalier kept the lights on in their body. A normal Lyctor's dormant shell responded with mechanical precision to threats mundane or fantastic. It could normalise its own temperature; it could filter poisons and toxins; it could repair damage with preternatural speed; and, of course, it could fight like a highly disciplined tiger. A Lyctor's limbs remembered all the training of her stolen second self, and would use it, ruthlessly and perfectly, until the Lyctor came back to reclaim them.

A normal Lyctor's body could look after itself. But it had become obvious to everyone: you were not a normal Lyctor.

III

NOT A NORMAL LYCTOR was God's favourite euphemism. Your assigned brothers and sisters favoured different terms. (The Saint of Patience quite liked "diet Lyctor." You sometimes planned Augustine's death, and you did not make it quick.) But you found chilly comfort in being within a range of normality, rather than on the wrong side of a binary. Within that range was also Ianthe the First. On that same night, after you came back safely to the arms of the Mithraeum, you found her sat in the tawdry quarters of her forebear glumly eating soup.

Her exquisite Canaanite robe hung from a peg—you noticed that the hem was muddy—and she was wearing one of the ridiculous skirts and shirtwaists she had unearthed from the wardrobe, all of which had *Valancy* carefully embroidered on the inside seams. The skirts and waists were all beautifully cut for someone of a different height and body type than Ianthe possessed. They were tight where they should have been loose and loose where they should have been tight. They looked like her burial clothes, and she looked as though she had emerged fifty years after that burial.

This particular garment, a deep spinel-tinged satin, exposed one shoulder entirely, and it was the shoulder of what you had come to think of as *the* arm: the right arm that Cytherea the First had removed just above the elbow, with somebody else's reattached wholesale. The new limb hung heavy from its olecranal point with a bluish seam. It looked fat and swollen and unused, which was ridiculous, because you had never been able to see anything wrong with it. It had been very nicely matched to the original until she had ceased using it altogether, and the difference was more pronounced each day. Unconscious of your critical eye, she scratched fretfully at the line until red hives appeared.

"Fifteen ten," said your sister Lyctor, as soon as she noticed you.

You said, "Eight thirty-four," and she said, "My God! Hark at the creature. *Eight thirty-four* . . . and such a dreadful pity that it doesn't even matter."

She was in a filthy mood, if she was wearing that thing, with her arm exposed. You were not in the best frame of mind yourself.

"Let us interrogate," you said. "Does it *not matter* because despite cutting three whole minutes off your previous time you could never hope to challenge me in this arena, or does it *not matter* because I'm going to die to Number Seven?"

"You're being damned optimistic if you think you'll live to see Number Seven," she said, blue eyed, those oily little freckles glittering almost pinkly above the dress. They reflected the red rims of her eyelids. You thought that she had been crying. "I'm amazed you made it here from the docking bay without getting assassinated, Harry."

"I will not answer to that sobriquet."

"Close the door and I'll call you *Nonagesimus*."

There were a few academic reasons that you closed the door, and from the inside, rather than behind you as you left. Her quarters held some measure of safety for you, as she warded with the paranoid focus of an escaped murderer, and therefore half as tightly as you did. You got better autopsies of her encounters with Beasts than you did from your own, as Augustine was wont to explain significantly more to her than either he or Mercy did to you.

But by the Sewn Tongue, those fucking *rooms*. Those candied, white-and-gold-striped rooms, those crystal-chandeliered rooms with a bed as big as some of the penitential cells back home. You'd hated them from first sight, as instantaneously as Ianthe took a fancy to them. You despised the cobwebby, overornate furniture, with filigree on curlicue on flourish, the masses of embroidery thread, the hangings on everything, swath of fabric atop another swath of fabric squashed down on a plush divan that rustled if you sat on it; and most upsettingly, the paintings. They were life-sized nudes in languorous attitudes, generally in oils, and all of the same two persons. They were enthusiastically executed. The duo posing held a variety of objects both likely and unlikely. You had once been fool enough to recommend that Ianthe take them down, at which point she had rustled up another from the bathroom and hung it in pride of place above an overpainted dresser. It was *not* that you were a prude. It was simply that sitting in a room with those paintings was like having a long visit with someone who kept laughing at their own puns.

But despite the violently awful nudes—the excess of latticework—Ianthe—you were a frequent visitor to her den. You took such a pitiful pleasure in *Nonagesimus,* now that you had spent months being Harrowhark *the First.* As God said, you might be the ninth saint, but you could never be Ninth again—except when you closed Ianthe's door.

"It's down to your want of ambidexterity, Tridentarius," you said, giving her the same sickly pleasure in nomenclature. "It's not exactly mathematics. You are trying to fight with a sword in your wrong hand. I am not even trying to fight with a sword. As I've been told tiresomely often, a half-cocked version of something is significantly worse than not being cocked at all."

Despite the fact that you had said *not being cocked at all,* Ianthe only slurped angrily at her soup, making a sound like custard going down a flute. "Tell me to stop breathing," she said. ("I have, on multiple occasions," you said.) "You won't understand. It's *utterly* instinctual. It doesn't matter if I try to fight from a distance. I'll flinch at something, and then Babs will kick in, and the arm won't work—"

"You cannot pass the blame on to your burnt-up soul. It's psychological."

"Bullshit," she said, with vehemence.

Babs indicated a very bad day. She so rarely mentioned her cavalier. "Augustine is critical, I take it."

"Augustine told me they might as well smother me along with you."

You were only astonished that you had any ego left to bruise. She took another spoonful of soup and said, her whey-coloured face dissatisfied: "He says the same thing you do . . . *psychological* . . . says I persist in being damaged for my own enjoyment."

Still cold and very weary, you laid your sword at your feet and sat yourself down in a high-backed armchair with a frill around the bottom, done up in citrine stripes. Ianthe's rooms were undoubtedly more luxurious than yours, and more interestingly appointed, having belonged for centuries to a long-dead Lyctor with time enough to come back every so often and furnish them to taste: but that long-dead Lyctor still seemed to sit in all the chairs and lie in the bed and shave by the water-pump sink, and you were relieved that your rooms contained no ghosts but your own.

You said, "There's nothing wrong with the arm."

"It's not mine," Ianthe said vehemently.

"Then cut it off."

"So typically *Ninth*—"

"Let your vaunted Lyctoral abilities kick in," you said. "See if it regrows."

"It won't," she said, taking you quite seriously. "Teacher said Lyctors don't survive decapitation, and that a lost limb would heal as a stump. And I know that if I try to make myself a new arm I'll leave something out. If it's not perfect it won't work, and I won't want it."

The once-Princess of Ida did not say this petulantly, but used the resigned, rather furrowed tones of someone mildly aggrieved by self-understanding. You suggested, "So get the Saint of Joy to do it. She can be relied upon for physiological perfection."

"Oh, you crack-up," said Ianthe, not lifting her eyes from her soup.

"I *personally* would not let our eldest sister regrow any of my limbs," you said, "but if perfection is what you desire—"

"Boo to that," said Ianthe.

You grew bored. "Teacher, then."

"He'd tell me how wonderful it would be to do it myself. We're not all Teacher's sweet little darlings for whom he would do anything," she remarked. "*I have never been good at attracting indulgent fathers.*"

You bristled, but had no adequate comeback. You were busy massaging your itching fingertips, which were still red and sore: the cellular degradation was subtle enough that you were healing one layer at a time, to ensure you'd got everything. Not for you the smooth stump of a regenerated Lyctor: you had to do everything yourself. Yet you also would not turn to God, who might heal you in one blinding, soul-nauseating instant, flensing you utterly from the bones upward, and who might also awkwardly pat you on the shoulder, or look at you with that solemn, half-troubled smile that you both craved and hated.

"Then I do not know what to tell you," you remarked, "except that if you persist in asking for my opinion, at least pretend that you want it."

Ianthe pushed away her empty soup bowl and sat up, looking at you, stolen eyes narrowing with a sudden spurt of inspiration. Her paste-blond hair fell lankly over a face that should have been beautiful and over shoulders that should have been exquisite, but only contributed to the general impression of a wax figure in a pink dolly dress. You had never been given the option to play with dolls, but given hindsight you could not see yourself ever volunteering to have done so.

"But *you* might do it," she said, softly. You saw her looking at the necklet of bone that peeked out from the collar of your shirt, the top of your homebrew exoskeleton. "You could do it, Harrowhark. And maybe I'd even let you, seeing as we're comrades-in-arms. Seeing as we're intimates."

You stood up, more than a little repulsed, and your exoskeleton creaked as you bent to pick up the two-handed sword. "I am not perfection yet, when it comes to meat," you said. "I'm not saying I wouldn't be close . . . but you want something I can't give. Nor is it something I'm *prepared* to give. Being honest, I am mildly disgusted you asked. Is there soup left in the kitchen?"

"Oh, heaps," said Ianthe, who appeared not to have taken offence at your rejection. It was so impossible to tell, with Ianthe. "I made it. It's vile."

Were there less likely bedfellows now than you and she, the daughters of mystical Drearburh and self-regarding Ida? It was not a connection formed of any mutual admiration; if anything, the more you saw of Ianthe the less likely you were to mistake her for likeable.

She made herself like an overdecorated cake: covered so thickly in icing and fondants and gums that it would take serious excavation to find any bread. As a necromancer she was a genius, though you thought she relied too much on shortcuts and circumventions. She had an exceptionally fine mind. She was not afraid of rigour. She was also obsessed with what might lie beneath the River and, though this was a touch hypocritical coming from you but never mind, a fucking crank.

But a crank who had attained Lyctorhood. A crank whom you were now obliged to call *sister*, though you thought it hurt her to call anyone *sister* much more than it hurt you. A crank whom a dead self had respected enough to include in the work. A crank who had found you, distracted nearly to death, beside yourself, disgraced, having thrust your blade straight through a dead woman's sternum, and simply said: *Wish you'd taken off her arms.* Perhaps there were more likely bedfellows, but yours hadn't killed you yet.

14

THE MITHRAEUM, THE SEAT of the First Reborn! The Sanctuary of the Emperor of the Nine Houses, the bolthole of God—the removing place of hallowed bones, and the ossuary of the steadfast! A space station hidden forty billion light-years from the ever-burning light of Dominicus, lit by thanergetic starlight, set in the midst of the circumstellar disc, an ancient jewel within so much dead gravel.

Your new homestead was perched in the middle of an asteroid field, made up of concentric rings, like a jeweller's toy. It consisted of habitation quarters—a doughnut ring of them on the outer edge—an inner ring of preparation rooms, a couple of laboratories, a reading room that was bigger than Drearburh, and a storage lazaret where the foodstuffs were held frozen in time, unperishable. The other Lyctors complained that there was a strange aftertaste to thousand-year-old food kept necromantically pure, but you couldn't taste it. There was also a water-replenishment plant and incidental rooms. The chapel, and God's rooms, were at the centre. Everything else was for the dead. Arrayed were the bones of the dead and the bodies of the dead and the mummified heads of the dead, and the retrieved flesh-and-skeleton arms of the dead, preserved immediately after they had been blown off the bodies of the previously living, and the ashes of the dead and the hair of the dead and the fingernails of the dead, and the folded skins of the dead and the eyes of the dead, jarred in long and exquisite crystal containers filled with aldehydes. A Lyctor sitting on the outside of the rocky ring that haloed the Mithraeum would not think it hidden: they would see it as a screaming beacon of thanergy—a burning gyre of death—letters writ large in space, HERE IS THE GRAVEYARD AND WE ARE THE GRAVES.

Your first months of Lyctorhood passed in an echoing, vaulted set of sterile rooms specially allotted to you. They were neutrally coloured in whites and greys and blacks, scrupulously clean, and relatively empty of bones. Unlike Ianthe's, they had never been used. They had been intended for a Lyctor who had never slept between their sheets, or hung their clothes in the closets, or bathed their face in the water-pump sink. To you, who had lived and breathed the aged dust of family members past, and worn their clothes and used their things, to get an unused set of rooms was new and enticing. You folded your clothes into drawers that had never seen clothes and kept the few small items in your bureau neat and organised, finding some measure of satisfaction in returning each night to such a place. You had never become content, and you were still helpless, but you might take chilly gratification in the small things.

No servants here, in the bolthole of the Necrolord Prime. Not a construct in sight. You all cooked your own food—or at least, Mercymorn cooked, and Augustine cooked, and even God himself cooked—you did not know about the other. Augustine was deigning to teach Ianthe, or at least make the attempt, but you did not see cookery in your future. You so rarely ate for pleasure that it was beyond imagining that you would become a normal human being who learnt how to make a sandwich. You were born of the Ninth House even if you had risen to the First, and you were happy with a cold collation. Ingredients could be taken from the storeroom and eaten as they were, in the broad steel kitchens so antique in their style: chrome-brushed countertops, wide square ovens, and a ring where a gas-lit fire came out if you swivelled a dial. Often you could find the Emperor of the Nine Houses there, sitting at one of the plex counters and drinking from a chipped mug of hot coffee.

He was wholly Teacher now. His personal sitting room, a quietly appointed little space with a few chairs and a low table all comfortably faded with wear, had become a familiar sanctum. The rest of his private chambers remained a forbidden tomb. You'd traditionally been drawn to forbidden tombs, but this one repelled even your curiosity. The doors were always locked, and you nurtured no ambition to see them otherwise. He often summoned you for a theoretical lesson, or the cups of tea you still hated but would have rather seen your skin flagellated off than say so, or simply to sit in silence. He had a trick of asking you to come over and talk, and then never actually talking, but sitting with you watching the asteroids continue their graceful orbit around a thanergenic star.

Once you found him with a sheaf of flimsy spread out over the low table—months-old reports—and he was *embarrassed;* God was embarrassed. "I still think about it," he confessed. "The eighteen thousand . . . the radiation missiles . . . Augustine says thinking about it before we endure Number Seven is folly, but the way I see it, if I fail with Number Seven nothing matters; if we win, then this is the thing that matters most."

It was always *I* when God ideated failure, as though the rest of you were not accountable for anything. You sat in your lustrous white robe, trying to appreciate the taste of black tea with milk in it, trying to look as though you might at any moment take the hard biscuit and place it *in* the tea as he did—the God of the Unstilled Mandible always gave you a biscuit—and you said, "Who did it, Lord?"

"BOE, I'm assuming," he said, a bit absently; then he paused at your confusion, and said, "That's an acronym for a group of maniacs. A cult who came to our attention maybe five thousand years ago. We stumbled on them during one of our pushes into deep space. *Stumbled* . . . they'd been looking for us the whole time. They hate the Nine Houses."

You said, "I have never heard of them."

"You might have by another name—or simply as nameless insurgents. They prefer to present themselves as a kind of organic reaction, not a single coherent group. In fact, their existence depends on a secretive central organisation that sends its agents to people we encounter outside the Nine Houses, to populated planets we're stewarding, and turns them against us from the shadows. But I know about them, and the Lyctors know about them. They upped their game about twenty-five years before you were born. They'd gotten a demagogue, a charismatic leader who wasn't content to work behind the scenes. Hotspots flared up, but we took them down . . . cell by cell, bone by bone."

You remained silent, fingering the biscuit thoughtfully, developing the fiction that you might eat it sometime in the next myriad. Teacher quirked his eyebrows close together and looked at you with those oil-on-carbon eyes, and said, "I think they were behind Cytherea's coming to Canaan House. That's a damned sight more terrifying to me even than old nukes they have in storage somewhere."

You said, "Cytherea planned to lure you back to the Nine Houses. To attract a Resurrection Beast to kill you, I surmise?"

"*Lure* is a strong word. I still think it was a crime of passion. I'm not saying she didn't have other reasons. It's just that I think some of them were heartbreakingly simple. I could've gotten through to her, given time," said God. "Time—it's always time—she was overworked and underloved. Whenever something needed doing, she'd always say, *Me, I will,* and because she *acted* as though she had a leaven of selfishness to her it was easy to say *Of course,* not recognising how many times she'd said *I will* . . . not recognising how she worked herself into the grave."

You said, "A Seventh House flaw. A fatal longing for the picturesque."

"I understand the Houses have crystallised into . . . types," he said, and he dipped his biscuit into his tea and ate it quickly, before the sodden part could lose coherency and fall into the mug. You did not understand why anyone ate these biscuits or drank this tea. "But they got to her, Harrow. I *know* they got her on side, though I'm damned if I know how they even got to be in the same room. BOE hates necromancers and necromancy. It's their fundamental tenet. And Cytherea? She would've been their bogeyman. A Lyctor. My Hand."

You were finding that if you held half a mouthful of tea in your mouth it cooled, and when it was cool it tasted more serene. Unfortunately, while you were still figuring this trick out, the Emperor of the Nine Houses leaned back and wiped his mouth with the back of his hand, looked at you seriously, and said: "Harrowhark, how many in your family? Your mother and father are dead, that much I know."

You swallowed in haste. *How* he knew that—the secret you had broken yourself attempting to keep hidden from the rest of the Houses, from the rest of your own House—*you* didn't know. But you looked at his kindly, open countenance, and you said with the refreshing candour that came from talking to God: "One, since my parents ended their lives. I was the only child. My mother miscarried multiple times before I was born; I don't know how many."

His gaze didn't leave yours. "How were you born?"

"I don't understand." You did understand.

"Harrowhark," he said, "You are a Lyctor. You generate too much light, or too much *darkness,* for me to look at you and make out any strong detail. But there are details I *have* surmised: you were awake during your first time in the River, and you performed necromancy, and believe me when I tell you only one other person has ever done that their first time in. Keep in mind that she was an adult necromancer who went on to found the Sixth House. You have achieved incredible things. I understand your personality and your background, and I understand how they might turn natural talent into . . . you. But it doesn't account for what I see in those moments when I can see you clearly. How did they *get* you?"

You put your cup of tea down, your biscuit still untouched, and you said as though pushed after long interrogation: "My parents gassed fifty-four infants, eighty-one children, and sixty-five teenagers, and harnessed that thanergy bloom to conceive me. My mother used the resultant power to modify her ovum on a chromosomal level, so thanergy ignition wouldn't compromise the embryo. She did this so I would be a necromancer."

The Emperor of the Nine Resurrections looked at you for a long time, and then he swore, very quietly, beneath his breath. You thought you understood, but then he said: "This was . . . all so different . . . before we discovered the scientific principles."

"I am assured they had no previous research to go by. They came up with it themselves."

God said, a little bewildered, "That's not quite what I mean. But to concentrate so much thanergy into so precise a task—like using a nuclear detonation to power a sewing machine . . . The ovum ought to have been obliterated at a subatomic level. Do you understand what they did?"

"Intimately," you said. "They explained it to me when I was very young. I could draw the theorem mathematics, if you gave me some flimsy."

"No, I don't mean mechanically. *Conceptually.* To all intents and purposes, your mother and father committed a type of resurrection," he said. "They did something nigh-on impossible. I know, because I have committed the same act, and I know the price I had to pay. Thalergetic modification of an embryo is difficult enough, but to achieve the same thing with *thanergy* . . ."

You gave a helpless half shrug. "My parents were not flesh magicians," you said. "But they were the greatest necromancers the Ninth House had yet produced."

"No doubt," said the Emperor. "But, Harrowhark—even as the product of two obvious geniuses—you are a walking miracle. A unique theorem. A natural wonder."

You looked at him, and you said: "I have just told you that I am the product of my parents' genocide."

The Emperor set down his tea and finished off his biscuit, and did that terrible thing that he did, on occasion: he reached over to touch your shoulder in that brief, tentative way, the lightest and swiftest of gestures, as though afraid that he might burn you. Your mother had guided your hands over bloating corpses. Your father had held down the corners of great tomes, and his sleeve had brushed your six-year-old-fingers as he showed you how best to turn their pages. Both of them had pressed a rough rope made of coated fibre into your hands—you recalled the pressure from their palms, their attempts to be gentle. When the Emperor touched you, your body recalled, unbidden, each rare and terrible touch committed by your mother and father.

God said, "I will shepherd your dead two hundred. I will take on their burden to mourn and cherish in more ways than you'll understand right now. And I'll remember your parents, who did such a godawful thing to my people and theirs. I will remember it until the universe contracts in on itself and wipes clean what they did, and makes blank such an indelible stain. I acknowledge to you and to infinity that I am the Emperor of the Nine Houses—the Necrolord Prime—and that their stain must be regarded as *my* stain. Consider it my crime, Harrowhark. I pledge myself to making it right."

A red heat had begun at your exoskeleton's necklet—travelled up your throat—darkened your face beneath your paint until you felt as though you had been held too close to a stove. You said, "Lord, you can't."

"Teacher."

"Teacher, have mercy on me. Please don't tell anyone."

A child's plea. *Nobody has to know.* To God! For a moment, he changed. He grew angry, and you thought it was at the rank foolishness, the irresponsibility of what you'd said. Those monstrous, unnatural eyes narrowed, and his mouth became hard as the stones and rocks that had made up the planetoid you'd later slaughter. For a moment you perceived a hint of his great immortal age—of an enormous distance between you, of an ignition too bright for you to conceive. You were an insect standing before a forest fire. You were a cell beholding a heart.

"Harrowhark, nobody has the right to know," he said fiercely. "Nobody has the right to blame you. Nobody can judge. What has happened, has happened, and there's no putting it back in the box. They wouldn't understand. They don't have to. I officially relieve you from living in fear. *Nobody has to know.*"

That night in your bed, you did not weep. Your body tried, and failed, to produce tears. Afterward, God was more careful with you than ever, and he had been careful before; sometimes you caught him glancing at you as if he was trying to see something in the confines of your face, but whatever he was looking for it was not what your parents had done. At the time you swore that you would tell him about the Tomb: you would find it within yourself to admit that also. You had never told anyone about the Tomb, but you would tell him—you would tell him if he asked—no, that was equivocation. You would tell him of your own free will, and be glad of any punishment he saw fit to give you.

Before you'd left him then, when your tea had cooled sufficiently that you were no longer required to drink it, you'd asked: "What does BOE stand for?"

"Blood of Eden," he'd said, slowly.

"Who is Eden?"

"Someone they left to die," said God wearily. "*How sharper than the serpent's tooth,* et cetera . . . Harrow, if you bother to remember anything from my ramblings, please remember this: once you turn your back on something, you have no more right to act as though you own it."

At the time, that had made perfect sense to you.

15

ONE OTHER CONSOLATION WAS THE BODY. She kept close by in the months that followed; she walked around in an old bloodstained copy of the scintillating First House robes, and you startled whenever you saw her. But you took enormous comfort in watching her pace your sterile, empty quarters, and in watching her kneel before the mummified assembly that lived within the corridors and apses of the Mithraeum. The greatest gift she gave you was that when you laid yourself down on your bed to sleep fully clothed, you would dream of her with an uncanny, profound regularity. You could not in fact dream of anything else.

In dreaming you would return to your old bed back in the sanctuary of Drearburh—your childhood bed, getting a little bit short in the toes for you now. You prayed at its foot, no longer bracketed by either gruesome great-aunt. Instead, opposite your cot would be the Body, her hands neatly folded on the ancient shawl that your mother had always laid on the bed—the electric light in the sconce shining down on the firm musculature of her forearms, the calluses upon those dead palms. Her eyes she kept closed, each wet and frozen lash brushing cheeks blanched by expiration.

"I'm afraid," you'd say.

She would say softly, in the voice that prickled each hair on your scalp with a sweet, deep electricity: "What of, Harrowhark?"

"Tonight I am afraid to die."

"That is the same fear as failure," she said once. "You don't fear dying. You can tolerate pain. You are afraid that your life has incurred a debt that your death will not pay. You see death as a mistake."

You said, a little bitterly: "What else is it?"

The dead corse of the Locked Tomb—the death of the Emperor—the maiden with the sword and the chains, the girl in the ice, the woman of the cold rock, the being behind the stone that could never be rolled away—said, in half-confused tones she had never taken with you: "I don't know. I died, once . . . no, twice," but then she had said no more.

Another time you said, "I'm afraid of myself. I am afraid of going mad."

Another time, "I am still afraid of Cytherea the First."

And, "I am afraid of God."

And again: "Do I have Ortus's eyes? Are these ones mine? I never really looked at them— Beloved, what were my eyes like?"

Unfortunately, that time she answered. Sometimes she didn't. Sometimes she talked to you, quietly, about discursive subjects, and sometimes she didn't say a thing. But now, that which was buried insensate said quite calmly, "She asked me not to tell you."

You awoke, flat on the floor in front of the water-pump sink, screaming until your throat was broken. When you stared at your bloodshot eyes in the mirror and tried to remember Ortus Nigenad's, you couldn't recall a difference: they were both that deep and fathomless black, the colour Ianthe called *black roses,* because Ianthe was overfamiliar and frankly a pervert. You tried to imagine Ortus's sad, heavy weariness staring at you from your own mirror. It did not work. You were both terribly relieved and terribly frightened.

16

IN THE FIRST FEW weeks you had created a new cipher, based off the original with a few mathematical changes just in case Ianthe *had* gleaned too much data from the envelopes. In this you started to collate your thoughts and findings on the Lyctors around you: a pitiful memorandum of opinion and perceived fact, mostly useless, gathered in the hope that by examining your findings in aggregate you might somehow receive wisdom. You had always liked to write notes. You grieved the loss of your diary from Canaan House, but your things had been filtered through Ianthe back to you, which meant that all you got was a small supply of sacramental paint and your old clothes. When you inquired about the diary, you received the blunt response that it had been burned on your own orders.

Your section on Ianthe was very short:

IANTHE (WHILOM TRIDENTARIUS) THE FIRST
Unworthy of trust. Suspects me mad.

You should have known the former, and the latter was all your own fault. The first slip was the matter of Cytherea's tomb.

The Emperor had laid the corpse of Cytherea the First in a small chamber off the central residential atrium, a little too close for comfort. This atrium was a well of corridor shafts off to other rings of the station, and its floor was an exquisite mandala of hand bones under glass—each metacarpal dyed the colour of its House, dominated by ombres of white to crimson for the Second and white to navy for the Fourth. Around the mandala were tiles of raised brown stone that rapped sharply when one stepped on them. There were no windows to speak of, just strong electric lights from round holes in the ceiling, and in the middle hung a delicate chandelier of white crystals. The room was pillared with three massive steel-edged columns on either side, each a cacophony of exposed wire under smoked glass. These wires were thronged about with bone, with glistening strands of fat wrapped around some of the threads of copper, instead of plex; they reeked of naked thalergy, and their purpose was still not immediately apparent to you. Every so often a whole arm bone would peek out of this nest of soft yellow fat-wrapped wire. You assumed it was not another memorial.

There were nine decorative arches on the east-most side of the room. You had by now investigated each arch carefully. The brown floor tiles were inlaid halfway up the walls in these arches, and then became glass of every different colour, and in the centre of each poly-chromatic sweep was a sword-bracket. Some of the brackets were empty, and some held rapiers. One in particular always drew you back to it: a black rapier with a basket hilt formed of ebon wires. At the termination of each wire was a single canine tooth, and the end—pommel!—was a soft, worn knob of black-dyed bone.

The side room they put Cytherea in was not so decorated. The door was always open to reveal her laid out on a stretcher, with candles all around her that never seemed to go out or melt down, covered by those chubby blush rosebuds that also never seemed to open or rot. In these two miracles you detected the hand of the Emperor Divine. Every so often you saw him in there, having a quiet conversation with the body in the same way one would talk to a sleeping child; some-times Augustine was there, and once Mercy. You never saw the other. You had ventured in there yourself often, even though it was gauche, even though you had done enough damage. Something about her troubled you, and you thought it was the paranoid madness, but you couldn't be sure. Your brain told you that the arms so chastely crossed over that skewered chest had been moved a little. Your brain told you that the lips were a little too parted. When you had told Teacher of your worries—you little imbecile—he had grimaced, and worried his forehead with his thumb momentarily, and said:

"Nobody would touch her, Harrow. *I* haven't."

"I know, I just—"

"Augustine wouldn't, out of love," he said. "Mercy wouldn't, out of superstition. And Ortus . . ." He looked at you carefully, as always when he mentioned the other; the name always came awkwardly to his lips. "Ortus wouldn't out of respect, believe me. He wouldn't even think of such a thing. Doesn't sound Ianthe's style either."

"But I thought . . ."

"I think perhaps you should try to avoid that room," he had suggested, sympathetically.

You had burned: you had been molten with shame and resentment: you had been reduced entirely to flame. Yet for all that you now walked devoutly past the doorway where lay the peaceful corpse of Cytherea the First, you entered that doorway in your waking nightmares: watched, lost in the hallucination of your mind's eye, as those frozen fingers twitched into arcane formations, as each bare toe on each chilly foot shivered as though the corpse had been touched with an electrified wire.

Your mistake was the time you stopped just outside the room, arrested by muffled creaks at the edges of your hearing; tortured past any shame, you turned to Ianthe and said:

"Do you perceive any sound from within the mortuary chapel?"

She said, "Do you *try* to sound as portentous as possible, or does it just sort of happen naturally?"

"Answer the damn question, Tridentarius!"

You did not call her *Tridentarius* outside of a locked room; so she looked at you queerly, and said, "No," and then, as though more enlightened by what she saw in your face, gently: "No, I don't, crazy-cakes."

And you did not ask her again.

There was so much more you might have written: *Eyes have not reverted to lilac since the River. Arm is continued weak point. Still cries at night. Cannot actually be anaemic considering diet primarily red meat and apples. Regularly undersleeps. Begrudges my relationship with Teacher. Knows too much.*

Your other sections were more substantial:

AUGUSTINE (WHILOM QUINQUE) THE FIRST, SAINT OF PATIENCE (WHY?)

The name had been easy to get. You had simply found him at his midafternoon cup of tea and cigarette—the Saint of Patience was as regular as a worm, and had no apparent fear of fire, or having to regrow his own taste buds—and asked him outright.

"Ah! Finally, my biographer," he had said, rubbing his hands together in a show of deep satisfaction. "I've been waiting for this, Harrowhark. *A, U, G, U, S, T, I, N, E, Augustine;* height six feet; visage can be described as *attractive but grave;* eyes can be *cinereous;* and if you're appreciative of poor little Cyth's tradition—" She was always *poor little Cyth,* while he smiled, and looked directly at you. "It's *Augustine Alfred.* Alfred was five foot ten—let's get that down for posterity. He was my other half—get that down too, for the human-interest aspect."

You were momentarily revolted by the apparent Fifth House tradition. "You and your cavalier were—wedded?"

He did not turn a hair at *wedded,* or, as Ianthe would, say back exactly what you had in a high-pitched voice, for which you would one day jerk her white and beating heart from her colourless ribcage and eat it dripping before her. You did not examine *eat it dripping* as you maybe should have done. He just laughed in the uproarious, slap-your-thigh way that the Saint of Patience always laughed. It was not a laugh that really ever seemed to find anything genuinely funny. When this peal of performative humour had died down, Augustine said, "Bless you, sis! He was my brother."

Killed own sibling.

Augustine the First was the closest thing you had ever experienced to human plex. On the outside, he was perfectly painted, in a sort of antique Fifth House style: all manners and politesse and over-easy familiarity. Yet there was nothing inside him but an equally easy contempt. It was as though ten thousand years had built up a shell and left a space at the centre. Nothing seemed to touch Augustine. He was effervescent and charming in a way you found a little tedious and flip, especially on those teeth-grinding occasions when God called you all to eat a social meal together. But there was never any real emotion, or reaction, or opinion—his mouth said one thing, and his face could contort itself into any number of silly expressions, but those eyes were devoid of substance. *Cinereous* was at least correct: ash also looked solid upon first glance, but was insubstantial filth on contact.

Poor relationship with Mercymorn.

You had written this understatement of the myriad when you thought that highly strung Mercy was easily out of patience with the sillier and more frivolous Augustine, in those first few weeks. He cultivated a specific expression whenever Mercymorn was talking: an expression that was meant to say to all assembled, *At least we suffer together,* and that more than once you had seen Ianthe smother a laugh at, so comical was the mouth. But that was the painted-on expression. The plex had been shaped differently. Though you often saw them pass in the hallway as if the other did not exist, you once spied a different encounter while safely ensconced in an alcove. They'd stopped in front of each other, with Mercy trying to pass left—Augustine made himself intangibly too much left to pass—Mercy trying to pass right—Augustine made himself intangibly too much right to pass—and Mercy saying, tightly: "Get out of my way, you miserable ass."

Augustine had said something you did not catch, but then something you did: "—back to the bad old tricks of decades past."

"Oh, as if you're my keeper, you chattering imbecile!"

"But does *John* know, my child?" said the Saint of Patience, smiling.

Mercy had bristled, the nacreous whites of her robe visibly shivering. "That," she said, "is a foul implication."

"I'm not *implying* anything. Does John—"

"—and it's *obscene* the way you call him that when—"

"Mercymorn!" said Augustine lightly. "I won't fall for any of your worn-out tricks, my girl. Now, look: do I have to kill you before you get us both in trouble, or not?"

From your vantage point, you could see that the Saint of Joy's face was a stiff white oval. Those hurricane eyes roiled within a face that was trembling and fixed. You could not see Augustine's.

She said, "Don't threaten me."

"Or what? You'll tell *Daddy?*" His tone of voice hadn't changed. "Good grief . . . You wouldn't get close enough to touch me, Mercymorn. No, I am not afraid of you. You are not very nice, but you are also not very clever, when it comes down to it. I'm going to give you three recommendations. One is to be in my airspace less. Two is to stop messing around with Cyth's body. Three is to stop playing the rather dangerous game you're playing—the one you said you'd stop."

"I won't do a thing you say." She sounded tearful now.

"Don't pull that face. I know you like I know my own soul . . . you're thinking, *If I move now, can I touch his neck before he can stop me?* And heigh ho, there goes my trachea! It wouldn't matter even if you *were* quick enough on the draw, you know."

"As though you could ever—"

"If you killed me, I don't think he'd forgive you, you see," said Augustine. The easy, confidential tone of voice had gone. It was now flat and immovable and bored. "But if I killed *you*—if I stubbed you out beneath my foot, which would still be more than you deserve—then I am convinced that it would take me a mere hundred years to get John to say, *I know why you did it, old chap, and I'm sorry,* and for everything to come up Augustine. You have shot your bolt too many times."

"How *dare*—"

"You have rendered yourself unlovable, Mercy," said Augustine.

"You're the second saint. He's sentimental over you. But don't forget that he's spent the last ten thousand years on a perpetual search-and-destroy mission out of, as far as I can tell, purely symbolic retribution. John is *never* as sentimental as you think. Do you need me to write this down for you, so you can read it to yourself each night? *You—are—unnecessary—to—him.* Worse still, you've become an embarrassment. I wouldn't set myself up as his replacement A.L. He doesn't need another bodyguard, and even she was significantly more lucid than you are."

You'd expected a response. None came. You looked at the Saint of Joy—and at her expression withdrew into your alcove, flattening yourself, lest she pick you as a target to vent her frustrations on. There was silence from the corridor. Then Augustine broke it: "Stay away from me, Joy. I find myself so profoundly tired of looking at your face," and his clickety-clackety bootsteps sounded down the corridor.

Mercymorn's voice floated back, somewhat strangled: "But I haven't even *touched* Cytherea!"

Afterward you stopped seeing them in the same room, except when the Necrolord Prime called you together for dinner, and then they sat as far apart as possible.

Favours Ianthe.

A source of continuing annoyance to you. You'd never been anybody's favourite anything and did not intend to start. But the idea that the *Princess of Ida* had managed to capture another's affection was bilious. Yet from the very start, Augustine had inclined toward her, and she had deployed her whole menagerie of coquettish smiles in return, each looking as though it had spent a month prowling the desert before being captured and put to this circus use.

She was often seen at his side, fully absorbed in whatever pearls of wisdom were dropping from the Saint of Patience's lips; drinking calamitous amounts of hot tea with much the same expression, one you thought ill-suited to her shadowed eyes and white mouth; and, though less calmly, taking instruction in the long training hall with its polished wooden floorboards, the wood so new you were hesitant to step on it. It was only then that they seemed at odds, as the so-called Saint of Patience ran out of it every time Ianthe put hand to rapier.

He smoked his fierce cigarettes as he put her through her paces. She was always so tremendously bored by sword exercises: "I thought the point was to outsource this, elder brother," you had heard her remark more than once. He would get cross quickly. From what little you could tell, her form was perfect. Her lines were exquisite. She never dropped the sword or fumbled with it, which proved again how inadequate a standard *what little you could tell* was. But there was something he did not like about how that right arm clutched that sword.

"Let go," you heard him tell her once.

"I'm assuming you mean metaphorically."

"Younger sister," he said cordially, "some nice boy spent his life learning that sword for you, now you are trying to add *your* opinions to his, and they are simply not worth half a toot in this hot and terrible universe. Stop holding it like it smells—or like a banana you're trying to burst—Emperor almighty, Ianthe! I've seen you do this perfectly, so *why* must you persist in doing it *poorly*?"

At that she had said a rude word, flung the sword down, and fled. Augustine finished his cigarette in a ruminative manner, and you stared at the rapier you had been given. The Emperor asked you to handle it, so you scheduled some time for handling it, with absolutely jack shit arising from the exercise.

"She *can* do it, you know," he remarked to the air. "She simply needs to quit steeping in self-pity."

You said, "Humiliating her is perhaps not the best curative."

"Harrowhark," he said, smiling, tapping his cigarette out on the skull of some long-dead Cohort hero, "if Ianthe's opinion isn't worth a fart in a hurricane, try to imagine how much less I value yours."

So far away from Drearburh; so far from your congregation, and the elders and laypeople who had blushed to kiss your knucklebone prayer beads. You felt you actually had valuable information in this instance, but Ianthe's secrets were not held in common, for you to spill so thoughtlessly. "Then that is your downfall," you said.

"You *are* Anastasia come again."

In a perfect world, Augustine's cool would have warmed Mercymorn toward you. She *did* cultivate a distaste for Ianthe, but did not become any less shrill, acid, or contemptuous in your direction. Naturally a large portion of your education fell to her—with Augustine busy, there was nobody left for you—but she more than once expressed her view that Augustine had nabbed the *"working* baby" on purpose, and left her the dregs to spite her.

Once when you were tired you had said to Ianthe, "Doesn't it chafe, carrying on after him the way you do? Picking up his things? Smiling with your teeth showing?"

"My teeth are extremely white and I brush assiduously, so I see no problem showing them off," said Ianthe.

"Lighting his cigarettes and cooing, 'That is so *fascinating,* elder brother.'"

"I intend to take on the habit myself," said Ianthe. "Cigarettes! On a *space station!* What a power play."

"Do you ever wake up and think to yourself, *When did the Princess of Ida become this grovelling slime?*"

She smiled at you, with those teeth so brushed and white. The eyes that had once been chill lavender were now blue, pattered with brown flecks, and as mocking as ever. "Most days," she said. "Oh, for crying out loud, Harrowhark, smiling and listening to some quite interesting stories about his ten thousand years is no hardship. Especially not when it may make him think twice about leaving me to be eaten by a Resurrection Beast. Carrying off Corona's con for over twenty years taught me that shame is a *privilege.* We're puppies, you and I: I with my lame paw, and you with three legs missing insisting you can make it on your own. And God help us both, because we are *surrounded* by wolves."

Ianthe ended this startling speech by chucking you under the chin. You were too outraged and befuddled to dodge her. She said, "Show your endearing side, Harry. It may save your life."

Spirit magician.

Another terrible understatement. Augustine was a spirit magician like the Mithraeum was a box with some bones. You did not begrudge him this expertise. Spirit magic had never been your forte. He had a Lyctor's power, and a myriad's refinement: he taught to a curriculum you had barely known existed. The dead Harrowhark of your letters had told you to take instruction: and so did God, shepherding you and Ianthe both to take lessons from the Mithraeum's resident expert in Resurrection Beasts.

"It's not my primary wheelhouse," Augustine explained. "But since our last expert vanished into a large intestine, unravelled by a troop of ghosts, I'm the last spirit adept standing."

"He's being modest," said God. "The barriers between us and the River are Augustine's. He could plunge half a city into it, if he wanted."

"What a gorgeously futile idea," said Augustine warmly. "I should chuck things in there more often. There's no way *that* could come back to haunt me. No, my Lord, I am not Cassiopeia; I am a spirit generalist, and happy with my lot."

"So we're talking about ghosts, and liminal spaces, and hell," Ianthe said. Ianthe always wanted everything brought back to liminal spaces and hell, as though her rooms were not enough. You could not deny an interest yourself.

The Saint of Patience never took this bait. "Dear one, I need the right moment to go to hell. But ghosts and spirits are as good a place as any to begin. You might say I like to follow energy trails back to their source. Revenants in particular are fun that way. Resurrection Beasts feed like revenants: they find thalergenic planets and guzzle them up wholesale, crack them open like clams, and take the soul for meat. Then they turn all that remnant thalergy into what we call the *corpus,* or the hive, and the thanergy—the dead clam itself—for armour. You can ask the Saint of Duty about the thanergy transfer." (You did not think this would be viable.) "When you look at a revenant on this side, what you're *seeing* is the thanergy mass that it's gathered. Usually revenants can only inhabit things connected to them in life— the best and most desirable would be its own corpse or skeleton, or planet if you're an RB: you've formed a bond with that thing through habit and genetics, it's your soul's preferred housing. Unfortunately, apopneumatic shock makes most of us do a blind dash away from the site of our deaths—Resurrection Beasts included. The card up the sleeve of the revenant, and the Resurrection Beast, is that it can inhabit anything it's got a connection to. Anything thanergetically connected with their death."

Ianthe suggested, in what you saw as a low-value suck-up play: "Burial implements. Grave goods. Any possession that they kept over time, that was exposed to their thalergy and thanergy. If they were murdered, the murder weapon."

"Bang on," said Augustine. "Even things that touched the murder weapon, though the connection's fairly weak there and the revenant would have to be particularly bloody-minded."

She pressed, "Could they use thanergy they generated *after* death? Thanergy directly related to themselves? I mean, things they kill."

"You are absolutely and beautifully right," said the Saint of Patience warmly, and you were not annoyed that she had won such approbation. It was not as though your brain had failed to come to the same conclusion; you simply hadn't felt like articulating. "This is how the RBs got on, having scarpered away from the Dominicus system. Resurrection Beasts add to their corpus anything they've done a good solid murder to. They eat planets; they suck up the thanergy, then add bits of the planet to themselves, getting bigger and meaner each time. Your average revenant doesn't kill human beings and stick them on its outside—for which I'm devoutly thankful. The last time we eyeballed Number Seven, it was over fifty thousand kilometres in diameter . . ."

"This is why you will be sent out to establish the perimeter," said God, as Augustine was lost in fifty thousand kilometres of reverie. "We can slow Number Seven if we take away its food. If we flip a planet all at once—a thalergetic death—the Resurrection Beast will ignore it."

("This is the way we used to prepare a thalergy planet for necromancy," God explained to you, much later, after Mercy began schooling you in the way of butchering planetoids. "No adept can perform any substantive work if they're reduced to scavenging trace thanergy. Even a master of the Ninth can only do so much with a few scattered bones.

So back at the start we'd drop in a single Lyctor, unnoticed, to start the thanergy reaction. Not to flip the whole planet, you understand, just to get the juice flowing." He made a hand gesture for *get the juice flowing,* which made your head hurt. "Then within an hour or two you could send down a team of adepts and be confident they'd have all the reserves they needed. Nowadays we can't afford to use Lyctors, so the first strike falls to the men and women of the Cohort, and they do a magnificent job . . . but the old way was neater, and kinder too, I think.")

Ianthe said, "If the Resurrection Beast is that big, surely the main worry is that we'll be drawn into its gravity well."

"Yes, but it almost never travels as a physical revenant. That's why it's so damned hard to track Beasts: much easier if they'd just leave flattened galaxies in their wake. They travel as River projections instead. 'Periscoping,' Cass called it. And once they *do* instantiate, they don't seem to want to get too close. This is where the Heralds come in. Unlike normal revenants, RBs have developed external actors, and those are the things that will attack the Mithraeum. We've nicknamed this the hive, and inside the hive are the Heralds. They'll look like independent creatures, but really they're just extensions of it. Spider, web. Hand, finger."

This whole lesson took place with you, God, and Ianthe sitting at the dining table, which still smelled like breakfast, and you did not like the lack of ceremony. Augustine was leaning over the table drawing a careful diagram on a piece of flimsy with a pencil he had borrowed from God. The resulting sketch was almost impossible to follow.

"You keep saying *creatures,*" you said. "That is a little—"

"Nondescript?" said Augustine. "I can't describe them, sis. The first time we ran into the tools of a Resurrection Beast—and this was just looking at them, I mean, they hadn't even engaged us—I watched a Lyctor, one I had never hitherto seen so much as cry out, scream like a colicky child. Another two, RIP since, simply vomited."

God added, "The Heralds and corpus sometimes vary between Beasts. They are the dead parts their centre has mashed together. Some Lyctors have seen them as insectoid. They're monstrous, and deadly, and there are often hundreds of them—thousands."

Once upon a time you might have asked questions: good, interesting, thorny questions, the difficult ones that showed you knew something and could be relied upon to run where you were directed, blindfolded. This time, you kept blessedly quiet.

"And they only halfway matter," said the Emperor, vindicating your choice. "Certainly they're dangerous. If you are devoured by the Heralds I cannot bring you back. But you can destroy them easily enough, if you've a blade and the facility to use it . . . or necromancy. But as a Lyctor, of course, your necromancy is needed elsewhere."

"Would *you* like to teach this one, John," said Augustine, patiently.

"No—sorry—keep going."

"I mean, I love the tack you're taking. I hadn't thought to scare the living wee out of them with, *They'll eat you alive, starting with your feet.*"

"Sorry! Sorry. Go on."

Briefly smiling at God, Augustine pointed at the diagram. "The part of the Resurrection Beast that we can destroy squats in the River, ladies," he said. "Just as the most important part of the revenant is where the soul is, the most important part of the Resurrection Beast is sitting over here. You'll leave your bodies, which protect you nonetheless—your good old cav's right there in your neurons and amygdala, ready to come out for exactly such a happenstance—and they'll fight it much better than you can because they're immune to Herald fear. I have lived for a very long time, and when I see a Herald, I still get the most appalling whim-whams. My cavalier doesn't care. I removed the part of him that did when I became a Lyctor . . . That's his main advantage. Your body can't, and won't, use necromancy without you. The power doesn't flow both ways."

Ianthe said, "But if we're in the River, then the ghosts—"

"You're a projection. They can't hurt you," said the King Undying. "And you won't even see them. No ghost will approach a Beast submerged."

He sat back in his chair. God had a quiet, ambling posture, an upright if slightly stoop-shouldered gait; he was mobile and alive. He was always somehow *more* alive than everyone else around him, and yet dislocated from what you considered living. A man-shaped eclipse. "And there we fight it," he said simply. "Much like fighting anything else."

Augustine said, "You ward against it. You hack up whatever it points in your direction. You wither its false flesh. It has form as we have form in the River, and it's vulnerable the same way we are. You get a good tight grip on its soul and you pull the damn thing to pieces. In the end, if you wear it down, you exorcise it altogether. It is a revenant . . . a revenant of a specific hell."

The Emperor said, "Once defeated, it can be forced down into the abyss, and from there it will not return."

"We hope," said Augustine. "Oh, Lord, do we ever hope."

17

MERCYMORN (WHILOM ???) THE FIRST, SAINT OF JOY (IRONY?)
Not forthcoming.

When you had asked Mercymorn outright for her House name, she had simply stared at you with disgusted astonishment, as though you were a turd who had learned to dance, and then said, "Go away!"

Unfortunately, Augustine had been no more forthcoming than Mercymorn. He did not recall Mercy's House name, would not remember if he could, and had most likely forgotten the information immediately to make room for something more worthwhile, i.e., anything else.

Poor relationship with Augustine.

"She might not have even had one," he said, shaking out an ancient sheet of flimsy newsprint. "Do keep in mind that our holy resurrections were staggered, and it took generations for our merry band to assemble. Alfred and I were there early enough to found the Koniortos Court on the Fifth, but Lyctors like Cyth wouldn't be born for years and years, and she spent her whole life suffering Seventh House woo-woo theories regarding the value of hereditary cancer . . . whereas Mercy is the oldest lag except for me, and she was out hammering at the Eighth House before the paint was even dry on the Resurrection."

Contentious cavalier.

When you asked God why she was the Saint of Joy, he simply said: "I really intended those titles to describe the cavalier, Harrowhark, not the Lyctor. Alfred for patience; Pyrrha for duty; Cristabel for joy. Mercy would be the first to tell you that Cristabel Oct was a delight." He paused and said, "Maybe don't mention her name to Augustine though."

Mercy was *not* the first to tell you that Cristabel Oct was a delight. When you mentioned her cavalier's name, she went rigid, as though stung. The Saint of Joy turned to you, scrunch-mouthed and nauseous with rage, and wheezed: "Don't you *ever—ever—*use her name with me, you useless *child,* you impertinent *cell,*" which was a discovery in and of itself.

Yet it was Augustine who said fervently, "A total delight. Effervescent. Kind to animals and children. A master of the sword. Did not have the intellect you'd ordinarily find in a sandwich or an orange, and was a sickening twerp into the bargain. The Eighth House will never see her like again."

Anatomist.

What else to call Mercy's power? As a Lyctor, you could read a human body's thanergy and thalergy like a book—but a picture book with helpful arrows pointing at places of interest, laying them naked and open to you. If you looked at Ianthe, however, you saw nothing. When you even *looked* at the nothing, it hurt the eye and wobbled the fat of the brain. Of course, she was no more immune to theorems than you were, but without the clarity of Lyctoral sight those theorems became much harder to use. You could press your hand to Ianthe's chest, if you wanted—which you didn't, naturally—and the blood-warm sternum beneath would gradually unfold for you. But it would take effort, and close contact, and you would need to know the sternum.

Mercymorn the First knew the sternum. Mercymorn the First knew the pericardial fat, the soft-tissue secrets of the mediastinum, the false-heart shape of the thymus. You might have to press your whole palm to Ianthe's breastbone—doubtless—and take valuable seconds to search out the bone, and the things behind the bone, their characters, their locations. Mercymorn could pinpoint your pineal gland with the merest touch to the skull. This was not due to some Lyctoral power that she alone possessed, no honed necromantic theorem; as God had told you, she had simply memorised the body, by rote, over the course of ten thousand years. She had studied the measurements and their range of differences, and on the rare occasions when she needed to assume where something was or how it worked, her assumptions had the accuracy of ten thousand years' experience. What Mercy didn't know about the body wasn't just not worth knowing, said the Emperor; if she didn't know it, it hadn't existed previously.

Over the dinner table you asked Augustine why, if it was simply a matter of memory, he hadn't done the same thing. Ianthe choked discreetly on a forkful of boiled flour-paste shapes in red sauce.

"Lord! I can barely remember what I had for lunch last week," he said. "Besides, anatomy has too narrow an application."

Mercymorn opened her mouth, hurricane eyes promising a coastal lashing, and said, "*Application!*" but Augustine said, languidly—

"One would only really *need* it to kill Lyctors, Harrowhark, and the rest of us never evinced any interest in that."

That broke up the dinner somewhat.

* * *

There was much you might have written about the last Lyctor of the trio. There was useful information aplenty—you held it all carefully in your head, repeated it to yourself day by day on the basis that it might yet save your life. In a way, you were more intimate with the Saint of Duty than you were with either Augustine or Mercymorn.

The thing was, life in the Mithraeum was very comfortable. You wanted for nothing. There was plentiful food and heat and water, none of which you could ever dismiss, having grown up in Drearburh—having pored so long over whether or not you had food and heat and water enough to support your dwindling population. You lived in the midst of a beautiful memorial to those who had offered the Nine Houses their bravery, and skill, and their lives, the very best of the best, whose deeds were proven now by the presence of their bones in the holiest temple in the holiest system in the holiest part of space. The House of God. The Temple of the Nine Resurrections. The Necrolord Prime.

Looked at objectively, there were really only two things wrong with your life. One was that you were not a normal Lyctor. The other was even less complicated.

ORTUS ??? (WHILOM ???) THE FIRST, SAINT OF DUTY
Wants me dead.

18

IT WAS ORTUS NIGENAD who took charge of the body, washing it and laying it out with the help of Magnus Quinn. Harrowhark was surprised that Ortus had the trick of it, let alone the will to do so. In the room off the kitchen, in the chilly little morgue that doubled as a pantry, their breath hung in diamond clouds midair. She found herself watching their process: dressing the eyeballs in spirits, supporting the jaw with a bandage tied neatly behind the dark head, doing up the shining copper buttons of the no-longer-white Cohort jacket. Harrow had questioned this, but Abigail said that once they had extracted the projectiles from the wounds, Captain Deuteros might be decently arranged. Harrow was astonished that decent arrangement could still be constructed: the body had been in poor condition.

There were eight bullets in all. On flimsy, Harrow had calculated the trajectories and forces needed to compromise the axial skeleton in such a way. Lady Pent had assisted. Her thick brown hair was pinned up high on her crown and supported her first pair of glasses, swapped out for another, apparently totally different pair of glasses while she leafed through an ancient gloss-pulp book, with gloves on to protect the fragile pages from her sweat. Harrow had sworn to avoid Pent at all costs, but the corpse in front of them had rendered that impossible.

Harrowhark said: "The first projectile caused enormous trauma to the heart, and would have been fatal. The second hit the clavicle. The third passed through the abdomen and lodged in the spine— and so on. The *important* note here is the first bullet. It accurately destroyed both atria."

Abigail turned another page and said, openly baffled: "So why keep shooting?"

"Panic," suggested her husband, straightening up from the corpse.

Ortus was still busy dabbing blood away from a popping bruise on the body's temple, but said, "Anger, perhaps. I have often heard that anger may carry one beyond the initial act of murder."

Abigail said, "Ah. *Here's* the puppy. Reverend Daughter, look at this."

Harrowhark stood and crowded in at the Fifth adept's shoulder. She was being urged to look at a diagram of a bullet. Harrow reached over to take one of the less-crumpled projectiles between thumb and forefinger, to hold it close to the picture and compare, and she beheld the drawing opposite: a long stock, an immense barrel, a jumble of triggers and mechanics and protrusions that she did not understand. *Carbine rifle*, read the key. For a moment she pitied Judith Deuteros's last seconds. To be killed with this ancient piece of grave goods! It would have been like being set upon by a ghost out of time.

A brief skim of the blueprint showed her the problem immediately. "This weapon can only fire six projectiles before needing to be replenished," she said. ("Reloaded," added Abigail helpfully.) "The assailant fired eight."

"And must've known that poor Judith had no hope after the first hit. So reloading is odd, to say the least. Did anyone get anything pertinent out of the lieutenant?"

Magnus said soberly, "She's waiting outside. I offered to wait with her, but she turned me down. Don't know Dyas very well and didn't want to push . . . It's a bloody business."

When Lady Pent went to the kitchens, Harrowhark accompanied her. They found Lieutenant Dyas not sitting down, or even leaning against the wall as anyone else would have spent the full hour or so they had been with the body, but standing ramrod-straight to attention. Her crisp white jacket appeared all the crisper and whiter after the wreck of her necromancer's. Her scarlet necktie looked redder too—by the time they'd gotten hold of Judith Deuteros the blood had dried hers nearly black. Ortus had sponged it, and was attempting to dry it over a stove. At their approach, Dyas drew herself up to her full height, and she looked at Harrowhark, not at Abigail.

She said, with uncharacteristic frenzy: "Why am I *here*?"

Pent said, "Just to answer questions, Lieutenant Dyas."

The lieutenant said, "I want to know—I just want to know—"

"What *you* know is of vastly more importance," said Abigail. "Please, if you can, tell us exactly what you saw down there."

Marta Dyas looked at her. There was no woe on her face, only a deep, almost thirsty terror, an enormous anticipation, which animated what was usually a schooled Cohort mask. "I was in the chamber when it happened," she said, "already engaged with the target construct. The room was closed off from the adjoining chamber where—the captain was." (There had been a brief pause. Harrow wondered if the pause had meant to contain *Judith*.) "I didn't hear a shot. The target disappeared—the chamber unlocked—when I came out, the captain's door was open, and she was inside. No . . . vitals."

Pent said, "How long from that chamber unlocking to you reaching her?"

"Five to ten seconds to exit the chamber and get there," said Lieutenant Dyas. Then she said, "In hindsight, the door must have opened when she died."

"Did you hear any subsequent shots?" Harrowhark asked.

"No. The test chamber was soundproofed." Dyas continued, a little mechanically, "I left Captain Deuteros. I moved to the corridor. I saw, at the very end, the Sleeper."

"Please describe it, if you can," said Pent. She added: "Take your time, Lieutenant. I recognise this is difficult . . ."

Dyas said, ragged, "I just want to know—"

"You will. I give you absolute surety that you will. What did the Sleeper look like?"

"You've all seen it through the glass," said Dyas. This was not entirely true. Ortus refused to go anywhere near the glass-faced coffin in that central room, or the somnolent corpse within, and quaked at his own breathing. Harrowhark did not fear to look more closely at the death Teacher had promised them, ensconced within that frozen, clouded plex. She had been nonplussed to discover that the Sleeper slept dressed for an emergency, as Dyas recited now: "Breathing apparatus over the face—orange hazard suit—oxygen hood."

Harrowhark said, "Easy symbols to fake. It could have been someone dressed as the Sleeper."

"It was carrying a weapon," said Dyas. "One I hadn't seen anywhere in or on the coffin before. I called out, but it wouldn't stop . . . I pursued it to the central atrium. The Sleeper's coffin was open and empty. The figure climbed inside. Pulled the lid down, snapped it shut."

Abigail prompted, "And then you escaped and raised the alarm."

The lieutenant of the Second looked at Abigail as though she had suggested *And then you went for ice cream.*

"I went and got a piece of tubing from the mortuary room," she said monotonously. "I hit the coffin. I hit the coffin repeatedly. I did so for maybe a minute. You found blood on the glass. It's mine. I tried my fists and my feet and the butt of my sword—that plex glass isn't plex. Or glass."

"That could have easily meant all our deaths," said Harrow; she had tasted hypocrisy on her own lips so often that she hardly felt the sting.

"Emperor's breath, Dyas!" said Lady Pent, white lipped, a little more tactful in her shock. "That didn't—rouse it?"

Dyas said, "No."

Harrow had only halfway noticed Ortus edging closer, ostensibly to check on Judith Deuteros's blood-crusted necktie. He had stopped in his ministrations to listen in the dreamy, part-transfixed way he always seemed to listen to everything, with slight tonal differences depending on the person. He listened to Harrow with the happy demeanour of a person far away in his mind palace, unless what she was saying had a direct impact on him, at which point he merely got very sad.

The Lieutenant's gaze—unsettling and part feral, giving the impression that she was now a bag with ten snakes inside—fell on Ortus, and the stained necktie he had been wringing out. Harrow stepped forward, trying to place herself between the sightline of the Second cavalier and her own. But she moved to protect the wrong cavalier.

Her cavalier cleared his throat—oh, damn:

> *"My sister, I envy your fortune; fearless you forge yet*
> *ahead, through the cold grey flood of the River.*

> *"Fallen in war for the fame of the House is the death*
> *every warrior fain would win at the finish;*

> *"Laggard I linger behind; hold fast on the far bank's*
> *beach-head! Blood shall repay your blood spilt."*

Book Eleven. For a moment, at the lieutenant's expression, Harrow thought that she might draw that practical Cohort rapier and go for Ortus there and then, which his turgid verse probably did not deserve but which his choice to quote it unwanted and in public very much did. She closed her thumb and forefinger over a chip of patella in her pocket. But then Dyas's hands trembled, and her eyes dropped to the floor, and she said lowly: "I can't hope for that anymore."

Abigail Pent said gently, "Lieutenant—" but Dyas was saying, low and fast, and this time to Harrowhark herself: "Is this really how it happens? You know of no hope for her?"

"She had eight metal projectiles spun at high speeds through her midsection," said Harrow. She knew that some people took comfort in the idea, so she added: "She would have died very quickly after her heart was destroyed."

"No," said the lieutenant, and now Harrow thought she seemed dazed. Her fingers kept working the hilt of her rapier, from which hung a neat scarlet riband. "That's not . . . Don't know why I thought . . . No."

"You have faced down a monster that is likely to be the doom of many, and many less able than Captain Deuteros," said Ortus. Harrow regretted not making him take a solemn pledge of silence, to walk the place as the mute and intimidating bulk his father had been; but only a very obedient idiot of a cavalier would have stuck to that. "I include myself among the latter. Is there no hint of our salvation?"

Abigail said, "Ortus the Ninth is right, Lieutenant. If there are any details, anything else you might be able to tell us—you've taught us so much already, even if the price was too high."

The lieutenant drew herself up again. Her mouth was now a calm line that betrayed nothing but classic Second House stoicism. Harrowhark admired her for that.

"One," she said crisply. "The Sleeper can move from its coffin. Two, the Sleeper can pass through necromantic wards. Three, Teacher told us not to wake it. I don't know what does. Noise doesn't." ("Not necessarily, no," said Pent, who never did truck with unconditional statements.) "Four, it's carrying a rifle."

"Like something from an old story," suggested Ortus.

"Like something. That's all the facts I have," said the lieutenant. "Don't want to guess. One more thing—I'm not saying this with absolute certainty. I only got a glance before the lid closed and the plex fogged up again. But there's something else in the coffin. The Sleeper's lying on it."

The lieutenant closed her eyes, though her precise posture did not shift. When she opened them, she said, "I don't know if this matters. But it *looked* like a standard-issue infantry sword." She added, with Cohort precision: "A two-hander."

19

THE FIRST TIME THE Saint of Duty tried to take your life, you did not anticipate it. If you had been a kernel less paranoid, a trifle less disturbed, you might have given Ianthe Tridentarius the pleasure of opening the note labelled *Upon the death of Harrowhark Nonagesimus.* Your only hope for that note was that it contained a single sentence along the lines of, *Get what joy you can from my corpse, you devious bitch,* but it was written by a previous self and you could not risk a guess.

It was only a few days into your internment within the Mithraeum. Ever since you disgraced yourself with Cytherea's midsection you had avoided all social meals, and you tended to scavenge food as you passed through the bizarre space that everyone called the kitchen. It was a long, clean, barren room where electric lights cast long shadows on pots and pans older than Drearburh, yet spared time's depredations. At this point you had not yet figured out your exoskeleton, but had managed to fix a prototype bone scabbard to your lower back, and spent most of the time limping around with it as though scoliotic. You had taken a portion of some kind of murky stew left warm on top of the stove, ravenous, not yet knowing what the Emperor would tell you later: that a Lyctor could persist perfectly well without food, but would not last long without water. ("Cyrus was half-mummified before we worked that one out," he would go on to reminisce fondly.)

Your mistake was not spiriting the food back to your rooms. Ianthe's room was not yet an option. In that first week you were still numb; you were tired, you were hungry, and you sat down at the countertop to eat your tepid supper, and had gotten through maybe five spoonfuls before the sword emerged from the middle of your chest.

The aim for your pulmonic valve was unerring, but he had put himself at the mercy of your third and fourth ribs. This was a mistake your assailant would never make again. Always your bosom friends, they unfurled for you then like the springtime. Thick ropes of costal cartilage burst from your breast to fix your assailant's sword in place: your ribs became jaws, your sternum the neck of a spring. Your blood sprayed into your indifferent soup, and the rapier stuck fast. You wrestled yourself backward; your phalanx bones burst through your fingertips like knives, and, too frightened for anything sophisticated, you raked blindly into the meat of the fatless and muscular thighs behind you.

Your claws turfed up the meat of his hips and pelvis, but you would come to learn that Ortus the First did not respond to pain. He moved—you were dragged with him, off your stool, away from your blood-spattered soup—and you let his rapier go, dilating the bone so that he stumbled backward and you went forward, rolling over the countertop, spilling your bowl, dislodging pots and pans, and causing a hell of a noise.

A chip of bone floated near where the rapier had clipped your rib. You popped it out of yourself and from that almost-living bone sprang femurs, melted on either side into patella, into pelvis, into a skeleton seething with regrowing ash. You tore one of your construct's ribs from its cage before it hurled itself at the necrosaint, and the rib you wrenched free had enormous and generous give: the bubbly innards separated from the strong, compact cortex as though created for that very purpose. The centre for shape, the outside for strength. The whole crumbled in your palms when you squeezed. You were borne up by a current of bone, twenty sets of arms sprung from tubercles you had made sticky and thrust into the ground, enfolding you in an armoured nest of skeletal limbs.

You marvelled at how easy it was. You barely had to think of it and it would be done, at a cost you considered negligible. But your blood was pouring out fast, and something bad had happened to some relatively important muscles, and you had no time to do anything but cut the flow and save the damage for later.

At that point, you took your first opportunity to really look at him. This was a fool's move: why didn't you run? You chose to *watch,* as though you could learn anything? A less critical party might've pointed out that you'd had a surprise gift of twelve inches of steel through the chest and made your pecs *sproing* the blade back out with your own ribcage, but you had never been party to excuses. You were startled by him all over again: by this ramshackle, burnt-out Lyctor, by the skin that clung to the skull, by that point-blank, stretched-thin face. Ortus the First did not look as though he needed meat or even water. There was a strangely burnt look to his dark brown skin, a burnt or otherwise oxidised look, not assisted by that shaven cap of rust-coloured hair. You hung, poised, for a moment not sure if you were hallucinating the whole thing. That hesitation cost.

From protoskeletal dust you conjured five full constructs: five constructs only as good as you were, tired and hungry. They scrambled like huge spiders across the counter and went for him. The Saint of Duty shouldered his goddamned spear. That first time you were absolutely affrighted: a *spear,* a spear for the *offhand.* He used the butt of his sword—it would be lying to say that you now regularly called it the *pommel*—to smash the first construct's skull to powder. The force was enormous. You tried to prop the skeletons back together from within your net, reknobble the spine, mould it with ash as a second skull's mandible got flicked off into the stovetop. A third construct was beheaded with the spear, swung through the cervical vertebra—it became a shrapnel of bones—and for the last two, your killer lost patience. He sucked the thanergy from their bones and it felt like a slap to your face. They disappeared into gritty puffs of bone smoke.

At this point you finally thought to run. More fool you. The nest of arms swung you around, prepared to be squeezed through the doorway. You shaped the net into a tight fretwork, springy, malleable. Although this was beautiful and worked a treat for mobility, you sacrificed resilience in the process. He threw his spear, almost casually, into this fretwork, and the net deformed fluidly on impact, and so it was *through* the bone that his spearpoint lodged into your large intestine. This sounded similar to a nail being rammed into a sausage. Your blood gushed like carbonated water. You tumbled through the doorway in a cascade of jostling, bouncing bits of bone, the scabbard jolting you roughly, rolling over and over until you lay bleeding at the feet of—

"Ortus!" said Mercymorn. She did not sound horrified, but deeply peeved. Your vision swam, and you smelled hot toast. "What are you *doing??*"

You curled on your side. The black haze was already starting to dim around your edges. You were not so apt with healing yourself, back then. You heard: "Is she *dead*?—Stay there, you idiot! Hands where I can see them! What were you *thinking*? Oh, he's going to be furious! You egg!"

It seemed hateful to you that in death you should be treated like a prey animal some domestic predator had brought inside. You heard the Saint of Duty say in his flat, joyless voice: "I don't answer to you."

The spear was removed. You still remembered acutely what that felt like. In the midst of that sensation, quick, light fingertips tapped a symphony over your back, arresting the flow of blood, seizing your flesh, cutting off circulatory shock; it was only then that you really began to understand what Mercymorn could do. With another fingertip, she tapped above your eyebrow, and your pituitary gland spewed out a flood of neuropeptides that immediately replaced the adrenaline squirting through your system.

She was saying: "It's not fair of you to try to bump them off when *we'd* get in trouble for it. They can die well enough on their own, you toad. This one's all of twelve years old."

This was not close to accurate, even given your lie, but fine. He murmured something. She said back, sharply: "Quick enough for anyone's satisfaction. Look! *Look!!* She can't even heal . . . *told* him her integration had retarded . . . *said* she couldn't stanch . . . and I'm *not* cleaning up this place, you are. Yuck. There's bone in the grouting."

Ortus the First said, "The Heralds will be here in eight months."

"I'm well aware of that, *thanks*," said Mercy. "*You* go flip some planets to give us a firebreak."

Ortus the First said, "Now you're telling me my own job."

"Oh, I *hate* you! I've always hated you, you dreary, repetitive *leg*," said Mercymorn passionately, and then you felt her thumb press down on your lower back, and your gastrointestinal tract—so interrupted by spearpoint—flushed, deep and warm, and you felt some of that twisting pain within you. You could barely feel it anyway, you were so running with hormones. It was the best you'd felt since before you'd gone to Canaan House. Then she said, more reasonably: "I know what you're doing, and it's not like I don't understand it, but if you'd wanted to smother the kittens you could do it more cleanly by knocking her out and dropping her out the airlock . . ."

She trailed off suggestively. The Saint of Duty said stonily, "I do things face-to-face."

"I am not trying to be cruel," she said cruelly, "but that *is* what got you into trouble nineteen years ago."

There were heavy footsteps on the tiles. You were rolled onto your back, where the scabbard made you roll backward and forward, like a tortoise with a knobble on its shell. You were filled with a great sense of calm as the world rolled back into focus. It had been psychologically dreadful to see Mercymorn tapping your chest and your midsection, mouth screwed up as though she were cleaning your vomit, but you were wrapped in a beautiful fug of oxytocin and did not care about other Lyctors, your assassination attempt, or anything much. It meant you could look up fearlessly, and nervelessly, into the eyes of Ortus.

Ortus's face, stretched too tightly over its frame and locked into a long, lugubrious expression, had no reasonable relationship with his luminous green eyes: a soft, buttery green, less startling or harsh than the green of a shoot or the green of a leaf, but instead liquid and fluvial.

The Lyctor leaning over you said warningly, "Don't you do a *thing*. I'll have to fight you, and I cannot begin to tell you how much I don't want to do that. Oh, why did I stop?" she wailed. "I should have kept walking. I hate reasonable culpability."

"I want that sword," said Ortus the First.

"*What?*"

"Give me her damned sword," said Ortus the First.

"You've already got a whole complement of oversized weapons, greedy."

Even an overexcited pituitary gland could not mask the sharp shank of fear that sliced down the length of your heart. You tried to raise yourself up on your elbows before you wobbled weakly back down. You said hoarsely, "No. No. It's mine."

Mercymorn lost her patience on an almost professional basis. "Oh, just get *out* of it," she said peevishly to Ortus. "Leave the baby alone." Before you could feel indebted to her, she added: "Next time, try this at night! When I'm sleeping! If I see you hurt her I *have* to intervene, or Teacher will lose his nana."

The Saint of Duty looked down at you, sprawled so awkwardly in a pool of blood, free of the two new punctures he had given you in such a short space of time. He took his spear and shook it like a bedsheet, and the bone haft folded in on itself until it was no longer or thicker than a mace handle. This short, fat handle and spearhead he shoved into his belt, then he sheathed his rapier, turned around, and left.

His sister-saint bawled after him: "I mean it! You clean this place up!" but he was already gone. She stood and smoothed out the front of her beautiful mother-of-pearl robe—the blood came off it in great gouts of reddish powder, dwindling to nothing—and she said, her placid face creased in complaint: "This place has gone to the dogs . . . What did you say, to make him try to kill you?"

"Nothing." The hormones were beginning to cease their pleasant flow, but you were still preternaturally calm when you said: "I came in to get some food. I did not perceive his entrance. The first thing I knew of him was when he stabbed me."

"Oh. Then he just wants you dead," she said, with perfect uncon-cern. "Good luck! Not!! That man is Teacher's attack dog . . . If he thinks you're a threat then I would advise you to settle your affairs."

You stared up at the ceiling and noted the bone-strewn scrollwork between the frames of the panelling, all about the long planks of electric light. And you said: "But why does Ortus the First want me dead?"

"Who?" said Mercymorn, indifferently.

IX

20

You had not left behind any notes about what you wanted done at your funeral. This was not due to a surfeit of optimism, though you were determined that your end would not come at the end of Ortus the First's sword or spear: it was because you found the idea of a funeral for you too pitiful—what would be said, and what would be done? What fitting epitaph for your fragile bones? (Perhaps: *Here lies the world's most insufferable witch.*)

In the following months the Saint of Duty attempted to kill you, by your count, fourteen times, and you never came to understand the motivation. Often you were saved only by intervention. Sometimes this came from one of the other two Lyctors. Once, vilely, from Ianthe; she had ensconced you in fat and rolled you down the hallway out of danger, and still laughed whenever she thought about it. Once it even came from God. He had walked in as your pelvis was run through by your elder brother's razor-sharp, scarlet-hilted rapier—so sharp you could never comprehend it—and God had laid you down on the big broad dining table of brown wood, and the world had whited out for you and reverberated up your nostrils and sinus cavities, then arced down the bottoms of your feet, as your skin and flesh closed over whole and perfect. Even your back ache had disappeared. Your body had hissed all over as it sealed, reborn in the hot white light of the Necrolord Prime.

And he had said: "Ortus, have pity."

"This is my pity, Lord," said the Saint of Duty.

"She's your *responsibility,* not your punching bag."

"I find the responsibility a hard one."

193

You'd lain dazed and stunned on the tabletop, and you heard the Emperor of the Nine Houses say: "I don't want to argue with you. This is ham-fisted. Get out."

If you had thought God's intervention might be final, might enforce some terms of peace, it had not. It had seemed—difficult—to raise the subject, when God did not want to bring it up himself. What would you say? (*One of your fingers and gestures is trying to kill me on the reg. Is this . . . fine with you?*) When you finally approached him about it, his wince made you wish that you had not.

The Emperor said, carefully: "He made a pact, with an authority I have no power to gainsay, that he would protect me from all dangers. Now it has been put to him that you are that danger. Harrowhark, forgive me. I need you to face him—each time—knowing your life is in danger . . ."

Here he broke off, and just said: "Will you wear a rapier, if I give you one?"

"For what *purpose*, Teacher? I could not use it, having misapprehended the Lyctoral process."

"Just in case," he said, and it was the first time you had seen him wretched.

"You say you misapprehended the process," said your Teacher, leaning forward and crossing his shabby-sleeved arms over his knees. "I don't believe you did, Harrowhark. I really don't believe you did. I've only seen one person get it . . . fundamentally wrong . . . and I hope I never see what happened to Anastasia and Samael again."

And thus, unintentionally, you also confronted him with *Anastasia.* You could not trip in the Ninth House without falling over an Anastas, an Anastasia, or an Anastasius; or, in later years, bumping into their niche. *Anastasia* had been the mythic founding tombkeeper and grandmother of the House, and the subject of at least two Nigenad poems (*'Twas deep in Anastasia's time, I wot*). She was namesake of the deep inner monument where lay the sacred bones of tomb-keepers past and those who fell in battle. You were profoundly upset to learn that she had been real; that the rooms you inhabited—the empty, tintless, quiet rooms—had been intended for her.

As you often sat, mute and still, a statue of yourself, opposite the Emperor of the Nine Resurrections, caught between pleasure and pain at listening to him speak, he did not wait for you to ask. He said, "Out of all of us, only Anastasia got it wrong. She'd researched it too much. Typical Anastasia. She'd seen some pathways in it that simply didn't exist. She spoke the Eightfold Word, and it didn't . . . work. After we—cleaned up—she asked me if I might end her life. Of course I said *no*. She had so much more to give. Later I would ask of her a greater and more terrible thing. I had a body and I needed a tomb . . . you might know of the body, Harrowhark, and you will know far better the Tomb."

At the time the Body had stood at the curtained plex window that stared out onto the field of slowly spinning asteroids, the mother-of-pearl robe slipping from her supple, naked shoulders, still moist as though just taken from the ice of her grave. You watched a droplet of water trickle down the column of her spine.

"The tomb that was to be shut forever," you said, and found the words so strange. "The rock that was never to be rolled away. That what was within should remain buried, insensate, with closed eye and stilled brain. Every day I prayed for it to live, I prayed for it to sleep."

Your voice dredged up from your brain, which dredged up from your heart, which dredged up from the oily, filth-stricken depths of your soul, and you said: "God, *who did you bury*?"

Teacher worried his temple with his thumb, and then worried his other temple with his other thumb. He took a biscuit and dipped it into his cooling tea, then ate it, then swirled the tea around in the cup and set it down again. "I buried a monster," he said.

From the glare of the plex window, beside some perfectly ordinary white twill curtains, the buried monster turned herself so that she was lit in the light of the undead stars. The curve of her cheek—the thick, black lashes that fringed her golden eyes—the thumbprint divot that lay pressed like a kiss within the bow of her lip—you had not known you were shaking until God himself reached out to still your wrist, so that you mightn't spill your tea over your knees. He unhelpfully passed you another biscuit.

"Eat up, there's nothing to you," he said gently. "Have two, get some fat reserves. Do you like poetry, Harrowhark?"

"I have never been a fan," you said fervently.

"Poetry is one of the most beautiful shadows a civilisation can cast across time," he said. "Go on . . . eat up, they're good for you. Here, I'm going to pretend to read this one off my tablet, when in fact it's been with me for over ten thousand years. Here's my favourite part . . ."

That night, the Body consented to embrace you. You so nearly felt those long arms wrap around your neck, your middle. You were so close to feeling that press of graceful forehead to yours, the long, lean, dead body chilling yours to the shivering point, as you all but perceived one cool corpse thigh touching yours from hip to knee. You had been nearly eight weeks in the Mithraeum. The sword that you bathed in your own arterial blood was sheathed in bone and heavy on your back. You no longer knew what it was like not to be afraid.

You—with your unfortunate memory for poetry—could still hear Teacher's verse, in his low, soothing, ordinary voice, chase itself round and round your head:

> For the moon never beams, without bringing me
>   dreams
>
> Of the beautiful Annabel Lee.

* * *

THE EMPEROR OF THE NINE HOUSES, THE PRINCE
UNDYING (WHILOM ??? JOHN???)
Who was A.L.?

21

RAIN STARTED FALLING ON Canaan House early one morning, and it never stopped again. For the first few hours it was the normal, leaden fall of water Harrowhark had become used to in her time at Canaan House. She found it merely unnerving now, not a killer of peace and sleep. Around midday a fog began to boil off the saw-toothed waters at the bottom of the tower. It rose up to the lower levels of Canaan, and kept rising. The fog was bitterly cold, and the rain stank like engine lubricant and blood; it tasted indescribable. Teacher and the other priests unearthed great spiny patchwork compasses of oilcloth and metal struts, which unfolded at the press of a button, and Harrowhark and the others were obliged to walk around with them over their heads even inside the main atrium, where the water leaked through the walls and ceilings.

At first, she trusted her hood and veil and let the rain wet her where it would. She was soon forced to acknowledge how difficult it had become to dry clothes. Ortus spent half his life wringing out tents of black fabric into the bathroom tub. Harrow was forced in bad grace to consent to him standing over her with one of these umbrella constructions, and listen to the hateful, arrhythmic *PLUT...PLUT... PLUT-PLUT-PLUT* of water on its waterproof skin. This incidental noise was very difficult for her: it was fertile ground for the false symphony inside her head, and those banging doors and murmurous half-heard ghosts were now joined by a thin background wail, which sounded for all the world like the mewling of a newborn baby.

"This has never *happened* before," Teacher complained at meals, fretfully, as though they were not Lyctors-in-waiting but instead sympathetic building inspectors. "The rainy season won't be on us for months. It ought to be ten degrees warmer than it is. I have had to bring in all the herbs and put them under a lamp. And this fog . . . I guess I might as well die," he concluded, something he now suggested hopefully at least three times a day.

Harrow found this a suggestion that lacked grace or tact, especially after they found the second round of bodies.

There were no witnesses to question, when they found the grey-wrapped figures of Camilla Hect and Palamedes Sextus laid on the stained, brushed-steel slabs in the mortuary. They had been arranged as though whomever found them had wished to present them scientifically. That they were Sextus and Hect was at first only educated conjecture: they were wearing their librarian greys, and one had the battered old rapier that had seemed to be all the Sixth House could proffer for this trial, and the other had ink stains on his fingers. Their faces had been obliterated by point-blank gunshots.

It was grim. Harrowhark was surprised by her own tranquillity, but concluded she was grateful for it. A strange, tomblike calm had fallen over her when Abigail had first taken her to see the bodies, walking briskly past the Sleeper's silent coffin with a lantern held high. Harrow admired her for that, for her lack of tiptoe or hush. Harrow had never seen Sextus or Hect except from afar, and had formed an impression that was all abbreviations: grey clothes, hushed voices, angles. It was Ortus who mourned for them, but Ortus was one of the Emperor's natural mourners. His mother had been the same. They'd both loved a funeral, which had been lucky for them, as funerals were one of her House's natural resources. When they brought both facially obliterated corpses upstairs under the direction of Lady Pent, she watched Ortus weep stolid, stony-faced tears, which once again turned his sacramental paint into an underwater skull.

To properly identify them, Abigail's husband-cavalier scared up the only flesh magician he could find. Finding other magicians at all was becoming difficult: the day-jewel and night-rock Tridentarius twins were so elusive that Harrow grew confused even trying to remember when she had last seen them. There was not enough room in the chilly morgue upstairs, and the dropping temperature was not immediately compromising, so they put the faceless bodies out on rubberized sheets in the dining room. It was there the Seventh cavalier brought his adept.

She must have seen them both on that first day—that muggy, sun-struck first day, when Teacher had given them the rings and the keys, and told them about the monstrous hypersomniac in the basement—but Harrow found she was startled when they arrived. It would have been difficult not to have been. The cavalier was bronzed and vigorous, an enormous, musclebound man in green, with a seafoam-coloured kilt and tooled leathers. This well-muscled individual was guiding a wheeled chair down the wide aisles between tables, and in the chair was what appeared to be a dead body, holding a little lacy umbrella of her own to keep off the drips. It was gowned appropriately in spindrift white skirts, and inappropriately in a little crocheted scarf of pilling white wool.

Harrowhark had known Ortus too long not to register the slight curl to his lip and the lack of maudlin suicide in his eyes: he was almost rigid with contempt. She had thought Ortus would find contempt too exhausting an emotion to bother with. The ghost holding the umbrella had her pale, sugar-brown hair cropped short, its curls gathered into a cap of silky ringlets. There was a gracile delicacy to her—a starved, wasted, childlike mien—and when she gave her umbrella to her cavalier, she actually rose to stand. A fine length of tubing emerged from her nose and was discreetly taped into the collar of her dress. Harrowhark had never seen its like before; it was a thin, stiffened cylinder of mucous epithelial tissue.

"It's great, isn't it?" she said to Harrow, by way of *hello.* She had a sweet, modulated voice, only a trifle breathy. "It's a pulmonary drain. It goes all the way down to my lungs."

"I have never seen such a thing before," admitted Harrow.

"You wouldn't have," said the Seventh necromancer rapturously. "*He* came up with it, when he was fifteen."

It seemed too stupid for Harrowhark to believe, but there could be no ambiguity in that woman's gesture. Her paper-skinned hand pointed to one of the faceless corpses, the one without a rapier. It oughtn't to have surprised her anymore that the relationships between every other scion of the Nine Houses seemed intimate, or incestuous, or familiar, or antipathic. She did not feel left out. She merely felt dislocated as Abigail said, "Are you sure it's him, Dulcie?"

"Give me a minute," said *Dulcie*, apparently, though who would have let themselves be called *Dulcie* unless faced with water torture was a question Harrow did not want the universe to answer. "I took a swab from the doorknob—I've got two prints, so if they correlate, that will tell us something . . ."

The grossly named Dulcie sat back down in the chair, and her cavalier pushed her alongside one corpse, and then the other. Harrowhark watched her work. She gently grated a bit off the heel of each stiffening hand—she took a minute sliver off each thigh, unbuttoning both sets of trousers without a blush or grimace—she cleaned under the fingernails ("Just for bacterial thalergy, you know"), and, in the end, sighed.

"The one on the left's Cam, the one on the right's Pal," she said, proving her desire to saddle the world with diminutives. "Did the Sleeper get them?"

"Only by assumption," said Harrowhark, while Abigail's dolt of a husband said, "I bloody hope so."

"Magnus," Abigail said, a touch disapprovingly.

"Well, if the Sleeper didn't, that's *two* maniacs with an ancient weapon and a love of blowing off faces, dear," said Magnus.

Maniac did not seem apt. The first death was maniac. Deuteros was riddled with far more holes than necessary. This had been a simple execution. The effects were grisly. It would be difficult ever to get a clear picture of what Sextus's and Hect's faces had looked like, as they were now sprayed indiscriminately across the back wall of the mortuary. From what Harrow had been able to reconstruct, and the relative time stamps of the deaths, it looked as if both representatives of the Sixth House had stood quietly with their backs to the wall, about an arm's length apart from each other, and had their faces forcibly removed from very short range. First went one; the second had waited; then the other.

Harrow said, "The projectile exited out the back of the skull, and we haven't been able to dislodge it from the wall. Fragments suggest a similarity. There is reasonable doubt, and then there's unnecessary caution. I say the Sixth were killed by the same entity that killed Deuteros."

"A thesis I agree with," said Ortus heavily. "The Sleeper, who sleepeth not. Perhaps a better name would have been . . . . *the Waker.*" (She searched her cavalier thoroughly for any evidence of humour, but found none, as per usual.) "It lies in an impervious coffin. It kills with a legendary weapon. What can we do against such a supernatural assault?"

The dreadfully named Dulcie was stroking a soft, wet lock of very dark hair between thumb and forefinger, quite close to the ruined ear of Camilla Hect. "The only thing you can ever do, when faced with an enemy too great for yourself," she said. "Fight like a trapped animal in a sack."

"I agree," said her bronze statue of a cavalier. "Better that we make the first move. What is *impervious*? What is *coffin*?" (Harrow was astounded to hear the older man beside her mutter, "An adjective and a noun.") "I say we muster all able-bodied cavaliers for an initial assault."

"And die," suggested Ortus ponderously.

"Better not to die as Deuteros and Sextus and Camilla the Sixth have died," said the man. "If you *think* of the enemy as unassailable, shadow-priest, then the battle is lost already."

Then this bronze statue cleared his throat, and added:

> *"I held to the faith of my fallible flesh;*
> *Why should I think of the irradiating star?"*

Harrow's cavalier swung his head to confront this act of spoken poetry. He looked like a man who had stood on the bailey, beheld the enemy at his gates, and found them manifold and terrible. He stared as though the Seventh cavalier had revealed himself to be the Sleeper, done awful and inadvisable acts with Ortus's mother, and compared Matthias Nonius to two shits.

202 / TAMSYN MUIR

"And that is how you would have your master end," said her black-swaddled swordsman, "with her cavalier filled with shot, before a box that does not open?"

"Interesting hypocrisy, from a black cavalier of the Ninth sepulchre," said his equally tedious opposite.

"All right, gentlemen," said Magnus Quinn, with a slightly forced cheer. "*Protesilaus,* if I'm not wrong? I'm not? Good— Respectfully, I don't agree with either of you. Ninth, you're too good a man to roll over and wait for another death. Seventh, the last time I attacked a box I couldn't open, it was my birthday and my wife had tied the ribbon too tightly. Let's get everyone on side, inasmuch as that's possible. Duchess Septimus. The Reverend Daughter. Lieutenant Dyas. United we stand, divided we fall, or so the saying goes."

"I don't know how much I can do," confessed Dulcie, who was most likely *Duchess Septimus,* and who had wrinkled her nose when a fat drop of rain had fallen on it. The gleaming Protesilaus thrust the umbrella over her head. "I've . . . I didn't really prove myself . . . there was nothing much to prove, on Rhodes. When I came here I thought it might be my chance to *do* something."

She finished this rather helpless little speech by playing with a fold on her virginal white skirts. Harrowhark said bluntly, "Listen to your first instinct. There's a tube in your chest, and you can barely walk."

"I've felt heaps better since I got here," Dulcie said defensively. "I've coughed a few times, but it's mainly for show, isn't it, Pro?"

> "*Do not mistake the thaw for the spring.*
> *Our bud is not yet certain,*"

quoth her cavalier.

Harrowhark deliberately did not watch for the hot flash of murder in her own cavalier's eyes, though it at least leavened his thick, porridgy sadness. It must have been traumatic to see his only cultivated personality trait co-opted by someone who looked like the hero of his very own epics. It was more interesting to look at Abigail Pent—to look at those slender, workaday hands turning over the forearms and elbows of the body that was apparently Palamedes Sextus, examining. "No defence wounds," Pent murmured. "Just like Judith . . . I wonder."

The wind had picked up. It suddenly screamed shrilly over the glass-covered, vine-choked roof, bringing bullet sprays of hard rain in its wake. For a moment, Abigail shuddered. Then she straightened up and clapped her hands together, as though she led a class of unruly small children. "We're all in this together," she said, which was a typically Fifth assumption. The Ninth didn't think anyone was in anything together, or if they were, they all had to disperse as soon as humanly possible to avoid splash damage. "I am beginning to suspect I know where the danger lies. Or at least, I've got a perfectly baseless assumption, and every scholar knows that this is where you begin. Dulcie—Lady Dulcinea, do you mind if I ask you to get Silas Octakiseron with us? He's neither to hold nor to bind to *me*, but he might listen to you."

"Fine," said the woman in the chair, drying her nose carefully with her crochet necktie, so as not to disturb her shunt. "I don't love you for asking, but I won't say that the renowned Abigail Pent asked something of me and I didn't do it. And you've been kind to Cam and Pal. I'll go."

Abigail said, "Magnus, will you ask the lieutenant—" ("Anything for you, even that," he said promptly.) "—and, Reverend Daughter, if you can, when you can, Coronabeth Tridentarius. And her sister, of course," she added, though Harrowhark thought that addition a bit belated. "With the cavalier. Again, if you can. I haven't been able to check . . . I'll get any leftovers. Ask everyone to leave the facility alone, to come together. And find out whose room doesn't leak," she added, struck by inspiration, "so we can put down mattresses, as—I tell you for free—we're *flooded*."

It was left to the cavaliers to transfer the faceless body of Camilla Hect back into the frozen morgue—Abigail had removed all of the cavalier's effects from her pockets, and was brooding over them like a crossword—and the intubated flesh necromancer wheeled herself over to the grisly remains of the skinny Sixth boy. He was a perfectly normal sight, except from the neck up.

"Is this how it happens, Lady Pent?" she asked soberly.

Abigail picked up a worn leather strap that must have belonged to a clockwork watch face, and said gently: "No. It's not."

"Does it get—better than this? Do you know?"

This did not seem to Harrow like a question that could ever be answered. She did not fully understand it. But the Seventh did love questions that were as beautiful as they were unanswerable. This oblique sally did not get a response from the other woman, who had taken off her glasses to examine a crisscrossed piece of wax and a fragment of darning thread. Harrowhark felt bounden to look at the things they had taken from the Master Warden's pockets: a scrap of soft cloth that you might wipe your glasses with, a pen, a little fold-out examining lens, a crumpled-up piece of flimsy. When the cavaliers came to bear away the Warden (less heavy than his cavalier: only Magnus and the Seventh, Protesilaus, bore him, with Ortus hovering on the sidelines), the chair-bound girl gave a woeful little sigh.

"Oh, goodbye!" she called out suddenly, to the corpse borne aloft. "Goodbye, Palamedes, my first strand—goodbye, Camilla, my second . . . One cord was overpowered, two cords could defend themselves, but three were not broken by the living or the dead."

Harrowhark suddenly felt something, in her core, though she did not know precisely what it was. Somehow in Canaan House her ability to feel had been blunted, leaving only a sense of dislocated longing, a bizarre yearning as though flipping through the pages of a book for a proverb she remembered but could not find. She focused on what was in her hands, instead of on a stranger's farewell to strangers.

The piece of flimsy was rolled up so tightly that it resembled a kind of fat pill. She took off her gloves, and with the edges of her fingernails—bitten to the quick, and never much help—she started to prise open one wrinkled corner. She was thoroughly surprised when a deep shadow fell over her: when her cavalier primary laid one black-gloved hand down on her naked ones.

"My Lady Harrowhark," whispered Ortus, "perhaps . . . maybe you shouldn't . . . in case."

"You presume overmuch," she snapped.

He withdrew. "I have often thought so," he said sadly.

By the time she swept into the corridor, the rain driving through the holes in the roof and the walls and lashing in with gusty, bad-smelling sprays, Ortus three-quarters of a step behind her, she had nearly gotten the whole thing open. She opened it, hummocked and humped all over with little rills from being over-folded, and she read:

> *HIM I'LL KILL QUICK BECAUSE SHE ASKED ME TO AND BECAUSE THAT MUCH HE HONESTLY DESERVES BUT YOU TWO MUMMIFIED WIZARD SHITS I WILL BURN AND BURN AND BURN AND BURN UNTIL THERE IS NO TRACE OF YOU LEFT IN THE SHADOW OF MY LONG-LOST NATAL SUN*

"It is a drawing of the letter *S*," said the deep, solemn voice from over her shoulder, and she realized she had stopped midstride. "The letter in question is constructed from six short marks stacked vertically three by three. There are two triangles on the top and bottom, which, along with some diagonal strokes, form a calligraphic *S*."

"Nigenad," said Harrow, without turning. "I did not ask you."

"Three people are dead, my Lady Harrowhark," said her cavalier. "One ranked Cohort necromancer. Two scions of the enigmatic Sixth House, quick in learning and wisdom if not in martial prowess. Am I to act only on your command, when the Sleeper comes for me?"

"Were you *planning* to do anything other than lie down and die?" she said, waiting for rage; dying for rage; hoping for the simulacrum of rage, if nothing else. "What do you think you can do, Ortus? Did you have a tactic, beyond stopping bullets with your body?"

"It would be within the family character, I agree," said Ortus, meditatively. "My father died, simply because your mother and father asked him to. He took his own life when your parents handed him the rope, though he had a wife at home and, if he acknowledged it, a son."

Harrow lowered the flimsy more out of instinct than intent. She found herself turning around to look Ortus full in the face, as best she could with the umbrella over his head, and the hood half-plastered to his scalp with rain despite the oilcloth's best efforts, and his painted skull now a sad melange of alabaster grey and black. She looked at his underslept, roly-poly face, his deep black Drearburh eyes. They were not true black, as she had usually thought: in the shadow she could finally see a deep earthy undertone, like the ploughed-up additive ground in the planter fields. His grown-up features were suddenly ancient to her. She wanted to panic, to feel the icy knives of despair.

"You knew," she said. "You knew the whole time that Mortus the Ninth died at their command."

Now Ortus's face changed. It slid a second time into paint-splattered, black-irised, hooded contempt. He looked at her as though she were tedious. He looked at her as though he did not know who she was. His contempt made the doors she heard in her ears slam in an orchestra of unfathomable sound. He looked at her as though she were a squalling infant; as though she had not spoken, but rather opened her mouth and vomited.

"Harrow," he said curtly, "you are not the only person who can add up two and two, and arrive at four."

Any reply she might have made was aborted by a sudden gust of rain through a broken window. A curtain of murky water splattered through the glass maw. The water carried with it a handful of flashing brown-and-steel objects, which fell in a tumbled heap on the rotten Canaan House corridor carpet. When they came to rest, she and Ortus stared down at a collection of large, rusted pipette needles, the hard plex type with measurement markings up the side.

"Would you like to know if I can see them also?" Ortus asked humbly, after a long rain-swept pause.

22

THE NIGHT AFTER YOU killed your thirteenth planet, you were beset by a dream wherein you sat down to dinner opposite the Body. This was far better than the normal travails of dinner, with its partakers all wearing the filmy mother-of-pearl Canaanite robes that clung to Mercymorn like starlight, turned Augustine ethereal, gave Ianthe jaundice, and rendered you a sacrificial parsnip; that trial where, if you did not eat enough, the Emperor of the Nine Houses told you kindly, "Try just a few more spoonfuls, Harrowhark," as Ianthe repressed not her smirks. But in the dream you wore your thick dark vestments of the Ninth House, and sat only opposite the monstrous dead of the Locked Tomb, who wore the shabby black shirt and trousers of some particularly slovenly penitent. Both of you wore the sacramental skull paint, and you talked comfortably of very little—yet it felt as though it meant very much. And nobody made you eat.

Then the Body looked at you with those direct, incalculable eyes, and she said: "Harrowhark. Wake up."

"Pardon?"

"Wake up. Now."

You opened your eyes to the ceiling the long-lost Anastasia had never seen, twisted in the bedclothes she had never slept in. The thickly insulated blackout hangings covering the plex windows projected the high ceilings into an eternity of shadows, and you could barely perceive your hands in front of your face. You pushed away the coverlet. You were cold beneath your nightgown, which had been short in the leg when you went away to Canaan House and was a sorry affair now, and your exoskeleton scraped quite loudly in that black silence as you took the bone-sheathed sword from its loverlike position next to you on the bed. You held it with the swaddled blade flat on your shoulder, your hands cupping the bottom of the hilt—still the pommel—and you did not strap on the rapier that the Emperor had given you.

It was lighter outside your rooms, in the corridor. The low yellow panel lights cast warped, skeletal shadows up and down the memorials of the Mithraeum. They had been turned down to faint blue-hued ambers to acknowledge the hours of sleep, and gave texture more than vision. To your Drearburh eyes, however, the passageway was flooded with light. That was why you saw her so clearly.

She stood at the curve of the passage, perhaps fifteen metres from you. She struck weird shadows in that low halo of cold yellow, the softly gleaming whites of her shift glowing like a shaft of light through green water. There were still smudges of petal in her pale brown curls, and her eyes were too dark to see, but you recalled their nightmarish blueness. Cytherea looked at you, turned toward you, and began to walk.

That walk! That shuffling, disconcerting, slithering *walk*! The body flung its arms before it for momentum, the legs stiff-thighed and lock-kneed, right-side arm moving in time with right-side leg, ridiculous, appalling. Those fixed dead fingers caught a skeletal arm wrapped in gold foil, amethysts studded like so many eyes between the knuckle-bones, and it clattered to the ground, and Cytherea tripped over it— without the head losing its tracking focus on you, those unblinking eyes adhered to yours—and the body splayed and juddered on the ground. Then the corpse began moving inchworm-fashion, pushed forward by the action of the legs, the forearms banging on the tiles, thrusting the blessed bones of some fallen faithful out the way as though unnoticed. It was as though a magnet were stuck in the meat, a magnet that craved some polar force within you.

This assemblage writhed closer. You were a holy Lyctor: Harrow-hark the First, ninth necrosaint to the King Undying, heir to a hard-won power that burnt in you like fusion. It was not arrogance to name yourself one of the most powerful necromancers in the universe.

You took one look at that relentless, freakish argument of limbs, and you fled.

You hurled yourself back inside your room and locked the door. You scrabbled inside your mouth—drew blood with your fingernails, bit your tongue—swabbed your reddened saliva on the door in the hasty whorls of a blood ward, and pushed a chair up and beneath the handle, mindlessly. You threw yourself to the ground, your heart rattling the bars of its ribcage prison.

There was nothing but silence. Your body was the greatest source of noise: your chattering breath, your noisily pumping blood, your mashing teeth. Everything else was profoundly dark and still.

And then, from the door, the warded door that should have burst its theorems outward upon even the touch of foreign magic—from the door there came the soft, scraping noise of someone dragging nails down steel. The handle eased downward in its latch, and hit the chair, and stopped.

Great, greasy silence. Then another desperate rattle. And then: nothing.

How long you lay on the cool glassy tiles, forehead pressed into a red welter against clear obsidian glass, one of your fists bunched in the rough knotted fretwork of the rug, you did not know. You could only mark the passing of time when the habitation settings kicked into action and the panels around the room diffused pre-waking light, intended to mimic a circadian sunrise. You were cold all over, shivering in your exoskeleton until the bone cuticles rattled into your skin. At some point you stood, mechanically, and you went and lay back down in bed. There was nothing else you could do.

* * *

It seemed unlikely that you slept. When you thought it was late enough in the notional morning you put on your mother-of-pearl robe and you rapped on Ianthe's door. It was not late enough; she answered after a long, scuffling minute, with sleep in her eyes and her hair in dilute whey tangles over her neck and shoulders, wearing a bewildering short garment of violet chiffon.

You said instantly: "Septimus is walking."

It took a moment for her to understand the name that had never been Cytherea's. After long seconds, recognition flashed in those adulterated blue eyes; you saw understanding replace the grouchy morning crossness; you saw it fade before an overwhelming boredom, and you knew that Ianthe would not help you.

"Tell her I want my arm back," she said, and slammed the door in your face.

ACT THREE

23

YOU WERE AWARE, as a hand thrust into cold water might not notice until too late that the water had begun to boil, that an atmosphere of greater unease had settled over the Mithraeum.

It would have taken an absolute straight-up idiot not to notice though. When you were all called to the interminable dinners for which Augustine hinted you should "dress"—which you took to mean that you should wear your mother-of-pearl robe by way of ritual, and which Ianthe took to mean that she should wear things beneath hers that were not worth looking at, and pin her mass of pale hair on top of her head, and which meant that God never came in a shirt that didn't badly want a new collar—it became brutally obvious. The Lyctors now ate all their dinners staring at tablets. Sometimes Mercymorn spread open a system map of local space, triangulating things that the elders frowned over and talked about in a way that did not include you or Ianthe. Quite often you two ate dinner in stony silence while, as Ianthe bitterly put it, the adults talked.

You began to find Augustine alone in the training room. He did nothing so pedestrian and comforting as *training*, but stared—paced—*thought about* reaching for his rapier, then abandoned the idea and left. Augustine had been in training for the past ten thousand years. You did not know what his idea of *training* looked like. More often you found Ianthe with him, going through motions with an unresponsive, fat-fingered ham-handedness that was not in keeping with her poise. She always wore an expression of exquisite, hardened

213

surrender on her face, as though to say: *You do realise I'm not going to do this?*

You only ventured in there yourself far too late into sleeping hours for anyone else to be up. Then you would strip down to your shirt and exoskeleton, and your trousers and your bare feet—and you would hold the two-handed sword in front of you, and lift it up—and point it down—and do a long and unutterably dull series of minute movements, trying to feel normal, trying to understand. You tried hard, in a way that would have broken the heart of any actual swordswoman. If your arms responded more ably now, if you were able to lift, and slowly strike, then it would not save your life at the hands of a Herald, a thing that none of your teachers had yet managed to describe.

"Imagine," said Augustine meditatively, when you asked, "imagine—the *worst* bee, but with a blood aspect, if you knew the whole time that it was a multitude of bloods. I'm talking at least three different types of blood, here."

"The last time I fought one, I did it with my eyes closed," said Mercymorn in her turn, and finished as though her punchline was a triumph: "When I opened them—*they had bled anyway*!!"

"Do you know, I have rarely seen the Heralds?" said God, when you finally came to question him. "Whenever they come I am bundled off to a sealed sanctum at the heart of the Mithraeum, so that their insanity can't touch me. Despite all that soundproofing, I hear them . . . I always hear them."

You said, "Lord—"

"*Teacher*—"

"The Saint of Joy will be active, when we are all in the River," you said. "And the Saint of Duty, and the Saint of Patience. And Ianthe. Four Lyctors, fighting with their cavaliers' perfect sword hands. Teacher, is it so sure a thing that I am going to die? I will be dormant, I know, but are they not enough to protect our bodies, as we destroy the brain?"

"Ianthe is far from a perfect sword hand."

You did not know why you defended her: "She will perform on the day, Teacher. It's a pose."

"We cannot afford to *pose*," he said, but there was a faint smile at his weary mouth. "Ianthe the First is a continual surprise to me. If I was going to pass out a fourth epithet, I'd call her the Saint of Awe."

You thought that had not quite suited Naberius, though it was hard to remember the Prince of Ida, these days. He was a face and a set of eyes and very little else. It was as though your brain had formed a scab over everything that had happened to you. But you pressed: "Lord, it's not certain that I'm going to die."

He did not correct your *Lord*, then. In those oil-slick, inconceivable eyes, you saw a flicker of something you did not understand. God said, "Harrowhark, to that, to everything, all I can say is that I live in hope. And that you need to keep handling your rapier."

So you kept handling your rapier. It was on one of these late nights, coming back to your room with a heavy heart and bare feet, running with sweat, arms screaming in the wrong places, your fingers red and raw beneath their coats of cartilage, that you came to the flesh-pillar atrium before the habitation ring, and noticed that the autodoor to Cytherea's tomb was shut. It was never shut. Its wounded openness, the thin smell of perpetual roses that always seemed to drift from that terrible monument, was a constant. Now it was closed.

You stood before that door, hearing the quiet injunction of your Emperor to *maybe . . . not.* In a very real way, he was correct. You did not understand your fears enough to confront them. You did not even understand if they were real. Back when you were a child and hung up on something you thought you had seen or heard, Crux would say: *You saw what you saw, Lady, and the only thing you control now is your reaction thereto.* You had seen the corpse walking. Now you would react. The steel of the door was very close to your face, and misted up with your breath.

With one swift movement, you pushed it open.

What confronted you was Ortus the First, his back bare to you, in a pair of soft flannel sleeping trousers and nothing else, so that you could see the protruding, tumorous knobbles of his spine and the wads of muscle atop his shoulders. Cytherea's limp corpse was propped upright, her fingers dangling over his forearm, the dead-dove whiteness of her face, half-covered by his own, rosebuds crushed to deep yellow shadows at his feet. His palm supported the exhausted lily stem of her neck; the press of his fingers on that faded skin was so gentle that it left no mark. You, who had been so familiar with his hands in all their violent attitudes, had not thought them capable of that kind of gentleness. It made them seem alien from the rest of the man. And he was . . .

Crimson heat scoured your neck all the way up to your ears. The Lyctor who so often tried to kill you did not turn around, though you had in a split second already thickened your exoskeleton to double density and slapped big layers of enamel over your heart.

Ortus stiffened to the point that his shoulder blades showed real danger of bursting through his back. He had become one enormous hunch. You were frozen in a welter of adrenaline confusion, ready only for his inevitable murderous blow: you were not ready for the un-Ortuslike tenor of his voice when he said, calmly, back so vulnerably offered to you: "Close the door, and *go away.*"

You closed the door. You went away.

"I caught the Saint of Duty in the throes of grave lust," you told Ianthe, about a minute later: she was not asleep either, but sitting up in bed with the lamp on, making complicated notes in a little journal.

"Oh my God," said the Princess of Ida. She looked enchanted. In the lamplight, the bags beneath her eyes were very pronounced. Two apple cores sat in a perpetual state of perfumed rot by her bedside: her attempts to halt decay had progressed admirably. "The classical vice. Oldest sin in the book."

"All flesh magicians," you said coolly, "should be drowned in boiling blood."

"Don't tell me the Ninth never—"

"We do not."

"Ah, but my beautiful naïf—"

"No."

"Never mind that. Was he *actually* . . . ?" (Here she made an evil gesture with her hands, which you took a moment to comprehend.)

"You know. Waxing necrolagnic? Committing the love that cannot speak its name?"

You told her what you had seen, and she was immediately dismissive and mildly crestfallen.

"Oh, but who hasn't done *that*," said Ianthe. She reopened her small journal; you noted that whatever she was doing involved some quite substantial mathematics. "Dull. You obviously walked in too early. At least now you know who's been moving her—*so to speak.*"

She did contentious things with her eyebrows, and then, apparently no longer interested, turned back to her mathematics. "Good night, Harrowhark."

You were not to be so lightly disregarded. You stood with your sweat cooling inside your shirt and your flesh adhering to the exoskeleton, and said: "The depredations of a bad man do not cause Cytherea to walk."

Ianthe closed her notepad and rested her pale head briefly against the headboard. "Bad man," she murmured to herself, and then: "*I'd* walk out on a date with the Saint of Duty. Nonagesimus, this is no time to interrupt grown Lyctors committing acts that probably seem perfectly normal after ten thousand years with such limited romantic options—though you should *hear* some of the things Augustine has told me, my God!—nor is it a good time to advertise that you are not merely a failure, but a mad failure."

"*You* should not advertise your utter lack of imagination," you said. "Tridentarius, my position is not so precarious that I am going to ignore things that happen in front of my face."

"Yes, but are they actually?"

"Don't presume you know what you're talking about."

"Your position *is* that precarious, my dear," said Ianthe, and reached over with a long left arm to place her journal on the rightmost table. "Did you know that Teacher asked Mercymorn if they could store you in his chamber when we go after the Beast? Mercymorn said no, they decompress that chamber for a reason, unless he thought it would be nice to asphyxiate you personally?"

You said, "And did *you* know that Teacher himself thinks you *far from a perfect sword hand*?" At her expression, you added, "I personally loathe tattletales for the purpose of insult, but it seems to be your main weapon in our conversations."

Ianthe's mouth had thinned to a purple slit where, you noticed, the skin was torn. "Those were his exact words?"

"It's no secret that I'm going to die," you said. In no way were you resigned to that. You had never died before. "I am most likely lashing out. Nevertheless, those were his exact words."

She stared off into the distance, her eyes fixed on the huge painting of the long-dead, clothing-optional Lyctor. "God is a dickhead," she murmured.

You were astonished by the force of your immediate anger. You were amazed by its intensity. You drew your two-handed sword from your back: your wrists weren't quite in the right position, but it was a good attempt. The sword's matte, calcified surface sucked in the lamplight, casting strange shadows on her eiderdown. You said, "Do not blaspheme in front of me."

"Don't draw on me with that ridiculous thing. You don't even know where you got it."

"God gave it to me."

"And you've never asked yourself *why*?"

At those mere six words, your brain revolted. You felt a hot, thick sensation in the back of your top sinuses that you had not felt in a very long time, never approaching your limits enough for it to occur: a nosebleed. "So tell me why," you said evenly.

"Can't," she snapped. "You ensorcelled my *jaw*, you fucking psycho shadow vestal! Yes, I worked that one out! So unless I want to do homebrew mandible surgery, I can't squeal to anyone. And I have *thought* about homebrew mandible surgery, but I have no idea how far back your curse extends, because I'm not a blackened, tedious little *bone witch*. Now sheathe your sword; you don't want to go toe to toe with me."

You said, "There you are fundamentally wrong."

"I'd strangle you with your own visceral fat before you raised one shitty skeleton."

"Try me," you said. "Oh, *try* me, Ianthe."

You stared at each other: you at the foot of her bed, sword as still as you could make it, its weight a comforting and familiar pain—her sitting up in the fallen bedclothes, eyes like ice and frozen ground. You knew how you would do it: she was still fool enough to keep two jewelled candlesticks by her bed, thick with topaz and delicate flecks of polished tarsal, and from these you would smash two ropes of petrous bone straight into either side of her skull. You might run your finger up the inside of your sword blade, curling bone matter from there as though it were butter, fed and strengthened with your own heart's blood. You might scatter it and thrust squamous pegs of thick phalange through her palms, the fissures between her tibiae and fibulae. At that point you'd get on top of her, use everything you had ever learned from watching Mercymorn the First, and fuse her spine like a hangman's rope.

Ianthe looked at you, and in the paleness of her skin and in the shadows of her lips was her death, and yours.

Then she rolled over and covered her head with her satin pillow.

"Go ahead. Kill me," she said, muffled through a thick layer of down and pillowcase. "I have to train with Augustine in less than five hours anyway and I've stayed up too late. Death is preferable."

There was no answer to that, naturally, except to sheath your sword, return to your bedroom, and put yourself to bed, defeated.

24

IT WAS NO SECRET TO YOU, or to anybody in the claustrophobic, smothering schoolroom that was the Mithraeum, that Ianthe's sword-fighting training was at the end of the line. The Saint of Patience had none left for her. Her ineptitude would have been a negligible problem had it not continued when Ianthe was in the River—had her doubts not gummed up the mechanism of Naberius Tern's mindless sword-arm. You had watched the submerged Ianthe's strong, upright, boyish posture flounder as the right arm dropped the sword. A psychological block, certainly, but one projected into the dead soul that stood to defend her body when the mind went voyaging.

There was more pressure on her than on you. The eyes that fell on you were now less critical, because in those eyes you were a woman already dead.

Your eighteenth birthday passed without anyone noticing, even you. One night before you went to sleep you thought to yourself, restlessly: *another year.* You recalled it as you always did: the memorial to the two hundred who had died seizing, kicking, and choking as their neurotransmitters were poisoned into overdrive. You silently begged them to stay their hands, as you always did. You never asked for forgiveness. Then you slept. Most people would have iced a cake, or something.

It was soon after your seventeenth year passed that you acknowledged a truth you had known for some time: Ortus the First had to die.

His Ninth House name no longer bothered you, now that you knew about Anastasia. It seemed reasonable that the foundress responsible for establishing many of your House's naming conventions had chosen to honour her fellow Lyctors, in the days before their names were veiled in holy secrecy. It was just a banal and uncomfortable coincidence, as though he'd carried the name of a dead childhood pet.

The Saint of Duty's death went from *option* to *necessity* the day you realised his true power.

Your narrow foyer was a necromancer's dream: easy to ward, and to ward thoroughly. You had washed the whole little vestibule with a gossamer-thin layer of regrowing ash, and pressed bone of each type into whorls in the walls. On breach, anyone passing through would have their arms ripped from their sockets and their legs whirlpooled down into deep bogs of boiling-hot bone that crept up their bodies like incendiary gel. To follow up, they would be run through with 4,987 sharpened, flexible needles of your own temporal bone: unbreakable, reactive, instant.

Only an idiot would have stopped there. Your quarters had windows. If *you* had wanted to invade anyone's space, you would have put on a haz—you knew a real Lyctor didn't even need that—crawled over the outside of the habitation ring, and found the inevitable gap in the room's armour. There were no such gaps in your quarters. You had studied the floor plan and spent hours perched atop a ladder of skeletons, sliding hot gobbets of your blood and spit into the crawlspaces above the wall panels. You had stood at the docking bay and opened the airlock on a sack of bones, and walked back inside with them pattering parallel over the outside hull as you guided them to your windows and warded the plex with them. You had sent them down the plugholes in your pump sink and in the shining white edifice of the tub. You got the beginnings of a tension headache merely from the wards' reaction to Ianthe Tridentarius visiting your bedroom. If she had noticed the fine bone dust you'd blown all over her clothes—a glitter of thanergy on all her robes—she had not said a word, which made you suspect that she knew and was doing worse to you in secret. You'd found none of her traps, and it made you jittery.

Naturally, none of your spaces could be considered *safe*. You slept with your sword in your arms. You often woke yourself up suddenly, to practise how quickly you could throw yourself into action. Without a properly ingested cavalier, you had only yourself to rely on; you had to work nine times harder. But you thought you at least knew your vulnerabilities.

You were eighteen years old now and a Lyctor of the First House, but in some secret chamber of your heart you clung grimly to the ways of the Ninth. Despite dead Harrow's insistence that you become a generalist, you were on first instinct a bone magician. Your wards were bone wards; to some extent, blood wards. It was not that you did not account for spirit magicians—you had reasonably warded for everything, for every scenario both certain and uncertain: but your magic was at its heart still the magic of a Ninth House necromancer. *This* was your downfall.

You were in the bath when it happened. The Mithraeum's quaint bathrooms had no sonic appliances. You could only bathe in water, which you had grown to accept. Ianthe openly enjoyed it, and kept saying you weren't running it hot enough; but you did not quite believe that hot water wasn't injurious. You bathed in a few centimetres of water somewhat below blood temperature, wrapped in your exoskeleton and behind your multiplicity of bone wards, and for some benighted reason you considered yourself safe.

The central ward in your bathroom was near the light fixture, where the protruding light made the ceiling tiles fragile and non-contiguous. You did not notice anything amiss until you saw fine grey grains in your bathwater, until you cupped this water in your palm, thinking it was soap, or that you were unusually dirty. Even when you saw the soft trickle of dying, pulverized bone drifting down from your ceiling ward, you still did not fully comprehend.

The milled bone lay in your hands, unresponsive and inert. Only when you tried to join it together did you realise it was dead, in the way only the oldest bones in the most historical part of the monument of Drearburh were dead: the bones whose remnant thanergy had trickled out of them over nearly ten thousand years, like water from a pinhole in a bucket, leaving behind calcium dust too far gone to answer a necromancer. If the bones interred in the Mithraeum had been subject to time's full ravages, not stalled by the gentle touch of the Prince Undying, only their most ancient stratum would have resembled the specks in your hands.

It took perhaps five seconds from speck, to trickle, to realisation: your wards had been destroyed. And then you heard a crash from the foyer—and then your bathroom door exploded open.

Your immediate reaction was to cocoon yourself in a thick shell of tendon-fused bone. This would have been a good trick if it had worked. Nothing responded. Your exoskeleton slid off your body as though embarrassed by you. The bone studs in your ears were numb. The bone chips you kept tucked in niches throughout the bathroom did not twitch as you pulled on them. Every bone in reach was dormant and immobile. You were far more naked than if you had simply taken off all your clothes, which you had in fact also done. And the Saint of Duty stood in the doorway with his spear, and his sword, and his tender green eyes in his hard concrete face, as though your wards were nothing.

He drew back his arm and hurled his spear at your heart. You flung yourself so violently to the right that the entire tub swayed and tipped onto its side, with an enormous porcelain *crack* and a rush of tepid water that sluiced across the tiles to lap against the toes of his boots. The sword you had balanced across the bath, its bone scabbard flaking away in chunks like the candied coating from a sweet, clattered onto the floor. You grabbed for it but he stepped forward and kicked it away.

You were grovelling in half a centimetre of soapy water and gritty skeletal residue at the feet of your assassin. The spear he had thrown, and the sword you could barely use, were out of your reach. Your layers of traps and contingency plans had been rendered abruptly useless. You were soaking wet, and you were naked.

It was probably desperation that saved your life. You had trained your whole necromantic career to move for space: to fight from a distance. The Lyctor must have anticipated that. He had seen you do it before. He did not anticipate you throwing yourself *at* him with the only biddable bone you had left, which was your own. Great spurs burst through the heels of your hands from your carpal bones, and you slashed, wildly, at his chest, at his face, at the arm holding the crimson-ribboned rapier. You had extended your curved, bloodied talons of trapezoid and capitate into him, through the fabric of his shabby shirt, into the meat of his pectoral muscles, before he bounced your head back against the doorjamb. The back of your skull smashed into the steel casing, but he was falling back, and he was taking you with him. As Ortus staggered over the threshold into the bedroom you had a split second's perception of your broken wards lying in heaps and desiccated clumps by the door, your regenerating ash all dried up on the threshold like so many ancient clags.

He dropped his sword to wrench your claws out of his chest, and you understood what he had done. He took your bloody spurs between his fingers, and the blood fell away into powder as he *stripped away the thanergy*. He did not absorb it or try to turn it back on you; he simply *undid* it, with the dismissive ease of upending a jug of water over a drain. The spikes of living bone, freshly grown from your own body, faded in seconds into brittle twigs. They snapped off in his hands and he tossed them aside.

You were dazed. You were horrified. The sword was in his hand again, vaulted neatly back into his grip by the blood streaming down his arm. He was too close to bring the blade to bear, so he simply swung the butt hard into the side of your face. Your cheek staved in; you felt your jaw splinter, and a couple of teeth tumbled loose in your mouth like ragged little dice. You staggered away with the force of the blow—he stepped clear and sliced inward and down, opening you somewhere under the ribs—and you spat in his face. The blood sprayed feebly from your lips and spattered to the floor.

The *teeth*, on the other hand, hung in the air for a moment, blossoming into perfect four-pronged flowers of sharp enamel, each one angled toward a verdant eye. You shot those teeth forward like bullets. They flew as you fell sideways, your balance lost. You could feel the depression fracture at the back of your skull; you could feel your brachial arteries spraying, panicked.

Your collapse against the wall meant you did not see what happened next. Neither, however, did he. There was an unpleasant, wet sound as tooth met eye.

Ortus did not cry out in pain. You might have respected that, once. He merely turned away—his sword in his hand and the spear dragging behind him—and exploded back out through your ravished front door, your untidy, ward-strewn foyer. You were left slick with bathwater, wet with blood, half-dead and dismayed on the floor outside your bathroom.

The injuries could be seen to. Arteries could be stanched, then snapped back together. Meat could be sewn up and skin made whole. Dentine was easily reconstructed, and so was enamel, though you might have to re-form your jaw a few times before your bite was correct. Nothing cracked in your skull had driven itself into your brain, and the bleeding could be corrected. But your peace was gone, forever.

The Saint of Duty could bypass your wards at any time. The Saint of Duty was a thanergy void. The Saint of Duty was the ultimate nemesis of a bone adept. You would never be able to sleep again.

It was at this point that someone, obviously drawn by the noise from down the corridor, tiptoed over the mess at your front door and peered inside. You did not have to feel her presence to know it was her: you knew the sound of her shoes.

"Harrow?" Ianthe ventured, from somewhere near the door. Then she obviously stopped and saw you naked, bloodied, flayed in your own anguish, with soapsuds still on your feet. You hallucinated that you could smell her: sweat, musk, vetiver.

You saw your probable future clearly. You had not until that point understood the danger.

If Ianthe Tridentarius knelt beside you then, no matter with what sugary contempt or filigreed Third condescension, you would press your diminished bloody terror into her; you would creep naked into her lap, shamelessly, and weep. You would crawl like a worm to whatever clinging scrap of solace she would give you. All your slithering, degraded desperation for condolence you would give to your sister

Lyctor with a brazen thirst that you would never come back from. She would be your end, as surely as the hammer to the oxygen-sealant machine of your childhood. You would have reached for her with the mindless desire of an infectious disease. You would have whored yourself to her as necrosis to a wound.

So maybe it was for the best that after a pregnant pause the Princess of Ida said: "Wow! *Not* how I imagined this happening, at all," and you heard her hasty footsteps retreat, away, back down the corridor whence she came. Then she was gone.

You lay prone on the cool black tiles, staring up at the smears on the ceiling where your wards had been—dazed and despairing, nearly too dead to sew yourself back up. In the back of your head you heard the Secundarius Bell pealing, pealing, extents beyond any Ninth sacred composition, and never called by any Tomb ringer.

Aloud, you said through swollen lips: "The Saint of Duty must die."

And on the bed, the Body said, "Yes."

25

YOUR LETHAL OATH WAS not reflected in any more general solemnity in the Mithraeum. Despite the apocalypse you had suffered, not much seemed to change. Everyone was far too busy to care. The next time you sat down to talk to Teacher, your heart in your throat and your tea stubbornly undrunk, he did not even mention it. Surely he knew. Surely he must have known everything. You were too prideful to beg salvation, but too stupid not to blurt, as a diversion from your own panic: "Lord, I saw the Saint of Duty kissing the body of Cytherea the First."

Part of his biscuit dropped off in his tea. He looked at it with genuine consternation, then at you with equally genuine consternation, then back at the biscuit. "Harrow—Harrowhark, I hate to ask, but are you *certain*?"

Even God distrusted you. "Teacher, I swear by the Locked Tomb."

"I wouldn't swear by that in this instance," he murmured, and took his dented teaspoon to fish out a quivering and deliquescent glob of ginger biscuit. Then he looked at you. There were sleep marks beneath his eyes, he was not wearing his halo of infant phalanxes and pearl-coloured leaves, and his hair looked only hastily brushed. He ran one hand through it, as though conscious of your critical gaze. "Well," he said, eventually, "that's unfortunate."

"Is it not a sin?" You knew you sounded like a quisling. You knew you sounded like a prattling gossipmonger. What you really wanted to say was: *Lord, I was in my bathtub, and he drank my wards dry of thanergy, and I burst his eyeballs before he could destroy me. I have not slept in forty-eight hours. I asked Mercymorn how best to stimulate my own cortisol, to keep me awake. Lord, she did, and I fear I have done something to my hypothalamus.* "Don't you think it's *strange*?"

"Only in that the closest thing to interest Ortus ever showed in anybody was in Pyrrha, and in the criminals he hunted," said the Emperor of the Nine Houses. "When he kicked that Edenite commander out an airlock, it was like seeing a man on his wedding day. Not exactly romance though . . . Harrow, over ten thousand years I've known that man, and he is *legendarily* unamorous. I have watched six other Lyctors carry out a myriad's worth of inadvisable love affairs with one another, because it is a very long time to be alone, but never him. He was unassailable. I won't believe he's doing anything to *Cytherea*. Everyone liked her, he liked her, but there's a huge leap between liking and—corpse compulsion."

You stared, feeling mildly drunk and unutterably pitiful, at your repeatedly uneaten biscuit.

Teacher said quietly, "You must think us all a depraved set of immortal criminals."

You said nothing. He pressed, "Harrow, do something normal. Learn how to make a meal. Read a book. Go ahead and prepare— our lives revolve around us all preparing . . . but take the time to rest. Have you slept lately?"

It was the first time you realized God could not understand you.

And nobody cared, and nobody paid you the slightest bit of attention, including the Saint of Duty, who was as whole, and as normal, and as two-eyed as ever. You had not held out much hope that you had done anything permanent. The only surety that it had even happened was the lasting smell of damp on your carpets.

So you went to Ianthe, and you asked her how to make soup.

"Oh, it's easy," said the Princess of Ida breezily. Despite Augustine's increasing critiques she showed no signs of temper, as might have been anticipated; in fact she seemed to get *more* carefree with every failure. "You cut up an onion, burn it at the bottom of the pot, put in a few vegetables, and then some meat. It won't taste like anything, so put in a few teaspoons of salt, and then it'll taste like a few teaspoons of salt."

In obedience to the Emperor, you made soup. You had never seen anybody cook before. You did not like it. There were technical manuals on the subject in a kitchen drawer, and you pored over those, rather than attempting Ianthe's air on the theme of salt. By the evening of the third day after your interrupted bath, you had not slept for eighty-six hours, but you had read a book, and you had made soup three times. During sleeping hours you lay beneath your bed, in the dark, hardly breathing, staring up at the dustless ribs of the steel mattress slats—you prayed to the corpse of the Locked Tomb, or you said to yourself, "Oh, God! Oh, God! Oh, God!" until it slurred together on your tongue and joined the orchestra of whispers that thrummed between your ears, waiting for the assault that did not come.

It was also on the third day post-Ortus that the tension in the Mithraeum gained weight and sharpness, like salt water forming crystals. This had nothing to do with you. It was the countdown that Augustine had issued to Ianthe.

"Five more days," he had said to her. You knew, because he had said it over breakfast, right in front of you and Mercy. "You've five days left, my chick. If you don't start using that sword arm properly by then, I shan't bother to teach you a damn thing more. I'm not interested in charity cases. If I were, I'd be teaching Harrow."

In another lifetime you might have been icily furious, or at the very least chagrined. In this one, you were simply looking at your knife, and your fork, and your spoon, and trying to remember which did what. The spoon, with its concave pit, was probably for transferring liquids. In its back you caught sight of Ianthe, who had put her colourless chin in her hand and was leaning her head into it, as though listening without much interest to a bedtime story.

"As you will it, brother."

Everyone was snappish and cross—except Ianthe, and except you. You drifted through the Mithraeum with your great sword on your back and your hand never far from the end—pommel—of your rapier. And you made soup.

Two days after Augustine's ultimatum, perhaps impressed with your newfound understanding of soup or hungry for social cohesion, a frazzled God asked you to make everyone dinner. You opened more of the recipe books—you spent some time cleaning out your weights and measures, and picking through the warehouse-sized supply rooms for the most appropriate ingredients—and, for a long time, you locked yourself in the bathroom, to do what you had to do. One hundred and twenty-six hours. You no longer felt pain. Sometimes your jaw rattled to itself, but it was almost musical.

That night you made soup more carefully than ever. The recipe said it had to cook for a long time. You paced up and down the kitchen, distracted and startled by lights as the air grew steamy and a little sweet-smelling. When the alarm sounded to say it was done you nearly screamed. It took you a while to turn it off. You tested the result of your labour, after a moment's hesitation: you still hated strong flavours, and it took you a while to understand tastes. The soup did not taste like anything very specific, but you did not add Ianthe's teaspoons of salt.

You transferred it to a big tureen, and when you all sat down around the table, the Emperor served everyone, like he always did: on those first few days in the Mithraeum you had been terrified by the idea of the God of the Nine Houses serving you food, but it was just his way. He was pleased with you. He smiled that rueful, dented smile, and he rested his hand on your shoulder, very lightly, when he filled your bowl. "As I said, Harrowhark," he said. "Make a meal. Read a book. It's the little things . . ."

There were two days left before Ianthe's deadline, and all the Lyctors ate with a distinct lack of relish. You watched Ianthe take a spoonful of food as you struggled with your cutlery. Your soup did not look like a bad effort, and you had been vaguely proud of it: the thick, translucent gold-whiteness of the pot liquor; the unburnt onion floating in white, stratified wedges; the candy-orange of the stored carrots. You had read up on vegetables carefully, trying to overcome your aversion to their colours: you had not wanted anything that might dissolve entirely in the soup over the length of cooking called for. "Needs salt," was Ianthe's judgement.

"Too much water, but not a bad effort," said Augustine with forced jollity. "Broth needs to thicken over time, Harrow." (You had let it thicken for hours, then added a great deal of water, in a panic.) "Do not get me wrong, sis. Eating a new cook's food after ten thousand years is frankly exciting. Let me give you a list of my favourite meals so that you can get them interestingly wrong."

The Saint of Duty ate your soup at a stolid, uninterested, mechanical pace. You had noticed at previous dinners that he did not like some particular vegetables, so you had put them all in. Deprived of solid choices, he was mostly drinking stock. God had taken a spoonful, eaten it, then put down the spoon, then taken a discreet sip of water. He said nothing. The next sixty seconds were occupied with the wet, semiashamed sounds of people eating soup.

"If we're going to do these awful shared meals, at least someone provide *conversation*," said Mercy waspishly. She was removing thick pieces of root vegetable and eating them delicately off her fork. "I can't bear to sit here and eat mediocre food in silence. I can do that by myself."

You said, after a moment to peel up the edges of your words, "Is it mediocre, elder sister? I followed a recipe."

"Cassiopeia's? Now, there was a woman who could cook," said Augustine, and his granite-coloured eyes grew soft and nostalgic in his long, hawk-featured face. "Not without injuring herself, mind. John, d'you remember that time she took half her finger off getting the meat out of that coconut? She didn't tell anybody until after we'd eaten the meal. That's a lesson for you, Harrowhark: confess, first thing, before we find a finger in the soup." (You flinched, then tried to smile; perhaps that was called for. Ianthe looked at the expression on your face and shuddered visibly.) "What's the meat in here flavouring the broth? If there's chunks, it's all rendered down."

You closed your eyes and tried to think. It was so difficult. You so badly wanted to sleep. You were doing so many things at once—your sole remaining powers of concentration were given over to this moment. For a second or two you forgot the word that you were looking for—it was on the tip of your tongue—while you were building, minutely, stromal cell by stromal cell.

"Marrow," you said.

The Saint of Duty exploded outward as your construct emerged from his abdomen. Your soup was watery and mediocre, as soup went, but as a delivery method for gelid explosives—marrow rendered through so much water as to not pass comment—it was perfect. Half a dozen arms shattered him in the soft electric light from the overhead panels. You let out your breath, and coalescing scythes destroyed intestines—lungs—heart. Then you fired upward, toward the brain.

And God said, "Stop."

The world slowed down. Augustine and Mercymorn stopped, arrested in the act of half-rising from their seats. Ianthe stopped, left arm paused, outflung, to shield her face. You stopped, sitting upright in your chair: your bones somehow rigid and still, and your flesh chilly and rigid around those bones. The shrapnel spray from the Saint of Duty did not stop—it cascaded across the table like the crest of a pink waterfall, *pitter-pattering* down on bowls and the tablecloth and the polished dark surface of the wood. But what remained of him stopped too, half man, half rupture—his prurient details hot and white, naked insides clothed with the sinus-drying burst of the power of God.

The Emperor of the Nine Houses—the Resurrection—the First Reborn—sat at the end of the table, his plain face splattered with gore, and his eyes were the death of light.

The Necrolord Prime said, very calmly, "Ten thousand years since I've eaten human being, Harrow, and I didn't really want an encore. Now tell me what you have done."

Your body was unyielding, but your mouth had purchase. You said, "I reconfigured a clump of marrow stem cells into sesamoid bone. From the sesamoid bone, I made a construct."

"Harrowhark," he said, "you cannot have perceived foreign bone marrow within the body of a Lyctor. I'm not sure *Mercy* could perceive it with her arms draped around Ortus the whole time."

"The cells weren't foreign."

"What?"

"I sectioned my tibia for the soup," you said.

God's eyes closed, very briefly. He pushed his bowl another fraction away. You stared down the table at him: at the blank, remote faces of your two nominal teachers—at the frozen ivory stillness of Ianthe, her hair now whitish pink—at space outside the window, where the asteroids themselves seemed to hang in tranquilized arrest. He said, "You must know that I won't let either of you kill the other before my very eyes, Harrow."

"He attacked me in my rooms. He drained my personal wards."

"Coming from the Saint of Duty, that's a compliment."

You said, "Lord, I am hunted. I perish."

"Harrow—"

"I don't come to you as Harrowhark the First," your mouth said. "I come to you as a supplicant. I can't live like this. Lord, do I displease you, that you shield him and not me? I understand that I am a sharpened twig beside your keenest sword, but why do you suffer this twig to live? I can't live this way. I cannot live this way. I have nowhere to go. I have nobody to turn to. I am a nonsense."

You looked at each other down that long, bloody table.

God said, "Harrowhark, when was the last time you slept?"

It was with all the dignity of the Locked Tomb, the chill of the stone that had been rolled and of the bones that had been laid, and of the still salt water that shimmered before the whitened monument where your holy monster lay, that you said, "Six days ago."

The Emperor of the Nine Houses stood.

The spell, whatever it had been, dropped like a white sun setting. Your body collapsed back into your chair. The construct gamely clambering out of the Saint of Duty dwindled to a powder of pink dust. The shard you had been driving up the cervical vertebrae to the base of the spine and the brain within its casing simply disappeared: destroyed or removed, you could not tell. The concatenation of Ortus the First's insides, laced and crocheted over the dinner table, sizzled away to a soft mist. Everyone's breath spewed from their lungs in one unholy gasp. Ortus's hands flew to his middle.

The Emperor did not give anyone time to react further. He said

234 / TAMSYN MUIR

evenly: "Dinner is over. Let us leave the table. Ianthe—take your sister to bed."

Everyone began clattering out of their chairs in a wild scraping of wood and tile. Augustine said, "My lord—?" and God said, "Go. Just go."

You felt strange and unreal as a white-lipped Ianthe hauled you up from your seat. The skin she touched was merely a thin and pervious netting keeping in your meat, which consisted of ten thousand spiders. She slung your arm across her shoulders, as though you were an invalid. Perhaps you were. Your legs did not feel correct. Your eldest sister, looking distinctly green around the gills and checking long strands of her overripe-rose hair for globs, had also risen—but the Emperor said, "You. Stay," and she froze.

There was no thought in you of fighting Ianthe as she walked you away. You could have gone meekly to the slaughter without a muzzle or a leash. Behind you, the Kindly Prince was saying, in far more ominous tones than you had ever heard him use: "Six days. No sleep. She still manages a full skeleton commencement from *diluted marrow*. What else have you failed to see, Mercymorn—?"

You were already at the door when her peevish response came: "But this is insane! She's only *nine years old!*"

* * *

The Saints of Duty and Patience were out in the corridor. If either had wanted to run you through, you could not have stopped them. You looked at them despite Ianthe urging you away: at Augustine, looking as though he had seen the ghost of someone he did not particularly like, and at Ortus.

Ianthe kept trying to turn you to face forward, but you kept watching even as she hustled you down the corridor. You saw Augustine fumble for a cigarette, light it with the little silver arc lighter he kept in his breast pocket, and pass it silently to his brother Lyctor. Ortus was impassive. There was not a trace of blood on his clothing. There was not a stray lump of viscera upon the shabby shirt, nor on the mother-of-pearl cloak still slung over his shoulder. There was no betrayal of any emotion on his face: not the surprise that had dawned over his heavy-lidded eyes earlier, nor anger, nor even dissatisfaction. He caught your gaze. You held his.

And the Saint of Duty lifted his lit cigarette to you in an unmistakable salute.

26

ONE DAY, HARROWHARK'S EYE was caught by the rain drizzling outside on the docking terrace, and by black figures rising in the fog. They were on the very edge of the terrace. She tugged her hood deep down over her head, walked outside into the rain—she kept bone chips clutched between her knuckles so that they would not grow wet from sweat or weather—and approached. One of the black figures resolved itself in that grey, stinking blanket of cloud: large and imposing, like the midday sun amid clouds. It was Coronabeth Tridentarius.

She was turned away from Harrow, and her riot of hair—half-caught in a fillet, half-escaping—was soaking wet, a dark and crinkling amber in the rain. She was not fighting or arguing. She was still as a statue, and ready and waiting as a dog.

The figure behind her was much smaller and slighter, the aseptic robes of his office a bleached, blued grey with the water. The braid pinned high on his head was so pale as to be white, and his rain-sodden chainmail kirtle gleamed, wetly, amid the fog. At her creeping pace, Harrowhark had covered only half the distance when she heard Silas Octakiseron say, clear above the patter of falling drops:

"And somewhere out there, may all the blood of your blood suffer even a fraction of what I have suffered."

He pushed. The eldest princess of Ida dropped from the side of the docking bay with swanlike ease. She simply tipped off the side, neither folding nor seizing—there one moment, a golden star, and then gone. There was no question of going to her aid. The Eighth House necromancer stood there with the wind flapping his wet alabaster robes, his braid torn to wisps and ribbons, and he did not even look over the side.

But he did look to Harrowhark.

"Defend yourself, Octakiseron," she called out. "The black vestals have only one answer for murder."

"The black vestals only ever had one answer for anything," was the reply, in his profoundly deep, gorgelike voice. He looked at her: from their distance of about five bodies apart his eyes were umbrous in his white and stricken face. "The question came, *Why*... and the black vestals said, *Because*. Now you have come to me, you cur of the nighttime, you fry of slavery, you have done what you have done, and you say to me, *Defend yourself*? How could I?"

"I don't give a damn about White Glass mysteries or cryptics," she said. "I care that you just pushed one of the Tridentarii to her death."

"Death?" said Silas.

He looked out again at all the rolling fog, at the clouds that obscured the grinding sea down to which Coronabeth was most likely still falling. From closer up, Harrow saw that he was all in disarray: his clothes were smudged and a few of his buttons were not done up. The rain and the fog had lashed him terribly.

Harrow took her hands from her pockets and strewed her chips upon the ground. From each chip—she felt a *pop, pop, pop* at the back of her brain from the thalergy expenditure—she unfurled a full appendicular skeleton, extending the bone in a hurry so that none of the cortex could mix with water. The dull gleam of their compact bone shone like marble in the wet. Silas Octakiseron looked at her five full constructs with his lip curling.

"Her filthiness is on her feet," he murmured. "She has not remembered her end."

"For God's sake, raise your hands, Octakiseron," she said. "Or make me strike down an unarmed man."

And Silas said, "Is this how it happens, then?"

He turned away. She saw what he meant to do, and her skeletons skittered forward on the rain-slick concrete of the docking terrace. But it was for nothing: Silas Octakiseron had launched himself fearlessly into space after the tumbling body of Coronabeth Tridentarius. He fluttered in the wind and rain briefly, like a dirty white bird, and disappeared.

She pushed through her skeletal crowd to stand at the edge—they held her arms back, for safety—and stared down into the virginal and unbroken bank of salty, reeking fog. There was no sign of either adept. From far below, the ocean howled. Harrow thought she perceived a tatter of something penetrate the cloud. Her heart pounded rhythmically in her ears, and she thought she saw, absurdly, a sudden gush of watery blood, as though the fog itself had been knifed; but it was gone almost as soon as she had seen it.

27

You lost a great interstice of time. The next thing you knew, you were staring at the shadowy bowels of a room, lit only by a soft yellow puddle of light—a bedside table–lamp—sheets slippery and cool over you. For the first time in your life, when you tried to let yourself panic and generate an adrenaline spike, it did not work. That trigger had broken. After too many days of generating cortisol, your pituitary gland was taking an unsanctioned holiday somewhere far away from you, and all you could do was lie, bewildered, in these unfamiliar surrounds.

Not so unfamiliar. After many long and stupid moments, you realised that you had been laid to rest in the white-and-gold confection of Ianthe's bed, with its chilly satin coverlet and the lilac flowers embroidered in silk floss on almost every inch of the bedclothes. You willed yourself into panic again, flailing against the mattress, and sputtered out dolefully.

"Lie back down," said the Princess of Ida.

She was standing before the windows. The amethysts dripping from her rapier's basket hilt flashed and glittered in the darkness: she had her left arm tucked behind her, and her feet arranged a hip's width apart, and her right arm extended before her, holding her sword. She was moving the sword into mechanical attitudes: blade pointed high, blade pointed low, wrist twisted to sweep the blade into position.

You struggled to sit up. Your head felt as though someone had studded your skull with fine little spikes that stroked your brain with hooked barbs whenever you moved.

"I said, lie *down*," said Ianthe. "You absolute madwoman," she added, without any particular emotion. "Can't believe I ate a whole bowl of nun . . . I should've made myself throw up."

The Princess of Ida sounded unlike herself: this was a more detached Ianthe—Ianthe as an arm pulled from the socket; Ianthe as a tooth torn from the root. Your head was so heavy. For a moment it was as though you were back on the *Erebos* again, when you had been made of cotton wool and black fog.

She changed form. The rapier came down low over her left side—swung slowly to cover the right—flicked up in a steel shimmer so that the tip of the sword pointed at the ceiling, on guard. Then to the left again, then swinging high to absorb an imagined blow to the head and shoulders. Parry positions, which you should have known but didn't. Ianthe was training in her nightgown—a grisly floor-length concoction of pale golden lace that made her long, limber body look like a green-veined mummy—and even you could tell that her movements were ungainly and belaboured.

It took you a long time to say, "Augustine," and she answered, immediate, impatient: "Are you *still* awake? Yes. One might've hoped that your light dinnertime entertainment would have given me an extension, but not so much."

You said feebly, "The Saint of Duty—Ortus can suck wards."

Ianthe said something very coarse in response. Then she said, "So that's why you stopped sleeping. Well, if he wants to attack you while you are here, I tell you truthfully that I welcome that inferno."

"But—"

"*Sleep,* Harry."

You were very weak. You felt an exhaustion beyond tiredness; a drugged, unstable fatigue. When you laid your head back against Ianthe's pillow, you smelled the thin putrefying off-apple smell from her bedside table, and you smelled her, and that scent was now familiar. It was the animal yearning for the familiar that undid you. You closed your eyes, and you were asleep.

* * *

How long you slept you did not know. You did not know what dawn of which day you woke to. The daytime lights filtered through the hangings of the four-poster bed with a warm whiteness, a lemony warmth limning the naked paintings that festooned the walls. It felt as though you had slept for a hundred years. The satin coverlet was cool against your arms, and you lay in Ianthe's bed insensate, comfortable.

Gradually you felt a heavy weight in a depression next to you. You rolled onto your side, suddenly and deeply frightened that you might see the bed's owner; your sword had been laid atop the covers beside your body, on the eiderdown, the bone scabbard gleaming a dull grey in the imitation sunlight. This was in every single way a better thing to wake up to than the face of Ianthe "Love My Twin, Also Murder" Tridentarius.

Then you heard breathing. It was with unexpected clarity of mind and soul that you pushed the eiderdown away and crawled to the end of the bed. And you found Ianthe before you, on the floor.

She was belly-down on one of the cream-and-gold rugs on the deep honey-coloured plush carpet, and all around her was a growing crimson mat of blood. She sprawled in a puddle of red as though it was her shadow. Her long hair tumbled over her face and shoulders like a veil, and she grunted hard through her teeth, breathing in long terrible breaths like a dying animal. As you watched—a silent spectator on her mattress—she propped herself on her elbows and grasped the ruddy crimson blade of her trident knife in both hands, and she thrust it furiously into the intolerable seam of her right arm.

Ianthe struck again and again. The wound kept healing over—the skin sewed itself back up even as she pulled the blade away. Blood coalesced around the seam in a serried row of teeth, of needles, and these she used to try to lever herself apart, but her elbow wobbled beneath her and she collapsed on the sodden carpet. She dropped the knife from nerveless fingers. She slapped that almost-imperceptible seam, then again. Then she gave a low and broken moan, and fell over onto her side, curled foetally inward.

Your mind was clear. Your thoughts were warm and tidy, as though they had been put through the sonic cleaner. It was with very little trepidation that you dropped to your knees beside her. You rolled her onto her back—and she looked at you with terrified eyes, half-blue, part-brown, with fragments of lavender. Her mouth was an ugly twist, contemptuous of herself. You had seen that expression a million times in your mirror, but never on her.

"Harrow," she said unsteadily. She was trembling.

"You're a fool," you said.

"How I crave your honeyed words," said Ianthe. Her mouth was almost purple from the pain. "How I love your tender compassion."

This was rank hypocrisy, but you were too focused to care. You said, "It needs to come off all at once."

"What—"

"Get something to bite down on."

She looked at you, her eyes a wild confusion of colours; she lay spread before you in her hideous buttercup nightgown, which was now a parti-coloured mix of gold and pink and red like a liver. After a moment, she nodded: she ripped a bloodied swatch of yellow lace from her skirt, and she compressed it into a tight cylinder and pressed it between her teeth. Her teeth were very white, and her tongue was wet and red.

You raised yourself up on your knees, swaying a little, and you pictured her for what she really was: an exquisite conglomeration of bone beneath skin and meat, pocketed in the middle with soft treasures of parenchyma and muscle. When you placed your hands upon her ribs you were able to see her skeleton as though she had shyly undressed herself for you, as though in the orange hues of the daytime light she'd sloughed capillaries and glands off the budding rose of her scapula. You saw the curve of her clavicle, bowed softly as the line of some drooping bellflower.

It was so easy. Now that you had slept, everything was easy. It was as though you had been walking in a lead casing, and now you were free. As before any difficult work, you prayed out loud: prayed for the rock to go unrolled and for the closed eye and the stilled brain; prayed for a woman you loved to assist you in disrobing a woman you did not, but whose bones you would sacramentally adore. You kneeled on her thighs and unsheathed a great shank of bone from your knuckles—Ianthe bucked, just the once—and you sharpened the edge to a translucent, liquid thinness.

With one cut you took the arm: you scythed through the knob of ligament and scapula and removed the humerus. Ianthe screamed through her mouthful of lace. The blood came like a spring tide over your front, and you felt it soak through your clothes and trickle down your navel. You cauterized the meat all at once, pinching the vessels closed, reaching down to press your fingers against where the humeral head had been. Then you covered over the gap with spongiform bone—to give you a platform to work on—and you spun her shoulder beneath your fingers, and it squirmed at your touch. Ianthe's screams had subsided to ravenous whimpers.

Her arm had to be her own. That was no difficulty. You coaxed fine webby strands of red marrow from the wing of bone that girdled her shoulder, and from that—from minute osteoblastic grit—from the mazelike netting of the bone that swaddled the sponge and the marrow—you remade her. The humerus was child's play, and you took genuine pleasure in socketing it into the lovely cup of the radius, the forked embrace of the ulna. Her trochlea you sculpted while holding your breath, easing it into its wet white housing.

The hand was almost an indulgence. The skeleton recalled itself. You did not need to know so intimately the lover's knot of carpal bones—the long tooth of her lunate, the jutting promontory of her trapezium—nor did you need to know the arch of the distal phalange, the shaft, the base. The new bone sprang avidly to meet your fingers, as though you were lovers joining hands after a long time apart. Your role with the bones was more guide than artist. The artistry would come at this point, and you warned her: "This will hurt."

Ianthe rocked upward.

You knew your limits. You had understood what to do with her body innately, and it was not what she wanted, but you thought it would suffice. You blistered the bone in tendons only where you thought it was necessary for range of motion. You bubbled nerves into that shining periosteum where nerves had never been before. Not a full complement, but just enough. Bone would call to bone, and nerve would call to brain. When you trailed your fingers up that new trunk of electrified humerus, she almost spat out the chunk of lace—when you pressed your palm into her shoulder and plugged her in, she sobbed, rhythmically, beneath you.

What was left at the end was not an arm. It was a construct: a sectioned skeleton, defleshed. When you sat down beside her you were chilly with sweat and pleasantly tired, as though you had run a good distance. You watched as Ianthe took the saliva-sodden wad of nightgown from her teeth, and as, shaking, she raised her new arm up to the light: the warm electric lamplight made her naked arm bones an iridescent gold.

The old arm lay on the carpet, abandoned and dead, looking a little sorry for itself. You said, "I didn't bother about the meat."

Ianthe said wonderingly, "But I've got some feeling in it."

"Most of the nervous glands are in your elbow."

"Why even—"

"You *have* worked out that the Lyctoral healing process is dependent on your nerve fibres?"

"But you don't—"

"I lack entirely what you all have," you said, "and have had to work out a replacement. I watched, and compared. In the beginning I thought maybe I could implant the process in myself . . . but it's not just a matter of nerves, even if those signal the reconstruction. I thought if I experienced enough pain, something might kick in to save me. It didn't."

She spread her rightmost finger bones wide, then back, experimentally making a fist. You said, "You will still need a mat of tissue or cartilage on the palmar bones, to hold the sword. Think of it as a glove."

Ianthe rolled away from you, damp with drying blood. You watched as she stood before the amethyst-studded rapier she had left in its scabbard, and you watched her slide it out, slowly, with a soft metallic sound that set your teeth on edge. You watched her web her skeleton hand with a neon pad of fat—not your preference, but she had her own proclivities—and raise the sword behind her, gauging the new weight in an arm substantially lighter than the one on the floor, and close her eyes.

Lunge. The arm answered. The movement was reactive, liquid, smooth. She cut a sweep before her, then flicked her naked wrist; each action was clean. The sword was as light in her hand as the bones in her arm. Her body was not her body—it was strange to you how you could see no trace of idle Ianthe in the parry and the thrust. Instead you saw a cavalier who had known from the cradle what life intended for him, and had a rapier placed in his hands not long after.

You might have changed your clothes, or washed the blood from your body. All your sister Lyctor did was throw her nacreous white robe over her shoulders, where it settled like snow under an aurora—all she did was belt her rapier to her waist, and slide the trident knife into the special scabbard across the hip, and point at you, and say: "I'll be back in fifteen minutes. Do not leave the room."

You were still weary and frightened, and Ianthe leaving reminded you how vulnerable you really were. But Ianthe did not heed your protests. Nor did she take fifteen minutes. You sat yourself back on the bed and pulled the covers up around your shoulders, and very slowly and surely your heart rate returned to normal.

It was fully twenty-five minutes before the door opened again. You coiled for flight, but it was, after all, just Ianthe—an Ianthe who had changed. She was a sorry sight. You had an artist's fondness for the right arm, but recognised the shocking juxtaposition of it, of the bloodless flesh and then the bloodless bone, that unexpected and violent nudity. Her yellow lace nightgown had dried to a crust of brown, and her hair had dried in patches of much the same colour: a sort of carroty stain at the temples and the ends.

But the expression on her face was that of undressed release. It was the expression of an awed child watching their raised skeleton totter forward for the first time without falling. She was incandescent, softly luminous in a way that gave her bleached skin a creamy colour, and which made the death-mask lines of her blank face animated and alive. Her eyes were blue again, with those mountainous flecks of sea-parted brown, and for the first time you thought how much she resembled her twin.

She was still grasping her lovely Third rapier in her skeleton hand, the blade naked to you, and she said, not bothering to hide her excitement: "It's shit. It's going to break."

"Not in a hurry, Tridentarius. That's regenerating ash."

"There wasn't the same weight behind my thrust."

"He didn't compensate?"

She swung her sword in a slow, glittering arc, revolving her wrist. Ianthe said, not unhumourously: "Naberius always compensated."

You asked, "What did Augustine the First *say*?"

"Nothing," she said, and she started to laugh, peals of bell-like laughter. She dropped to sit on the bed, and exulted: "Nothing *much*. He dropped me into the River, went two rounds against my body—it worked, Nonagesimus. It worked. He says it's hideous and he'll gild it for me—" ("Tacky," you said.) "—but I can fight the same way I fought after I became a Lyctor, before I lost the arm. I'm real, I work. Harry, I am a *Lyctor*."

Her jubilance was infectious. It did not hurt you. You were not a Lyctor.

You said, "You may feel free to thank me anytime you so choose."

Ianthe was suddenly beside you on the bed. She had dropped her rapier among the bedclothes and for the very first time brushed the dry distal tip of her new pointer finger against your cheek. You were vulnerable, but you did not pull away. She tapped you on the cheekbone, and once on the tip of your nose, and then lastly pressed her naked finger to your bottom lip.

"*Thank* you?" she said. "Harrow, you *loved* that."

The smooth claw of the finger joint felt cool against your mouth. Her head was quite close to yours. The lace nightgown gapped, somewhat, at the front. The Princess of Ida said, "I already know how I'm going to thank you," and you were bemused. You absolute idiot baby, you were mystified. You were tired, and you were embarrassed, and you were riding high from the satisfaction of doing one half-perfect thing—of having committed a low miracle of your own devising—of, for a handful of minutes, being Harrowhark Nonagesimus again, the greatest necromancer produced by your dark and sacred Drearburh.

Ianthe took her finger from your lips, looked at you, and smiled a phosphorescent and confidential smile.

She said, "I'm going to help you kill the Saint of Duty."

28

DAYS LATER, THE ENDLESS rain and lubricious fog turned suddenly to ice. Harrowhark woke up in the unfamiliar annex where she now slept, red and chapped with cold. The Second's chambers had been deemed the least leaky of all their rooms on offer, helped by their placement quite low down Canaan House's southmost side, and Lieutenant Dyas had invited them to move in with no enthusiasm whatsoever. They had arrayed makeshift beds and mattresses on the floor of her parlour, the broken furniture pushed into corners and stacked up at the sides, and there they all lay like victims after a massacre.

They were a ragtag bunch: Abigail Pent and her husband, who shared the decomposing four-poster that the dead Judith Deuteros had slept in; Protesilaus the Seventh and his intubated adept, who slept like a healthy baby swaddled in carpet rugs, and robes, and all her spare clothes; Dyas, who seemed never to want to sleep again, but only to sharpen her rapier, to the point where it must have held around nineteen edges; and Ortus; and herself. Ortus had placed his mattress between all concerned and the door—"I will be that bulwark," he'd said portentously, although Harrowhark *had* noticed that it was the driest and warmest spot. That was that, that was all of them. When she had asked after the remnant Fourth children, Pent had remarked a little cagily that she had already moved them on. Harrow read between the lines and found that she could not resent their being—squirrelled away—so that the rest of the group presented a larger and juicier target.

Her breath sparkled in front of her mouth, and her fingers ached, even though she'd slept in gloves. The sun shone thinly through lacy patches of feathery, tessellated mist on the glass, glass on glass: ice! All at once Harrow was homesick for Drearburh. The fog outside was so thick that Canaan House seemed to have ascended into the heavens overnight—risen up into the atmosphere within a thick wet fleece of cloud and mist, a dirty ovine colour. Harrow could not see the sea or sky. She thought the rain was falling less heavily outside— but then she perceived that instead of the dreary, murmurous fall of precipitation, each drop had hardened into a pellet of ice. The wind whipped them up against the thick plex window, and they sounded like shot from the barrel of a gun.

It was not much past dawn. She'd slept in her paint, and her teeth tasted like pigment. Harrow wrapped her veil around her mouth as a muffler, and rose silently from her bed. The others slept on, in silent hummocks like graves: Ortus before her, a black and faintly whuffling hill; on her right Protesilaus Ebdoma, who slept with his sword on his breast like some soldier's monument, one where the sculptor had gone overboard on the muscles; on his right, his necromancer, her short buff-coloured curls falling on her childlike cheeks; and on her left, Dyas, who lay with her eyes open and her sword on her breast. Her gloves were very white against the steel hilt of her rapier, and very white against the bared sepia of her wrists.

The door to Pent's room opened on silent hinges to reveal her kind-eyed, curly-haired, and abominably silly cavalier. He had his slippers on, and two coats over his pyjamas: on seeing Harrowhark, he touched his lips and beckoned her through to his room. Within, Abigail Pent was curled up on an enormous windowsill, a decrepit love seat tattering itself to pieces beneath her, watching the hail come down in calm fascination. There was a roasting smell, like chocolate and dust. A little electric heater blarted out tepid air on the floor, its fans wheezing hotly. To Harrow's numb fingers, it seemed to be warming approximately jack shit.

"Pretty foul out there," Pent said in low tones. "Coffee?" (That must have been the chocolate scent. Harrowhark accepted a cup, mainly to warm her hands.) "The pressure's dropping freakishly . . . though of course, you aren't victim to atmospheric conditions on Drearburh, are you? Are you getting any sleep?"

Harrow said merely, "I don't care about surrounds. It could easily be less advantageous." Often her cell had been worse.

"Hear, hear," whispered Pent's cavalier, holding the coffee pot, which was wildly belching steam. "That's the stuff. We'll make a Fifth of you yet, Reverend Daughter. *Not that bad—can't complain—it'll be a damn sight worse in the River.*"

"Just so long as the Duchess Septimus is holding on," said Abigail, unperturbed by a fresh smash of icy pellets next to her head. "I tried to make her take the bed—she was so upset that the Templar pair weren't on board. I told her that I didn't think we'd get Master Octakiseron first time round . . . She won't tell me what he said to her, just that he 'was *horrid*.'"

"Cheeky little so-and-so," said Magnus. "If he were my son, I'd give him something to think about. I'm not surprised he's gone to ground."

"I would hope your son might be of different character," said his wife, half-smiling.

"Protesilaus should have biffed him."

"It's strange," said Abigail, ignoring her husband's exhortations to biffing. "The Eighth are not generally the type to hide."

Harrow came to an internal decision to tell the truth. It was not particularly difficult. She had only been holding on to the knowledge because a woman whose tongue wagged did not love the silence of the Tomb. Also, she was frankly uncertain that what she had seen had been real: but now it was nearly a week later, and she was tired of what Magnus Quinn's eyebrows did when he uttered the word *biff*.

"Silas Octakiseron is not hiding," she said. "He's dead."

Both of them looked at her. The Fifth necromancer's glasses were misting up with the cold, so that her tranquil brown gaze was seen as though through a filmy cataract. "Pardon?" she said.

"So is Coronabeth Tridentarius," Harrow added. "I cannot confirm the fates of the rest of the Third House."

"*Both* of them—" began Magnus, and his wife cut in quickly, "The Sleeper—"

Harrowhark said, "No."

She told the Fifth House the story of what she had seen; though she left out the blood in the fog.

Magnus and Abigail shared what seemed a very long glance. Magnus looked troubled, and his wife looked set, and strangely resigned. After the awkward length of what passed between them, the cavalier meekly slurped at his coffee cup.

"We should have made him a greater priority," said Lady Pent.

Magnus said, "I'm not certain."

"And now he is gone," she said, and added: "To say nothing of the Third . . . Reverend Daughter, you say this was nearly a week ago? A week, and you didn't think to tell us?"

There was a slight accusatory note in Pent's tone. Harrowhark did not feel great about it, but neither did she feel particularly bad; she just felt small and empty and hard, like the hail battering itself so fiercely on the window outside. The heater produced another helpless splurt of dust-smelling heat. "I had to be sure," she said.

"Of *what*?" said Magnus.

This did not require an answer, so Harrowhark did not give one. She merely held her hot coffee between her hands and stared with what she knew to be a slightly smeared but still discomposing painted face, with all the white and black of Ninth House sacrament. It was not difficult to win a staring match against Magnus Quinn; he wilted in about five seconds, and stared out the window, and sighed very heavily.

"We didn't need him," he said bracingly.

Abigail said, "We need everyone."

"I never thought he was quite the thing."

"Tridentarius's loss is the greater here," said Harrowhark repressively, and she thought Abigail sounded somewhat distracted when she said, "Yes—yes, I do think so. I just hadn't expected . . . If she's gone, then perhaps that means . . . Reverend Daughter, will you do me a very great favour?"

"That depends on what the favour is."

"I would like you to read this for me," said Lady Pent.

252 / TAMSYN MUIR

She set down an empty cup of coffee on the frigid windowsill, and she took a little flimsy bag from her pocket. She unzipped the plex tab on the top and removed, delicately, a piece of yellowing paper. The Fifth adept used the very edges of her fingernails to unfold it, carefully and tenderly. Harrow stood up at once, but the cavalier was somehow between her and the door. The sweat beaded behind her knees and prickled behind her ears as she glanced down at the paper.

Harrow said, "I would like to bring my cavalier into this conversa—"

"You need Ortus the Ninth to read a piece of paper with you?" said Magnus Quinn, with broad good humour, the type that was as resolute and inflexible and polite as a summons. She had been stitched up. She was a fool. She had lost her fear of the Fifth House, and now she had been boxed in as only the Fifth House might box you: smiling the whole time, and acting as though the whole thing might be a bit of a joke. Harrow made her face imperturbable, and swallowed slowly, so that her throat did not so obviously gulp.

She stalled. "The text is small."

Pent said, "Do you think so?"

The Fifth necromancer did not let go of the paper. Harrowhark looked down at its bloodred, panicked writing: a hasty, furious scrawl, written with such fury that the pen had bitten the paper.

> I WILL REMEMBER THE FIRST TIME YOU KISSED
> ME—YOU APOLOGISED—YOU SAID, I AM SORRY,
> DESTROY ME AS I AM, BUT I WANT TO KISS YOU
> BEFORE I AM KILLED, AND I SAID TO YOU WHY, AND
> YOU SAID, BECAUSE I HAVE ONLY ONCE MET SOMEONE
> SO UTTERLY WILLING TO BURN FOR WHAT THEY
> BELIEVED IN, AND I LOVED HIM ON SIGHT, AND THE
> FIRST TIME I DIED I ASKED OF HIM WHAT I NOW ASK
> OF YOU
> I KISSED YOU AND LATER I WOULD KISS HIM TOO
> BEFORE I UNDERSTOOD WHAT YOU WERE, AND ALL
> THREE OF US LIVED TO REGRET IT—BUT WHEN I AM

IN HEAVEN I WILL REMEMBER YOUR MOUTH, AND WHEN YOU ROAST DOWN IN HELL I THINK YOU WILL REMEMBER MINE

Harrow read this screed in a flat and affectless monotone, her voice dying away on *mine*. The cavalier looked at the paper, and his necromancer looked at her.

"Read it to me," she said, knowing her voice was still flat and hard as the hail.

Abigail turned the note back to herself, still with the care reserved for some priceless antique.

"*I still get an erotic charge from snakes, sorry to say,*" she read.

There was a brief silence. The hail slapped at the window's glass as though wanting to hurl itself through. There was a growing rime of pale blue frost at the edges, and a cleared mist from where Abigail had sat. Deep in the fast-moving fog outside—unmoved by wind and unresolved by gouts of chilly hail—all three of them watched, a little detached, as tiny particles of ash joined the hail in the storm, as though the already overcrowded weather had been augmented by the eruption of some distant cinder cone.

"It differs mildly, then," said Harrow, and Abigail admitted, "Somewhat, yes."

Magnus said, "But why—"

"I am mad," she interrupted. "I have always been mad, since I was a child. I hallucinate sounds. I see things that do not exist. Ortus has masked much of it, but as you have identified and exploited, my vulnerability only requires his removal. I did not tell you of Silas Octakiseron's death because I was not sure I was an accurate reporter. I am insane."

Abigail Pent took off her glasses and popped them down into the top fold of her robe. She reached out to touch Harrow's arm, and Harrow flinched away; she winced a little in sympathetic apology, and removed her hand.

"You have kept that close to your chest," she said. "I would like to hear more sometime, if you are ever inclined to tell me. But, Harrowhark, that squares perfectly with another theory I have, if all this time you only looked to your own frustrations—have you ever considered the fact that you might also be . . ."

"Here it comes," said her husband wearily. "The ghost agenda."

"Magnus! Haunted," his wife finished, in triumph. "Harrowhark Nonagesimus—I really think you should consider the idea that you might also be *haunted*."

29

AUGUSTINE WAS ALL SMILES now that Ianthe the First had passed her final hurdle. His open delight did a lot to ameliorate the reddened, swelling tension that had permeated the Mithraeum. You found his frank and open relief patronizing, but your sister Lyctor did not, or at least made a very good show of enjoying it. You went to watch a bout between them in the training rooms, sitting quietly and holding your rapier—it was full of unnecessary formality even to your Ninth House eyes, all antique niceties and duelling condescension that had been long forgotten back home. Ianthe was a saint of the Third House, and Augustine an antique of the Fifth; neither did anything without putting down a little carpet first, and introducing themselves to an audience of a thousand quiet-eyed memorial bones, and you.

But after the ceremony came the sword. You remembered so little of Naberius Tern, either of his death or of his life, but from what you had gathered he would have been the last cavalier in the whole star-less universe to think his sword-arm better off defleshed. Despite that, Ianthe was cured. It had been your faintest and most childlike hope that Ianthe would consider your bondage over; that your saving her life would be enough to release you from the collar of debt she had placed around your neck.

"As if," she'd said. "When I ask, you will know you have been *asked*, Nonagesimus."

The Saint of Patience had held to his promise to gild the arm, and now you often caught Ianthe marvelling at her metal-shod finger-bones, at the buttery shine of gold upon her triquetrum. Your eldest sister, whose discomfort and annoyance only grew with Augustine's delight, confronted you about it in the corridors: "Did you *really* erect that ghastly edifice?"

"Yes," you said.

"And it's really self-synthesizing bone?"

"Yes," you said. "Though I wouldn't call the process *synthesis* when the construct is merely perpetually growing to fill a pre-realised skeletal map. It's yet more proof that topological resonance can be manipulated."

Mercymorn's eyes narrowed to hurricane slits with short, thick lashes. Her prismatically white Canaanite robe was wrapped very tightly around her, as though she were cold, and she had bound back her peach-coloured hair as though it were a wimple. She said, "I see," and then, "I see. I see. What's two plus two?"

"Four—"

"Smallest bone in the body?"

"The auditory ossicles, but—"

"What's the name of the Saint of Duty?"

You said, "Ortus the First," and you were too slow. She reached out and tapped you on the side of the head. What Mercymorn the First could do with a simple tap on the side of the head might have meant your end far more easily than the Saint of Duty, a run-up, and his spear—but she said out loud, "Ortus," and then hurriedly again, all in one single *Ortus—Ortus.* The back of your skull ached, and you felt the chilly stab of pain in your sinuses that you sometimes felt in the dry atmosphere of the Mithraeum. You jerked away—your fingers flew to the bone studs in your ears—but she was not attacking you. You, so aware of your body, could sense no gland overworking, nor chemical coursing, nor vessel constricting.

The only change was in Mercy. Her placid oval face had taken on much the same look as you had seen, through a thin veil of viscera, the day you had fed the Lyctors your own marrow. She looked at you, quiet, and perhaps even a little lost; and she said: "I can't tell if you're a once-in-a-lifetime genius, an insane imbecile, or both."

Then she said: "Children as fists! Infants as gestures! Yuck! Pfaugh! I live in the *worst* of all possible worlds."

And without saying another word, Mercymorn stalked off down the corridor in the opposite direction, the lights making rainbows of her tightly shrouded robes.

When you reported this conversation to Ianthe, she was not particularly interested. This was, you thought, your sister-saint's downfall: she had pre-defined a set of things that merited her attention and consideration, and everything else she put aside. ("*You* brood over everything," she had said once, to this accusation. "You read unholy omens in the way people say *good morning*.")

"She's a crank," said Ianthe. "Augustine says she went funny years ago, and that much like a stopped clock, she's 'right twice a day, by coincidence.' Avoid, avoid."

How you loathed any sentence beginning with *Augustine says*. "But she touched my head," you said. "She was changing something, or looking for something—and I have no idea what."

"Your brain," suggested Ianthe.

Later you lay together in her lavish bed, far apart enough that if you reached out your hand, you might just brush her with your fingertips. It was, you had admitted, the only place you now felt safe to sleep, what with your wards so eminently destroyable. The mockery you endured for needing her proximity was exquisitely painful, but humiliation was steadily becoming your existence whole and entire.

But sleeping side by side was—awkward. It had been her idea. You would have slept on the carpet, if you hadn't thought it would leave you more vulnerable to the Saint of Duty—it would have been too easy to see you from the window in the case of a spaceside assault. Trauma prevented you from simply taking a pillow and sleeping in the bathtub. You lay flat on your back in borrowed blankets, wearing third-hand clothes. Ianthe had given you a daffodil-coloured nightgown, rummaged from some ancient drawer of artefacts belonging to a long-dead Lyctor's cavalier. It made you look like a liver inflammation. You stared glumly at a painting opposite the bed of an exquisite woman with lots of ruddy golden hair, a dreamy smile, and no clothes—though she *was* holding a rapier and, for no reason you could see, a melon.

That first night in her bed, you'd placed your bone-dressed sword between you, and felt better; she had, unsurprisingly, ragged you for it. "Relax," she had said. "I haven't invited you to an orgy, Harrow."

From this lying-down angle, the painting of the nude and obstreperously beautiful woman was in full sightline. You had murmured, "I believe you . . . albeit many wouldn't."

"This is why I cultivate you, Harrowhark," she had remarked, "the suspicion that you might possess a sense of humour."

You had said, "I'm not so gullible to think that your only reason."

"Of course I want something from you. But it's not *personal,*" Ianthe had said. "Understand me, Harry. I always take the smartest option first . . . burn any bridges that need to be burned . . . try to get in before anyone else can. It was the first thing I ever admired about you, back at—well, I promised not to talk about that . . . I'm very good at seeing the big picture. And your being alive is, right now, part of my big picture."

Both of you had stared, in the bedtime silence of blankets and darkness, at the big picture in front of you.

"They're all self-portraits, you know," she had said gloomily. "Cyrus the First and his cavalier constantly painted portraits of themselves and each other in the nude, hung them up everywhere, and gave them out to people for their birthdays. Augustine said Cyrus had them all brought over from Canaan House."

"Why do *you* keep them around?"

"It is the type of energy I wish to take into my future," Ianthe had said.

You both lay now in the low blue habitation light of the sleeping hours, not so close that you could semantically be said to be *lying together.* You were very aware of her nonetheless: of her skimmed-milk hair and discontented mouth, and of the amber satin she wore that made her arm so gold and her veins so green.

"The Saint of Duty is killable," she said. "You've shown that you're capable of killing him, even if you're not a genuine Lyctor. So if it were up to *me,* he'd be dead already." (You did not remotely believe this.) "The real problem is Teacher. I'm not sure you can kill Ortus quickly enough to avoid Teacher bursting through the wall with a merry, 'Not on my watch!' and bringing him back from a deathblow."

You said, "Then what do you propose? Distracting *God*?"

"That is exactly what I propose," said Ianthe. At the sound you made, she continued eagerly: "I mean it. Augustine says he'll do it . . . I asked him as a favour to me, and he said yes."

"Augustine said *yes*? Augustine agreed to the murder of his brother Lyctor?"

"There are very complex power dynamics on this station," said your sister Lyctor, with whom you had a very complex power dynamic. "I told him the whole story—don't make that face, Harry, it'll stick that way—and *he* said Ortus was on too long a leash and what he thought he was doing Augustine didn't know, but that gunning for you was stupid when you're just going to be eaten by Heralds anyway . . . Sorry, direct quote."

You said flatly, "I appreciate the sentiment."

"In any case, *he* said they can get by with just three Lyctors to take down Number Seven, so if I can step into Ortus's shoes now that I'm not 'problematic'—you can see I took my lumps, Nonagesimus—he can buy you an hour, after dinner."

"When?"

"Tomorrow."

"How?"

"Didn't say—but it's *Augustine the First,* my child. He's the first and oldest Lyctor. These three are all the oldest—and the last—that's why they're Patience, Joy, and Duty . . . three virtues. If Augustine is going to distract God, that means he's going to distract God. He's very old, and I hate to admit it, but he's enormously quick . . . and sophisticated . . . and devious. Anyway, I've taken care of him, and he'll take care of Teacher, and you'll take care of Duty."

"You've really—ensured this?"

"Fight him and win, Harry. Call it payment for the arm . . . You sound surprised."

You found yourself murmuring, almost more surprised with your-self than with her: "*Warrior proud of the Third House! Ride forth now as my sister.*"

There was a rustle from her side of the bed, and you saw that she had sat up a little, her exposed and metal-skinned humerus garishly propped on the covers.

"Was that *poetry*?" she demanded.

"Debatably," you said, and she lay back down. Then you said: "I accept your help. I am forced to admit that I cannot do this alone."

"I live for your forced admissions," said Ianthe. "It would have been a pain if you'd said no. I've already organised everything."

You both fell silent. The canopy of the four-poster bed obscured the fresco on the overdecorated ceiling, which was a relief to the eye. Her covers were softer than the covers in your room, though you thought the mattress too squashy for real comfort. One sank down into it like a bog. You were not used to so many pillows, nor were you used to the slippery chill of satin on your skin, nor were you used to hearing someone else's breath, insubstantial, beside you. For a moment you thought Ianthe had fallen asleep.

Then she said, idly: "Coronabeth and I spent three nights apart in all our lives, and the second time she cried so hard that she threw up . . . I hope she's sleeping easy now. When she doesn't, she gets bags under her eyelids you could carry water in."

It seemed as though a response was expected, but you did not want to speak of dead twins. You simply said, "I have always slept alone."

"You don't say."

You heard the primness in your voice when you said, "I am be-trothed to the Locked Tomb, Tridentarius. I slept on a cot in my cell."

"I always forget you were an honest-to-God nun . . . and six years old to boot, if you listen to Mercymorn. How old are you, really, Harry?"

"Eighteen, and my tolerance for *Harry* wears thin."

"Eighteen," she said, in the tones of the jaded, fagged-out socialite. "I remember being eighteen."

"You are twenty-two."

"It's a universe away from eighteen."

You lay in that bed like a marble sculpture, your body remote and faraway. Sleep and safety had blunted your panic, but not arrested it wholesale. If Ianthe reached out to touch your arm, you were afraid you might not understand whose arm she was touching. You were so afraid she might touch you. You were so afraid anyone might touch you. You had always been afraid of anyone touching you, and had not known your longing flinch was so obvious to those who tried it.

But she did not touch you. Instead, sleepily, she asked: "Do you really keep all those letters on you?"

Since you were living in exile from your room, they were now tucked into hollow capsules within your exoskeleton, the location of each of the twenty-two locked into your memory like so many theorems. You'd tried just tucking them into your robes, but you'd rustled. "Yes," you said, and did not elaborate.

Then she startled you by asking, "Any regrets, Harrowhark?"

"About?"

"About any of this. Going to Canaan House. Becoming a Lyctor. Coming to the Mithraeum."

You were not at all certain. "No."

"No, I suppose not," she said thickly. "You were more farsighted than I was . . . Me? I've never regretted anything, as a rule. Good night."

For a long time in the darkness you wondered at that, her *good night* hanging unanswered. *You were more farsighted than I was.* It was the easiest compliment to you that had ever passed her lips. You did not set store by compliments—it was vanity to accept them, and patronizing to give them—but this one echoed in your head. *You were more farsighted than I was.*

You looked at Cyrus the First's cavalier before you closed your eyes, though not to appreciate her details. You were more struck by the idea that she must have died back at Canaan House, when the work was finished—when the Lyctoral theorem had been cracked. Her necromancer had brought these ghoulish remembrances on purpose. He had surrounded himself with pictures he had painted, of him, and of the cavalier whose soul now fuelled the battery of his heart. You were lucky that the memory of your own cavalier did not hurt you—except sometimes in the form of a sick headache in your temples, or in words stuck on repeat in your head.

Some of those words were eating at you now, and you recited them to yourself in the quietude of your brain:

> *Warrior proud of the Third House! Ride forth now as*
> *my sister! Ride we to death, and the proving!*
>
> *Ride we with heads held high; we shall bloody our*
> *blades in the foe's heart; death shall we bring to the*
> *foul ones—*
>
> *Death shall we win for ourselves, as the prize for our*
> *high deeds done on the ash-choked plains of the*
> *ravens!*

Book Eleven. Matthias Nonius and the cavalier secondary of the Third House would proceed to destroy a whole legion in exhaustive detail, after which the grievously injured daughter of the Third had to be carried over a thanergy-irradiated desert while Nonius mused aloud on the nature of fate all the way into Book Twelve. You fell asleep.

* * *

By the next afternoon, an envelope had been slipped under Ianthe's door. It was paper of a deep, creamy brown, and sealed with wax. When Ianthe broke it open, you peered over her elbow at the contents. A single page—also real paper, also dyed a creamy tan colour, lettered artistically in flawless handwriting and deep blue ink:

AUGUSTINE THE FIRST, LYCTOR OF THE
GREAT RESURRECTION, FOUNDER OF
THE COURT OF KONIORTOS, FIRST SAINT
TO SERVE THE KING UNDYING

REQUESTS THE HONOUR OF THE PRESENCE
OF HIS YOUNGEST SISTERS

IANTHE THE FIRST, EIGHTH SAINT
TO SERVE THE KING UNDYING

&

HARROWHARK THE FIRST, NINTH SAINT
TO SERVE THE KING UNDYING

DINNER WILL BE SERVED AT HALF AN HOUR
PAST EVENING COMMENCEMENT

ATTIRE: FORMAL OR CEREMONIAL DRESS

Your head pounded with a tedious recognition.

"No," you said.

Ianthe tapped your shoulder with the invitation in her usual parody of playfulness, which was a little like being batted around by a predator while still alive. "This is the *plan*, Harrowhark. Just sit back and watch my teacher work."

You said, "I do not understand the faith you place in that man."

It was no good. You would have preferred a time that was not hours hence; you would have preferred a plan that did not involve a formal invitation, a dress code, or dinner. The last dinner you had attended had not gone exactly to plan, and you thought another dinner in poor taste. But you had not reckoned on your roommate, who—as a princess of the Third House—thought of dinners the way you thought of morning orison.

"I still have my robes of office," you said as she tore apart her wardrobe, fingering each article therein before tossing it aside.

"It's no longer your office. No—no."

"It's *technically* correct."

"Not this time, my child. I'm sick of being associated with a half-snapped stick of liquorice, dressed in a tent— No—hideous—not even Corona would wear that. No—no."

264 / TAMSYN MUIR

"My shirt and trousers will suffice, then. Beneath my Canaanite whites."

"Even worse," said Ianthe, and wrestled from its housing what appeared to be a full tulle skirt in midnight purple; skirt and woman scuffled momentarily before she heaved it across the room. "No—yes, for a different and much better party—no—no. Sometimes I think the Emperor of the Nine Houses favours you because you've got the same taste in clothes. God, what's *this*? That's a bit risqué—"

You grew desperate. "Let me pick."

Ianthe looked at you; her blue-and-brown eyes were beatific. "Harry," she said, and she said it tenderly, "have you never read a trashy novel in which the hero gets a life-affirming change of clothes and some makeup, and then goes to the party and everyone says things like, 'By the Emperor's bones! But you're *beautiful*,' or, 'This is the first time I have ever truly seen you,' and if the hero's a necromancer it'll be described like, 'His frailty made his unearthly handsomeness all the more ephemeral,' *et cetera, et cetera*, the word *mewled* fifteen pages later, the word *nipple* one page after that?"

You said emphatically: "No."

"Then we have no shared point of reference. Thankfully, however, this is not that part," she said. "Not even one of the Emperor's fists and gestures could give Harrowhark Nonagesimus a sexy makeover. Sometimes I think you look like a twig's funeral. In the right light though— Oh, this might do, it's even your colour. Come here."

She was holding a mass of black fabric, but no black such as ever existed in the House of the Locked Tomb. You approached with naked horror. Ianthe shook out a long piece of starry sable stuff and held it against you; it appeared to be some sort of—enormous handkerchief. It was not a dress.

When you pointed this out she said, with some asperity: "Valancy Trinit was my height, weighed more than both of us put together, and—judging by her portraits—had a body that did not quit. *Your* body, by comparison, gave up at the starting line. Take off your clothes."

Take off your clothes was an imperative you never thought you would obey. You did not take off all your clothes, but you consented to strip down to your shirtsleeves, because the shirt was long. The exoskeleton provided some coverage, though not remotely enough for comfort. You stood there with your chin thrust out, expecting a steady flow of crude japery, but all she said was: "Will you take off that grotesque skeleton corset?"

"No."

"What about your face paint?"

"No."

"I do not know why I ask these questions," she said.

She wrapped the scarf around you, pinned it, grunted, then took it away. You were left to sit on her bed, eating one of the apples she had not yet used for practice. As you ate you watched her, and you reread the invitation, while—typical of a flesh magician—Ianthe took out needle and thread, and quite happily occupied herself with sewing. She pronounced it "very easy, actually" to thread the needle with her defleshed hand.

Written on the back of the paper:

My room, ten minutes beforehand.

"Try this on," she said, eventually.

It amounted to little more than a veil. She pinned it over one shoulder and left both your arms chilly and bare. The material was water-thin and slippery; when you emerged from behind a gaudy screen, she cinched the black, scintillating stuff tight to your body. It was not true black, but shot with a deep chemical indigo, and as you looked in the mirror the shade made your eyes lightless hollows. Above that field of navy-black, little white scintillae trapped inside like luminescent filaments growing in a charred corpse, your irises were devoid of any colour at all.

Ianthe circled you, tugging and pinning, and you suffered it only because her touch was disinterested and clinical. Neither the touch of her living fingers nor her dead ones lingered. It was as though you were simply her patchwork corpse. You would have been impressed at her craft, except that she dismissed your compliments: "This is nothing. Naberius could embroider you a full overskirt without pricking a finger." This might have veered close to sentiment had she not added, "I wish killing him had given me his needlepoint too."

Your sister Lyctor brushed your hair and fluffed it out with her fingers. It was long enough to do this. Only a little while ago you had shaved it down to stubble: it had taken fright, and regrown at speed. Terribly afraid that this was your lone symptom of Lyctor regeneration, you had not cut it since. You would not let Ianthe fill any of the holes punched in your ears with metal earrings or pearls, and you refused all other jewellery not bone, and so there was not much else to be done. When she finished, you did not look upon your reflection with revolted shock, merely with a dull and uncomfortable distaste. The worst part was your sudden resemblance to your mother.

"I am very satisfied," pronounced Ianthe.

You said drearily, "I look like an imbecile."

"You look just good enough that I'm proud of my handiwork, but not *so* good that I'll be consumed with lust and ravish you over the nut bowl," she said. "I walked a fine line, and I walked it admirably. Go and fix your paint; your skull's dribbly."

As an act of meaningless rebellion, you applied the sacramental skull of Priestess Crushed Beneath the New-Laid Rock, the least beautiful skull in the canon. When you came back, she was smoothing her hair at her dressing table with a bone-backed brush. She wore a gown of achromatic purple—pale and almost grey, like the smoke from a fire banked with lavender, and made of what appeared to be a few layers of gauze. The back was open, and you could see the fine dents of her spine—her bleached skin bluer and sweeter against the pallid gossamer—and the twin blades of her shoulder blades looked strangely nude and vulnerable to you. She said languidly, "Button me up," and you obeyed by sprouting three skeleton arms from the bone-impregnated inlay of her chair, glad to hide her vertebrae.

Ianthe wore her Canaanite robe over her shoulders, but did not slip her arms into the sleeves: you were glad for the feeble, diaphanous cover yours offered. She buckled her rapier belt loosely at her hips; your two-hander you carried on your back. As you followed your coconspirator down the habitation corridor to Augustine's rooms, a prickle of anticipation washed over the insides of your stomach.

Just as your rooms bore very little resemblance to Ianthe's, Augustine's rooms bore no resemblance to either yours or hers. His interiors were of dark wood. Floor-to-ceiling bookshelves ran up most of the walls, and the floor was not tile but deep plush carpeting. It was a much more crowded, lived-in room, and on every surface was a book, or a stylus, or a folded pair of socks. There were baroque leather armchairs with pale weals on the arms and seat from years of sitting, and tasteful paintings with wooden frames, and a general smell of wood polish and book glue. It was a friendlier room than you had expected, insofar as you had expected anything. The wide tapestry sofa was thick with fringed cushions in comfortable disarray. There were vases of eggshell-thin ceramic on the table set before the vast plex window—currently hung with primrose drapes, shut—filled with, though you had no idea where he had procured them, cut flowers in shades of orange, red, and gold.

The Saint of Patience was bent over a mirror above a wooden washstand, wearing a suit of antique make beneath his robe. You were grudgingly impressed by the sight of a historical artefact actually being worn: black trousers, black jacket, a plain white shirt with a high white collar, very starched. Augustine had combed his hair into a flat cap against his skull, faultless and shiny, with not a strand out of place. Within the collar sat a funny little black tie that was cut in a curve, and he was knotting it into a fat bow.

"Nicely done, my dove," he said jocularly to Ianthe, taking her hands and kissing them. There was a tightness around his concrete eyes that belied the good humour. "You put me in mind of a statue of some lost goddess hauled up from the waters, painted lineaments removed but marble intact."

"Covered in moss, mould, and gunge," she suggested, consenting to be kissed on each cheek. "You should see my sister."

"You always say that," said Augustine. He looked at you, and relieved your mind by not kissing you anywhere; he simply raised his eyebrows and said, "And so the crow can be a swan! Ah, this is like the old days . . . you should have seen the shindigs we pulled off, when we dared congregate. We partied as though it were the days before the apocalypse. I will remember them always. John laughed more then. Mostly at that madman Ulysses, and Cassiopeia, under the table because she'd had a single glass of wine . . . . All right, kiddies, shall I tell you how we'll play this?"

You asked, "Why are you helping me commit murder?"

He checked his little tie in the mirror again, corrected some imperceptible skew, and straightened up.

"For reasons of my own, dear girl," he said, with the glacial cheer that seemed to be his first line of defence. "Once upon a time, if my younger brother had deemed it fit for you to exit this vale of tears, I would not have stopped him, but I admitted long ago that Ortus no longer listens to anyone. He always did get his own bizarre obsessions, and you could never get them out of his head with a pneumatic drill. He has caused me more pain over these last scant forty years than I dare to admit. No, there's no question of me barring you here. I'll get Teacher's undivided attention. You'll both skedaddle. Harrow will finish her bloody business . . . if she can, which I am not at all sure of."

"She can," said Ianthe, ruining it with "probably," and the Lyctor said: "She can *try*. I once watched that man fight a city. The city didn't win. He'll leave the dinner first, and be in the training room afterward, that's his habit; you'll leave on cue."

This seemed nonsensical to assume. You said, "He'll leave?" at the same time the Princess of Ida said, "On cue?"

"Won't tell you what it is; if you're waiting for it, our Emperor will smell a rat. Just believe me when I say that when I want Ortus to go, he'll be giddy-*gone*." (This did not make much sense to you, as a joke.)

There was a brisk knock on the door. You immediately pressed yourself to the wall, out of direct sight if it opened, and Ianthe tightened bony fingers on the shining end—pommel—of her Third House rapier; but Augustine merely said, "Come in, lynchpin."

The lynchpin walked in. It was the Saint of Joy.

Your erstwhile teacher ignored you, folded into your alcove, and she ignored your sister, whose pallid eyebrows had shot up so fast and so far that they were in danger of breaking the atmosphere. Mercymorn wore a long slip of peach-coloured silk, and her white Canaanite robe was tucked over her forearms and had slipped entirely off her slender, aggrieved shoulders. She had scraped her hair into a merciless and shining coil at the back of her head, and she had no eyes for either of you.

She said, "You have some nerve."

"Not remotely; I never have," he said, affably. "Do you accept the terms of the offer?"

"Tell me what you're—"

"Accept first."

"I'll accept if you swear on the sword," said Mercy, with unholy eagerness.

He raised his rapier up within its scabbard. It had a bright conical hilt of what looked to be copper, with pricked designs all over it. "I swear by the sword of Alfred Quinque, best of men and cavaliers, that the details of your, ahem, *business* will not be told by me, or revealed by me, or let fall from the lips of my mouth nor the pads of my fingers—even though I think it will be the death of us," he added. At this, there was a fractional relaxing of Mercymorn's frowzled brow: not relief, but the germination of the seed of relief. "Accept."

"Fine! I accept," she said. Then she looked around herself, and said: "You *do* know the children are present? Should I kill them, or what?"

"Ignore 'em," said Augustine. "Better you don't know why they're here. Look—I need you to fully commit to this one, Joy, and if you don't, I will consider the oath I just swore tampered with."

"Commit! *Commit!!*" she said scornfully. You noticed she was wearing short strings of apricot-coloured seed pearls in her ears; they vibrated as she folded her arms across her chest. "Stop wasting your breath and tell me the plan."

"Once you hear it, whatever you do to me, don't do it below the neck. None of my other shirts are pressed."

"Stop drawing this out! Tell me!"

He cleared his throat and said: "*Dios apate,* minor."

You had a front-row seat to Mercymorn's dreamy eyes going quiet; the eye of the tempest, before she reared back and punched him full in the face. There was not much force in that blow, which barely snapped his head back, but he whitened as though her fist had been a battering ram. He gagged, doubled over his washstand, and ejected a mouthful of teeth—a tumbling, plinking bowlful; he held his hand over his red and dripping mouth and closed his eyes, and after a few moments straightened back up, a trifle greyer, running his tongue over his regrown incisors.

"Minor," he repeated when he could, taking out a handkerchief and dabbing his mouth. "*Minor*—how many times must I say it?"

"You've lost your senses," she said unsteadily.

"You think I am *joking*, Mercymorn?"

They looked at each other. Then followed the type of conversation you had only seen once before, between her and God—that exchange of shrugs, and words begun in the mouth and aborted at the first breath, and at one point she said, "Gradient?" and he answered, "Radial," and then they devolved again into a shorthand of facial expressions. In its own way, it was swifter and less coherent than what you had seen pass between the Emperor of the Nine Houses and her, that lifetime ago leaving the *Erebos;* but at the end, her hand fluttered around her mouth, and she halfway wailed:

"I'm not wearing the right dress."

"It's perfect. You look like a melon."

"But I *hate* this," she said, quite genuinely, and Augustine looked at her with his insubstantial eyes and said: "I understand. Buck up, Joy; it won't kill you."

Your gaze met Ianthe's. She had followed the whole thing in rank fascination; now she quirked her own eyebrows at you in what you had come to understand was, *Who knows?* For a moment you worried that, come another myriad, you and she might be able to carry on such a conversation: that you would know her intent by the twist of her mouth and her exhalation, to the point where you could speak without dialogue.

In the end, Mercymorn said, "*Blech!*" and turned on one heel and stalked out. She flung open the door, said anxiously, "*White* wine!" and with that cryptic epigram, disappeared.

The Saint of Patience said, "That went significantly better than I thought it might," without a glance at his sink of bloodied teeth. "Come on—I want one of you on each of my arms on this battlefront. On my right, Ianthe. I'm not clutching that bone; I never did like 'em skinny—Harrowhark, you really didn't get any height, did you? Lord! Imagine being crystallized a teenager, forever! Whatever you see tonight," he added, suddenly serious as the grave, "do *not* get involved."

Behind his back—as you walked down the corridor—the Princess of Ida mouthed at you smugly: *Quick! Sophisticated! Devious!*

IT TURNED OUT THAT AUGUSTINE THE FIRST—
Saint of Patience, founder of the court of Koniortos, genius of the
River—ten thousand years old and oldest among saints, quick and
sophisticated and devious—had a shrewd plan to assist you in the
murder of his dutiful brother. His shrewd plan: to get everyone profoundly drunk.

Two hours later you sat amid a pillage. The remains of a meal lay
before you, more than you had ever eaten of your own volition. You'd
had to. The only other option was unconsciousness. A pyre of candles
cast their radiance across the snowy white linen and the silver cutlery
that the Saint of Patience had so carefully set, and on the crumb-strewn
plate that had once contained rolls of some description, but they had
been eaten—or put somewhere—you did not know, and you didn't care.
The shining bones of Cohort heroes hung as silent observers on either
side of the room, and you fancied weariness in their eyeless expressions.

You were not sure how it had happened. It had seemed to begin
as all previous dinners had, just more formal. Maybe Augustine's
cooking was more careful and more lavish—he tended to cook in
short bursts of violence, serving many parts of a meal but not all at
once, which coming from the Drearburh table you found bewildering. You hadn't been able to focus on what you were eating; only that
by the third course, you had to continue or suffer the consequences.
You did not really like the taste of wine, which Augustine had served
you before, and had not imagined there could be that much of it. He
refilled the glasses before you ever finished one, so that you never
made it to the bottom of the first.

Now, in the smoking ruins of dinner, he and the Saint of Joy, and God and Ianthe, had moved their seats to a cluster at the end of the table. Ianthe's First House robes were somewhere on the floor, and her elbows were on the tablecloth, and her cheeks were pink, which gave her a spurious loveliness. Augustine had removed his jacket and was sitting in his white button-up shirt. The tie at his throat had come undone entirely to hang limp and black beneath the points of his dishevelled collar. Mercy had it worst: the knot of hair at her neck had come down, and now was springing loose in pale, rose-gold strands, and she was actually sniggering.

God sat between them. Teacher had his sleeves rolled up to his elbows; if it was a tidier or nicer shirt than he usually wore, you could not tell. The coronet of bones and leaves had fallen from his brow, probably in among the napkins, and his top button was crooked, and every so often he would come around and fill up everyone's water glasses, and say with increasing earnestness: "Keep drinking *water*, Harrow," as though water were the greatest and most impossible boon granted to the Nine Houses. His smile kept crinkling the edges of those white-encircled eyes.

Every so often you would look over the table at the man you intended to kill. The Saint of Duty had drunk just as much as Augustine, but had an expression like stone, with not a button out of place. He had more than once shared a glance with you that you were very afraid was solidarity. You weren't sure. You were drinking water. You were drinking a great deal of water.

"To absent friends," said Augustine suddenly, and raised his glass.

And everyone said, "Absent friends," and raised their glasses, and drank. *That* was the invention of torture; you had no doubt that either the Third or the Fifth House had come up with the damned rule that whenever you raised your glass and proposed a sentimental toast, everyone had to drink with you. You sipped. You did not have any absent friends.

"And to our cavaliers," said the Saint of Joy, quite suddenly, after everyone had drunk.

Augustine raised his glass again. "I'll drink to that. To cavaliers—we didn't deserve 'em . . . and they didn't deserve us, as I always say. To Alfred—Cristabel—Pyrrha—Loveday—Naberius—to them all."

You saw the Emperor darting an impassive glance at the increasingly disarranged saint at his right, but she did not greet this toast with anger. She simply said, "To Cristabel," and drained her glass in one single, violent motion. When God briefly pressed the tips of his fingers to the tips of her fingers, she said instantly: "I'm not drunk!!"

"I'd never think it," he said.

You watched Ianthe take another swig of the pale, apple-yellow liquid in her glass. She leaned over to you and murmured, breathlessly: "*This is the greatest night of my life.*"

"I've drunk enough to Alfred over the years, so let me drink to Cristabel," said the Saint of Patience, and he drank, and then he swirled the contents of his glass meditatively. "Here's to Cristabel."

Mercy said, with less rancour: "You never liked Cristabel, even before what happened."

"Bullshit I didn't like Cristabel," he said instantly, with the careful, measured reasonableness of a man you had personally seen get through two bottles of wine. "You know what I feel . . . you know I don't think she was the best influence on Alfred . . . you know I thought they brought out the worst in each other, and I don't think you disagree."

God said, "They were very similar people."

"No," said Augustine. "They weren't, John. She was a fanatic and an idiot—yes, she was, Mercy—and he . . . was a man who regretted that he wasn't. It took surprisingly little to lead my brother astray."

"Nobody could lead him where he didn't want to go," said God, and his patience took a solemn edge. "You know that."

"Lord! Don't tell me that," said his Lyctor, faintly smiling. "I have built an entire myriad on the idea that I could've made him come around, given five minutes."

His sister-saint said nothing to this. She flicked her eyes down to her own glass, instead, and he quickly filled up the awkward pause with, "Anyway, let's drink to a woman who never divided opinion. Here's to Pyrrha Dve."

All eyes trailed fatally down the table to the Saint of Duty. Your gaze was among them. You grasped the stem of your wineglass in your hand, and you looked at the face of the man who had been necromancer once to a woman called Pyrrha: the inscrutable lack of expression that had greeted you in the bathtub, and the first time he'd walked into the Mithraeum's chapel.

He said flatly, with a note of warning: "Augustine."

"I mean it. Don't you think that's astonishing, after all this time? Even Mercy doesn't have a bad thing to say about her." ("Why am I constantly painted as a critical person," came the inevitable critique.) "I say, here's to Pyrrha, the woman I cultivated a smoking habit to impress—the cavalier, the legend, the stone-cold fox . . . John, please stop joggling my elbow, I have heard *stone-cold fox* from your own holy lips."

The Emperor protested, "Respectfully! *Respectfully.*"

Ortus said, "Another topic."

"Right," said Augustine. He took another gulp of wine as though to fortify himself, and Ianthe suggested: "To our enemies, older brother."

"Yes! Great," he agreed heartily. "A classic. This is why you are my chosen apprentice, chick. To our enemies—the enemies of the Empire—to those safely in the River, that is. I won't drink to enemies alive, but let's drink to enemies fallen, as we can afford to be gracious. Let's drink to the dried-up Blood of Eden."

Both the Emperor and Mercy said, immediately: "They're not gone."

"Fine, pedants—I drink to the best of them, gone for absolute certain . . . not the remnant kooks, idiots, and zealots who think a nuclear missile could give us pause. The commander would never have settled for a nuclear missile . . . Lord, that was a merry dance she led us. It deserves something. Perhaps it's a toast."

Across the table, you noticed that the Saint of Duty's knuckles had clenched, just slightly. You had a good sense for knuckles. The Emperor mistook your focus for puzzlement: "It was before you were born, Harrowhark." ("*Long* before you were born," added Mercy owlishly, "because you are three years old.") "This isn't really a story that deserves to be told after . . . three glasses of wine."

"That was never three glasses of wine," said the man to his left.

"Four glasses of wine," amended God, which was probably still inadequate. "This is a good lesson for you, girls, not to underestimate anyone. A quarter century ago these fanatics found out about the Resurrection Beasts. Which are classified to the upper echelons of the *Cohort,* mind, so that was an intelligence effort and a half . . ."

"They knew about them," said Ortus. "They just didn't know what they were."

"Finding out what they were didn't stop them. They searched one Beast out . . . threw away half their ships separating a Herald from the pack . . . *killed* that Herald, let's drink to that—" ("To killing Heralds," said his two elder Lyctors, and they drank, and so did Ianthe, and you put your lips on the glass.) "Even a dead Herald can drive a necromancer insane. They took that thing *apart.* They made it into knives. They made it into axes. They made it into armour. I mean, extremely frugal, but honestly—that commander had Herald bullets."

"Bullets," said Augustine, "Darts. Throwing knives. Dead shot. Got me right between the eyes once. Mad as a cut snake, and three times as vicious. We nearly lost you to her a few times, didn't we, Ortus? Should we drink to Commander Wake?"

The glasses rattled as the Saint of Duty stood, and said the most words you had ever heard him say. "Probably not. Excuse me. I'm tired."

They watched him go in pursed-up silence. Teacher rose from the table, silently, as though thinking of going after him. When the door shut behind the escaping Lyctor, Mercymorn hissed, "Augustine, you ass," and he protested calmly: "He's fine."

"You call that *fine*—"

"—sudden access of sympathy a little uncharacteristic when—"

"—not *difficult* to imagine that maybe—"

"Don't," said God, sitting back down with some difficulty. "Don't. Not when you're finally talking again. This is more amicable conversation than I have seen you two exchange in . . . it must be decades. Don't. I've had a very nice evening. Harrow, you haven't drunk too much, have you?"

You had drunk exceptionally too much, and were dying to purge your kidneys manually. "No," you said, at the same time that your seatmate said, "Very obviously, yes."

"Nobody *asked* you," you said, but Ianthe was moving her chair over, and she was slinging her living arm around your bare shoulders— which made them feel less bare and less cold, which you resented— and she was saying, "There, there, Harry." (God repressed a smile at this vile nickname, for which you once again assured Ianthe slow death.) "Let me introduce you to the special world of sisterhood—I will reveal everything you do, contradict you at every turn, and hold back your hair in the morning."

You did not want Ianthe to reveal everything you did, nor did you want her to contradict you at every turn, and you especially did not want her to hold back your hair in the morning. But God said cheer-fully, "Here's to sisters," and the other Lyctors reached for any glass that contained anything, and you had to take yours—Ianthe pressed it into your hand—and you drank.

Augustine said, "To sisters, and the women we've left behind."

God's mouth was cheerful as ever, but his eyes were not when he said, "Do I have to drink to that?"

For the first time, you were witness to the Saint of Patience dis-combobulated. "Apologies, John. Wasn't meant as a jab."

"It doesn't hurt anymore—most of the time," said God, and he was still smiling.

The Lyctor at his left was combing out her hair—it tumbled in a heavy mass around her shoulders, that curious heart-of-a-yellow-rose colour, that pinkish, reddish, goldenish shade that was not entirely appealing. Her glass still had wine in it, which seemed unrealistic, and she said: "Here's a better toast . . . . To the Emperor of the Nine Houses. To the Resurrector. To my God."

"To Emperor John Gaius, the Necrolord Prime!" said Augustine, and he drained his glass.

This was the only toast you were willing to drink to; you drank, because you held to your convictions, and also because Ianthe was looking at you with the mocking and faintly pitying expression of someone who did not expect you to drink. This made you drink twice.

"I'm not going to drink to *myself*," Teacher was saying. "I'm not the best man who ever lived, but I'm not quite that much of a narcissist."

The Saint of Joy said, with uncharacteristic ferocity: "You *are* the best man who ever lived."

"I'll drink to that," said Augustine.

You could not behold God's expression for any great length of time. Augustine stood, and he refilled his glass, and he refilled Mercymorn's. He clinked his wineglass against hers with a little crystal tinkle—she beheld him with dim and unfeeling eyes—and they drank in silence, at either side of the Emperor of the Nine Houses.

Eventually, she said: "I think I wish Cytherea were here."

"I don't," said the saint on the other side. "We would have had to suffer her favourite conversation of *Who had the hottest cavalier?* And my answer hasn't changed for anyone's money. I don't care that she was ten years my senior, Pyrrha Dve was hotter than the very fires of Hell."

"Agreed," said God.

"John, you dog."

"An absolute bombshell," said God. He looked deeply into Augustine's eyes, took another slug of wine, and then said in graveyard tones: "Though maybe not quite such a bombshell as *your mother.*"

It destroyed some cavern of your reverence to watch Augustine punch the Prince Undying on the arm, and to watch the Prince Undying gamely cuff him back. Part of your brain temporarily calcified into atheism. You had not thought it would be like this. From the day the letter arrived in Drearburh, you'd thought that your Lyctoral days would be spent in prayer, training, and the beauty of necromantic mysteries. You did not think any part of it would be spent honestly quite drunk, wearing a piece of material no larger than a towel, and with Ianthe Tridentarius's fingers idly caressing the hair at the nape of your neck. For a moment, you wondered wildly if you had hit your head quite hard entering the shuttle out of Drearburh, and had hallucinated everything subsequent.

Mercymorn said peevishly: "*I* always thought Nigella was prettier," and both men assured her, "You're not wrong," "Good choice, et cetera," until Augustine said gloomily: "Try getting a look-in with Cassy around, though."

You turned your head and muttered into Ianthe's ear, knowing your desperation was naked: "When do we leave?"

"The time has not yet come," she murmured. You looked into her shining brown-flecked eyes and were stricken with panic that the time might never come.

Mercymorn finished off another glass of wine—Teacher removed her wineglass, and then, thoughtfully, removed the bottle closest to her, and then removed any bottles of wine within her reach—and she placed her tranquil oval of a face into her slender hand, and she said: "You're wrong, Augustine. You still hate Cristabel . . . you hated my cavalier long before what she did."

He was arrested in the process of refilling his glass. You had no idea how anyone could drink as much as the Saint of Patience had and remain coherent. He put down the bottle and said, "Do I?"

God said, "This isn't a conversation either of you have to have. Not now. Especially not after five glasses of wine."

"Lot more than five. No. No, it's fine. Judge ye not. Let her dig him up again," said Augustine, though now he sounded a trifle unsteady. "Do I, Mercy? God help me, I don't think I do."

She said, "Look me in the eyes and say that."

Augustine stood, with nary a tremble. He wiped his mouth carefully with his handkerchief again, and although God had half-risen too, again—put his hand on Augustine's arm, and looked at him, and whatever passed between them was too swift to classify—he moved next to the Saint of Joy's chair. He crouched a little so that they were eye to eye—in the candlelight you could not tell whether you thought they looked appallingly old, or no older than Ianthe—and he said, "Joy, what's done is done. They're dead. The crime is punished. I don't hate Cristabel."

Her face was savage and smooth and implacable. "Say it again," she said.

"I don't hate Cristabel," he said lowly. "Dear, I barely hate you."

For a moment you thought you were about to see a replay of what had happened in his rooms, and that the distraction would consist of a battle between two Lyctors that you would have been somewhat sorry to miss.

It did not. Wild eyed, tumultuous, unbalanced, Mercy leaned in and kissed him.

An alarm crescendo of horror went off in your head. She did not kiss him placidly—he responded immediately and without restraint. The Lyctors kissed each other in the manner of two people who either held a decided passion for one another or were attempting to slide a hidden object mouth to mouth. The Saints of Joy and Patience kissed each other with a fervid, drunken familiarity, without preamble, or frankly any shame.

God was trying to say something. Augustine parted from Mercymorn with a noise vaguely like a vacuum hoovering up mincemeat, and—with no crash of unholy thunder, and without the rent of the universe in twain, and without his skin melting from his unworthy bones—*he turned and also kissed the Emperor of the Nine Houses.*

You were glued to your seat. You were hot from your temples all the way down to the top of your ribcage, with outrage and mortification vying for top place within you. You were frozen as Augustine carefully, thoughtfully, and with a great deal of intent, put his mouth on God's mouth. As though this were not fodder enough for the coming apocalypse, Mercymorn stood, swaying; one thin dress strap was sliding precariously off her shoulder. When Augustine detached from the Emperor's solemn mouth, Mercy reached up, grabbed great fistfuls of his shirt, and kissed God too.

It took Ianthe two attempts to get your attention. Eventually she stood you up wholesale, and with absolutely nobody paying attention to either of you, she propelled you out of the room. You looked over your shoulder as she opened the door—God had just picked up the Saint of Joy bodily and sat her at the edge of the table, and the Saint of Patience had his mouth at God's neck, which was *horrible*—and Ianthe hustled you through as though escaping from a fire. You had never seen three people get their hands on one another before—you had never seen two people get their hands on each other before. Ianthe closed the door just as Augustine's fingers reached the buttons of the Emperor's shirt, and you had never been so grateful to her in your entire life.

31

"*THAT* WAS THE CUE?" Your voice sounded humiliatingly high-pitched.

"Harry," said Ianthe, thankfully also a trifle strangled, "when three people start kissing, it is *always* a cue. A cue to *leave*."

You said, "I feel unwell."

"Yes. Yes, me too," she said heatedly, in unexpected accord. "That was disgusting, to say the least. Old people should be shot."

The underfloor lights glowed their cool blue, trying to soothe you into circadian sleep. A Cohort officer with grey tags at their sleeves lay enshrined in a niche opposite, an eyeless steel mask laid heavily on their face. Both you and Ianthe were breathing as though you had run a footrace, laboured and loud. Ianthe's hair was in long margarine tangles down her neck, and her mascara was smudged beneath her eyes, and her ribs were heaving as though she were in an asthmatic fit. She carried her high-heeled shoes in her gilded skeleton hand, and they made for a strange juxtaposition. The breath-soft lavender gauze had a tiny violet stain on the front, and her mouth was red: she had been chewing her lips, and they had broken, and split. You realised with an uneasy start that you were both, in fact, quite drunk.

Ianthe ran a tongue across those wounded lips and said, "I suppose this is it."

You said, "I appreciate your part in this, Tridentarius," but before you could stop her, she drew you close with her living arm, and she bent her head to yours. You understood this inevitability only a second before it happened. Perhaps there was a dark universe in which you reached for her; in another you exploded her heart in her chest.

In this one, as she lowered her mouth, you turned your face away, and her kiss fell on the side of your jaw. Both of you reeked of alcohol. Minute traces of blood smudged your cheek with tiny perfume blots of thalergy as she brushed her broken mouth across it with unanticipated tenderness. There was a rigid trembling somewhere in your sternum. When she raised her head again her gaze was cool and mocking, as though your inability to receive a kiss was yet more proof of limitation.

Your mouth was very dry when you said: "My affections lie buried in the Locked Tomb."

"And let them lie," she said, laughingly, and not very kindly. "Somebody might even exhume them for you. Good luck, Harry . . . try not to die."

She walked off swinging her dancing shoes in her dead arm, and she even hummed tunelessly beneath her breath, before she disappeared down the corridor: a lone wax figure in pale purple chiffon, tall and colourless—except in the greasy metal of her bone arm, which the lights rendered all the colours of the rainbow. You could hear her carefree humming even after she disappeared, as you stood outside the dining room stock-still and frozen.

When it died away, you turned to your assassination.

You kicked off your shoes and left them, as you were still drunk enough to find that reasonable. Most of the alcohol was already in your bloodstream, but quite a lot of it was racketing around in your small intestine. As you walked in silence down the tiled hallways, past the pillars of tendon- and plex-wrapped wire, you focused on working it out of your capillaries and then out through your pores until you were running wet with sweat. Easier to move ethanol through water membranes than anywhere else. The fog in your brain and body burnt away, and you peeled two long strands of articular cartilage and hard calcium from your exoskeleton. These you melded and worked between your hands like clay, until you had a smooth greyish globe of bone.

There was no question of proceeding by stealth. Stealth required advance preparation, scouting, mapping, and you had not been given time for any of those. You had not known until ten minutes before dinner that your target would be in the training room. You had been forced to come up with tactics that would work on any battlefield. The buzz of adrenaline and remnant alcohol sang through you and made you feel prickly and overwarm, despite the fact that you were as soaked with cooling sweat as though you had stood in a spray of blood. You had been the subject of attempted murder more times than you had fingers and toes. You had sat through a long, agonising dinner culminating in two elderly Lyctors getting their tongues on God. Your mouth had been very nearly kissed. The calm that came over you as you went to murder Ortus the First was the weary calm of someone who had already been tried within an inch of her fucking life.

You stood before the autodoor of the training room, bowered over the black lintel with rainbow-coloured bunting and tessellated butterflies of pelvises and spines. There was nothing to sense within, but you would never have been able to sense him. You pressed the obsidian tab that opened the doors; you rolled your ball through with a swift underhand movement; you shut the doors again before they'd had the chance to part fully.

You had thought this through in detail. The Saint of Duty was a thanergy void. This you understood. Send a skeleton construct in, and within a few seconds it would be an inert pile of bone upon the floor. You had wondered about trying to build some complex mechanism with multiple layers—interlocking tiers of thanergy-rich bone, freshly grown from your own body, forcing him to waste time chewing through it all—but then you had remembered the ease with which he had crumbled bone even as it sprouted from your wrists, and realised the risk was too great. You did not know how fast he could work, and you could not base your whole plan on a guess.

When Ortus the First had dried up your wrist spikes, you had felt him do it. There had been an appreciable jolt, as of a switch being thrown. He had gripped the periosteum in his hands and made something happen. That meant it was a conscious action, not passive. That was only logical, since a necromancer who *automatically* dispersed the thanergy from his surroundings would be a desperate liability to his fellow adepts. If the drain was a conscious action, it required some measure of concentration. He needed to focus. You could not give him that chance.

Your bomb exploded into a myriad of bone shards. You felt their thanergy light up like an electrical impulse, through the walls. You made that training room a goddamn hailstorm. Each fragment was no longer than four centimetres; that was long enough to kill, given the pressure with which you shattered them outward. There was a muffled eruption of rattling—a vigorous *THWACKETA-THWACKETA-THWACK* as thousands of missiles hammered into the floor, the ceiling, the walls, the foot-thick plex window. You thumbed two studs out of your ears, dropped six full constructs behind you in a spirit of pure optimism, and slammed the pad open again.

The training room was a smoking ruin. The wooden floors were a jagged carpet of embedded bone caltrops. The electrical lights overhead were smoking, crackling bars of broken housing and tungsten fibre; your bones were cilia inside a cavity, bristling spines on a rose's stem, fine hairs on the legs of an arachnid. Razor-sharp spikes powdered harmlessly beneath your tread as you ran into that destroyed room wearing little more than a scarf and your paint, with your collagen-coated hands clutching your two-handed sword; and you readied yourself.

The Saint of Duty wasn't there.

You said, "Fuck."

Then, more aggressively: "Fuck!"

The smothering caul of disappointment around your heart was an unhelpful distraction. You sheathed your sword to the back of your exoskeleton and—reminding yourself, yet again, that reliance on others was as taking a brute-force blow with your vulnerable lacrimal bone—you turned off the lights, and you covered the ends of the wires in a thick cap of cartilage, heading off the fire alarm. Then you removed yourself from that bone-strewn ruin, somewhat chastened, thoroughly aggrieved.

Ortus the First was not in the training room. Fine. He had surprised you before. There was one other place on the Mithraeum where you had found him, at a time like this, when he thought he might not be disturbed; and so it was on swift feet, and with rising determination, that you retraced your steps toward the outer ring and the habitation atrium, and the room where one last Lyctor lay in state.

The Saint of Duty was not there. Neither was the body of Cytherea the First. A trail of blood emerged from the open doorway, smiled on dimly by the electric lights. It led away from the bier where once the necromantic saint had slept so restively. Your heart and brain responded when you bade them both be still, and for a few seconds you stood before that continuous ribbon of blood, almost without thinking—and then you retrieved them both, along with whatever madness-tattered sense you retained.

You crouched. The blood was minutes old, a tangled skein of oxygen-rich carmine and oxygen-poor scarlet: blood from the right atrium, expelled straight from the heart. You stood and stepped carefully into the room on your bare feet. Behind the abandoned altar there was a criminal crimson splatter of blood on the back wall, more sprayed across the incorrupt petals of the increasingly blush roses. And discarded on the floor lay Ortus's spear, slick and red from its point to almost halfway down its shaft.

You did not need a Sixth House dust-botherer to reconstruct this particular tableau. Someone had stood behind the bier, their back to the wall; the spearhead had been thrust through their chest and exited their back with one almighty push—blood had spurted from the exit wound, and then sprayed forward when the spear was pulled back out, with that same prodigious strength. Judging by the mess it had made of the roses, the attacker must have received a liberal coating. Then the victim had been dragged past the altar and out into the atrium, and from there to who knew where.

The weapon belonged to Ortus; but to whom belonged the blood? You had wet your hands before with the blood of Cytherea's unbeating heart; this was not hers. One possibility was that Ortus had stabbed a third party, and then chosen to abscond for reasons of his own with both their body and Cytherea's. That might be the most plausible explanation. But it was not the simplest.

You followed that long, snaking trail back out of the room. It led down the hallway, then turned an abrupt corner into a feeder corridor to an inner ring. You spurred your exoskeleton into a trot; your chilled feet spattered through the still-warm blood, and you left cooling crimson prints behind you as you ran. You moved along a dimly lit statuary corridor, between the gilded and bejewelled skeletons of Third and Seventh heroes dressed in gold and green robes of necromantic office, with amethysts and topazes and emeralds for eyes; you turned abruptly, skidding a little in the blood, through a low service doorway.

You had passed through the habitation ring, and the storage ring. You were in the engineering and environmental ring now, with the power systems, and the life-support, and the exhausts and waste. The lights were dim here. There were fewer portholes, and the effect was immediately more claustrophobic, more tubular. Even here, no space was wasted: ten thousand years of memorial meant that even in the sharp yellow shadows of the filtration panels, and past the enormous gurgling vat of the water tank, the inlaid bones of the Nine Houses sat forever watching switchboard lights marked things like END EFFECTOR SUCK—END EFFECTOR WINNOW—END EFFECTOR SIFT. Better to decay to powder in the Drearburh oss than keep watch above END EFFECTOR SUCK until the end of time.

The blood was still wet beneath your toes, although thinning out somewhat; it trailed in a nearly black ribbon down past the filtration rooms, and you followed it out to the exhausts. It dripped down a short flight of metal stairs into a wide, deep room within the station, not so thickly built up with the accretion of computers and mechanisms from upstairs. You could understand the great scope of the Mithraeum in here. Tall oblong plex windows were set high in the walls, and wads of thermal foam nuzzled up against a little bunker, windowless and solid, with huge valves set in it travelling up through the walls and into chambers unknown. You did not yet know why the station had an incinerator: as far as you knew, it recycled rather than destroyed its waste. Mechanical arms dangled overhead, waiting to place things into the incinerator via a roof-hatch. Partway up the main wall, above the bunker, was a tiny plex-fronted control booth, which you could see no way of accessing; the door must have been somewhere back up the stairs.

The blood ended abruptly at the door of the incinerator. As though in a dream, you followed it to its terminus. Set in the door was an immensely thick plex panel, yellowed from old fire, and you peered through it.

Ortus the First lay propped against the wall at the back of the incineration chamber. His chest was a neat, bloody void where the spearhead had gone precisely through his heart. It would have meant instant death for a normal human being, even a skilled adept. He lay with his chin lolled down on his chest. There was nobody else in the incinerator with him.

The showdown between you and the Saint of Duty was already over. Your enemy had been killed without you laying a finger upon him. You felt, dimly, cheated.

The Saint of Joy and the Saint of Patience were—distracted—with another matter, that matter being God and a heretical three-way division of saliva. Ianthe had walked away from you, all split lips and gay loneliness; had she walked, less drunk with every step, toward the little room where Ortus bent over a dead woman? Was his ruined heart a gesture for your benefit? Would she leave so much blood; would she come here?

Ortus's corpse heaved for breath inside the incinerator, and coughed, though you could not hear the sound.

You watched as, trembling, he slapped a hand to hide his nude and livid wound. All around him, the incinerator mechanism rumbled to life. You spun away and looked up. In the protected plex booth stood Cytherea, spotlit by the strong white light from the panels above her, leaning heavily upon some handle within; a dead woman staring at you through dark and filmy eyes, her face freckled with drying blood, petals in her limp ringlets.

The flesh was dead, but the hate in that face was alive and well and living. You looked at the walking corpse within the cramped control

booth, that wraith of irradiated loathing, and as you were frozen by
that gaze she shouldered forward—moving as though throwing her
limbs; moving as though she wore her body weightily as lead, and
each joint's flexure meant heaving an enormous mass—and, keeping
her eyes on yours, she flipped a switch.

The valves groaned and popped with heat. They sounded like the
acceleration of some great engine. And Cytherea turned, and with
each limb dangling out of time with its mate, she limped away.

Within the incinerator, Ortus looked at you. In the shadows of
the incinerator, his eyes seemed very dark. There was no bloom of
necromantic power, nor move to save himself: the third saint to serve
the King Undying stared at you with something very like helplessness,
lying there with his heart exploded, a man before the flame.

You thought that you might gather up his ashes in a box and keep
them. You imagined what kind of construct might be made from the
bricks and mortar of the bones of a sacred Hand, a man who in an act
of sacred transgression had used another human soul to fire the ravenous battery of his heart. You thought about sleeping for six whole
hours a night, in a bed alone. You thought about proving your sanity:
to Ianthe, to Mercy, to God. You prepared to follow Cytherea—to
run on bare feet back up those stairs, into the filtration rooms, and
to head off that loping, shambling cadaver at the pass. You imagined
the answer to that mystery.

And then you iced your hands over with thick wads of cartilage,
slid them into the handle of the door, and pulled with all your might.
It did not respond. Living bone burst from your fingertips in grossly
exaggerated distal tips, and you snapped them off at their bleeding
edge. The pain distracted you, and you screamed aloud, to focus.
This bone you unfolded into a seething web of phalanges and nug-
gety clumps of palm bones, pressed into the door; then *those* distal
tips you turned into fluid, and this fluid you turned into liquid ash
a micrometre thick, a very—weeny—construct. You syruped this
broth through the microscopic crack in the door's seam. The incinerator's mechanism ignited somewhere in the vents above you with

a thump—the Saint of Duty followed the flow of a nozzle spraying transparent liquid before his feet—and you wrenched the door from its hinges; you tossed it down the breadth of the room, in a mad, idiot, beautiful rush, and you walked straight into the petals of a chemical fire. An alarm shrieked overhead as though it too were roasting to death.

In the second that you saw the ruddy white surge of flame, you did not know it was hot enough to melt steel. You only saw the steps of what you had to do. One of the arms with the liquid-ash fingertips had resolved into two skeletons behind you, their outside layers wet with regenerating ash. You rocketed them forward to drag Ortus by the legs. You exploded their spines into a solid wall of regrowing bone, into a rushing avalanche of reeking, liquid, perpetual marrow, plunging it into that fire as a thousand-layered barrier, the fire versus the bone, unfolding and unfolding and unfolding as the flames burned and burned and burned. You stripped the fucking enamel from your own teeth and added that to the squelching, scorching layer. It was the first time, as a Lyctor, exploding such tonnage of bone into an incinerator's flame, that you looked upon the limit of your power: and that limit still stretched so far out into the goddamn distance that it was out of your sight.

The incinerator buckled. The alarm screamed. You grabbed Ortus and pulled him down the side of the room as a mass of hot melted bone sludged from the door. You dragged him away from that singeing, choking, killing mass, and you laid him against the bulkhead.

He was almost totally incapacitated. His eyes were closed. You moved his hands away and looked more closely at that shattered heart; the wounds were closing, but slowly, far more slowly than you would have expected. His cyanosed lips bespoke terrible effort as his heart knit back together. He was a myriad-old Lyctor. You did not understand.

The Saint of Duty said, with a kind of hoarse solemnity: "Fresh blood wards. Every night."

You said, too surprised not to sound like a moron: "What?"

He said, "Can't bleed thalergy . . . not fresh thalergy. Thanergy, easy. Mixed with thalergy . . . much harder. No bone wards. Blood wards. Understand? Fresh blood wards. Each night. Can't break those."

This was all said in staccato, at the apex of each wheezing breath. The incinerator continued to spew out a white-hot lahar of semi-liquid bone, and it smelled ferocious. The Saint of Duty did not open his eyes. He just concluded doggedly: "You'll be safe from us."

There were smarter questions to be asked in response. The one that came to you first—and in your defence it was not a bad one—was: "*Why?*"

He did not answer. He buckled as he turned his head and coughed, more wetly. Then he reached out, and he put his bloody hand to your head, nearly covering your face, the tips of his fingers to your temples and your cheeks, like a smothering, or a benediction.

"I know you're there," he rasped. "Kill me all you like. I would know you in the blindness of my eyes . . . in the deafness of my ears . . . as a shadow smudged against the wall, annihilated by light . . . stop. Not here. Not now. Let it go, love. I just want the truth . . . after all this time."

Ortus dropped his hand and said, with intent: "Just tell me—back then—why you brought along the ba—"

A voice down at the other end of the room bellowed: "*Harrow!*"

It was God, at the stairs. Mercymorn, dishevelled, was beside him. A few steps behind was Augustine, even more dishevelled, with lipstick on his collar. Ortus did not continue. You stood, the air sizzling the ends of your hair, slapping your face. The Emperor stood on the bloodied steps opposite you, amid the wail of the alarm. The incinerator wheezed dolefully—someone was moving in the little plex office—and then clanked off. With a sudden white shock to the sinuses the bone gunge melted to fine powder, and then, as you looked, dwindled to invisible soft dust.

You said insistently, "Why I brought along *what*? What do you *mean*?" but Ortus had opened his eyes now, with all their bizarre green sweetness, and he was staring up through you and up through the ceiling as though he could see through the very hull of the Mithraeum; and he looked up, and beyond you, and he said no more.

* * *

How much God believed your side of events—how much you believed, in relating the story, hot with adrenaline and regret and the helpless self-doubting rage of the psychotic who knew what she saw and was still able to dismiss it—was not clear. He was very weary. The buttons of his shirt had been done up with the wrong buttons in the wrong holes. You were acutely aware of his displeasure, but did not entirely understand it.

As God, Mercymorn, and Augustine looked over the incinerator, they left you alone, sitting in the filtration room with Ortus. You did not often trust instinct, but you were not afraid of him then, seeing him sit on an upturned box the same way you were sitting, wiry, and empty-faced, and defeated. You were just angry.

"You saw what you saw," you said. "You must have seen her stab you. The blow was from the front, with your own spear."

Ortus said, "I don't know."

"You were conscious. You spoke to me."

He said, "I don't know."

"We had a conversation. I want to know what it meant."

He said, "I don't remember."

You looked into his clear green eyes; his expression had not changed, and neither had his voice. You could not keep the disbelieving contempt from yours when you said, "You don't *remember*?"

The Saint of Duty turned his body toward you. He was clutching his rapier; but it was idle, in the crook of his elbow, in more the manner of an abandoned broom than of a weapon ready for war. His eyebrows were very slightly drawn together, a sort of exhausted crinkle. He looked at you, and he said in a voice you had known since you were eight years old: "I sometimes—forget."

It was the tone—clinical, enamelled, half-defensive, half-endangered—the tone of someone admitting a final frailty. It was familiar because you had used it yourself. *Understand I am insane.*

Later on, when the Mithraeum was searched, Cytherea's body was no longer on its altar; and God said he could not detect it anywhere on the station at all.

* * *

When you were back in your rooms—your now-familiar, almost-welcome, neat and empty rooms—you opened a vein and set about replacing all your bone wards with blood. It took you hours. You did not fully ward the plex outside, which would have needed complex and careful remote construct work, but you placed an extra skein of wards around the interior windows, and hoped the quick fix would do for one quiet night. You were standing in your little foyer blowing a fine grit of bone dust over a wet blood ward when you heard footsteps outside your rooms.

You stood very still, and you listened.

"I hope you're happy."

"Not a bit."

"What a *farce* . . . what a grotesque, awful, miserable *farce.*"

"Well, for goodness' sake, how was I to know they'd trip the incineration alarm? God, it's always the one you don't turn off."

"As though I meant that."

"If you mean the other—you were in serious danger of overegging the pudding. Nobody would ever believe you would get *that* drunk accidentally."

"Piss off," came the response. "I nearly slapped you. Don't you *dare* use her as a lever, ever again. Bringing her into it . . . and your nincompoop brother with her . . . almost isn't worth the payment."

"She should be so lucky as to be any kind of use, as she wasn't any in life. Damned proud of my straight face. *Oh, Cristabel, all is forgiven!* Good night, Mercy; my lips are sealed, but if you're going to make deals with the devil, do ask to see the goods beforehand. I hope you choke before I regret it, and I hope you know that one day I'll wrench Cristabel's rotten ghost from your corpse, and *eat* her . . . Where *did* you stash Cytherea?"

More footsteps. A voice rose: "I told you once and I'll tell you again:

I haven't *touched* her, you vile, condescending son of a bitch . . ." And then—nothing. You ducked back into your room.

At last you were able to wrench off the scarf that posed as a dress, and button yourself into a nightgown of your own, and you were able to brush your hair, and scrape off your paint, and wash off the blood from where Ianthe kissed you, and you were able to lie in the silence of the night with your sword beside you and the evening behind you.

Next to you, the Body said quietly, "The water is risen. So is the sun. We will endure."

ACT FOUR

VIII

32

TWO MONTHS BEFORE THE EMPEROR'S MURDER

THE FOURTEENTH PLANET YOU were sent to kill was the thriving, thalergenic satellite of a hot little star. It was lush and terrestrial, with a thick carpet of vegetation and plenty of animal life, and nobody particularly wanted to be responsible for taking it out. Unfortunately, it was right in the current path of Number Seven; and Number Seven, as Teacher put it, would view such a planet like a hot pie. You were the youngest. It was left to you, and to Mercymorn.

Cytherea's body had never been found. An attempt was made, in those first few days, to search for it, but it seemed that the only one still anxious about it was the Emperor. You knew that Augustine suspected Mercymorn, though you did not know why; Ianthe suspected Ortus of squirrelling her away, no matter your doubts. ("You know," she persisted in saying, "for . . . *sex reasons.*")

She had not blamed you for failing to murder him. Surprisingly, nor did the Saint of Patience, who had allusively apologised for his failure to account for the incinerator alarms. You had not seen any great changes between him and Mercy—except that they were fractionally more short-tempered with each other—or between him and God or her and God. There was no embarrassment, nor any pause when they met at breakfast, or in the corridor, and clasped arms with the same warmth or lack thereof that they had always shown. The total absence of appropriate shame made you suspect that this had happened between them before, a thought that made you want to give yourself a lobotomy.

And, despite the overwhelming disappointment of God, the Saint of Duty had tried to kill you twice since then. But even he seemed to be weary of it. And your wards had held.

At the start of your latest excursion your teacher surprised you: when you landed on the planet's surface and confirmed that the atmosphere was breathable ("Keep an eye on what you're breathing in anyway," said the Saint of Joy. "Planets are dirty."), she had given you a pack, and a water canister and a beeper, and told you to go away. There had been no room to land the shuttle at the planet's lush and forested pole, and so you were faced with a short hike.

"You can do it by yourself," said Mercymorn. She was snappish and fretful, but Mercymorn was always snappish and fretful. She had not become any less snappish and fretful in the last handful of weeks: simply abstracted, as though her eyes already looked to the River. "I'm going to go do the moonlet next door. It'll be covered in reflected thalergy. Time yourself—don't let it get away—most of the life on this thing is in the ocean, but if I've made a mistake, don't get eaten by some sort of *creature* while you're under."

You said, "Sister, how am I meant to protect myself when I go under?"

"I'm not the genius two-year-old, am I," she barked. There were red rings about those hurricane eyes, and she kept wringing her hands together and looking down through her lashes when she spoke. "I'll be back in about six hours. Goodbye!"

It was the first time you had been left alone on a foreign planet. The earth beneath your feet reeked of moisture, and little worms and beetles moved within it. The foliage was a violent effusion of greens— fresh, lemony greens, and dull dark piney greens, and in-the-middle dun greens, and a rustling, bristling canopy of leaves. The air was hot and wet, like the inside of a mouth. The sun beat down on your head in gouts of ultraviolet radiation—your eyes squinted against the light—and the sweat made your hair start to curl thickly about your neck. It very badly wanted cutting now.

Two days ago God had taken you into his little sitting room and given you a glass of water, which showed that he had learned, and a biscuit, which showed that he lived in optimism. And the Emperor of the Nine Houses had said, "Harrowhark, when the door comes down behind me, I want you in that room."

You had said, "No."

"Harrow, there has been no progress. That's fine. I understand. But I want to give you more time . . . I want you to have a future."

You had said, "Augustine the First has trained me in the River. My necromancy there is nonpareil, and has been since the first. When the Beast comes, I will be ready to meet it, on its turf."

God had looked at you, and he had quirked his mouth in something like a smile, and said: "You're even stubborner than I am. I thought I'd cornered the market."

There were many days when you felt his disappointment as a vise, as a long-imagined hessian pressure against the bones of your throat. There were equally as many days when his nightmare eyes relieved your dry exhaustion like a long, chilly drink of water. Your love for God was akin to your love of the beautiful riverbed edge of the iliac crest. Your love for God was like those moments of reprieve, immediately after waking, when you were not sure who you were; those moments of living in another Harrow's skin, a Harrow who understood everything with a purity of completeness. It was a relief, to worship thus. You had once thought your capability for adoration had been consumed when your eyes had bent upon that face in the Tomb, dead and irresistible, the interment of beauty. You were relieved to find some scraps left over.

You raised the hood of your mother-of-pearl Canaanite robe over your head. The sunshine beat down through it and pattered prismatic light over your face. Birds shrieked above. They were not large creatures, and you were not afraid of them, but you almost pitied them. It was an uncomfortable thing, to remove the soul of a planet like this: it would be the first time you had done it, and the first time you had killed any planet alone. The creatures would not die immediately when the planet did. But they would—slowly—come to change, and in the end they would be thanergy mutants who could not reproduce. A rather Ninth House death, and the death that came for all flipped planets, in the end.

The forest floor was gnarled and uneven—for the first hour you walked stoically, and you sipped your water. When you grew tired, you spent the second hour in the arms of a large, hulking, ambling skeleton, and you had to brush away the branches and leaves as a second skeleton stormed ahead, cutting down all this boil of thalergy as it went. It was with an ache like nostalgia that you thought of Drearburh, and home: that you thought of the vast gyre at the very apex of your temple, which seemed like a pinprick from the bottom tier, that thin, watery cloud of pumped atmosphere and the dead of space beyond. You thought of the murmurous prayers within the chapel. You thought of the Secundarius Bell, its booming profundity, its black tongue's clangour, of waking to the *CLANG . . . CLANG . . . CLANG . . . .* as some ancient bellringer hyperextended his biceps in trembling, sacred eagerness to yank that rope.

The Body walked beside your construct. The sun did not dry the melted ice upon that indistinctly coloured hair. The moist warmth of the jungle around you did not impede her, and exertion brought no flush to those long, thinly muscled arms, nor to the slender, gracile legs, nor to the dead cheeks. She had been with you very often, of late.

You saw all the signs of your undoing. You had few months to live. It could be quite easily counted in weeks now. God had been correct: you had not changed—you were not fixed. You were the last, lone, assailable Lyctor. The others were now distant from you, looking to the Resurrection Beast that came to punish their mortal sins and kill their Kindly Prince.

And yet—there, in the alien slather of forest, among the ferns, and fronds, and greenery arching against a skyline that was a more reticent verdancy paling into navy blue—you could almost believe that you had the capacity to be happy again. You were an unfilled hole, but even a hole might be content in its emptiness.

At that point, though you did not know it, you were a mere kilometre from this insubstantial contentment's obliteration. A hole might also be filled with worms.

VI

INTO THE FOURTH HOUR, you realized you were being followed. A very dim awareness of some large presence pierced the curtain of so much other thalergy, and you were instantly irritable—Mercymorn had failed to gauge the planet's character. It was plain there *were* large mammals in this region, and you'd have to come up with some way to carefully plant yourself so you wouldn't get chewed on while you severed the planet's soul. Your annoyance turned to suspicion when it became clear that the thalergy signature was following *you*—it was keeping careful pace about a hundred metres behind you, stalking your path. This was not hard. Your skeletons trod heavily. You were leaving a trail that a blind idiot might've followed, in the middle of a dark and moonless night; you went back to being irritated, this time at your own foolishness, and you stopped.

You waited in a clearing for your predator. You caulked a space over that rich red earth with bone, so that you could stand on a little platform of it with the tip of your sword touching that mat and not worry that some annelid was about to squirm over your feet. You checked yourself over to make sure that no airborne foreign body was making inroads on your immune system. You pulled your hood deep over your head, and you waited.

The thalergy made its approach. You realised with a deep and slithering horror that it belonged to a person.

And then a woman was standing at the edge of the clearing. She wore a peaked cap to keep the sun off her dark-eyed, scissor-slash face; a woman in a grey robe with the ends tied in a fat knot about her middle to keep them from dragging in the dirt. There was a rough canvas bag around her neck, an arresting, festering mass of thanergy amid all that clear and comprehensible life. She had two shabby scabbards peeking up over her shoulders, and chin-length, slate-brown hair tucked behind her ears, the colour of ancient tiles in an abandoned temple.

Your voice did not feel like it belonged to you when you said, "I saw your corpse."

"Well," said Camilla Hect steadily, "don't tell everyone, or they'll want to see it too."

From the distance between you, you considered her; you also considered a body with a ruin for a face, lying on a long length of plastic sheeting. The sobbing, shrieking birdcall around you resolved into an indistinct burble, and you raised your hand to your right ear, and your fingers came away thick with blood so dark that it was almost purple. She took a step toward you; you retreated one, equalizing the distance, and she did not close the approach. You looked at the cavalier of the Sixth, and you bled.

A file opened in your mind. Your hands scrabbled within your robes—the exoskeleton gave up one of the twenty-two letters, with a reminder long memorised:

If met, to give to Camilla Hect.

This had not troubled you. Many of the letters required impossible contingencies. Now one impossible contingency was standing before you. You gave the envelope to your hulking skeleton, and it crossed the clearing, admirably navigating the lumpen forest floor, to deliver the letter to the previously dead Hect.

She took it, broke open the envelope, read the contents, and blinked; all while you siphoned blood out of your ears. She looked at the letter; she looked at you; she looked at the letter. Then she balled it up between her fists and ripped it to shreds.

"Okay," she said finally. And: "It's coming out your nose."

You wiped your face, quashed your growing annoyance, and said, "Am I required to know the contents?"

Hect cleared her throat—you flinched—and recited perfectly: "*For service previously rendered by your House: invoke the rock that remains ever unrolled, and understand that I will both consider your life as inviolate, and aid you if I can. Thanks."*

You said, appalled, "I did *not*."

"It was there in black and white, Reverend Daughter."

Reverend Daughter was still a little sweet to your bloodied ears; but you said, and knew you sounded irascible: "Then I have been seriously promiscuous with my past favours."

"I suppose you thought you owed us," said Camilla.

It had been a long time since you had been around those who were not Lyctors. You grasped for her, thoughtlessly, with your construct; you were astonished by the speed with which Hect drew those big, balanced knives from each shoulder, and hurled herself at your skeleton like a stone from a sling. Her first sweep with the butt of a knife shattered the ribcage—it coalesced back; you now disdained skeletons not made of permanent ash. She swept in with a foot, aimed at the fragile place beneath the knee, and sent your construct stumbling forward. You said, "Cease," but she levered one knife into the base of the spine, severed it, pulled the spine back toward her with a *twang*—and you heard your voice rise to say: "I need to know you are *real*!"

She kicked the skeleton away from her; it was in two surprised parts, wriggling to fuse back together, slow to understand the damage. Camilla Hect sheathed her knives with as much speed and fury as she had unsheathed them, and she said: "No sudden moves."

"I am Harrowhark Nonagesimus," you said. "I am the ninth saint to serve the King Undying. I am his fingerbone; I am his fists and gestures . . . I am a *Lyctor*, Hect. What hope would you have against me?"

"None," said Camilla.

And then she added calmly: "Yet."

You were silent. Your head throbbed. The birds were very loud and shrill, and a multitude of smells drifted from the forest—of damp air, of damp earth, of all the things that crept upon it, with their insensible quantities of legs and little frondy parts. You sat down on your bone-plated log, and you wiped your face, and you said: "I watched your body be laid out. I examined it myself. And now you are here, forty billion lightyears from the Nine Houses, and you tell me that you are real."

"If you're going to sit around feeling sorry for yourself, you've changed," she said. And then: "I'm going to come closer. All right?"

You watched with cold apprehension as this resurrection approached. She was not puppeted as your mother and father had been; nor was she a Seventh-style simulacrum. Her thalergy lit up with the pure combustive light of a strong, healthy human being, and the minute deaths throughout her body—bacterial, apoptotic, autophagic—produced a thanergetic embroidery you could see as easily as her breath heaving within her chest. You startled badly when she dropped to her haunches before you and looked you over coolly; looked into your left ear, then your right, peered into your eyes, glanced up your nose.

"Nice intercranial haemorrhage," she said. "Kills most of us non-Lyctors."

You said, "Why are you *here*? Why are you here *now*? How are you here? This planet orbits the sanctuary of the Emperor, Hect, reachable only by necromantic means, and you are dead."

"I'm really not," she said. And, after a pause, in her dry abrupt voice: "I came to find you, Reverend Daughter."

"You have found me. Tell me for what purpose."

Camilla took the bag from around her neck. She held it between her hands, and you could see her hesitate; she did not appear to be the hesitating type. Her thumb gently stroked the leather thong closing the drawstring neck—rested there lightly—and then she offered it to you. She silently proffered this shabby little bag, about as big as your two hands cupped together, as if it were a casket filled with jewels. You knew before you touched it what was within. What you did not understand was why.

You opened the bag and removed its contents before her dark and stony gaze. It was not particularly full. You cupped the thing between your palms, and marvelled.

It was a cracked piece of human skull—a ridge of supraorbital bone and a cut-off curve of parietal, a bulge of zygomatic cheekbone, a shard leading down to the maxilla. That was all. As a skull, it was not particularly interesting—male, early twenties, maybe eight months dead—but as a reconstruction, it was incredible. The piece had been assembled from fragments, manually, and not by a bone magician. The smallest would have been no bigger than the moon of your cuticle. It had been painstakingly—passionately—laboriously reassembled, from the skull of someone who, soon after death or symptomatically during, had exploded. There were miniature cracks where it had been glued. You turned it over and over in your hands.

"Eyes," said Camilla.

A thin stream of blood was emerging from your right lacrimal duct. You wiped it away. Your headache was quite bad now.

You said, "Your necromancer."

She said, after a moment's pause, "Yes."

This was also impossible, as the last time you had seen the skull of Palamedes Sextus, it had been speckled with firearm propellant from the bullet that had shattered his face—inward. You wiped your left tear duct before the stone-faced cavalier could say a word.

You asked, "What do you want from me?"

Camilla stood up.

"The Warden's still in there," she said.

You waited, with that work of astonishing labour between your hands. After a moment she said, "He's attached. To the skull. I want you to confirm. That's all."

That's all. You beheld the skull again. The six-month-old bone was yet lively with thanergy. All scraps of flesh had been carefully removed; there were no hunks of hair on that pulverized skull, nor fragments of dried brain matter within the parietal bone. You tried to recall Palamedes Sextus, and your ears renewed their liquid assault. When you hastily scanned your brain for the source, you found nothing particularly wrong, and it made you bleed more. You shook blood out of your right ear, and said: "Elaborate."

"Thanks for not smiling. He's in there," she repeated, a little doggedly, but with that same dry calm. "He's a revenant."

You had been too honestly astonished to do anything so coarse as smile, or laugh, or say, *You have got to be kidding me, that is a good one.* "No, he's not," you said. "A ghost attached to an immobile object—a ghost attached to an immobile object for this length of time—it would have lost coherency and drifted away long ago. He could not walk. He could not speak. He could not perceive. A ghost does not cling passionately for months to a few fragments of skull."

"He would," she said.

"I'm certain he had a—forceful personality, but—"

"No, I mean he deliberately fixed his soul to his body, with spirit magic," said the cavalier. "We planned for it. In the event of his death. I know he did it, because I got the message. I only want to make sure I snagged the right part of the skull. We didn't account for—pieces. If he's not in here I have to go find the others."

You looked up into her face. Camilla Hect was a closed object, with locks and snaps; she had an expression like the rock before the Tomb, inexorable, giving nothing away. But her eyes—her eyes were dark as the grit mixed with the soil, neither grey nor brown but both. They were the eyes of a winter season without any promise of spring. In comparing the eyes to the face, you saw into a zipped-up agony.

And she said, with that same dull, blank, diamond-hard pain: "The Cohort took the rest of him away. And I don't know where they have put him."

It was not pity that moved your hand. It was open curiosity about the kind of man who would have sealed his soul to his fragmented corpse before he died. You tucked your knees up and you put the parietal bone lightly beneath the print of your index finger: you scoured every cell of that bone for some remnant soul.

And you could find nothing.

It was not the first time you regretted your unfamiliarity with spirit magic. You had flayed yourself in writing with the accusation: *Your understanding of flesh and spirit magic is execrable.* Now your regrets reached their pinnacle: you were not even sure that your inability to find a dead boy was due to the dead boy's absence, or due to your lack of study.

You said, "If his ghost in any way travelled to the River, it would have driven him mad. If he released his hold for even a moment, or if he was unable to bear the prison of his bones . . ." Camilla just looked at you. You relented: "One moment."

The ninety-six puzzle pieces this cavalier called a skull did not warrant what you were about to do. Your construct skeleton you compacted neatly back to a chip of bone, and your exoskeleton you made inert. If you left them, they would crumble to pieces, and it was better not to give her any indication of your vulnerability while you were under. You moved to sit on the grass. It crushed beneath you, and the smell made you anxious. You deliberately did not think about all the insect life squirming and seething beneath the seat of your robes. You planted your feet flat on the ground and made your spine a soft curve. The ghost wards were already painted on your belly and the back of your neck, though they were superstition only, placed for the unseen emergency where you were forced to physically move your body through the River. A mind without its meat would not attract a ravenous ghost. There would be a thronging populace here, all uninterested in you if you were not attached to your bright, delicious flesh, and anyway you only intended to take the briefest look. You took the weighty sword from your back and placed it beneath your feet, and then you took the partial skull from your lap, and you waded into the River.

You had intended to use the skull to triangulate its owner. It would be otherwise impossible to pick out one ghost between the billions upon billions—innumerable spirits, a nearly infinite mass—making their way through the dark waters.

Time and space works differently in the River no matter how you enter, my chicks, Augustine had warned. *Anchor yourself as you're leaving the old meat robes behind, and as you wade through the waters. Attach to worldly geography; be aware of your body; let it be your harbour, unless you're dying to be pulled somewhere you don't want to go.*

You used the skull as your geography instead. The water was very cold when it closed over your head. It felt thick and slippery as oil. Augustine had ducked you and Ianthe in the River, to train you for this—to get you used to a River teeming with the mad, the insane, and the ravenous—and you knew what to expect. You would be in filthy water, with the teeth, and the rotten flesh, and the bloody, unseeing eyes. You might, if you were lucky, look down upon the mad ghost of the skull. You could discharge your duty by confirming that he had long ago drifted away, and that Hect might drift away from the buttoned-up primal grief a ghost story had frozen in place. You prepared for the ice, and the initial panic of ghosts exploding outward from your body, that safe predatory entry of your brain—the cloudy water, foggy with old blood—

—and you were standing in a room. Your wet robes were dripping onto a scrubbed wooden floor.

The room was penitent-sized, big enough for a bed and a table. Less penitential, the bed was strewn with pillows and cushions and comforters; the table was similarly scattered with preparations, little paper packets, and a stained enamel bowl. An old chair was pushed close to the bed, its back re-stapled to its frame and some of the stuffing coming out in square, foaming chunks of yellow. Above the bed, a dirty little window that had resisted someone's attempts to clean it looked down upon a dying courtyard where a thick array of salt-choked vines were the only greenish things among an array of spindly leafless trees. A shelf held a few desiccated books, one standing out like a fleshy corpse among skeletons. Your eyes fell upon the title: *The Necromancer's Marriage Season.*

"It's a historical," said a voice behind you. "Abella Trine, inevitably of Ida, is considered a poor prospect on the marriage market because she's too skinny, her tract-specialist flesh magic is *too* good, and she wears her thick chestnut hair in an unflattering bun, which is mentioned at least twice a chapter."

You turned around.

A man stood in the doorway to the tiny room. He was taller than you. His dull robes lapped around a body of starvation thinness. He was toying with a pair of glasses, and he stared at you with naked eyes of exquisite, pellucid grey: the softness of charcoal burnt nearly white, with the glass clarity of quartz.

He continued, "There're a few suitors vying for her affections, though Abella's such a pain in the arse I've got no idea why. There's a spoiled swordswoman I'm quite fond of, but the narrative doesn't like her because she goes to sexy parties every night, which I'd regard as a blameless enough hobby—and then Abella meets an insanely tedious widower from the outskirts of Tisis, whose saintly husband ate a grenade in the war. After two massive misunderstandings, they hook up, and then there's a time skip to their adorable baby, who talks with a phonetically impossible lisp and can already form a kidney. The whole is unspeakably sordid." He slid the glasses back on to that beaky nose. "Long time no see, Reverend Daughter."

Then he did a very terrible thing. He stepped forward, and he pulled you into a wild embrace—the hold of a man drowning in deep water who cannot help but drag his rescuer down to the bottom with him. He dug his fingers into you in a way you were a little familiar with: tight against the chance that the person in front of you might be a cloud, or a mirage. He lifted you off the ground in his impatient, overfamiliar eagerness, and then he set you down again and saw your face.

"*Excuse* me," you said, with sodden asperity.

"Oh. Apologies," said Palamedes Sextus. "Misread the moment. Let's call it cabin fever. Nonagesimus, is Camilla—"

"She sent me," you said, wringing out your wet hem. "She is alive and well and living."

He whistled a sigh.

"Oh, thank God," he said a little unsteadily. "Thank God for that mad, stubborn, lovely girl. Speaking of. Harrowhark, you are a sight for sore eyes."

You frantically clapped your hands to your exoskeleton, but knew as your fingers touched the representation of bone that it was no good. There were no letters there; they could not transfer when you did not know their contents—and there had never, in any case, been a letter addressed to Sextus. The previous Harrow had never bothered to think of it. You knew full well she had seen Hect and Sextus dead; why account for one's reappearance, but not the other's? This was a mystery you had no answer for; you were utterly on your own, in this nonsensical miracle of a room.

You said instead, "A *projection.* A projection in the *River*?"

"I'd call it *on the bank,* though that's not accurate either," he said promptly. "I couldn't anchor myself to my body properly when I was about to render myself down to my component parts. So I established a kind of bubble attached to the Riverbank and anchored it to myself at the cellular level—not one thick rope, but lots of tiny little strings. Like a spiderweb, I suppose. As long as anyone could find any bit of me, be it never so small and soggy, there'd be a couple of strands still clinging to it, and me on the other end. Or that was the hope. Couldn't test it, of course."

You said: "I have been inside the River, Sextus, multiple times, both in spirit and in flesh. You cannot build a *bubble* there."

"Okay, wrong word, perhaps, but—"

"You cannot *build* in the River! It is a dimension of perpetual flux—defined space is nonsense here—you might as well try to wall off time with bricks and mortar."

"Yes. Sort of. But by our very presence in the River, we briefly exert space on non-space. Think of how, when you blow air into water, you make bubbles. The water can't be where the air is. It's like the air temporarily enforces its own rules over a localised area. If you were *in* one of those bubbles, you could do things under air-rules—like talking, or lighting a fire—that water doesn't permit. Like water rejecting air, the River instinctively rejects what lies outside it—it doesn't want any *here* in its *hereafter.* So you can impose your own rules on it, to a very limited extent . . . I could write at least six very good papers about this, Harrow. There's so much work to be done."

You quickly scanned the room again and were struck by its nagging familiarity. You should have known it. You did know it. "This is Canaan House," you said.

"Moment of death," he agreed. "I said the rules were limited. I can hang on to my sense of self in here, but not my necromancy. I can't *do* anything. All I have is a single still image of the room, and for some reason a single romance novel, which I have read upward of fifty times. Thank God I had a pencil in my pocket; I'm in the process of crafting the sequel on a section of wallpaper."

"How much were you able to retain?"

"Look out in the hallway," he suggested.

Cautiously, you stepped out of the doorway. What you had taken for an exit consisted of no more than the view from the door, with some leeway for peripheral vision. It extended maybe a foot in either direction, and then gave way to an enormous white blank: when you walked toward it and pushed ("Steady," Palamedes warned), the white was solid, though with a vague sticky jellified quality to it. It was an abyssal whiteness. It was an absence, resolved into touch.

When you stepped back into the room and knelt on the bed to peer out the window, it was the same. The vision was all the same dead terrace, and a sliver of ocean, and stone: craning to look either way revealed that great and terrible whiteness. The window was solid and did not open.

You said, "The barrier begins where your line of sight ended. It's derived from everything you saw."

He said, "And it doesn't change . . . the sea is still. It looks like it's moving, but it's not—it's like one of those holographic pictures where turning it up and down lets you see another part of the image. There is nothing here, and that nothing never changes."

You sat down on that overcushioned bed, and you looked up at his long, grave face; you tried to remember if you had ever seen it, before it was summarily blown off by gunshot. You really did try. When you closed your eyes, there was nothing cauterized upon your eyelids— except a little redness. You said, "A human mind cannot live this way, Sextus. Being stuck in place is any revenant's undoing, unless it has a very specific anchor. Eventually it will lose purchase—it will let go—it will return to the River. I cannot imagine the type of mind that would hold on to that edge, and keep holding."

"I can, and it scares me," he said heavily. "Look. How long have I been dead, Nonagesimus?"

"Eight months," you said, "give or take."

He took off those thick lenses and looked at you with diamond-grey horror. His face was homely; he looked somewhat like a beak, a chin, and a jaw put together as a joke—but the beauty of his eyes made the whole attractive, as though they were a mould colonizing the rest of the stratum.

He spluttered, "*Eight months?*"

"I don't have an exact record, but—"

"What? Why did it take you so long? It should have taken you a week, tops."

"Excuse my *apparently* sluggard pace," you said, feeling that this was an unjust accusation, "but your cavalier only just brought me your bones, and regarding *that* I have more than one question to ask her—"

His brows were crisscrossing like swords. "How did you and Cam get separated in the first place?"

"I was not aware I owed a debt of care to—"

"I mean *she* wouldn't have left *your* side, if you'd given her half a chance—"

You lost your patience. It was difficult to say if you'd ever had any; you'd just spackled over the hole with curiosity.

"Warden of the Sixth House," you demanded, "why are you acting as though I should know you? Why are you acting as though your cavalier knows me? I am Harrowhark the First, formerly and in everlasting affections the Reverend Daughter of Drearburh: I am the ninth saint to serve the King Undying, one among his fists and his gestures. I did not know you in this life, and I will not know you in the next one."

He stopped dead.

"*You* became a *Lyctor*," he said.

"That was always the plan."

"Not for the Harrowhark I knew. Tell me you did it correctly," he said, and there was a quick, questioning eagerness to his voice, something beneath the confusion. "Tell me you finished the work. You out of everyone could have worked out the end to the beginning I was starting to explicate. Your *cavalier*, Reverend Daughter—"

"Has become the furnace of my Lyctorhood," you said.

The dead Warden stopped. He looked at your face as though his eyes could peel through dermis, fascia, and bone. And he said, quietly: "How God takes—and takes—and takes."

There was an enormous rumble overhead. It sounded like some great mechanism grinding against itself with unlubricated joints, a turbulence of machinery sobbing to life. There came another, farther off, and a bright white light at the window that made you think of the Emperor. Thunder, and a sweep of lightning. Palamedes's lovely eyes widened, and he said, "That's not possible," and darted to the window.

You went with him. A squall of rain tossed itself at the window like a bird. Through the smeared glass—the still and static light outside was suddenly overcast—you looked down.

On the terrace stood a figure in haz orange, swathed in crinkling safety material from neck to feet. A breathing apparatus obscured the face. And in one gloved hand, clear even from this distance, you saw it: a huge two-bore gun. The figure stared with empty goggle eyes as the wind lashed, and as the thunder boomed, farther away now.

Sextus was saying, "The hell is—"

You said, and your voice sounded strange to yourself, as though you had heard the word only in dreams and never articulated by waking tongues: "The Sleeper."

The Sleeper looked at you both. There came another sudden violent burst of obscuring rain, and it was gone. You and the necromancer of the Sixth House moved as one: shouldered both of your bodies against the door to the room until it shut fast, as you slid a crude deadbolt home. You leaned your full weights against it. This was not a very impressive mass. He said, quickly: "Ninth, this place is powered by *one single* theorem, held together with the fragility of spirit magic. I cannot manipulate it. I cannot change anything about it, not the room, not the cushions, not the astonishingly shitty book. *I* can't change a thing about this space—but anyone coming *to* me could change the parameters, and you've brought something with you that's changing them. *Go.*"

Both of you froze as you heard shuffling steps outside the door, a low, asthmatic wheezing from the apparatus. Then you shoved your pathetic necro bodies more forcefully against the door. You said, "Don't be a fool."

"Go and go *now*, Nonagesimus!"

"I'm not about to leave you alone with something I have *done*, Master Warden!"

"That's more like the old Harrowhark—but I mean it, get out! I'm banking on it going with you. I'll be fine. Just tell me, what's Cam got of my bones?"

"Three inches of right-hand parietal, full right-hand frontal, leading down to—"

"That's enough. Just so I know what to focus on— Can you change that into something more useful?"

You said arctically, "I am a *Lyctor*, Palamedes Sextus."

"And I'm so sorry about it," he said. "Point taken though. Anything that articulates, okay?"

"But—"

The crash against the door rattled you all the way down to your toes. You had no magic in that River bubble; it might as well have been the vacuum of space, before you had built the furnace within yourself. Your necromancy was as still and dead as the room itself. It was surprising, how badly it frightened you. It was only you, and your mind's outline of your body, and the ghost of a dead man, and the thing that followed you inside.

The door held as both of you strained against it. The next rattle made the hinges squeal in agony. Palamedes looked at you and opened his mouth to say something as a third rattle flung you both back a little; your heads knocked together, and then you heard the deliberate steel rasp of a trigger being cocked.

Sextus was rubbing his temple and looking at you, awestruck, as though he had seen some stupefying glimpse of the beyond; you did not remotely understand the sharp smile that suddenly crossed his face.

"Kill us twice, shame on God," he said, and he leaned forward, and much to your intense distress he swiftly kissed your brow. Then he said: "Harrowhark, for pity's sake, *go!*"

You dropped back under, and you did not hear the gunshot; you were, not for the first time, overwhelmed with the suspicion that you were standing in the middle of what you had thought to be scenery, only to reach out and discover that it was all so much flimsy. You were not a central lever within a mystery, but a bystander watching a charlatan display a trick. Your eyes had followed a bright light or colour, and you realised with a start that you ought to have been watching the other hand. You were standing in a darkened corridor, and you could not turn around: and then a brief explosion of light revealed to you that it wasn't a corridor at all, and it had never been dark.

But you were always too quick to mourn your own ignorance. You never could have guessed that he had seen me.

34

WHEN YOU SAT UP, struggling for breaths you did not need to take—wet only with the sweat trickling under the dormant bones of your exoskeleton—you saw not the canopy of trees overhead, but a filmy white length of sheeting. You had been moved. You were lying down flat, not bent in the curved posture that you had been taught to adopt, and your sword was tucked beneath your arm, and you had been upended onto a thin blanket that nonetheless let you feel each blade of grass and uneven mound of turf beneath, and feel the beating sun overhead and hear the shrill host of outside creatures.

Camilla Hect sat beside you, and she did not flinch when you sat up all at once. You were in a larger clearing, with a huge mess of crushed boughs beside you, some of which had been pressed into service to hold up the tent you lay beneath; beyond the tent curved the great metal belly of a shuttle.

Your mind idiotically focused upon its bizarre shape and style: it was not a Cohort shuttle, nor any kind of shuttle of the Nine Houses, and not only because it had not been adorned with even a single bone. It was made of very shiny silver steel, and its heat treatment made it sizzle, with a sort of wobbling radiance sitting just above the hull. It was also thoroughly battered and singed: you would not have flown it ten feet above the ground, let alone into atmosphere or the black depths of space. It was small, no more than three bodies wide and three bodies tall, and the thought of being forced inside curdled you. But your distaste and paranoia were stopped in midswing by Camilla saying with barely repressed intensity: "So?"

You said, "He's in there."

The cavalier of the Sixth House looked at you; then she collapsed back in a long, controlled movement. She lay flat on her back staring sightlessly at the sky, half-shadowed by the sheeting, half-glowing in the light. At last she gave a long, shuddering breath and sat back up with the same abruptness.

"Good," she said, and she smiled, very briefly. This smile lit the corners of her face like a rising comet. It made her look, in fact, ridiculously like her adept. "What now?"

You held the carefully assembled fragments of skull between your hands, and hoped that *he is* had not become *he was.* Then you crushed the bone between your fingers—the cavalier next to you reached out reflexively, then stopped herself—and you kneaded the fragments within your palms until you could winnow out the glue, which, thank God, had been chemical in nature. It might have very easily been derived from keratin, which would have been a momentary confusion and annoyance. The glue was expunged as a knotty collection of gummy nodules, which you discarded, and left you with a thanergy-rich clay. You considered this malleable stuff for a moment before knitting it between your hands.

Phalanges spurted from the mass; then a distal row, then a proximal row of carpal bones and a length of articulated wrist. It was not the sheer animal pleasure of Ianthe's arm, but it was easy and it was satisfying. You said, "I could simply give you a full skeleton frame."

"Don't," said Camilla quickly, and paused, and said: "That's going to get me in trouble."

"The Warden specifically requested movement."

"I don't mean him," said his cavalier.

You tossed her the hand bones and she caught them on reflex. You grasped your sword and stood, and, before she could prevent you, you walked around the side of the bizarre shuttle. There was some manner of open cargo-delivery hatch, or means of entrance, with the door hoisted up on a jack so that fresh air could circulate within the shuttle. You stood in the blinking sunlight before this open door, on the flattened grass, and you looked inside. The three inhabitants stared back at you.

The first was Captain Deuteros, a woman whose stretched-out corpse you had last seen riddled with bullets. She was sitting, not in her Cohort whites, but in a drab long-sleeved shirt of indeterminate colour, and dark trousers. She looked like a shell of the crisp adept you had seen back at Canaan House, and less robust even than her corpse. She had lost significant weight from her already fragile necromancer's build, her cheeks were dark hollows, and she clasped two crutches in her lap.

Another woman sat close beside her, wearing her own shabby shirt of indeterminate colour, but as though it had been designed for her royal use: a woman you had last seen calmly falling to her death. Ianthe Tridentarius's features stared out of Coronabeth's face—an aurora of a face, with deep lustrous skin and burnished hair, and eyes of genuine violet, like plums. Both women were seated in the back of the poorly furnished shuttle, amid crude engines set in oil-reeking array beneath a thin metal grille, and a mess of boxes piled in every corner. Yet the Crown Princess of Ida, missing and presumed dead, filled up that space like a mass of flowers on a midden. She was in as blooming good health as could be, as vigorous as Deuteros was frail.

The third staring inhabitant was not a person. It was an enormous flimsy poster in a chipped frame, the only sign of decoration in that untidy little shuttle. A head-and-shoulders photograph of an unsmiling, adamant person, in all assumption a woman, stared fixedly at you as though calculating how much effort it would take to snap your neck. She was dressed in black to the chin, and her red hair curled thickly about her neck and shoulders. Thick, itchy streams of blood began to ooze down your sinuses.

That portrait frightened you more than anything you had seen since becoming a Lyctor; it scared the irresolute piss from your body. Yet you had never seen the face before in your life.

The Second House captain said, somewhat hoarsely: "Ninth?"

You wiped your face before your hands flew to your exoskeleton again. It disgorged one of the twenty-two with ease, and you pulled open the letter marked: *To open if you meet Judith Deuteros.*

You translated without conscious thought:

ADDRESSING THE LADY HARROWHARK NONAGESIMUS,
KNOWN AS THE REVEREND DAUGHTER BY HER OWN
DESIRE, NOW HARROWHARK THE FIRST, FROM THE
SAME, NOW DEAD.

LETTER #12 OF 24.
If you meet Judith Deuteros, silence her. Kill her if necessary.

The bones of Deuteros's jaw fused shut; you glued her bottom molars to her top molars immediately, and cleaved her tongue to her palate. She said, "Nnnngh?"

You took out a second letter to be sure, although this one was in plain script, and you had read it already:

ADDRESSING THE LADY HARROWHARK NONAGESIMUS,
KNOWN AS THE REVEREND DAUGHTER BY HER OWN
DESIRE, NOW HARROWHARK THE FIRST, FROM THE
SAME, NOW DEAD.

LETTER #5 OF 24.
Protect Coronabeth Tridentarius at all costs, even if this endan-
gers your life. The work is forfeit if you contribute to her death
by direct or indirect action. In the interests of the work, you may
silence her, so long as this causes her no significant pain.

In different handwriting:

P.S. Or any pain at all.

In yours:

P.P.S. I cannot guarantee a total absence of pain.

The first amender:

P.P.P.S. There must be a total absence of pain actually.

In yours again:

P.P.P.P.S. We have jointly agreed on "as little pain as may be achieved via the fullness of necromantic effort."

And in the first:

P.P.P.P.P.S. xoxoxoxo

Coronabeth Tridentarius had already leapt to her feet and unsheathed a rapier you knew very well, and which froze you to the core to behold. It was a Ninth House rapier. The blade was black metal, with a plain guard and a hilt of the same colour. She stood before the mute shell that now constituted Deuteros, neatly at the ready with the rapier brandished and her left arm tucked behind her back. It was so like looking at Ianthe that you were differently bewildered; but you had already done the same to her—the tongue to the roof of the mouth, the teeth to the teeth—and so all she could say was, "Nnnngh!"

You drew your two-handed sword.

"Stop it." The Sixth cavalier had joined this shitty tableau; she narrowed her eyes to slits in the sunshine. "I warned them already."

"I do this on a greater authority than your own."

"Balls," said Hect succinctly. "Let them go." Then: "Why is that sword gummed up, and who taught you to hold it like that?"

"I refuse to— What?"

"Your hands are too close together. Put your left hand at the bottom of the pommel, tuck in the arm close to the chest. Right hand high on the hilt, close to the cross guard, up a bit with your thumb—yeah—that's more like it." You did all this, and she said: "Good . . . not like you have the muscle for a rising strike. Okay. Now let Coronabeth and Judith go."

Your grip adjusted, you found it significantly less difficult to hold the sword pointed down than previously. You asked, "Why are you here? Why are you all *alive*? Why are you on the other side of the universe—in your own shuttle—innumerable years away from the Nine Houses? Why were your bodies not found at Canaan House?"

With her mouth a gruesome, stuck-together distortion, Deuteros had stood with a crutch shakily clutched beneath one arm, and was now hauling herself toward you with an uprightness of posture that belied her physical weakness. It was still the Cohort captain who silently approached, her dark eyes cold and level; you kept your bone-sheathed sword steady, though you would not in any case use it to *kill her if you have to*. The captain shouldered past an obviously reluctant Coronabeth—their eyes met, and Judith shook her head in a minute *no*—and she stopped about a step before you.

Then she grabbed a fistful of mother-of-pearl robes. You did not flinch. She said, "Nnnnngh—mmmmf—*nghaaaagh,*" as though sheer force of desperation could wrench coherent sound from a fused mouth. Camilla flew to her left side and Corona to her right, but she swung her crutch at them. Her grasp was surprisingly strong, and as she said, "*Nnnghhh!*" you unfused lips, tongue and teeth. You always were too curious for your own good.

"*Ngghyaaar*—warn him, Lyctor! He has been infiltrated, damn it, and I can do nothing! I am a prisoner of war! If you love him, tell the Emperor that the traitor has already—*Nghhhyughh—*"

This last *nghhhyugh* was nothing to do with you. Coronabeth, face set, had clasped her hand over the Second House's mouth and manhandled her backward, which was very easy for someone of the Third's stature to do to someone of the Second's. Ianthe's twin was stone-eyed, and the expression she and the captain gave each other was antagonistic, to say the least. Judith was humiliatingly bundled back within the confines of the shuttle—Coronabeth kicked a lever close to the door—the great shady overhead hatch started whining down, and you watched the darkness claim her and the furious dignity of the downed soldier beneath the cold gaze of that too-familiar portrait. Judith was signing something to you, but you could not make out Cohort signals. You'd never bothered yourself with the military.

Camilla was picking up the crutch. She said, restlessly, "Look, we should go. We weren't meant to be here."

You said, "You are a fool if you think I will let you leave like—"

"I evoke the rock that is never rolled away," she said instantly. She was a quick study. "Let us leave. Tell no one we were here. Don't ask any more questions. We're not on the same side anymore, Ninth. I owe you. I owe you everything. But—things have changed."

It was your turn for your tongue to cleave to the roof of your mouth. The once-cavalier of the Sixth House looked at you impassively, and she said: "I'm sorry, if that helps."

You said, "It doesn't."

"Fair."

"Let me ask one thing," you said. "One single question—just the one—for the sake of what I have just done for you, and for the Master Warden of the Sixth House."

Camilla looked at you distantly, and eventually said: "Ask. I'm not going to promise that I can answer."

You said, "Who took you away from Canaan House? Who are you *with*, Hect?"

"You call them Blood of Eden," she said.

* * *

That evening, Mercymorn came to fetch you from the surface of a planet you had killed, with almost no thought to its murder. Indeed, you had felt almost nothing, and you said very little, which met your teacher's needs excellently as she had nothing to say to you except, "You smell like dirt." She piloted you back to the Mithraeum in silence. You watched the retreating planet out the window, and it looked no different, except that perhaps the deep water that lined the equator in chilly juxtaposed slabs of ice seemed more cracked and turbid than previous. It was safely dead, with its cavorting animal populace unaware of their long-term death sentence. Worms crawled within the miserable, foetid pit of you.

35

"I AM SORRY, NINTH," Abigail said, in the same hesitantly kind and careful tones you might use to tell someone that their cat would never grow up into a tiger: "I'm not at all an expert in psychometry, and with such an old rapier you'd need both a Sixth House specialist and to get *awfully* lucky. It was your grandmother's nine generations back, you said? And it was handled, briefly?"

"That," came the soft, funereal voice of Harrowhark's cavalier, softer and more funereal filtered through his muffler, "was the nature of the condescension."

"And the blade has been replaced?"

"The hilt is original, barring the grip." Pause. "And parts of the basket."

"Right. No chance of it being . . . bled on?"

"It was handled. She told stories of how the balance of the sword was complimented. It would have been touched for, perhaps, twenty to thirty seconds."

"With gloves on."

"That is customary."

"Ortus," she said. "I'm not trained for this. I think our chances are very small. I think we've got a similar chance of Magnus tripping over the secret entrance to the lost chambers of the Emperor Undying. Actually, that's significantly *less* unlikely, as I've come to believe they run sidelong to the facility rather than—never mind. Sir, I am truly, truly sorry, but—Reverend Daughter, is that you?"

It was not likely to be anybody else standing on the threshold, unwilling to cross over and listen to the rest of the conversation. Harrowhark had been standing in profound silence, without so much as the rustle of a fold of robe, but the necromancer of the Fifth House had demonstrated extraordinarily acute hearing for eavesdroppers. "We're used to Jeanne and Isaac, you know," she had said, as though that constituted an explanation all by itself.

No hope of disappearing back into the corridor, or taking refuge in audacity and answering, *No.* The Reverend Daughter swept into the frozen library as though she had been noticed at the moment of entry, and found the Fifth and her swordsman-apparent standing before a rack of old and crunchy maps. He had his fragile, rusty sword balanced courteously on his palms before the mild-eyed adept, and she had been rubbing a sort of clear balm over the knobbled base. Ortus, as blackly gowned, deep-eyed, and sadly painted as ever, had taken to wearing his black canvas panniers all the time. His hood was recklessly pushed away from his freshly shaven head—it took a sense of duty shading into martyrdom to shave in these conditions—and he looked rather as though he had been caught opening birthday presents a day early. His breath emanated from the black scarf around his face and nose as a pale mist.

The bloody fog had turned to sleet; the sleet had, in its time, turned to ice. A soft snow began falling like volcanic ash about a week after the first hailstorm. Banks of snow piled up through the cracks in the windows and blew loose into everyone's faces in the more exposed halls and ways of Canaan House. Sometimes the snow fell red, and the ice settling into the cracks of the paving stones and the steel of the dock terraces was a deep, unsettling carmine. The fresh vegetables had died, and they were down to preserved food. The rainbow-girdled constructs had kept fishing in the still-moving salt sea, but Teacher had taken one look at their catch and refused to have it cooked, or to let anyone else even see it.

Nonetheless, the snow and the bloody ice proved to be the least of the changes facing Canaan House.

Ortus sheathed his rapier with more care than finesse, and he asked: "How fare the preparations, Lady?" at exactly the same time Abigail said, "You shouldn't really be walking unaccompanied, Harrow."

"Quinn and Dyas were with me until the end of the corridor. We've laid all the wards," she said. Harrow had not bothered with scarf or muffler, and every so often regretted it: her lips were cracked, and so were her paints, no matter how much she powdered herself beforehand, which gave her skull the appearance of a worn-down fresco. "No matter their efficacy, they'll tell us something—if the Sleeper trips them while moving, that will tell us one thing; if the Sleeper *doesn't* trip them while moving, that will tell us another."

"You did not attempt to move the coffin," her cavalier said, with only the faintest flicker of hope.

"Of course I did," said Harrow, and he briefly closed his eyes in a full-face wince. "Nothing. It is absolutely immovable. Dyas pried up the panelling to see how far down it extends—it is laid like a pillar. I didn't hold out too much hope that we could simply drop the thing into the ocean, but I admit to being disconcerted."

He said, "Mistress, you might have woken it up."

"And that would have told me something else," she said.

"I wish that you would not take such enormous liberties with your own life."

Harrowhark said, "Would you rather I took enormous liberties with yours?" and did not intend it to be unkind; had thought it even faintly reassuring. But Ortus's dark eyes chilled in their sockets, as though the icy cold had reached them also, and his lips curled downward, and he said, lowly: "That is my purpose, yes."

"You hate the facility. It makes you sweat. You have begged not to be taken down there."

"Yes," he said.

"Then try to not to mourn when everything goes according to your request," said Harrow, and then they were both irritated—she knew that he was irritated because a conversation had not gone the way he'd overplanned it, and she knew that *she* was irritated because each time she tried to blunt the razor edge of her tongue, he somehow grasped the blades of her anyway. Nothing in their exchange had been less than typical of the Locked Tomb, and yet ever since she had come to Canaan House she had found it all—*wanting,* somehow. She did nothing to stanch the flow when she said, "Are we in agreement? Are we clear?"

"Thoroughly," said her cavalier sadly.

Abigail had been making herself look busy as only a member of the Fifth House could. Harrowhark was learning that a scion of the Fifth House might busy themselves politely during a murder, or an orgy. Now she said briskly, "I'm glad you're here, Harrow. I wanted to talk to you about what happens next."

She sat down at the table and tossed her thick, painstakingly brushed sheets of smooth brown hair behind her—Abigail Pent would present smartly in earthquake, fire, or flood—and Harrowhark said, "I assume you mean the organs."

"Yes. Those aren't great," said Pent.

The snow had settled; the ice, in pinkish, crackling drifts, had formed miniature fernlike cherry-shaded patterns on all the ancient glass. In their wake, great slithering, pulsing tubes had worked themselves up through the cracks in the floorboards, or wound down among the frozen weeds. The tubes were a fresh, clear pink, with redder veins beneath the translucent topmost layer. At intervals, black clusters swam within, this way and that, like frightened fish. When one cut them, they bled a gush of filthy water, then the wound closed up as one watched. The cold had deepened to the point where a few hours would freeze this substance solid, a sort of brownish cloud with a misty, gelid surface.

The tubes were not homogenous: every so often they would pouch out, or fall in dramatic drapes along the wall or from the ceiling, with whitish, pearl-bubbled globules secreted away within their flesh. The surviving inhabitants of Canaan House were united—even Harrow—in agreement with Dulcie Septimus's pronouncement that it was "absolutely ghastly, bordering on shitty."

Abigail considered Harrow gravely, with her hands tucked into a pair of her husband's outsized woolly gloves, and she said: "Reverend Daughter, we look to you."

Harrowhark had been looked to before, though rarely by anyone under seventy years old. She kept her gloved fingers within the folds of her robe, flexing them occasionally, and waited. The Fifth historian continued: "My necromantic scholarship is specific, my general practice—scattershot. I never did hold ambitions in that quarter. I can command a skeleton, but I can't create one. I can work tendon or a muscle, or settle skin into a gash, but if that can be weaponized, I'd love to know *how*. And as for the Duchess Septimus . . ."

All things considered, Dulcinea Septimus was a medical miracle. By her own account, her lungs were blown-out sacs of inflammation from the last round of pneumonia she had fought before her voyage to the House of the First; the cold ought to have already buried her beneath those deep, cerise snows outside. But there was seemingly very little wrong with her, apart from the occasional cough. Harrowhark had been ready to denounce her as a lifelong hypochondriac, except that Septimus herself was the first to insist as much: "I have always said that *thinking* one is sick is probably what *makes* you sickest," she once said hopefully, while avoiding attempts on her cavalier's part to feed her evil-smelling linctus from a spoon.

Abigail said, "She should be incapacitated. It's marvellous that she isn't. But her flesh magic is inward-supporting—she says the Master Warden of the Sixth House gave her instruction when they were children, though goodness knows he would have been what, nine years old—and that she neglected her other studies. You, the lieutenant, and Protesilaus the Seventh constitute our front line."

Harrowhark very specifically did not look at her cavalier to see how he took this pronouncement. He had formed a violent passion against the heroic knight of the Seventh House; she thought it was nice that he had a hobby. She said, "If the temperature drops further, I am in danger of becoming less useful. I have been experimenting with heating marrow to stop it from freezing, an art I have as far as I can tell only just invented, but it is fiendishly difficult. I do not admit this lightly."

"Oh, damn!" the Fifth necromancer said softly. "Damn, damn! I hadn't even thought of that. I mean—gosh, that's fascinating, you ought to tell me the details at some point, but—damn!"

Harrowhark rubbed her hands against her ribs through her robes and gloves, and said: "This is all precaution. I'm still fit for purpose, so long as the temperature doesn't fall."

"Then time is against us," said Ortus.

"Time was always against us," said Abigail.

"Oh, time . . . *time*," said a voice from the doorway. "Time means very little . . . *mastery* does. This temple stood for ten thousand years untouched by all but time's clumsiest pawing . . . but then its master was the Master, for whom even the River will part. Time is nothing to the King Everlasting."

It was Teacher. He wore his white woollen tunic with its beautiful rainbow sash, and his sandals and a little white half cape, but nothing else to keep out the cold. He had a bottle of apple-coloured liquid in his hand that he took a pull from every so often, the sharp reek of which made Harrow's nose crinkle.

To their silence, he added: "I believe we are now being punished for what they did. Even the devil bent for God to put a leash around her neck . . . and the disciples were scared! I cannot blame them! I was terrified! But when the work was done—when I was finished, and so were they, and the new Lyctors found out the price—they bade him kill the saltwater creature before she could do them harm . . . Oh, but it is a tragedy, to be put in a box and laid to wait for the rest of time. It happened to me, but I was only a man, or perhaps fifty men . . . Reverend Daughter, your whole House treads upon a knife's edge, as keepers of such a zoo."

He caught her gaze on the bottle, and his very blue eyes twinkled a little madly, and he said with greater calm: "It's thistle shrub, child. I could not get drunk on it if I tried. And how I have tried."

Ortus said, "You speak in riddles, old man."

"Then let me speak plainly," said Teacher. "You worship a monster in a box and play at being the masters of its tomb. Now *we* have a monster in a box, and it has become obvious that it means to master us all. Canaan House has never changed its colour, nor its shape, nor with the seasons. I should know; we measured summer to winter, temperature and precipitation and the acidity of the very sea beneath us, and it never hailed, and it never snowed, and we certainly never saw fimbriae hanging from the rafters. Let me prophesy in my old age: the Sleeper is getting up the strength to wake completely, and colonize what it finds. I fear! God! How I fear!"

Abigail said, "Teacher, please come and take up residence with us. We have beds—we keep watches," but he cried out: "And miss out on the chance to *die*? I've been wandering these halls at three o'clock in the morning, saying at the top of my voice, 'It would be terrible to be shot,' and the Sleeper still does not come . . . It is dreadful to be shown a monster's pity."

He pivoted abruptly and took another long suck at the bottle. "Your swords will not rend its armour," he said, with his back turned to them. "Its weapons will ruin your flesh. It will not stop until it has subsumed its quarry. And it would only acknowledge the blade without . . . all we have are the blades within. It has seen them and made them dull. There is no hero left among us . . . and I say, hooray!"

Teacher, in a mad sprightly dash, clicked his heels together with the ardour and energy of a man a quarter of his age. "Hooray!" he said again. "Into the River with us, boys! Fifty can school like fishes!"

And he threw his bottle violently at the nearest section of tube, out in the corridor. Harrowhark watched as the shiny red organ gave out a wet, squishing *blarp*; the bottle bounced off it dismally, and as Abigail and Ortus drew close beside her, it rolled sadly beneath another fold of wet, curtaining pink. Some of the bitter fluid within spilt out onto the battered wooden floor. Within seconds, even the ends of that alcohol began to flake into shards of ice.

"It's coming for you, Reverend Daughter!" said Teacher. "Oh, it's coming for you—and once it's got you, once that rock's rolled away, once that tomb's levered open, the Emperor of the Nine Houses will never know peace ever again! The King is dead! Long live the King!"

Teacher capered madly down the hallway like a child—slapping at long, shivering droplet-shaped lumps of viscus, and whooping as he went. His hooting and hollering rang off the antique walls long after he disappeared.

Harrow felt the cold as an old friend inside the thick black canvas of her church robe. Her fingers burnt as though she had held them too close to a fire. Her cavalier and the historian did not warm her as they stood beside her: it was as though she were alone in the room. She was startled when the latter touched her: laid her hand on her shoulder as though she were no older than one of the vanished Fourth House duo, a gawky little girl in the face of death.

"Well, bugger Teacher," said Abigail Pent crossly.

36

ONE WEEK BEFORE THE EMPEROR'S MURDER

In those last long, terrible days before the end—those strangled, claustrophobic, white-faced days that stalked the borders of your nights like predators waiting for your collapse—you began to pray again. This was not because you had anyone in particular to pray to. It just helped, in its own ineffable way, to read your knucklebone prayer beads, and to recite childhood meditations you had learned when you were yet too small to look out over the pew. You were filled with the baffling memory of Mortus the Ninth lifting you up to see your mother leading Mass; before you were allowed on the sanctuary, you were seated in front and held by your father's cavalier, so that you might not stare at a softly powdered stone chair-back for the whole session. You remembered that you had far preferred the strong, sad hands of Mortus to being sat next to your great-aunts and given a stinging piece of peppermint candy to suck, as though you ever needed to be kept quiet. It had been the last assumption of immaturity you would ever enjoy. You had been three years old, maybe.

If you prayed for anything, you prayed for clarity. You prayed that you might look upon the face of each remaining Lyctor and that the Body would quietly point to the apostate. You prayed that it had been Cytherea, traitor even in death, and that her body had somehow been tossed out of the Mithraeum's airlock. You prayed that the whole thing had been an illusion, and sometimes nearly convinced yourself that it was; that you had imagined the dead of Canaan House alive again, impossibly drifting through the jungles of your victim planet, far away from where their bodies had gone to rest. But then why had their coffins on the *Erebos* been empty? And why now was one of your letters missing, and another two freshly opened?

Whenever you thought about it, enervated lines of thick, hot blood drooled from each ear, so that your canals were perennially stained deep brown. You prayed to live just a few more weeks.

* * *

One month ago, after you distractedly slit the jugular of your fourteenth planet, you were praying thus when a great alarm began pounding through the halls of the Mithraeum. You did not recognise the klaxon—red lights replaced the soothing blue glow of the habitation lamps lining the walls, strobing anxiously on and off.

And then a huge shutter slid over your window. You stood in front of the weirdly bending, echoing light in front of the plex, and you watched a great metal panel crunch into place with a silent grinding and huge vibration, slowly cutting out the light. Your rooms grew profoundly dark except for that excited red blinking; the klaxon continued as you were left in that red-hued darkness, tight with anticipation, ready to die.

The voice of the Emperor of the Nine Houses rasped over the comm speaker beside your door, and you rushed to stand before it as he said: "J. G. calling in. All clear. Lyctors, do you copy?"

"A. A. calling in. All clear."

"G. P. calling in. All clear."

A pause. Then you heard Ianthe's cool, detached tones, as if she hadn't even been asleep: "No one has yet seen fit to grace me with a callsign, but nonetheless, all clear."

Augustine: "You're I. N., of course. Harrow's H . . . Yes, Harrow's H."

"H. O., calling in," you said instantly, and you ignored Ianthe's audible sniggers. "All clear. What's going on?"

And God said urgently, "Mercy, do you copy? Who pulled the alarm?"

The communicator crackled. Somebody breathed deeply. Then

there was a lowing over the system—a terrible animal call of un-comprehending pain—and it did not sound like the Saint of Joy. It sounded like a shower of static, and a bitten-off sob, and then a great, wet, horrible thump.

The Emperor said, "Someone unlock my door so I can get to her."

Ortus said, "I'm closer."

Another wet noise of contact. Then Mercy said hoarsely, "No. No. I am coherent. I just . . . less than a second of visual. I looked away, Lord, but it was optically magnified . . . there in the centre . . . It is here! The Resurrection Beast is come! The seventh colossus, brood of that which murdered Cyrus the First, packmate of that which murdered Ulysses the First, the one and the same that Cassiopeia died for. Oh, God, John, sometimes I wish I were capable of dying—I saw it! I saw it, and it is blue like Loveday's eyes! It knows what you did to its kin, and it sees my cavalier's mortal soul burning in my chest!"

The mechanical *clank* of a door unlocking was also audible over the line. The Emperor said, "Thanks," and then his side of the communication cut off. Nobody else spoke on the line.

The klaxon ended. It kept ringing in your ears long after it was gone. Augustine's voice crackled over the line, quite wearily: "What a dolt. She knows not to look within a kilometre of the thing's predicted arrival. Well, it's here early, and so are we. Back to bed, everyone."

And you went back to bed. The shutters did not come up again. You would learn that they would not; you would learn that the Mithraeum would only be privy to even more shielding in the days ahead, lest the Emperor of the Nine Houses look upon what approached. But that night you just lay next to the Body, and you noticed that her eyes were open very wide, and that in the darkness they were death-mask gold.

You said, "Beloved?"

She said, "It's coming," with the most anticipatory astonishment you had ever heard in her low, many-personed voice—right then she used the voice of your father's cavalier. And: "It's near!"

Had she ever been astonished before? Had she ever been uneasy? You were lying face-to-face with her, centimetres from the wet sheen of her skin that ought to have made an imprint on your pillow, facing that crinkled lower lip. Her eyes, which the night lights had turned the sick amber of a healing bruise, stared through you. The Body was troubled: in that hovering place so close to the end of your life, it seemed only natural that you should reach for her. The fear of death had remade your worship into desperation, or maybe desire. You reached one hand out for that frozen tangle of hair at the back of the skull; you closed the gap between you, and you kissed that lovely corpse mouth.

Of course, you could not. There was nothing there. Contact made her drift away, just as with any of your hallucinations. You had not touched her. Maybe you had not even reached for her. The Body watched you with an expression you were terribly afraid was pity.

You said, "Please," and you reached out again. A wave of dizziness rocked you. You pushed at the robe lying crooked at the slope of her shoulder; you pressed your hand low to her belly. Her dignity was untouched by this gross urgency, this coarse frenzy; or maybe, again, you had not done it. You said again, "Please."

As though you had crossed no boundary, and above the soundless rough shouting in your ears, the Body said: "I have to go away for a while," and you regretted everything.

"I have done wrong," you said.

There was the tiniest suggestion of a furrow in that cool unbreathing brow, and she said, "How?"

You did not begin to know how to answer that. The Body reached out, and stroked her fingers forward, as though to close your eyes: you were too tired to imagine how those fingertips would feel on your lids, how that thumb might brush down the bridge of your nose. You closed your eyes in obedient response. And then—you poor broken-hearted sad sack—you fell deeply asleep.

In the morning, the Body was gone.

* * *

"Here is the strategy for engagement," said Mercymorn.

She had wheeled a large piece of opaque white plex before the dinner table where you and Ianthe and Augustine and Ortus were seated, clustered close to her, with the Emperor at the end of the table busying himself with his own work—with his tablet and his diagrams, with his styluses and flimsy. By this point, it had been nearly two months since the death of the fourteenth planet. All the window shutters had been down for weeks. This contributed to a general sense of living inside a box, which you did not mind: there were no windows in Drearburh, though there *had* always been a sense of depth that made you feel freer than you did upon this flat collection of rings and corridors.

Your teacher stood before this assembled throng in her Canaanite robe, looking fragile as a white flower with a rotten-peach heart, and she said, "The engagement could go on for three hours. It could go on for eight. It could go on for a week . . . Assume that timing is labile, and proceed accordingly. Next!"

The Saint of Joy drew a large cylindrical tube on the plex whiteboard, with a fat black soft-tip pen. She segmented and labelled the cylinder from top to bottom, each a neat interval apart: EPIRHOIC. MESORHOIC. BATHYRHOIC. BARATHRON.

"The greatest portion of the fight will take place here, as normal," she said, emphatically underlining EPIRHOIC. "We must use the bank as much as possible. Once the Beast tires—you'll know because it will try to run—we wrestle it down to the mesorhoic layer, then the bathyrhoic, and then to the barathron. Once we're there, the stoma will open—and we push it through. Simple!!"

"*Not*," Mercymorn added acidly, in case anyone had mistaken her.

Ortus said, "I maintain we should drive it downward at the start."

"No thanks! Not all of us are spearfishers! Next!" she said, but the Saint of Duty wasn't done; as he occasionally did, he ground forward with the force of gravity, and added doggedly:

"Our swiftest fight against a Beast took place in the bathyrhoic layer."

"Yes, and Number Eight wasn't tired by the time we got to the barathron, and Ulysses the First had to wrestle it through the stoma, and he is as we speak languishing in Hell! It's a Resurrection Beast, honey! Thank you! Next!!"

From the end of the table, his white-ringed eyes still bent down upon his papers, the Emperor said quietly: "His was the action of a hero."

"Oh, but the problem is that heroes always *die*," said Augustine, who was worrying an edge of tablecloth between his long and elegant fingers. "You can't even really pronounce one a hero until they die heroically. I thought the downward assault was a good wheeze when you two first came up with it, Ortus, but we know now that the last push against a Beast *has* to be sudden and conclusive. I'd rather have fought nine more hours and have Ulysses sitting here right now, inciting a sexy party, than have watched him wrestle that thing out of sight."

"I *hated* the sexy parties," said Mercymorn, with an almost tearful vehemence, and Augustine said, "We know, Joy. We know."

You had been watching Ianthe. She could not bear meetings, or any kind of organised activity where she might be forced to deal with anyone else's opinion, which you found strange considering that she had spent her entire life at the hip of her twin sister. She was sitting in her chair with her pallid arm crossed across the shiny gold of her skeleton one, both framed hideously against the coalescing rainbow whites of her robe. Her hair fell in thin, straight sheets over her shoulders, and she rested the back of her head against the chair-back as though she might nap at any moment. She looked to you; you looked away quickly, but you had been caught watching.

Lately you found yourself praying that the traitor was not Ianthe, all the while having seen for yourself the living Coronabeth in the arms of Blood of Eden: the twin who, as far as you could tell, was the only human being Ianthe loved more than herself. For the sake of this sister Ianthe had held your gaze while sliding a knife through the palm of your hand.

Why did you pray for Ianthe's innocence, when it was so dubious? It was not the way of the Ninth House to pray with such wilful credulousness; yet you prayed all the while knowing Ianthe's facility for tergiversation would have given the whole universe pause.

That wanton backstabber said idly, "What about the physical form? Is it really invulnerable?"

"At its current trajectory I have triangulated that it will perch—
here," said Mercy, and fixed a map of local space to the plex with
round magnets. You were bewildered by how far the perch seemed
from the Mithraeum; your erstwhile tutor had pegged its location at,
if the diagram read true, somewhere in the orbit of a planet five billion
kilometres away. "The asteroid field means that we'll only get waves of
Heralds around twenty-five thousand strong—it can't all-out rush us."

Ianthe said, "We know where it is. Bomb it."

"We tried that, duckling, as I've told you," said her teacher, but
quite kindly. He had removed his kit of rolling papers and pouch of
evil-looking innards, and had begun to roll a cigarette. "The layer of
dead matter and Heralds is two thousand kilometres thick."

"Send a Lyctor to penetrate the layer, plant the bomb close up. I'll
do it, if courage fails in the hearts of my elders."

Ortus said, "Tried that," and Mercy said, "Cytherea was mad for
weeks. And I do not mean mad *cross*, I mean mad *insane*. She didn't
even touch on the surface."

"It's not that getting rid of the corpus wouldn't be useful," said the
Emperor. "It *would* be. When Cyrus drew the corpus into a black hole,
Ulysses said that it was the simplest thing in the world to dispose of
the brain, that it fell into a dormant state, and he could bring it down
to a stoma singlehanded . . . but that cost us Cyrus. And Cassiopeia
drove the body into the River alongside its own brain, but only Cassy
could have ever done that . . . or Augustine."

It was halfway to a question. Augustine said, "I'm not Cassy, John.
It's all theoretical to me."

And God said, "I hope it *stays* theoretical. Anyway, the damn thing
hardly seemed to care. Put the Heralds aside, Ianthe. Leave them to
your sword-hand."

You said, "And how to defeat the Beast? What does it look like?
How will it attack us? What must we expect?"

Mercymorn took her fat-tipped marker and scribbled on the plex,
placing her new object squarely in the epirhoic layer. "This is the
Beast," she said.

Augustine said, "That's a muffin."

"I see a cloud, but with a face," said Ianthe. "If you take that main squiggle for an eye."

You said, "I thought it was a flower," and God said, "No, yes, I agree, there's something—florescent about it."

And Ortus said, "Thought it was a snake in a bush."

"I hate you *all*," said Mercymorn passionately. "I have hated you for *millennia* . . . except you, my lord."

"Thanks," said God.

"I merely want to put you in a jail," said his Lyctor, now meditative, "and fill up the jail with acid once for every time you made a frivolous remark, or ate peanuts in a Cohort Admiralty meeting, or said, 'What would I know, I'm only God.' Then at the end of a thousand years, you would say, 'Mercy, I have learned not to do any of these things, because I hated the acid you put on me.' And I would say, 'That is why I did it, Lord. I did it for you, and for your empire.' I often think about this," she finished.

The Emperor of the Nine Houses said, "I ate peanuts, discreetly, the once."

You said, "Let us continue on the assumption that the diagram is the Beast."

"Yes! Thank you," said your teacher, "except that I noted your use of *the assumption,* and I would like to remind you, infant, that I also hated you on sight. The Beast's brain will sit in the epirhoic layer, and it will attack us in—any way it chooses. Each Beast is different. I have fought numerous now, and each Beast is quite unlike any other . . . Number Two spewed quicksilver and remade itself into hundred-foot spikes. Number Six kept sucking us into enormous sphincters and spraying us with worms. I cannot even remember what it looked like. I remember Number Four . . . it was a humanoid creature with a beautiful face who held me under the water, and it spoke in a lovely voice but it only repeated, *die, die*—and I recall Number One as a great and incoherent machine . . . when I saw it I thought it had a great tail, and a thousand broken pillars on its back, but Cassiopeia saw it as a mechanical monster with swords for wings, and great horns of myelin, tessellated over with graves."

It was the Saint of Duty who said, restlessly: "Number Eight was a giant head."

"Finned like a fish," said Augustine, lost in reverie. "Its ribs were bloody bandages, and its teeth protruded through its own skull, tangled about its face like a nest. It was red, and it had a single eye of green that moved all about the body . . . Look," he said, coming back to himself, perhaps seeing something in your and Ianthe's expressions. "They're not great, is what we are saying."

Ianthe said, "Then this is a waste of time, eldest sister. We can't plan on fighting it."

"We can arrange our formation," said the Saint of Joy primly. "Take your own section of the Beast, and concentrate. You, idiot baby, will take the east. Augustine will take the west, Ortus the north. I will take southmost to its central point, whatever that point looks like, and whatever it may be—it may be we can't even comprehend it spatially, but at that point, *fight it and get out of everyone else's way.*"

You said, "What about me?"

No one looked at you, except for Mercymorn. Ianthe's gaze was fixed in some totally different direction, perhaps her appointed east; Augustine was lighting a neatly rolled cigarette, and the Saint of Duty simply studied the shield pulled down over the wide window that had used to look out into space. Even God did not look up from whatever administrative work concerned the Prince Undying. The only eyes for you were Mercy's: that endless, red-shaded hurricane, sinking into those sandy brown depths, moving over the face of grey waters.

"Just don't get in the way," she said.

Augustine said smoothly: "See where you're needed, sis. It may be that the Beast has some vulnerability you can mark. Or it may try to attack us from without, which means you'll be useful on the perimeter. Keep flexible."

This would have been a perfectly reasonable request had its meaning not been so obvious. *Do not distract us with your death.*

The Kindly Prince said, idly: "He's right, Harrowhark. From what I can tell, it's useful to have someone who can move laterally, rather than being obliged to keep to one place . . . and in any case, like most best-laid plans, this one won't survive contact with the enemy. Do what you feel is best, and everyone else will endeavour not to swamp your skeletons . . . Can we have a tea break, Mercy? I'm gasping."

Your sister closest in age did not stand, as everyone else did, at God's request to put the kettle on. She was still looking at the black diagram, and she asked, quite unconcernedly: "What *is* the stoma?"

Mercy said, "Augustine, you did *tell* her about the stoma," in tones of accusation, but he simply said: "No. I saw no reason to frighten her. Why—did *you* tell Harrowhark?"

Naturally, you had not been told about the stoma. Your teacher simply said, fractiously, "She'll never see it! Why bother?"

"If I have my way, we'll leave Ianthe safely in the mesorhoic. We three old lags will be more than enough to take it down," said Augustine sharply. Ianthe's languid brown-spotted gaze dragged up to him as though it barely had the energy to do so. "That thing has a ferocious gravitational pull. It's not for neophytes."

"Excuse me, we may not all of us be alive by the time the thing is exhausted, so I would stop swaddling your squalling baby—"

"You never *did* take the stoma seriously, which is why your whole damned House sucks at it like a grotesque teat—"

"Don't be *coarse*—"

"It is the mouth to Hell," said God.

He stood in the liminal space between dining room and kitchen, the biscuit tin clutched in his hands. There were crease marks on his clothes from too much wearing, and there was a faint smudge of blue where he had been writing with ink and touched his temple. He said, "A genuinely chaotic space—*chaos* in the meaning of *the abyss* as well as *unfathomable* . . . located at the bottom of the River. The Riverbed is studded with mouths that open at proximity of Resurrection Beasts, and no ghosts venture deeper than the bathyrhoic layer. Anyone who has entered a stoma has never returned. It is a portal to the place I cannot touch—somewhere I don't fully comprehend, where my power and my authority are utterly meaningless. You'll find very few ghosts sink as far as the barathron. If I believed in sin,

I would say they died weighted down with sin, placing them nearer the trash space. That's what we've been using it for, in any case. That's where we put the Resurrection Beasts. The rubbish bin . . . with all the other dross."

Then he said, "So who wants a bikkie?"

37

THE ATMOSPHERE ON THE Mithraeum crystallized into hot, waiting agony. You would walk down a hallway and find Augustine and Ortus fighting—their eyelids glued together in pink, smarting lines as they sparred blind, in tight corners, rapiers flashing like light over water—then stopping apparently at random, before the Saint of Patience would say something like, "Okay; again, but airless," and you would hear a sudden pounding wheeze as both of them emptied the air from their lungs. Generally, you then took another corridor.

The Lyctors also did what they perhaps should have from the very start, and organised loosely planned, often contradictory sessions of instruction for Ianthe—and for you. You went en masse into the River, leaving your bodies behind to slump into C-curves—or at least, yours did, the rest of them stood—and crunched the silvery sand of the bank beneath your feet as the three saints led you both to assemble wards. No blood or flesh or bone here: the first two might be scavenged, the last swept away by the capricious tide. You collected bits of dried wood—dried wood?—and empty-coloured stones—stones?— from the banks of the River beyond death, and you collected armfuls of the sharply unkind osiers and tall, feathery plants, the ones with long fibrous stems as tall as you were and thin, tangled leaves. Filthy salt wind whipped your faces as you formed wards from the flotsam that grew, apparently, on the bank. And no ghosts passed you to wade down to the water—no ghosts heaved themselves out of the waters of the layer that Mercymorn had called the *epirhoic*—they had fled for different climes.

342

"The poor bastards are terrified," said Augustine.

There was nothing to see in the River yet; no brain, no hint of Beast, no far-off haze that indicated anything amiss. When you came around, you found that you were the only one sitting in a circle of standing Lyctors, their faces like blank flimsy, their rapiers in their hands, their offhands at the ready. The Saint of Duty with his spear. The Saint of Patience with his smallsword. The Saint of Joy with her net. Ianthe, with her trifold knife. You stared numbly at these faces, wondering which one would betray God at the last.

At the beginning of that last week, you still believed you might live, despite the briefing's assumption that you would not. In the middle of that last week the Emperor of the Nine Houses, the Necrolord Prime, invited you to his rooms after supper, to talk; when you sat in that now-familiar armchair before that now-familiar coffee table—the great window now a flat darkness, the ship a belly you were all nestling within—he surprised you by only offering you water and a very plain cracker. You found yourself able to nibble its edges, and tasted only flour and salt.

"I know you said no, the last time," said Teacher. "I respected it. I won't offer again, except to say—if at any point, before the final shutters come down—if at any point before Mercymorn locks me in—you come to me and ask to get locked in with me, it will be done. You have ten thousand years before you, Harrowhark."

You did not address this. Instead, you said: "Lord?"

"*Teacher.*"

You said, "You are the Prince Undying. You are the Necrolord Highest. Why do we lock you inside an airless room?"

He rested back in his chair and locked his fingers together over his belly. "You've hit upon a sore spot, Harrowhark," he said affably, brown brows crinkling together. "I am your salvation and your light. Who should *I* fear?"

"I never meant to," you said, leaning forward. "I just want to understand. Please."

"What happens to your body when you go under, Harrow? When you go into the River?"

You had long passed the point where you needed to think about it. "The body enters a senseless state. The Lyctor doesn't perceive anything around them in any sense; even their necromancy fails. Instead, the secondary soul comes to the fore—the protection mechanism—that can wield a sword even if their mind is gone . . . without conscious thought or awareness of its own, but with a perfect sword-hand." If they were functional.

The Emperor of the Nine Houses drummed his fingers over his belt. It still hurt you a little, to look into his terrible eyes: the irises like black shadows of the Canaanite white, that iridescent absence of colour, a shade rather than a tint; the purity of the white ring; then the matte black of the sclera. You had never become used to it.

"A myriad ago, I resurrected nine planets," he said. "And I reignited the central star, and I called it Dominicus. As a reminder. *Dominus illuminatio mea et salus mea, quem timebo?* God is my light. Harrowhark, if I went under—I'd enter that senseless state, and I am God. What if, forty billion light-years away, my people looked up to see Dominicus falter and go out? What if the very House beneath their feet died all over again, as I turned my back upon it?"

You said, "So if you die, the Houses die with you. The star warming our system fails, and—becomes a gravitational well, as I understand it?"

"Yes. A black hole, like the one that took out Cyrus," he said. "I can only hope you'd all be dead already. Oh, there'd still be Cohort ships . . . hold planets . . . a scattering of us . . . but we would be so few, and so many people hate us, and my work is not yet done. I cannot behold that apocalypse, Harrow. I think you are one of the only Lyctors who can really and truly understand *apocalypse* . . . It is not a death of fire. It's not showy. You and I would almost prefer the end, if it came as a supernova. It is the inexorable setting of the sun, without another hope of morning."

Both of you fell into silence.

"If I fought the Resurrection Beast I'd leave my Houses to die," he said. "If I fought the Heralds, I might well go mad, which would be the same thing. So I'm shut in here—walled in, really—to prevent the Nine Houses becoming none House, with left grief."

He looked very tired. He looked very rueful. He said, "Once again. You're not the only one with limitations."

"May I ask you a question, Teacher?"

"You're not sick of them yet?"

You said, "Who was A.L.?"

His eyes flew open. God sat up straight in his chair, looked at you in open astonishment, and he said, "Are you sure you want to go with—that one? Let's go through all the other, less awkward ones first. *How is a baby made?* I can do that, easy. I mean, I don't want to, but I'm ready. I have this little book about babies, bodies, friends, and family. Are you and Ianthe being safe?"

It was your turn to sit up straight in your chair and intone, constructing each syllable with the same rigid emphasis you might give to a skeleton: "We—are not—*intimate.*"

"Sorry—I mean, you're about the same age, I don't really know how this goes anymore, we've all been alive for too long . . ."

"Neither are we romantic—neither are we, frankly, *platonic—*"

"Sorry! Sorry. Sorry," he added, "I should not assume these things."

If your paint could have baked upon your face and crumbled off like clay, it would have. If you could have willed the Saint of Duty to burst through the door, skewer you through, and parade your gored body around the room, you would have. You began to get up. "If I have overstepped, Teacher, forgive me. I withdraw the question."

"No," he said. "Let's talk about her. Let's talk about my bodyguard."

Carefully, you sat back down.

God said, "You've been listening to Augustine and Mercymorn."

"Yes."

"It wouldn't be Ortus. Poor Augustine. Poor Mercy. They still feel badly . . . they still carry their apportioned blame. I think, yes, that it's time for you to know about A.L."

He pronounced her name, as both his wayward saints had, as two clearly separate letters: you could hear the *A* and the *L.* He said, "It stood for a couple of things. A joke, mostly. I often called her *Annabel Lee. Annie Laurie.* When I first met her I just called her *First, One.* She had a real name, but I buried it with her, and nobody says it anymore.

"She has been dead for nearly ten thousand years, but she keeps her vigil with me, as a memory, if nothing else . . . Annabel Lee was my—what do I call her? Guide? Friend? I'd hoped so . . ."

You did not know how to respond to this. He did not seem to need a response. God said, "She was the first Resurrection. She was my Adam. As the dust settled and I beheld what was left and what was gone, I was entirely alone. The world had been ended, Harrowhark. One moment I was a man, and then the next moment I was the Necrolord Prime, the first necromancer, and more importantly, a landlord with no tenants."

You said, "Teacher, what destroyed the House of the First?"

"Not much," said the Emperor, and he tried to smile. It was awful. "Rising sea levels and a massive nuclear fission chain reaction . . . it all went downhill from there."

This quiet admission provided the first details you had ever heard of the pre-Resurrection extinction. As mythologies went, it felt distant and unreal. He continued, "It wasn't gorgeous dust to be left in, Harrow. I was dazed . . . I was bewildered . . . and she was my defender and my sole companion, and my colleague in the scholarship of learning how to live again. It was bloody difficult. I had never been God."

He trailed off here. Then he said: "She lived to see what happened at Canaan House. Not that she took much interest. My first Resurrection was not a normal human being, Harrow, and she struggled to pretend. Anger was her besetting sin. We had that in common. And when the cost of Lyctorhood was paid, when the emotions were at their peak . . . we found out the price for our sin. The monstrous retribution. To be chased for our crime to the ends of the universe, to have our deed stain our very faces and follow after us like a foul smell. She died after that first terrible assault."

You did not say, *I am sorry;* you did not offer empathy. As with many mysteries, this one had turned out to be sad and dull: the Emperor of the Nine Houses had someone, and then, like all his Lyctors, the Emperor of the Nine Houses had lost someone. It was your story. It was Ianthe's story. It was the story of Augustine, and of Mercymorn, and of Ortus. It was Cytherea's story, and that of all the Lyctors who had died over that long dark sheaf of years.

"I understand why cavaliers primary carry their House titles," said God. "It makes sense. But it is a corruption of the original. D'you know why you're really *the First?* Because in a very real way, you and the others are A.L.'s children . . . There would be none of you, if not for her."

And then the Emperor of the Nine Houses set down his empty mug of tea with the residue of ginger biscuit crumbs within. You had no idea, in those seconds after the gentle *clink* upon the table's surface as the universe held its breath, that he was about to say the worst thing that had ever been said to you. The fine, forbearing lines at his forehead and at his eyes crinkled earnestly, and he said: "I like to think that she would like you. You'd make a hell of a daughter, Harrowhark. I sometimes indulge in the wish that you'd been mine."

There had been a moment in your life when you were convinced that you were about to spoil your substance at the foot of Ianthe Tridentarius's altar. You had been granted reprieve. There was no such reprieve for you in that moment. You had not sold the marrow of your soul for stolen eyes and a half-hearted kindness. What dismantled you—you bereft idiot—was not even the God who made the Ninth House, the Emperor All-Giving, the Kindly Prince; your end appeared in the form of a grown adult telling you that they might have liked you for their own.

You hurled the glass to the table. It shattered into a flower of water, with a crackling multitude of shards for sepals. You stood upon that table. It creaked beneath your weight. God had half-stood to stop you when you sank to your knees on the glass; you knelt into obeisance on the razor-sharp fragments, pressed your palms down into the shrapnel, and you folded yourself into wet and bleeding penitence before him.

He said, "Harrow, no." He was distraught. He said, "Please— Harrowhark, I'm sorry, I have obviously said something immensely stupid—I do that, eh—I never wanted to hurt you." He said, "Ten thousand years, and I am still such a fool."

You might have told him of the traitor. Instead you said: "I broke into the Locked Tomb."

After a moment God said, "You did not."

"The wards to the stone were easily bypassed," you said. "The line of Reverend Mothers and Reverend Fathers has been responsible for their upkeep for years. The barriers and gates beyond were more difficult. I was nine years old when I began, and ten by the time I could traverse the shaft. I spent a whole year working on nothing but those locks. When I came to the blood ward on the stone, the ward of the tomb-keeper, I did not know how to pass. It remains the most complex piece of magic I have ever seen. It was my first vision of the Necromancer Divine . . . but one day when I was ten years old I decided to end my own life, Lord, and sometimes I think it was that which let me cross the tomb-keeper's gate. I opened it; I saw the saline water that laps the stony shore, and I walked into the sepulchre. I have seen the Tomb and I have looked upon your death. My parents killed themselves over my heresy. I saw what lies within, and I will love it beyond my own entombing. I— Did I sin, Lord? Did I kill two of my fathers that day?"

You were panting tiny, sharp puffs of breath from the back of your throat. You knelt on the broken glass on the flat table before him, damp with blood and water; you did not weep, but only because you no longer knew how.

The Emperor of the Nine Houses could only have been quiet for five seconds. To you, it felt like a hundred thousand years.

And then he said, very gently: "No, you didn't."

You pressed your face into the surface of the table, and you closed your eyes so violently that the pressure stung your brows and cheeks. No star hung so still as you did then, at the end of its hard hydrogen burn, breathlessly waiting to slough off its outer layer.

And he said, "Harrow, whatever you thought you did, you didn't."

"I opened the outer door."

"Okay," he said.

"I went up the passage."

"I'll accept it, though that thing's a literal death trap," he said.

"I broke the ward and I rolled away the rock—"

"There's where you're wrong," he said.

You did not lift your head but said, "I was ten years old, but I was not a child. I set myself one task. I studied for one purpose. Don't consider my limitations, God: I am not a person, I am a chimaera."

"We won't get into that, but don't think I am discounting the genius of a single-minded, necromantically augmented ten-year-old," he said. "I'm not saying that you didn't do it because you weren't good enough. Harrowhark, I'm saying that *nobody* is good enough. There *isn't* a bypass. I built that tomb with Anastasia, designed every inch of it, and I did not include a way in. I never wanted that tomb opened, from either end. I made that ward, me alone, and it wouldn't answer to the greatest of my Lyctors any better than the meanest infant necromancer in all the Nine Houses. Their might would be one and the same."

The supernova of your heart went out; faded, as swiftly as it had shone; it became thick, and miniature, and dense. You lifted your head minutely, and an embedded fragment of glass fell from your temple, from a string of red blood.

"It can't be broken," he continued. "It can't be contravened. It can't even fade; its magic was my magic. The line of Reverend Tomb-keepers has laboured under a misapprehension if they think the rock *could* be rolled away, except by me. It's a pure blood ward, Harrowhark. Whatever you thought you did—whatever false chamber has been built around that tomb that you mistakenly stumbled into—there is no possibility that you breached the real thing. I am so sorry. You were party to a tragedy based on a misunderstanding."

You were rendered down to your incoherent parts. You wanted to say, *I saw the Body;* you wanted to say, *I saw the tomb;* but you were seized, all over again, by doubt in the face of fact. The uncertainty of the insane. The conviction of the mad. Nobody had seen you walk through that door. Nobody had watched you leave. What he saw in your face you had no idea; only that he crouched, and he looked at your blind, bleeding numbness with those chthonic eyes, and he wiped his thumb over the part of your temple where the glass shard had buried itself, and he tucked a stray lock of hair behind your ear with the thoughtless gentle tidiness of a parent.

Then God's eyes widened fractionally, and his voice became altogether different when he said: "Harrow, who the hell's been tampering with your temporal lobe?"

Your body rolled itself off the table, with such a reflexive suddenness that you were not sure that the action was through your conscious effort. Your meat floundered to stand, wild with shards of lead crystal and a dozen cuts through your clothes, and you turned away. The Emperor said, "Harrowhark?" as you stumbled away from the table, and more plaintively—"Harrowhark!" as you unerringly careened to the door, but he did not follow. Somehow your hand slapped the pad that slid it open—somehow your meat dragged itself away from him—and you walked, and you walked, and you walked.

As the door closed you might have heard, "Damn it, John—*damn* it." But the last thing you were going to do was trust your own ears.

38

You only started to accept your death after that terrible evening. It was impossible to ignore the manifold symbols of desolation. For example, the Body had made good on her word, and disappeared. She had been your quiet companion since your Lyctorhood—she had faithfully kept tryst with you—and in the morning after the sleep you could not remember and the walk back to your room you could not recall, it struck you that she was not coming back. Nobody would come for you. The path was cleared for you to die, and the lovely woman lying chained to the marble had not been able to bear to watch your progress on it; or perhaps it was just that she had never existed, except within a ten-year-old's fever dream.

The hours stretched themselves out to snapping point. You ate with a mechanical stolidity, even if you would rather not have. You washed yourself, and you dressed yourself, without a flicker of interest. Now when you caught sight of yourself in the mirror it was with a certain repelled bewilderment, as if you had never seen your face before, and it honestly seemed as though you had not. On one of the last days you discovered with distant consternation that you were trying to leave your rooms without even applying your paint.

You thought of trying to write a letter. To whom? Crux? Captain Aiglamene? Your wretched great-aunts? To God, to Ianthe? Should you plan your funeral, aiming to beat the Saint of Joy's frugal twenty-four minutes? Once you would have asked your corpse to be sent back to your House, to be walled up in the Anastasian, the last daughter in the tomb-keeper line: but perhaps even your empty vessel would attract a planetary revenant. No, your body could never go back home. You decided to write, *Toss me out the airlock,* but thankfully this puerile self-pity sobered you up a little, and you did not bother to begin.

The only real advantage to those last few days was that of the swordsman with the thousand scars: one more could not harm you. There was very little left to surprise, and very little left to sicken. But on the penultimate night before the Resurrection Beast was due, you dropped your glove down the side of the bed; you had to kneel down to retrieve it. And you found that far beneath your bed—hidden in the darkness where you had once lain, waiting for the Saint of Duty—lay an inert corpse: the missing body of Cytherea.

You lay in that gap between the frame and the floor on the outside of the bed for quite a long time. You had not sensed any foreign thanergy in your room, nor trace of hostile theorem. Even now, she lay docile and dusty, empty in your sight. You extended your fingers to brush her arm—and there was the ever-present sign of God keeping her preserved, with the hot lemon scour of his divine necromancy punching the back of each sinus. She lay still as an abandoned doll. You even said, "Get up. I can see you," but this command did not rouse her, for some reason.

At the time you did not wonder how the body had breached your wards, which you dutifully reapplied each night with fresh blood. You considered the corpse; you bracketed thick bone clamps to its dead ankles and dead wrists; and then you strode down the corridor, and when Ianthe answered your crabby knocking with a sleepy, "Nonagesimus, what do you—" you did not give her time to finish her sentence, but dragged her, by the icy gold of her skeleton arm, back to your bedroom.

She did not protest, or make a comment, coarse or otherwise. She was too surprised. Ianthe raised her eyebrows at you as you pointed her to beneath your bed; but she took her nightgown in her fists, and crouched down to look between the mattress and the floor.

And she said after a long moment: "What am I looking at?"

You experienced a hot moment of aggravated panic; but when you crouched down with her, the Lyctor's corpse was still there, dead and unmoving in her bracelets of bone. You said, "It's right there." She did not answer. You said: "The *body*, Tridentarius. Cytherea's body. Cytherea's body is *beneath my bed*."

She did not answer. You rattled, mindless: "On its back, arms at the sides, feet arranged at a thirty-degree angle."

Ianthe sat up and brushed down her knees. She looked at you with an expression you could not parse in the diminished light, only it had been made with great care. She said: "I—can't see anything, Harrowhark."

You stared at her. The Princess of Ida looked down, then away, and then slid her gaze deliberately back to you, as though it were difficult. You realised: she was embarrassed.

"Have you been sleeping?" she asked tactfully.

"It's no more than three feet away from us, Tridentarius."

"I wouldn't blame you if the answer is no; my beauty sleep is seriously impaired at the moment."

"Touch it. Get under there." She did not move. You said, "*Touch it*."

Ianthe rose soundlessly to her feet, and the long skirts of her nightgown—a brilliant ruffled canary-yellow silk that made her look like a formal lemon—rustled restively around her calves. She said, "I'm going back to bed."

Despite the layers of deadened scar tissue, there was still enough limberness in your soul for you to say: "Ianthe, for God's sake, have mercy."

She paused at your threshold. The violent yellow made her hair look white and gave her skin no colour found in skin. She said, light and careless: "Good night, Harrowhark," and she walked out of your rooms.

You looked at your door. You looked beneath your bed. You went to your sink, and you ran the tap until you could splash the coldest water possible on your face: you took five deep breaths in, and five deep breaths out. You closed your eyelids and rolled your eyes in your sockets. Then you went and looked beneath your bed again.

Cytherea was gone. There were cuffs of bone glued to the floorboards. You had left it for maybe three minutes. No ward brayed. You searched the rest of the room, but there was no corpse to be found. You lay down on the bed, and if you'd had the ability, you might have cried bitterly from sheer desire to feel release. But you could not; and no release came.

* * *

On the last day, for the last time, the Saint of Duty tried to kill you.

You were coming out of the habitation atrium—you had stood, briefly, at the entrance to the tomb where Cytherea's body no longer lay at rest, perhaps in the hope that she might coalesce before your eyes and rewrite reality—and when this inevitably failed to happen, you had walked away, hoping to find the remains of somebody's leftovers to listlessly gnaw upon in the kitchen.

Ortus hit you out of nowhere like the hammer of God. He tackled you just as you stepped into the corridor—body-slammed you into the wall with an almighty *crunch*, prematurely ending the long afterlife of an engraved skeleton inlaid with black pearl that had been fixed to the wall holding a big waterfall sheaf of ebon grasses. You automatically fixed the small cracked oblongs of your nasal bones into position as you flung him away again, reawakening the broken memorial into an array of shoving palms pistoning forward from one almighty synovial joint. He slammed into the opposite wall, and you backed away down the corridor, bleeding a little, measuring the distance between you and his spear.

He barked, "Draw your sword."

Immediately you reached for the bone-scabbarded blade you kept lashed to your back. He said with a touch of frustration, "Your *rapier*," and you just stared. He held his spear in his left hand, its point a razor-sharp omen, and his plain rapier with the scarlet ribbon in his right; an ancient funeral bouquet was in tatters by his feet. Ortus had not shaved his head in the last week or so, and the stubble on his bony skull was a cap of brownish russet fuzz like a splash of forgotten blood.

"There's no reason to kill me," you said, and marvelled at it, suddenly, the ease of the conclusion.

The Saint of Duty did not answer you. He stood in the corridor with an impassive face, and you said: "The Resurrection Beast will be here within hours. I am going to die. And yet you are here to kill me now?" He did not answer. "That isn't the act of someone removing a liability. You are either killing me for fun—doubtful—or out of anger—I'm unsure why—or for personal gain."

Ortus looked at you again. Then he sheathed that plain rapier and twitched the wicked point of his spear up to face the ceiling.

"You're wrong," he said.

"How?"

"You're still a liability."

"*Tell* me."

You thought he would not answer. But then he said, haltingly, in the manner of a man saying something difficult in a language he did not speak well: "Don't go to the River. End it yourself. Before they breach. Cut off your oxygen. Or however you like." At your expression, Ortus added as though it were an explanation: "So you don't . . . suffer."

"Why do you care if I suffer?"

"Because I was the one who failed you," he said briefly. "I pulled too many punches." And: "Sorry."

And, most horribly of all: "This wasn't my idea."

Then the Saint of Duty turned and walked away from you, disappearing out the mouth of the corridor, into the habitation atrium and beyond. You were suddenly seized with the conviction that the universe would not have judged you if you had lain down in that corridor, shed fifteen years, and thrown an absolute tantrum; if you had pelted the cool panel floor beneath you with hands and fists and wailed. It meant so much that you would die with so many questions unanswered, would go to your unkind grave understanding absolutely jack shit.

"Whose idea?" you called after him, and your voice rose to a shriek. "*Whose idea?*"

In a way, it helped. Nothing added to your resolution to live so much as someone else suggesting that you die. Ten minutes later you were eating leftover stew in the kitchen with something close to animation, choking down your last lunch before the apocalypse. And you were angry. You were always such a little bitch when you were angry.

39

THE HERALDS OF NUMBER SEVEN—the ghost of a swiftly murdered planet in the demesne of Dominicus—arrived that evening, around forty-three minutes before the habitation lights were due to go off. They had already been dimmed to preserve power, as apparently the defence mechanism locked inside a Lyctor did not need light to fight by—nor senses of any kind, in fact; Mercymorn said they did not even feel pain. Unlike them, you generally needed light and felt pain, but you were the Reverend Daughter of the Ninth House. The first was negotiable, and the second was irrelevant.

When the first Herald broke through the Mithraeum's honour guard of asteroids, it was not particularly terrifying. You had made your preparations. You sat on the floor before your window that looked out onto nothing. The great sword you had taken off and laid before you, as though it were a beloved talisman and not a sickening, befuddling relic, a back-breaking burden your dead self told you to carry. You were almost fond of it, except when you looked at it, at which point all fondness was dispelled.

The courier of the Beast landed on a part of the Mithraeum's hull very far away from you. You did not feel the impact or hear a sound. It was only when Augustine's voice came over the communicator, "Confirmed impact. West quadrant, third ring, engineering room," that you even knew it existed.

God's voice: "How many minutes before you're in the halo?"

"Depends. Impact, again. Also west, third ring, same location. Are they spearheading? Impact. North quadrant, habitation ring. Ortus, that's quite near you."

A crackle. "I'm fine."

Another crackle: Mercy's voice. "Less chatter on the line. Wait until they breach. They'll try to smother us first, and roast the station."

"No temperature change," said God.

Then you felt it: the first vibrational *thump*, and it sounded astonishingly close. From above you—direction was difficult; thanergetic sense irrelevant—what sounded like a small meteor had struck the hull of the Mithraeum. Silence before, and silence after. There was no distant roaring, perceived through the shudder of the hull and shutters—no monstrous noise, no pageantry. The messengers of the Resurrection Beast arrived without fanfare, and for a moment you resented the anticlimax.

Augustine, on the comm: "Confirmed. East quadrant, habitation. That's you, girls. Don't bite your tongues."

You thought it was one of Augustine's little jokes, until the fear hit you.

It hit as a smell. Your nostrils quivered, and your head was filled with a strange petroleum odour, redolent of old machines; but there was a sweetish underlayer to it, like vomit. It assaulted you in the manner of a migraine headache. Then the punch—like the Saint of Joy to one's kidneys—low in your stomach, racing up the central line of your body, seizing your heart in its teeth and shaking. Your palms ran wet. You made a gulping, golloping sound in the back of your throat—you tried to close your eyes as though that were some escape, but it was not—you tilted forward, gasping, your pulse bellowing, your ears deafened. You were suddenly convinced that there were little things crawling over your skin—you rubbed frantically at your forearms—you shivered convulsively, as though to fling them off; you touched obsessively at your ears; you cringed when a stray hair fell across your forehead.

But as you lurched—fretted—perceived—you fought. You made yourself one inhalation and exhalation—reduced yourself to one sensation, following it from down at the toes up all the lines of your body to the crown of your head. As the sensation rose, you filled with contempt for a stranger's insanity. You had enough of your own to contend with. After a few minutes, you came to with nothing more than a sense of embarrassment, a desire to itch, and a mild heat rash.

Ianthe was screaming over the comm. Everyone waited politely for her to stop.

You said: "Is that all?"

And with a crackle, God said: "It will be like this until they breach, Harrowhark."

The Princess of Ida's voice came over the communicator, a little ragged. "How long?"

"Over an hour," said Mercy.

And Augustine said: "Sit tight, kiddies. The fun starts now."

* * *

Your room had long ago plunged into near-complete darkness, leaving no distraction from the great rocking *thump—thump—thump*—of body after body flinging itself against the great mass coating the hull. There was nothing to see—the shutters were down—but you could feel the terrible vibration, hear the groan of chitin on metal, the cataclysmic rending of steel by fungous claw.

It was very cold. A fine shimmer of frost now coated your cheeks, your hair, your eyelashes. In that smothering dark, your breath emerged as wisps of wet grey smoke. Sometimes you screamed a little, which no longer embarrassed you. You understood your body's reaction to the proximity. Screaming was the least of what might happen.

God's voice came very calmly over the comm: "Ten minutes until breach."

* * *

And you walked to your death like a lover.

EPIDROΘOS

NINE MONTHS AND TWENTY-NINE DAYS BEFORE THE EMPEROR'S MURDER

"THESE TWO ARE INTENDED FOR YOU," said Harrowhark Nonagesimus. "They are to be opened only in the event of my death or of the other happenstance, though I have very little hope of you not opening them the moment my back is turned. The other twenty-two are written in an unbreakable code only I can decrypt, intertwined with a false chamber-code that, if even merely beheld, curses you, your family, and the restive bones of your ancestors, for as long as the name of Ianthe Tridentarius is whispered in necromantic hearing. Twenty-four, in all."

"I would have just gone with a blood ward, personally," said Ianthe.

"A blood ward is for those without imagination," said the astonishingly nude-faced girl. The Ninth necromancer unpainted was revealed to be a lean-faced, diamond-jawed nunlet, with very dark brows divided by a crisscross frowning mark—striking looking, certainly, even spiritual, a good subject for a painting if you were ready to settle for *The Ninth House Frowned*. "As I cannot reasonably expect not to bleed for the next myriad, I cannot rely upon a blood ward, and neither should you. Are we going to do this, Third, or not?"

"This may not work."

"You have reminded me."

"I'll say it again. The procedure could fail. Or it may work, but only temporarily. There could be any number of side effects—physical disorders—if you push your brain too hard, any surgery could simply heal over—and if you're doing what I have a suspicion you're doing, it could play merry hell with scar tissue. This is *profoundly* experimental. More to the point, it is totally fucking demented."

Their eyes met in the mirror. The ex-Reverend Daughter had set one up in front and one above her head, which was being held by two of the obedient skeletons of the sort she so obviously loved. Ianthe still did not understand the entrancing appeal of the dark aptitude of the bone; it was as though somebody had decided to make flesh magic less flexible, less subtle, and much less interesting to look at. What was the joke again? That the Ninth House knew a thousand shades of off-white?

She looked down at the tray of tools—scalpel, saw, little bottle of water with a spray nozzle—and astonished herself by saying: "Ninth. Maybe this is an eleventh-hour point to make, but I find myself making it. Tell me what you're doing. Tell me the details of your grim, dark, and shadowy plan. If you don't, I have no assurance that I am not about to have a front-row seat as you reduce yourself to a gibbering wreck—or lower. A vegetable. A hunk of wood. A Fourth House write-in advice column."

The nun did not answer. Ianthe made her voice as low and coaxing as it could go, and she pressed: "Make me understand what this is worth to you, Ninth. Think about what you've promised. Consider what I am, and what use you might get from me. I am a Lyctor. I am a necromantic princess of Ida. I am the cleverest necromancer of my generation."

"Like hell you are," said Harrowhark.

"So *impress* me," said Ianthe, unmoved.

In the mirror, that paintless, unfamiliar face tightened. The lips pressed together until they were the pale brown of roses, ashen. Ianthe found herself thinking what the face could have done to it— the top lip was softly curved, as though the painter had not been able to help embellishing where they thought nobody would notice; the arch of that philtrum was close to a poem. The cheek was unreasonably smooth, considering the amount of topological greasepaint those Ninth House pores must have seen; those heavy eyelids, deep-set, thick with black lashes, a vanity that nobody in that shuffling mausoleum had thought to shear. And that was not even considering that the face was taut and stricken with the starvation marks of agony; that she had shaven her head almost fully bald for this, leaving only pinpricks of black stippling her skull.

Then there were the eyes themselves: that solemn and lightless black that, whatever rictus the nun's face might assume, could not hide the woman; they stared out of Nonagesimus's face now with mute, flayed appeal, as stark and discomfiting as skinless muscle.

"I will impress upon you this," the Ninth necromancer said forebodingly, and stopped.

Then she said: "I asked you for a reason. That reason was not your genius, which I admit exists. Nobody who reverse-engineered the Lyctoral process could be anything but a genius. But I haven't seen anything that makes me believe you are more than—a kind of necromantic gymnast, doing showy tricks without concern for the theory. You're not of Sextus's calibre either."

"No," said Ianthe lightly, "but Sextus's head exploded, proving to the world that he hadn't accounted for everything."

"I may have been Sextus's necromantic superior; but he was the better man. You are not even so worthy of that brain as to wipe its bloodied remnants from the wall," said the Ninth. "You are a murderer, a conwoman, a cheat, a liar, a slitherer, and you embody the worst flaws of your House—as do I . . . Nonetheless, I did not ask you because you are a *Lyctor*, Third. I did not even ask you because you know significantly more about your subject than I do."

"Tell me, because I am hugely bored of hearing all my flaws," said Ianthe, with lessened patience.

The shadow cultist stared into the mirror. Those great black eyes were empty pools: abyssal holes—an oil spill in the dark—or unfilled sockets.

"I asked you because you know what it is," she said haltingly, "to be—fractured."

Of such banality was grief made.

"Harrowhark," said Ianthe. "Let me give you a little advice. It is free and smart. I'll walk this back now—I'll adopt the sweetest good humour about everything you've done for me already—if you admit that you are *running away*. And running away is for fools and children. You are a Lyctor. You have paid the price. The hardest part is over. Smile to the universe, thank it for its graciousness, and mount your throne. You answer to nobody now."

"If you think that you and I are not more beholden than ever," said the girl, "you are an idiot."

"Who is left? *What* is left?"

Nonagesimus shut her eyes briefly. When they opened, one was—not correct. She stared at her own heterochromatic, night-and-day gaze, at those celestially mismatched irises. One black. One gold.

Then the Ninth House Lyctor said tightly: "We are wasting time. Open me up."

"It will be worse for you in the end, Nonagesimus—"

And Harrowhark roared: "*Do* it, you faithless coward, you swore me an oath! Expose the brain—guide me—and let me handle it from there! There's still time, and you thieve it from me!"

"All right, sister," said Ianthe, and she reached for the awl first. The hammer would be second; the hammer for the living hand, the awl for the dead. She rested it high on the frontal bone, squinted, and gauged. "Time to absolutely fuck you up."

She struck.

* * *

Once Harrowhark was sleeping a sleep she might never even wake from, her face marked with the lines of weary, heart-heavy exhaustion, Ianthe sat and watched. She had not been allowed to watch the entire process; for a stretch she had been forced to sit behind a screen and twiddle her thumbs as those paranoid amateur hands rummaged around in a way that would hopefully mean Harrowhark couldn't coordinate enough to piss, if life was remotely fair. Now she pressed her fingers over that scalp, trying to work it out, trying to see exactly what had been done.

She gave up within a few minutes—impossible to tell with Lyctor privacy, even this close. No bleeds, certainly. Everything in the right place. Maybe a little reduction in the temporal lobe, a few out-of-order bumps in the temporal gyrus that might have been there already. As a last act of pettiness, Ianthe coaxed a new crop of that lightless black hair out of the scalp, and fidgeted with the follicles so that they would squirt out a little extra, cursing the Ninth House nun to almost *ceaseless* haircuts. It was the little things that mattered.

She stood at the doorway and watched the breath minutely fill those lungs, in—and out—and in. There were smudges of sweat on the face that in this light looked just like tears. It tickled her fancy to imagine Harrowhark falling asleep crying, like any lovelorn child. What a fool. What a destructive, romantic, ridiculous act. It was always a certain kind of ass who approached love like that—a certain kind of very good, talented ass, who had been overly used to their hands on the reins and never could cope when they were taken off—nor had the personality to put them back on again.

Ianthe had that type of personality. And she had a few years on Harrow.

"Someday I'll marry that girl," she said aloud. "It might be good for her." And: "Probably not, though."

And then Ianthe the First went to see a man about a queen.

ACT FIVE

4ō

??? ??? ???

HARROW NOVA HELD HER black rapier thrust upward in the direction of the top tiershaft. She laid her offhand arm across her chest, her knuckles against her collarbone, where the black chain of Samael Novenary—true black Drearburh steel, each link a death's head, the weighted end a carved butterfly of pelvis in lead-filled bone—clinked unmusically against itself. Her nerves were steel; her guts were some lesser material due to a curious admixture of fear and fury. They had assumed the qualities of gruel, or hot porridge. "To the floor," she said.

"Harrow," said the cavalier opposite her, "we don't have to do this."

"Then withdraw your claim and acknowledge me as the cavalier primary, you *weed*, you *worm*, you *slime*. I'm your superior in every way. I do not possess your size—I do not possess your strength—but I have trained for one singular purpose, and I will not be denied this chance."

"Yes, Harrow; but my father would kill me," he said.

Ortus Nigenad hulked before her sadly. Massive in his new robe and boots, with new panniers too, and his grandmother's rapier—the new boots and rapier she envied, but the panniers she did not. They were freshly crafted of obsidian and the strongest type of canvas, which must have emptied out the treasury. Harrow wondered bitterly if her parents had flogged something.

Ortus was all muscle and fat; he had the desired enormity of the modern Ninth House cavalier, and she never could have hoped to match it. She had never tried. Harrow realised early in her career that if she could not have the size, nor the weight, nor the sheer breadth, that she would have the speed, the technique, the agility. She had decided this at around five years old.

Denied of weapons, it had been Harrow who had climbed the Anastasian monument and retrieved the chain of Samael, the sacred relic of the long-dead warrior servant of the original tomb-keeper; for that sin she had been forced to strip before the very altar she stood before now as the Reverend Father whipped stripes into her back, until the Daughter had intervened. Now Harrow had the chain, but the Daughter never let her forget the intervention.

"Harrow," said the skull-faced cavalier of frightful aspect—upon stepping down from his post five years previous, Mortus had scari-fied the skull into his son, when the adopted necromantic heir had confirmed Ortus for her cavalier primary; the cicatricial lines showed clearly beneath the paint—"they will never let you go. I truly wish they would. I do not long to travel to the First House—I do not dare imagine to serve a Lyctor, let alone stand against one, as in the days of Nonius."

"Matthias Nonius never stood against a bloody Lyctor."

"It is clear in the histories—"

"Half the page was gone!"

"A suggestive emendation makes it clear that—"

"I am the daughter of the House of the Ninth," she said, cutting off whatever he had to say about suggestive emendations. "I am the un-fulfilled vow and the bloody teeth of the unkissed skull. I acknowledge myself as a cruel disappointment. I may have been supplanted—I may be no real heir to the mysteries that belong only to the Reverend line—but I *will* bear the sword! If I am no adept, it is my right to carry the blade instead!"

Ortus Nigenad wiped the sweat off his forehead. The candlelight limned the carved hurts of his face, but his expression did not match their fearsomeness. The panniers of bone at his back rustled pleas-antly, in the manner of a child's sandpit.

"Harrow," he said. "You do not even really want to carry the blade for her."

"No," she said. "I hope she gets boiled alive in oil. I hope she falls into a hole with a crowd watching. I hope someone takes a large pair of secateurs to the muscles at the backs of her heels. I so genuinely and wildly long to see that. I would buy tickets."

Ortus said tremulously, "But you know she quite—"

"No."

"And they say she is petitioning for—"

"Continue that sentence," she said, "and I'll make it *to the pain.*"

"Harrow," he said doggedly, "I would become cavalier secondary in the veriest heartbeat. How honourable still, to be a cavalier secondary of Drearburh! And to stay at home and look faithfully after the family, and not go out into the unkind arms of space, and to foreign houses! But even if I said, *Yes, I acknowledge Harrow Nova as my better,* your—the Reverend Mother and Father would not accept it. You would have to kill me before they would consider you. And it is the least of my desires, to be killed."

"You are right," said Harrow.

His relief was palpable. His shoulders sagged forward, though that was possibly due to the panniers hastening his scoliosis. Aiglamene was always scolding him about posture. *Look at Harrow.* She *stands like a monument,* she would say. *You stand like a damned fishhook.* Ortus leant heavily against the pews with a sigh of relief, and he said: "Thank you. Good. I am glad."

"And I consider it a salient point," continued Harrow.

She took the sword from her chest, and slung her chain from over her shoulder, and seized one weighted end between her gloved fingers. The welter of fury inside her resolved into a wet rush, like metal poured into a mould, and as it always had, the sword became an extension of her arm. "Prepare to die, Ortus Nigenad. Commit your soul to the Locked Tomb, and to the rock, and to the chains, and hope it floats high on the River."

"For God's sake, Harrow, *please.*"

Their voices had carried. The little sacristy door flew open; Marshal Crux emerged, hoary, wearing his most formal mouldering leathers, his raddled face aghast and his liver-spotted hands trembling with indignation.

"Swords drawn!" he cried. "Swords drawn in the narthex—before the altar, and before the vesting tables, and with the icons watching! You *besmirch* us. You *sully* us. You *debase* this place."

"Forgive me, Marshal," said Harrow.

"I do not speak to you," croaked Crux, with solemn dignities. Crux was the only reliable source of sympathy in Harrow's life; sympathy always delivered in such a way as to be horribly unfair to everyone else, but sympathy all the same, and as unpopular as it made her she would not have swapped it for—anyone else's tenderness. "I speak to the cavalier primary. Ortus the Ninth, fool that you are, you ought to know better."

"Forgive me, Marshal," said Ortus humbly, as was his wont, as though he had any part in it. Sometimes Harrow hated him for that.

"I will not," said Crux indignantly. "Go rush to your cuckoo's side. They are nearly done with the arrangements."

The cavalier primary stiffened, and with the faintest note of reproach he murmured something. The tone of his murmur did not quite make it to *defensive;* Ortus, even being well over thirty, could not do anything but mumble before the marshal.

Crux barked out a noise that was too old to be a laugh.

"What's that? What's that, you egg? *I oughtn't to call her such*? Choke yourself—*burn* yourself—bury yourself. If you have the bottle to tell that cockerel what I name her, I will think the better of you for it."

True to form, and with no more self-defence than a huge and aggravated sigh, Ortus set off in the direction of the sacristy. As he left, Crux was muttering, "Rueful day when we send flotsam to be our champion . . . rueful day when we send jetsam to be its sword. Harrowhark"—only Crux added on -*hark;* it was carefully elided by everyone else, for what it reminded people she was—"be gentle with your weapon, and do not make it naked before the altar."

He lumbered closer to her, coughed wetly, and added in a hoarse and patently audible whisper: "There are pilgrims here, even now. It would be pretty to apologise."

There *were* pilgrims; she was embarrassed not to have noticed.

They must have come in without her perceiving them. Two visitors kneeled toward the back of the pews, on the kneeling rail, their black church robes taped with brown around the right shoulders to show their House affiliation. She sheathed the rapier in its ragged scabbard, and reshouldered the chain she had polished so carefully, and performed a rather half-hearted bob in the direction of the altar as she made her way down the aisle.

At her approach, one of the pilgrims shook her hood back. She wore spectacles, and her thick brown hair was neatly bound back in a black fillet, as was customary; the man next to her had shaved his head and kept running a hand over it surreptitiously, like a child at its first cropping. Harrow was surprised to see the first pilgrim give her a weary, troubled smile, as though the woman knew her. It was a smile that was sorry you had missed the mark in your exams, but thought you had not quite studied hard enough. Harrow had never set eyes upon her in her life. She did not know her. She did not know her husband.

Except—how had she known that the man was the woman's husband?

"This isn't how it happens," said Abigail.

41

??? BEFORE???

THE MUSIC WAS RAUCOUS to Harrowhark's ears. The stringed instruments—viols—a piano—all played in carefully tasteful modulation, but to her affrighted senses it seemed as though they were blasting full bore directly into her tympanic chambers. It was very warm inside the amphitheatre, and despite the kindness of the candlelight—despite the electric lights being dimmed to an attractive submission, playing out over the assorted massacre of the crowd in its eye-hurting panoply of colour—her eyes still felt like they were bleeding. The Reverend Daughter's veil of office had been pinned back upon her head, precisely where it was no use to her.

The crowd at least thinned out considerably near their delegation: no matter the bewilderment of the occasion, no matter the crush in the room, nobody really wanted to get close to the House of the Ninth. Harrowhark was glad for this on two levels. One, because she hated the press of people; two, because in the dimness, and with distance, there was less chance for other guests to notice the shabbiness of their finery. The lacework of her robes had been patched with thread as close to the original black as possible, but not *quite* matching, as was the perpetual trouble with blacks. The brocade of her skirts was stiff from bad storage. She was not ashamed of the ancient diadem and torc collar she wore. Both had been taken gently from the corpse of an ancestor, before that ancestor had sighed into powder under the beam of the torchlight. But she did not like what their patches of rust signified of their poverty.

Harrowhark fretted with the edges of her veil. "It's no use the damn thing being down," said her captain, sotto voce.

"I do not intend to compete," said Harrowhark—not moving her lips but inclining her face very slightly toward the woman next to her. "If I did, I would never compete with my *face*."

"Yes, but you might as well have one," said the older woman calmly. "That's the first thing Her Divine Highness will look for in a bride: presence of a face. It's a precondition of attraction."

"That is *not* why we are here. Unlike every other House scion present, I will not—flaunt my goods in the shop window."

"Emperor knows what we'd even flaunt," grunted Aiglamene.

The other seven Houses present were flaunting as though they were birds in a particularly baroque mating season. Her so-called cavalier primary took great interest; he jotted verses on a scrap of flimsy that he palmed discreetly into his pocket every time her gaze fell on him. The other Houses had mingled into a spectrum of colours, interweaving in the dances like a living drift of spangles. Clean Cohort whites with coloured ribands vaunting colour on the pips or wrist; long dresses in iridescent white, a simpering tactic, with hued wreaths on the head to denote the House; necromancers in robes of all kinds, none of them practical. All except for the Sixth House, who did not seem to be represented among the dancers, but sat in a grey puddle by the wall in wallflower blessedness, as though they were a communal gawky child who could not find a partner. They all wore the same dead-dove greys and chattered among themselves. If the situation had been different, Harrowhark might have made an introductory approach to them, but she had other things to think about.

One tall, astonishingly built Third House princess had chosen to sit among their number like a butterfly in a grey bog: she wore a silk robe in gold and breeches that showed off a calf too fit to be called a necromancer's, and she was holding a glass of champagne and laughing at something she was being told. The rest of the noble House of Ida made intermittent attempts to chivvy her back, in case being seen among the Sixth House proclaimed her too hopeless to win the attention of Her Divine Highness, but the Third princess kept waving them off.

Harrowhark's anticipation was at a fever pitch by the time anyone approached her. She did not know why her heart was beating so hard; she did not know why she was afraid, other than that the crowd was unmanageable and that there was too much noise and light. She knew her eyes were too wide within her sacramental paint—the elegant skull called simply the Chain, which she had been practising for months—when a couple approached, without a retinue. A man and a woman, the lady with the hint of a necromancer's build: she was arm in arm with the man, and he appeared to be eating a canape on a stick with his other hand, and so Harrowhark refused to look at him. The lady wore a deep cocoa satin gown with a train, and when she stood before Harrowhark she coughed, discreetly, into one buff glove. The simplicity of the gown revealed little about her, but the cut said more, and the cursory little gold tiara perched on the gleaming brown braids of hair said a lot and loudly.

"Lady Abigail Pent," said Harrowhark, who had been practising that as well.

"To be honest," said Abigail, "I'm quite sorry to crash this one, as I would *love* to see where this mixer goes."

"I, also," said Harrowhark's cavalier primary, from behind her shoulder.

Magnus had finished his canape, and added enthusiastically: "Agreed. This is top. *Have* you ever eaten party food before, Lady Harrowhark? Because if you haven't, this is a very good approximation. No taste, but incredibly salty."

Harrow said frigidly, "*Pardon?*" before she remembered that she could not have known Lady Abigail Pent by sight.

"This still isn't how it happens," said the Fifth—

42

MONTH??? DEATH

"Lieutenant!" cried a voice. "Wait up—please."

Coming out of the briefing room, still a little bit pinched with space exposure—she had learned belatedly that after the first week it was considered namby-pamby to wear one's placket of grave dirt anywhere visible, and it made a bump within the uniform—Harrowhark stopped and pivoted to the two soldiers behind her. She came to the unpleasant realisation that she would be forced to salute, and duly did so: although the navy-rimmed pins in front of her denoted the same rank as her own, the burnished steel pins on the opposite lapel indicated that these two had seen action. This was not greatly surprising, in the context of the navy edging of the Fourth House. She had already heard a great many jibes to the effect that Fourth House arrivals ought to be issued with both a medal of honour and a coffin. But they were very young. They were younger even than her, which was grotesque. She recognised them before they had finished their responding salute, which was significantly worse.

She said stiffly, "Lieutenant Tettares. Lieutenant Chatur. Do you require the service of the Black Anchorite?"

"No, because who would, ever," said Lieutenant Chatur, whose corkscrew hair had been bound up at the back of her head. She did not resemble Harrowhark's idea of a cavalier primary, even with the rapier bound to her hip. She was looking Harrow over rather critically in return. Harrow had been allowed her paint—she had been granted her jewels of office—as a chaplain, she had even been allowed a bit of robe, though a cursory Cohort robe that pinned to one shoulder and was about as much use as a sugar-spun bone. The starched white shirt and trousers seemed to take away all her substance. The more substantial child before her was saying in a piercing voice: "I heard they actually had to *exhume* a book as to how your lot work, because we haven't had a black friar for *fifty years.*"

"Then I will take my leave—Lieutenant. Lieutenant—"

"Excuse her, please, she sucks," said her necromancer briefly.

("Thanks?"

"You do though?) Look—I wanted to introduce myself. You obviously know who I am. But we'll be going through training together—we're the only House heirs entering on the same footing—I don't think it would be stupid to keep together. And you're here without a cavalier. Nobody knows why the *Reverend Daughter's* signed up for action. But I can't judge—I'm the Baron of Tisis, and they're probably going to haze us all until we're half dead. Now we're all together, I'd like to be friends. Pax?"

Harrowhark stared down at the gloved hand proffered, then at the hand's owner. He had recently taken out quite a lot of earrings, and his ears were riddled with little empty punch holes, as though he were the recent victim of some guerrilla sewing. Both faces were, in fact, turned to her with none of the disgust she had initially fancied; their enthusiasm, she had to admit, was sincere. She did not shake the hand, but she reached out to briefly touch the fingertips with her own, and she said, "I would advise you against this. The Cohort were . . . opposed to my inclusion."

"Oh, you have to get over that," said the cavalier dismissively. "We could've papered the walls in strongly worded Cohort letters. It's not like you're the only one. The Cohort hates it when the actual *heir* joins up. They legitimately tried to give us mumps—"

("They did not legitimately try to give us mumps. My little brother gave us mumps.")

"—there's a whole bushel of rules about asking permission to engage, and if there's a war on we'll get packed off to the back, so if you're *smart* the first thing you have to say to your commanding officer is, 'Excuse me, I don't want my rank to get between myself and the troops,' and then she can 'forget' to follow the safety missive, and you can get put on the post-thanergy front, where it's interesting— Do you want to go to the cafeteria?"

Harrowhark did not want to go to the cafeteria. Lieutenants Tettares and Chatur accompanied her to the cafeteria anyway, a place she had contrived never to visit unless absolutely necessary. She felt acutely visible standing in the queue in full view of all the other officers-in-training; the massed necromancers and sword-handling men and women of the Nine Houses who had passed examinations, or paid money, or whatever it was they did in the other Houses, to acquire an officer's rank. She was the only one with a black-enamelled lieutenant's pip; she was the only one with black slashes at her sleeves. All the while, the Fourth pair kept up a stream of meaningless chatter, like two human waterfalls. Crux would have said that their tongues were hung in the middle. If, Emperor forbid, she had been a flesh magician, she would have been very sorely tempted to hang their tongues in the middle herself.

Harrow tuned back in to the cavalier-enlisted saying, enthusiastically: "—tried the coffee yet?"

The coffee had, in truth, been a long way down Harrow's list of priorities. In the face of Lieutenant Chatur's bewildering ardour, she could only muster a chilly: "No."

A strange ripple passed over the younger girl's face, as though she were trying very badly not to laugh. But she said, "It's not like anything you get back at home. It's got extra stimulants and things—like, acids—for space exposure. Bio-adaptive . . . *Can you tell me what it is, Isaac?*"

He screwed up his narrow eyes, sighed a little, and then supplied: "Bio-adaptive reuptake inhibitors."

"And what do we call it?"

"BARI," he said.

"Yeah, BARI! It makes the coffee taste *weird,* but if you make it the right way, with like spices and stuff, it's actually *great.* The Cohort wouldn't run without the on-duty coffee adepts. We wanted to try this deck's cafeteria, because they've got a hotshot new BARI star."

Harrowhark found herself at the front of the queue beyond which this BARI star apparent waited; and she found herself looking down at the counter, her tongue tied.

"Let me guess," said a voice. "You take it black."

She reached out for the cup. The server pushed it toward her in the same instant—their fingers brushed awkwardly in the act of transmission, and in a mummified moment of time, they looked at each other.

The coffee adept was a girl that Harrowhark had never seen before, though she must have been part of their training platoon. With the plain shirtsleeves and apron, and a cloth slung over the shoulder obscuring her insignia, it was impossible to tell her affiliation: the arms beneath the rolled-up sleeves betrayed lean, taut muscle, a little dewy with sweat and steam from the mess. But it was the face that sent her neurons in a thalergetic spin. When Harrowhark looked at that face, she found a curious heat travelling all the way up from the pit of her pylorus to the high collar of her Cohort shirt. It then traversed her cheeks, her nose, her brow, her temples. The other officer smiled a firm-jawed, long, crooked smile at her; Harrow was electrified by the fact that beneath the hastily brushed crop of red hair those eyes were—

"Absolutely *not*," said Abigail, from beside her.

43

ONE NIGHT BEFORE THE EMPEROR'S MURDER

HARROW THRASHED ON THE mattress and breathed in lungfuls of splintering air. She writhed like a shot animal; arms pinned her down—"Stay with us, Ninth, come on," someone was saying—and a sudden spasm seized her, shaking her from the inside until she was certain she would vibrate out of her skin. There was a susurrus of hushed mutters coming from above her, urgent voices, none of which made sense to her:

"Are we stable—?"

"I hope so; another pull like that and she'll bring the children back wholesale, and I don't think I can bear sending them out again—"

"Why *now*?"

"Wasn't that—?"

"I honestly preferred some of those to—"

"No. Better the rules we have," interrupted the second voice. "We have no idea of the limitations in those other scenarios."

Another breath—and her throat refused, closing up in protest; she turned her head and coughed, affronted, affrighted—she opened her eyes, and the world rushed up to meet her.

She awoke convinced that she was staring up at Dominicus framed within a blue sky, a lambent and unreal blue, a nonsensical backdrop. A familiar voice—Magnus's—said kindly, "You're fine. You're fine." The sky was the ceiling, and the ceiling was a decrepit room in Canaan House, veiled with the hot white breath from her own throat. When the world finally landed its long wound-up sucker punch, a tangled

379

howl came out of her throat, and she was shocked that she was able to make such a noise. Memory hit Harrowhark Nonagesimus with the inexorable gravity of a satellite sucked from orbit, flinging itself to die on the surface of its bounden planet; the world hit her like a fall.

There was a blur of faces, of movement. Harrow found that she was not shocked, after all. She was consumed. She was the kindling for the arson taking place in her heart, her brain dry wadding for the flames, her soul so much incandescent gas. She could not do this. She absolutely and fundamentally could not do this.

"Harrow?" said someone close by—someone familiar; her vision swam.

"If I forget you, let my right hand be forgotten," her mouth was saying. "Add more also, if aught but death part me and thee."

And, unsteadily: "Griddle."

The hands must have withdrawn; she found herself facedown on the mattress, sobbing as she had not sobbed since she was a child. Someone said, "Everybody out. Go—" But this was more than she could take stock of. Harrow was too amazed by her body's expanding capacity for despair. It was as though her feeling doubled even as she looked at it, unfolding, like falling down an endless flight of stairs. She dug her hands into the mattress and she cried for Gideon Nav.

She only stopped weeping when her body had physically exhausted itself. The tears could not flow from gummed-up eyes; nor sobs from a cracked throat. For a long time she pressed her face into the wet patch of mattress she had cried into, and smelled the old stuffing, and felt the grief that had multiplied into a universe.

She sat up. She breathed. She pressed her face into the front of her worn black robes, and dried her tears into chilly tracks on her cheeks. Harrowhark looked around her, and the bloody rawness of her throat made her guttural as she asked curtly: "What have I done?"

"That was actually a question I'd hoped *you'd* answer," said Abigail Pent.

She was the only one left in the room. Harrow looked her over with new eyes. Even with this new perspective, in all respects Pent was the same as ever. Neat, if a little scuffed around the edges, as though she really had been slumming in an ice-cold Canaan House and had not had a proper bath in a while—brown-eyed and fresh-faced, every inch a daughter of the Fifth. There was a scarf tied around that immaculate hair, and she wore large puffy mittens on each hand.

She was not, more to the point, the ruptured corpse she and Gideon had found at the bottom of the facility stairs: the body with the slit abdomen, with a key sealed neatly inside her kidney. She *seemed* alive, and well, and living.

"You died," said Harrowhark. "Septimus killed you. The Lyctor masquerading as Septimus."

"Yes," said the Fifth adept. "It was unpleasant. Look, I hate to ask, but did you—get her? None of us are sure."

"Nav and I drove a sword through her breastbone," said Harrow, and swallowed against a wad of saliva burning in her throat. Her brain was whirring like an overheated mechanism; she could almost smell the hot dust. It was long past the hour to put herself in order.

She said, "Give me a minute."

"Take your time," said Pent.

The cold did not worry Harrow until, as habit, she tried to warm her core from within, and found that she could not. She was somehow not a Lyctor here. Pushing her blood cells around made her feel that old, hungry pang for thanergy that she had not felt for the better part of a year. She closed her eyes so that the only senses assaulting her were the temperature—the reddening burn on her cheeks and hands—and the blackness of her lids, as blank as the pages of an unwritten book.

Sixty seconds. Anything more was indulgence. She opened her eyes and said, "Lady Pent. Tell me about your childhood bedroom."

"It was the size of this sitting room, perhaps," said Pent promptly. "Two beds with their heads against the far wall from the door. I liked to have my younger brother sleep in my room sometimes, when I was small. Primrose walls in paste-on flimsy, not wash—a pretty chroma of the Prince Undying, but a little cockeyed—a Vit-D panel in place of a window, with a repeated design on it. My grandfather's arm bones over the door. A little reinforced table where I played at dolls or read, with a cubby beneath it where I was meant to crouch in case a zonal jet made it past the winnow. Phosphorescent stars painted on the ceiling, a peg on the wall for my gloves and robe. I haven't thought of it in years. Why?"

"Initial test," said Harrowhark. "The flexibility of metaphysical solipsism aside, I have hardly any knowledge of the Fifth House and how its people live there. The more nonsensical your answer, the more likely you were to be a construction of my brain."

Abigail laughed, but it carried a tinge of rue: the laugh of a woman who had opened a long-lost book to find the most necessary page torn out.

"Reverend Daughter," she said, "I've been accused of many things, but this is the first time I've been assumed to be a delusion."

"But you are—"

"A ghost," said the woman smilingly. "A revenant, more precisely."

Then she said: "There was so much I wanted to ask. So much I'd assumed! I sought a deliberate pattern in your choices when, perhaps, none existed, which is a shameful mistake for a scholar. Therefore, let us debunk all my pet ideas. You *are* a Lyctor now, aren't you?"

"Yes," said Harrow. Gideon. Blood. A broken rail. "It was not my intention, at the end. But—yes."

Abigail's eyes grew intent; she leant forward. "That's one bet won," she said, with grim satisfaction. "All right. When did you become aware of what was happening to you? When did you realise what was going on with the other soul?"

It was easier to answer questions mechanically. "In the first days. I knew she would be absorbed. I understood that I would inadvertently destroy her soul—the process was already underway. But it hadn't finished. I had time. I decided to remove my ability to so incorporate her . . . by removing my ability to comprehend her."

Easier, now, to recall it. A litany. The same singsong recitation as the Eightfold Word. It could almost live apart from suffering. "I took the part of my brain that remembered her . . . that understood her soul . . . and I disconnected it. Then I made rather crude systems—so as not to be accidentally reminded . . . knowing that the pathways

might reopen if they were knocked about. I had an accomplice . . .
someone who knew how to manipulate the fatty tissue of the brain
better than I possibly could. I made my skull a construct, programmed
to apply pressure to specific lobes. And it worked, Pent. It *worked*,"
she said. "It was stupid. A brute-force solution. But it worked."

Abigail was looking at her very carefully, with a different expression than before. Harrow knew she sounded a little irascible when
she said, "What?"

"I think we are talking over each other," said the Fifth adept, rubbing her mittened hands together. "I'm not asking about the preserved soul that made you a Lyctor, Reverend Daughter . . . though
that's also filled in some of the pieces. Harrowhark, I am referring to
the *invasive* soul."

"The *invasive*—?"

"You are being haunted," said Abigail calmly. "I had assumed you
had picked this battlefield deliberately, and raised an army to fight
alongside you. I didn't quite know why you'd chosen *us*. Now I know,
but it seems you did not. You are possessed by an angry spirit, Harrow, and you are losing the war."

Harrow reflexively tried to pad out her fat reserves; it was really
shockingly cold. She was stopped when she realized she could not
identify where they sat under the skin of her arms, let alone augment
them. The limitation was familiar: it was the limitation she had lived
with all her life, when she was *Ninth*, and not *First*. Her furnace of
power was gone.

She reached for the memory of her other self—no; she under-
served herself by separating herself into two halves, Harrow First
and Harrow Secundarius, as though she were following bells. They
were all one Harrowhark, wearing different clothes. And she was no
better now that her vestments were black—in a way she was greatly
worse. But the memory was there.

Think of how when you blow air into water, you make bubbles . . .

It was getting chillier. The wind howled against the darkened
window. There was no good weather in her brain. She said, "We are
in the River."

"Yes," said Abigail. "That was my first realisation."

"This is my creation."

"Yes. You set the parameters," said Abigail. "We realized through process of elimination, as we each recalled ourselves in the end. You didn't. Ortus was convinced it was your creation from the start—I'm sorry that I disbelieved him."

That was for later mental delectation. "I made a *bubble* in the River, just like Sextus did. But unconsciously, shoddily . . ." Sextus must have thought her such a churl. It would have been an enormous relief to have Palamedes Sextus with her then, if only so that she could, perhaps, offer some paltry thanks. But to have him see her so slow on the uptake would be hideous— "Why Canaan House? Why Ortus Nigenad? To fill the hole in my memory."

Thankfully, Pent was quicker on the uptake. "You didn't *remove* the memories of your cavalier, Harrowhark. I think that would have been beyond even the powers of a Lyctor. You falsified them. You skinned them over with something that looked good." What a waste of a woman, to have ended her life at the bottom of a ladder.

"But why make so many changes? Why is this narrative so different? This isn't how it happened at *all*. I understand that . . . that Gideon had to be—absent, but why . . ."

"This isn't a picture you're drawing, Harrow," said Pent. "It's a play you're directing. You set up a stage in the River, you pulled in ghosts as your actors, and you enforced certain rules to keep your cast on-script. But now another director is trying to hijack the play, and the struggle for control backstage is leaking over into the action out front. You're being ousted."

"By whom?"

"I don't know," said Abigail candidly. "And there are other discrepancies I'd hoped you could have shed light on. Why did you only pull *some* of us as ghosts? Why did the others appear as—varyingly ludicrous constructs? Lieutenant Dyas was certain Judith was wrong before she even died, that she was like a confused parody of herself."

"I never could have called the ghost of Captain Deuteros," interrupted Harrow. "Deuteros lives."

Abigail leaned in eagerly. "Tell Dyas that. She'll want to know. The princesses . . . ?"

"Alive."

"Their cavalier—"

"Breakfast." At Abigail's bewilderment, Harrow qualified: "Ianthe Tridentarius is a Lyctor."

"Blast. It should have been Coronabeth. Ianthe never *was* quite the thing. The Sixth—"

"Camilla's alive. Palamedes . . . enjoys extenuating circumstances." At this second round of bewilderment, she qualified: "The Master Warden found the idea of dying inconvenient."

Abigail brightened. "Say no more."

The Fifth House necromancer sighed in obvious pleasure, a simple delight that some of them had lived where she herself had not. A deep guilt sparked within Harrow's ribcage. Pent even murmured, "The King over the River is good," which filled Harrow with another sensation entirely.

That brought with it a reminder so savagely stupid she was astonished that it had not been her first thought. Her hands flew to her midsection. She closed her eyes. She leant back into the soft curve of her spine—she took the reins of the River in her hands, and she walked out into the waters, and she walked, and she walked.

As her—cavalier—might have put it, absolutely butt-fuck nothing happened. She could not access the River. She was not aware of it. There was no awareness of the anchor of her body; just as with the removal of her Lyctoral magic, there was no exit route. She was trapped within the bubble, writhing like a fish. And somewhere back on the Mithraeum . . .

"Time," said Harrow urgently. "How does this track with *time*?"

"Based on my assumptions about spirit magic and the nature of consciousness," said Abigail, "this—stage—only exists when you have limited or no conscious awareness. While you sleep, or while you have been knocked out, or otherwise disconnected from outside stimuli. I have not experienced any breaks in time—it's seamless from this side. I imagine the simulation runs within your sleeping mind's understanding of time, if somewhat contracted *and* dilated . . . How much time *has* passed in the—er—real world?"

"Nine months."

"Good Lord." She was genuinely upset. "I would have put us at about eight weeks. Oh—my family's probably been told . . . They'll be wondering where the living hell my spirit is. My poor brother— Magnus's parents—my fern collection—"

"Lady Pent," said Harrowhark forcefully, "forget the ferns. In the real world, I have been fatally stabbed. The place that holds my body is about to be overrun by thanergetic monsters created by a galactic revenant. I am, put bluntly, on the verge of death. My soul is under siege, and I overwrote my real memories with a ghost-filled pocket dimension, which has now apparently been co-opted by some kind of poltergeist. From what I can tell I am *stuck* in here. I cannot get out. And I am about to die—I may even be dead already—which will render this all somewhat moot."

The window cracked. At first she assumed it was the howling, killing wind; but as she and Abigail watched, a questing pink tentacle, crackling with ice as it shifted and slithered, made a ropy trail down a broken hole in the glass. A long, pulsing tube. As they watched, a sphincter opened in the end, and from that hole emerged a clattering pile of plex scope slides, the type you would preserve a cell sample between. The door to the bedroom had been flung open: the previously dead Magnus Quinn was there, wearing a huge furry coat, cavern-cheeked from the chill, saying, "They're breaching the walls, dear."

"Tell Protesilaus and the lieutenant not to touch them."

"Too late, and I can't blame them, these things are vile—"

"Leave your body to your body, Reverend Daughter," said Abigail, rising shakily to stand, her teeth chattering. "If you were dead on the other side, we'd all be gone by now. If you die in *here*, your soul is gone forever. Right now, in this moment, you are alive—let us ensure that if your body survives, you will remain at the helm."

Harrow fought to be heard over the screams of the wind. "But I was stabbed through the stomach! What's *happening* out there?"

44

THAT SAME NIGHT BEFORE THE EMPEROR'S MURDER

THE BLADE OF THE rapier tangled in your skin. Big hanks of dermis kept wending their way up along the fuller, unsure where to head from there; as organs knitted together inside your abdomen—as interstitial meat threw itself against the invasive blade—the bloodied tip quivered, pushed this way and that by the regrowing tissue. You'd been stabbed from behind, and you'd collapsed backward onto the rapier's hilt. Its foible pointed upward where it protruded from your torso.

And you'd gone and left me behind.

I arched up on your hands, rested your weight on your feet—the blade stayed stuck—and I pushed up against the corridor wall, and I got you to stand. Your legs were trembling. The only thing I could think of to do was to wad up your hands in the robe, give myself a count of three, and push the rapier tip backward as hard and as quick as I possibly could. The noise that resulted—I'm not doing it justice when I say it went *SCHHHLIIIIICK*, which also doesn't describe the pain of a full foot of steel being pushed back through your innards and out the small of your back as carefully as I could do it, which wasn't very. The sword fell to the tiles with a sad rattle, and I took a couple of moments, and by the time I reached down to get it you'd just—healed up. No more pain. No more stab wound.

The hilt was so hot and slippery with blood that it was hard to grasp. Your hands were bare. It took a few goes to get it. The grip was made of polished wood or plex, and your fingers didn't close

387

the way I expected them to, probably because they were shorter than mine.

We were in a narrow, sweaty corridor, dark, lit only by a thin rail of overhead red lighting. There was an alarm blaring somewhere, and a distant white-noise buzzing sound, like you'd get from a piece of malfunctioning machinery. You were soaked through with blood, and where you weren't soaked through with blood you were soaked through with sweat. The air was shimmering with the heat. Standing in that hallway was like standing next to a bonfire, one that also made you wet.

Beneath you a bunch of blood was smeared playfully on the floor and lower walls, as though someone had rolled around in it, which I guess you had. But there wasn't *that* much of it. It hadn't been a fight. Whoever stuck you with your own rapier hadn't let you get a shot off. You weren't around to be furious, but if you had been, I would've told you not to bother; I planned on making them sorrier than they had ever been in all their fucking life.

Pool of blood: check. Air so hot: check. Surrounded by big and illicit bones: check. Looking at your hand to keep this tally—what hand there was, beneath the blood, and your fingers, and your small palms, and their absolute lack of thenar muscle—reality went through me. Kind of like a big iron railing, now that I think about it.

You were gone. You'd left me behind. Inside you.

"Fuck," I said. It wasn't my voice. "Fuck. Oh, shit. Oh, fucking hell. Help. Yuck. *Aaaargh.*"

In the darkness of that hot and bony corridor, something bumbled into view before you—us; me—which at least forestalled my full-on physical and emotional breakdown. It was a nightmarish nonsense of wasp, and bone, and meat, and it was alive, and when it saw me it stopped.

The thing's bulk was set on a stretched-out, humanlike frame—like a person walking crab-fashion, feet planted flat and hands flat backward on the ground, abdomen thrust ecstatically up in midair. But when I say *hands* and *feet*, think of hands and feet fed through a shredder, and then all the exposed bone and flesh banded back together with black-flecked orange shell. This was topped with great shiny plates of thorax, a big diamond-shaped thing, and a tiny-waisted abdomen. At its highest point sat a huge skull of something that might've been anything, so long as that thing wasn't human. Its lines were obscured by great slabs of pulsing, greenish, comb-chambered flesh, and here and there someone had slapped on long wicked hairs as thick as your fingers. Which weren't that thick. I'm just amending here; your fingers are fine. Great serrated beetle jaws emerged from either side of the skull's maw, dripping steaming liquid, and it snapped meditatively as it stood—hung, actually: transparent wings buoyed it up, moving so rapidly that what with the steam and the blood and the heat and the dark I hadn't seen them to start with. And as I watched, little pinpoints spun within the black craters of the skull's eye sockets, and then great wet black eyeballs emerged from those holes.

This would have been a terrific moment for you to come back. It would have been completely sweet. I don't care how much of a hot badass I'm meant to be, I was in the wrong body clutching a sword I'd never used, and you didn't have any muscles, and I absolutely did not feel well. I felt bad. I needed a time-out. But the monster screeched in a weird, double-throated bleating chitter, two sounds simultaneously and both of them shitty, and those eyeballs swivelled round and round and round.

I lined up your front foot with your back ankle, thumb wrapped low around the hilt of your sword, which proves that you can put the swordfighter into the necromancer but you can't, wait, hang on.

And I said, "Goddamn it, I told you to lift *weights*."

The creature skittered toward us at an incredible speed. What followed was an absolute shitshow.

For us. Not it. *It* was fine and dandy. Turned out that when it approached, its wings lifted it high enough to expose a fat, savage stinger on the end of that abdomen—the sawlike mouth shot a high-pressure squirt of transparent liquid directly into our eyes, which I *narrowly* dodged by swinging your blood-sodden arm across your face—fun times, because the liquid turned out to be insane monster acid. I heard the robe sizzling away on contact, then I heard your skin sizzle too—felt the strips fall away from your arm, first of cloth and then of actual dermal layer—and I took a couple of steps back and I bit about three holes through your tongue, but our pain receptors were still all fucked up. I'm not saying it didn't hurt like a top-notch bitch, because it did, but when I shook the worst of the unholy insect spit off our mess of an arm I found your skin *growing back as I watched.* Hell of a party trick, Nonagesimus, I mean, damn.

I parried a smashing overhead blow from the stinger, which was beading more clear fluid from a tip that could've jerked our heart out, and my borrowed arm clanged my borrowed sword into the saw mouth. I kicked the stinger with your booted foot, which was like hitting a wall with a feather duster, ducked under another stream of acid, and then, sorry, turned and ran for your goddamn life.

I burst into the nearest room. The bedroom. I kind of knew the layout, but I'd never really been able to use your eyes. Living inside you—if I start I'll never stop, so we have to move on—was like living in a well, and every time I bobbed to the surface I kind of got clothes-lined back down to the bottom. I'm not complaining, I just want you to know. Even so, I knew enough to bust through your foyer and to the remnants of that ash barricade you were an idiot to make, heading for the thing I knew I would find right where you left it, with its thick white scabbard cracked into pieces all around.

The creature squirmed through after me, made that shitty bleating half-curdled chirrup, and spat another stream of evil saliva at us. I hit the floor, ditched the rapier, and grasped the hilt of my two-handed sword.

Which was, by the way, in fucking *abominable* condition. There is so much I should have told you. I just didn't have time. I didn't know. I didn't know I'd have to say: *A sword doesn't hold an edge on its own, you sack of Ninth House garbage.* I didn't know I'd have to say, *If you dip a sword into melty bone, the metal gets more pitted than an iron mine, you cross-patched necromantic shit.*

I think the main thing I should have said was, *You sawed open your skull rather than be beholden to someone. You turned your brain into*

soup to escape anything less than 100 percent freedom. You put me in a
box and buried me rather than give up your own goddamned agenda.

Harrowhark, I gave you my whole life and you didn't even want it.

Actually, scratch that, the main thing I should have said was, *SQUATS ARE A START, OR A COUPLE OF STAR JUMPS, THEY'RE NOT DIFFICULT.*

As I stood with that sword grasped between your hands, the hilt of the two-hander bit our skin, but not fatally. There were a couple of callouses now on those soft necromancer's palms, and I was proud of you.

When I met the first strike of that poison-dripping stinger, our limits became obvious—the first strike ripped your extensors to shit, clanged down your forearms and up into your feeble upper arms like a miniature strike team had entered the tendons and set the whole thing to blow. The pain came in *waves.* But some ancient engine had revved to life for me in a way it never had done for you, probably because I am a good girl and you are an evil nun, and it tore through us almost simultaneously: renewed those shredded muscles, tied back together that multitude of miniature rips. *My* first overhead strike shattered the stinger, and the heinous thing reared and then sheared our cheek open before I could duck—but the only thing I cared about was the superheated steam feeling in our arms, and the swing, and the arc of my broadsword as I cleaved a neat arc through that creepy insectoid waist.

The creature toppled into halves. It curled up horribly in a death throe; those humanlike fingers and toes on the bottom of the frame curled in on themselves, and all the meat parts depuffed and shrivelled, and putrid-smelling guts squeezed out of the skull's mouth hole. In that panting dark heat, the death reek was intense. And your shoulders wouldn't stop shaking, even when I leaned against the bed.

It was only when I saw us in the mirror by the dresser—saw me, in you—still not saying anything—that it hit home what you had done. Your face was a mess. It was such a weird goddamn melange of us: *your* pointy-ass chin, *your* stubborn-featured, dark-browed face, less battered than the last time I'd seen it, but—wearier than I'd ever known it to be. Your eyes had little smudgy lines next to them, and they were there at the corners of your mouth, marks of this huge, exhausted sadness. You could always leave everything else behind, but you never got rid of being so absolutely fucking goddamn sad.

The skull paint dripped down your cheeks from the sweat, and from the blood, and from where I'd wiped it accidentally. Your hair was way too long. It was plastered down your neck, and it was seriously itchy. All of that was the same Harrowhark Nonagesimus. Angular. Ferocious. Terrible. But at the same time, it wasn't.

Main reason: my eyes stared out of your face. The shape was yours, but the yellow-amber irises were as out of place in your face as my sword was clutched in your thin, straining arms. The expression wasn't right either—my *what the fuck?* face was very different from your *what the fuck?* face. It was like watching a shell of you walk around; like the empty puppets you'd made of Pelleamena and Priamhark. Except that would've been easier. This was your shell, but it was all filled up with me. God, the double entendres were hard to resist.

I said hoarsely: "Get back here. Get back here right now, or I'll make you say the worst shit I can think of. Just mean and gross. Beneath even me, is what I'm saying."

No response.

"*Oooooh, Palamedes. I am measurably less intelligent than you. Put your tongue in my mouth, and I'll flop my tongue against it.*"

Nothing.

"*I think bones are mediocre.*"

Maybe you were dead.

"*Ohhhhhrr, Gideon, I was so dumb to think a tub of ancient freezer meat was my girlfriend. Please show me how to do a press-up. Also, I'm very obviously attracted to y*—no, damn it, this is just sad. This is garbage." My temper was going. Maybe your temper was going. "Come back. I hate this. Eat me, and let's go full Lyctor. I didn't fall on a fence for *this*, Nonagesimus."

Sound. Motion. Another chittering scamper, close to the door. Then another.

I had forgotten there were going to be more of them. Your memory hadn't happened to me, and even if I'd had a front-row seat for most of it, it was like watching a play through a blindfold. If I wanted to know something, I had to deliberately go looking through your shit. And I'd forgotten because I was an idiot. It was so hot in that room, and my insides—your insides—felt so cold. I shrugged off that stupid white robe—which looks dumb as hell, by the way, like Silas Octakiseron got into the glitter drawer—and I tried to get you back through sheer force of hope, and sheer force of want.

No dice. I shouldered my sword. Your arms blazed in response.

"Whenever you're ready," I said. "Don't worry, honey. I'll keep the home fires burning."

And the Heralds piled in.

45

AN AMOUNT OF TIME BEFORE THE EMPEROR'S MURDER

THE ROOMS OF CANAAN HOUSE were thick and silent with falling snow: red with new blood, and brown or black with old. Ductile, organic tubes and lymphatic nodes pulsed pinkly everywhere: in the corners, bubbling up along the doorframes and the pillars. Outside the windows, stretched webs of organ had wrapped themselves around the tower like nets of sticky venous spiderweb. They choked the stone. They burst through windows, and every so often they would tremble uncertainly and erupt in floods of bloody, foamy water.

That was wretched; but Harrowhark was more interested in the strange garbage littering the snow and the rotting furniture and the underfloor squish of tube and fossa. Pipettes, again; broken glass-fronted containers filled with dark fluid, mysterious lumps floating suspended within; and shattered skeletons, lying in the slithering mass of tubes or on mountains of what looked to be capsules or pills. At first her brain skimmed over the skeletons—it was Canaan House, ergo, there were skeletons—but then the familiarity dawned on her: some of the skeletons were not wearing First House sashes or raiment, but bearing Drearburh tools.

"Keep moving," said Magnus Quinn, with the friendly and unyielding iron of a parent taking a small child to the bathroom. "No time to take in the scenery."

She fell in step again and said, "Where *is* this room?"

Abigail said, "Close by. The others will be there already, if all's gone according to plan—take my hand; we're heading outside."

The cold hit like a slap in the mouth. The snow was falling in driving, vision-obscuring sheets, smarting the skin, with a smell that made them all retch. The Fifth led her along a rope attached to an outside terrace—the obscuring fog could not disguise the roar of the sea below, nor the fact that most of the terrace had *gone*. Then down again, into a corridor so choked with gurgling pink tubes that they brushed Harrowhark as she followed close at heel, to descend a flight of stairs.

This was familiar territory. A vestibule, dark and claustrophobic. Malfunctioning lights overhead, fizzing madly. At the bottom of the stairs, glass doors showed the space where the pool had once been—filled now with bloody water, dark, bobbing shapes within. River water. Abigail turned to a tapestry that had been pinned up over one wall, and shouldering it aside revealed a cramped entryway to a hall that Harrowhark knew well. She said, "Surely not."

"It's not locked," said Magnus. "And it's been left alone—no blood rains, nothing jiggly."

Harrow was bewildered by another layer of recognition and realisation as Abigail approached the great heavy-pillared Lyctoral door with its reliefs of horned animals and its crossbar of black stone and carved marble, and rapped a sharp sequence of knocks on it that were, after a moment, answered by a scrabbling from within. This was not simply one of the locked rooms of old; it was a *person's* room. And as for whose—

The door yawned open. The rail of electric lights shone down on the old laboratory area: a row of benches with scoured, pitted composite tops; books and ancient ring-binders pushed into a far corner; the inlaid tessellation of bones in the walls; and the flimsy poster of a six-armed construct with a hulking body and a flat-skulled head, the old ruler of the Response chamber. The real Septimus was here, poring over a sheaf of flimsy, flipping through it as though looking for something. Nearby was a pushed-together arrangement of chairs, a leather-covered sofa, and a long table where Lieutenant Dyas was laying out the ancient, rusted collection of guns. And then the little staircase up to the split-level platform with its bookcase, and its armchair, and its two beds; sitting in the armchair was Ortus Nigenad, her first—second?—cavalier.

Septimus's cavalier had opened the door. Harrowhark was bemused all over again by Protesilaus Ebdoma, whom she had never seen alive; if anyone *had* seen him alive, they never would have mistaken that shuffling zombie for his real self. Cytherea was a Lyctor and could have easily done better; she simply hadn't bothered. Harrowhark had thought from the start the woman showed signs of suppurating ego, but she had never convinced Gideon to see past the appealing eyes and softly clinging dresses. Protesilaus bowed cordially to them, and he said in his deep and resonant voice: "Teacher declined to join us."

"Oh, dear. Still hanging out to die, I suspect."

"Couldn't say, Lady Pent."

The spacious apartment was cleaner and more . . . lived-in than when she and Gideon had first opened its doors and ransacked its mysteries. At her expression, Pent said: "I needed somewhere to keep the children, at the beginning."

"The *who*?"

"You summoned Jeannemary and Isaac along with the rest," said Abigail calmly. "I worked out how to return them to the River first thing. They didn't want to go, but I overruled them. I would have done the same with anyone else—if only Silas had asked me; what has happened to his soul worries me horribly."

This sharpened Harrow's focus. "You have the means to leave?"

"Yes."

"Then why don't you?"

"Everyone who has stayed," said Abigail, "has chosen to stay, and risk their lives—or souls, I should say."

"What *is* the risk? Can a spirit be harmed?"

"A spirit can be trapped," said Abigail, "trapped as every spirit in the River is trapped . . . I know it must sound puzzling, Harrow, so I'll elaborate. The River is full of the insane, who attempt to cross—"

Magnus coughed in a genteel Fifth House way, and said, "Who wait for our Lord's touch on the day of a second Resurrection."

"Who attempt to *cross,* my love," said his wife patiently, "to get to what lies beyond; who throng in their great and endless multitude, mad, directionless; or worse, have been trapped at the bottom, about which I know very little but fear all I know. Jeannemary and Isaac, who already endured so much, and never did anything wrong, other than the time they tried to pierce each other's tongues, should have travelled lightly through those waters. Harrowhark never should have been able to stop their progress—no, dear, *don't* shush me. She knows something of heresy."

This was in its own way a dreadful slander on the Locked Tomb, and on what lay within it, and on the Ninth House in perpetuity. When she had been younger, and significantly stupider, she might have cared. But Harrow did not care now. She was utterly distracted. She held the even brown gaze of the woman before her, with her tidy hair and her squashy mittens, and she said, "It has been thousands of years since anybody bothered to believe in the River beyond."

"Yet I believe more than ever, now that I am dead," said Abigail, smiling.

"But God—"

"I firmly believe that the Kindly Emperor knows nothing of that undiscovered country. He never claimed omnipotence. I longed my whole life to give him my findings," she said meditatively. "I think there is a whole school of necromancy we cannot begin to touch until we acknowledge its existence—I think these centuries of pooh-poohing the idea that there is space beyond the River has stifled entire avenues of spirit magic, and I believe the Fifth House was waning *entirely* due to us reaching a stultified, complacent stage in our approach . . . Oh, I hope so desperately that my brother found my notes! Something has gone terribly wrong in the River, Harrow, and I wish you'd find out what."

Lieutenant Dyas did not look up from lugging another gun to the table as she said, "Let's address what's gone wrong in here, first."

"Right. *You* don't think I'm a mad heretic, do you, Marta?" Abigail suddenly said beseechingly.

"No. The Second House doesn't overthink the River," said Dyas. "If we did we'd just have to fill in forms. Quinn, show me where you found those bullets."

Harrowhark had found her eyes avoiding the stairs, and the armchair; that was cowardly, and now she looked there straight and true. Ortus met her gaze quite tranquilly. He sat in the chair with his hood down, and he had opened up a book; he had been using it as a prop to unobtrusively write something on a scrap of flimsy. She mounted those stairs like a tremulous bridegroom, climbing toward a man who had known her all the days of her life.

At the top, she said: "How long did you know? Did you see it from the start?"

"I didn't," he said. "Not fully, until talking to Lady Pent and Sir Magnus, a week or so ago. At times I would recall, and then in the next few seconds, forget I had recalled anything. At times I knew, and at other times I did not. I realise that does not make much sense," he added humbly.

"Ortus," she said. "Do not bow and scrape to me. My family killed you."

"No. Marshal Crux killed me, and my mother too," he said, and he bent his nearly black eyes to the page balanced within the book, and he scribbled something down. "I knew that, when we discovered the bomb. The pilot found it midroute, and he stopped the shuttle so we could look at it; and my mother wept and wailed as he and I tried to work out its mechanism, but obviously—neither of us were experts in bombs."

Her heart crushed within her. She said, "I take full responsibility."

"I wish you wouldn't," said Ortus.

"I asked him to put you on the ship—I was trying to—"

"It does not matter what you tried to do," he said, and he took the flimsy away and put it in his pocket. "If you are culpable . . . you are culpable only of giving the marshal the means to murder me. Marshal Crux was not a good man . . . and yet, perhaps, he did what he saw was fit. Perhaps if I had said, 'No, I must stay and do my duty, and aid the Reverend Daughter whatever her will,' then I would have lived. But I was a coward, and I let my mother overrule me. My mother was strong . . . so strong, I hear, that her spirit lasted beyond death. I was weak. I always was weak, my Lady Harrowhark."

She said tightly, "Don't call me that."

"My apologies, Reverend Daughter."

"Don't call me *your lady*," she said. "You owe me nothing. You don't owe me fealty. You don't owe me duty. Though the way I treated Gideon Nav defies description, I treated you in a manner that rejects any claim I had to your loyalty. You don't have to stay, Nigenad— tell Pent to get you through the barrier and back into the River." As though the River was the better option. She said, "In the River, you'll be relatively safe."

Ortus laid his pen on the arm of the beaten-up chair. He settled his hands over his body awkwardly—there was always so much of Ortus, too much of him for his own comfort: he did not know what to do with his fingers, he did not know how to settle himself into the chair he filled or accept that he occupied space. He asked, "How did Gideon die?"

She closed her eyes and lost herself in that dizzy unreality of blackness: of swaying minutely, of lost balance. So many months had passed: and yet, at the same time, she had only lost Gideon Nav three days ago. It was the morning of the third day in a universe without her cavalier: it was the morning of the third day—and all the back of her brain could say, in exquisite agonies of amazement, was: *She is dead. I will never see her again.*

Harrow said, "Murder."

Ortus said, "I thought—"

"We were pinned down by a Lyctor, our backs to a wall," she said. "I was utterly spent. Camilla Hect, our companion, had suffered multiple injuries." It was a blow to her dignity all over again, her unconscious gracelessness to Camilla Hect; a girl whom, in reality, she should have taken by the hands and thanked profusely for every time she tried to save her cavalier. "Nav had a fractured kneecap and a broken humerus. She pierced her heart on a railing because she thought I would use her to become a Lyctor. I will spit in the face of the first person who tells me she committed suicide; she was in an impossible situation, and she died trying to escape it. She was murdered, but she manoeuvred her murder to let me live."

His face was very sad: a wistful, light sadness, not the ponderous sadness that he wore like his sacramental paint.

"What is better?" he asked. "An ignoble death by someone else's hands, or a heroic death by one's own? How should it be written? If the first—that she was cut down by an enemy—I would feel such hate for the enemy . . . If the second—an ugly death at her own devising—who, then, would be left for me to hate? Who does the poet judge? The eternal problem."

"Ortus, this is not a poem," she said.

"I think you must hate her," he said, and she thought she knew what he meant, until he said: "Don't. If there is anything I know about young Gideon . . . if there was anything in her that I too understood . . . it is that she did everything deliberately."

Very little in Harrowhark's life had embarrassed her up until that moment. She had been caught naked in front of a stranger. She had been kissed by a half-drunk Ianthe the First. She had admitted to God her apocalyptic transgressions, and been gently told that she did not know herself. She had been outplayed by Palamedes Sextus, outgunned by Cytherea the First, undone by Gideon Nav.

None of that humiliated her so viscerally as her strangled, bellowing, unchecked shriek now, a child's cry that whipped every head in that busied room round in her direction: "She died because I let her! *You don't understand!*"

Ortus dropped his book. He rose from the chair. He put his arms about her. The dead cavalier held her with a quiet, unassuming firmness; he petted her hair like a brother, and he said, "I am so sorry, Harrowhark. I am sorry for everything . . . I am sorry for what they did . . . I am sorry that I was no kind of cavalier to you. I was so much older, and too selfish to take responsibility, and too affrighted by the idea of doing anything difficult or painful. I was weak because weak-

HARROW THE NINTH / 401

ness is easy, and because rebuff is hard. I should have known there was really nobody left . . . I should have seen the cruelty in what Crux and Aiglamene encouraged you to bear. I knew what had happened to my father, and I suspected for so long what had happened to the Reverend Father and Mother. I knew I had been spared, somehow, from the crèche flu, and that my mother had been driven demented by the truth. I should have offered help. I should have died for you. Gideon should still be alive. I was, and am, a grown man, and you both were neglected children."

She should have loathed what he was saying to the very depths of her soul. She was Harrowhark Nonagesimus. She was the Reverend Daughter. She was beyond pity, beyond the tenderness of a member of her congregation rendering her down into *a neglected child.* The problem was that she had never been a child; she and Gideon had become women before their time, and watched each other's childhood crumble away like so much dust. But there was a part of her soul that wanted to hear it—wanted to hear it from Ortus's lips more, even, than from the lips of God. He had been there. He had witnessed.

Harrowhark found herself saying: "Everything I did, I did for the Ninth House. Everything Gideon did, she did for the Ninth House."

"You both had more grit at seven years old than I ever had in my entire life," said Ortus. "You are the most worthy heroes the Ninth House could muster. I truly believe that. And that is why I am staying. I am not a hero, Harrow. I never was. But now that I have died without hope for heroism in life, I will hope better for heroism in death. And therefore I will fight the Sleeper with you."

It was difficult to know what to do with this type of touch. It made her whole soul flinch, but at the same time opened some primeval infant mechanism within her, as though the embrace were a mirror: having someone hold up an image by which you could see yourself, rather than living with an assumption of your face. It was not like the touch of her father or mother. When she had first sat by the tomb in shivering awe, she had fancied that the Body's ice-ridden fingers had shifted for hers, minutely. Gideon had touched her in truth; Gideon had floundered toward her in the saltwater with that set, unsheathed expression she wore before a fight, her mouth colourless from the cold. Harrow had welcomed her end, but suffered a different death blow altogether—and she had become, for the second time, herself. She untangled from Ortus, more reluctantly than she'd expected.

Ortus said, "Come down. Hear the plan. I helped craft it—it is not complicated, but it is the only plan we have."

"I will," she said.

Harrow bent to retrieve the book he had dropped when he had stood—it fell open at the flyleaf. A message was still readable, written in faded ink, in strong, cramped letters:

ONE FLESH, ONE END.

G. & P.

She and Gideon had looked over the contents of the drawers. Cigarette ash. Buttons. Time-abandoned toothbrushes. An ancient emblem of the House of the Second. Whetstones and guns. She now knew what the *P* stood for: Pyrrha Dve.

But what about *G*? What if one had altered one's temporal bone to affect the tympanic lobe to overwrite a specific word with something different? Her adjustment had been meant to catch a name, but it had ended up catching two. Mercy, and Augustine, and God must have thought her mad. As for the Saint of Duty himself—

"His name isn't Ortus," she said, totally bewildered.

She found Ortus looking at her with a helpless and equal bewilderment. He offered, "Pardon?"

"I thought you were named for him—you're not," she said, conclusions spooling out in front of her like an unravelled tooth, in hideous naked majesty of enamel and nerve. "My mechanism worked too well. It did not account for context. *Ortus* doesn't come from a Lyctoral tradition. But what if *hers* did? What if we named her, accidentally, for him?"

But what could that mean? Mercymorn had said their names were considered sacred and forgotten, except for Anastasia's, who had never attained Lyctorhood. Why would a necromantic saint's name be evoked in such a way?

The page fell over her thumb. On the second page—much fresher—Harrow read:

> **THE ONLY THING OUR CIVILISATION CAN EVER LEARN FROM YOURS IS THAT WHEN OUR BACKS ARE TO THE WALL AND OUR TOWERS ARE FALLING ALL AROUND US AND WE ARE WATCHING OURSELVES BURN WE RARELY BECOME HEROES.**

She opened her mouth to ask her dead second cavalier a question about her dead first cavalier—a pattern that was starting to look less like tragedy and more like carelessness—but downstairs, Abigail was saying:

"Harrowhark? Ortus? If you are ready, we might want to move. Dulcie's found some good-quality candles of animal fat—there's no hope of blood, of course—but 'fire and words' were scourging enough with the children . . ."

Both Fifth adept and cavalier had the happy, quasi-contented faces of people about to embark on a favourite activity, like a hike or a game of chess, and the cavalier of the Second House had two guns slung over her back and the pressed expression of a Cohort soldier about to embark on her *least* favourite activity. Harrow knew with a sinking bone magician's heart what everyone was about to do before she asked the question, but asked it anyway.

"What *is* the plan, Pent?"

"Why, to let ghosts bury ghosts," she said. "With everyone's help, I am going to exorcise the Sleeper."

46

THE NIGHT BEFORE THE EMPEROR'S MURDER

Look, I had the best of intentions for your body. I was very aware that I was walking around in borrowed clothes, and I did not want to scuff them, mangle them, spindle them, or otherwise do long-lasting damage. All of the moral high ground I got by falling on a spike for you would have been undone immediately if you came back to one arm, half a foot, and a disfigured ass.

But the reality was this: it took me five nightmare bees to learn how to deal with your grip, your core strength, your arm strength, your thigh muscles, and your height, and the operating thing I had to deal with in all cases was *lack thereof.* Even if you'd ever toned a muscle, you weighed half of me. They tossed me around like one of your skeletons, and I died three times in that buzzing, filthy, hot bedroom.

The only thing that stopped them from coming at you all at once was a lack of space: they moved as one coordinated, buzzing, snapping posse. To win, they only had to swarm us and they knew it. I played for space and position, kept the two-hander low on the hip because I needed whatever cover I could get you—locked three of them at bay with big cross strikes, and then I overcompensated because the weight of my sword pulled you with it, and one of the death bees did a little jiggly skull dance to the right and planted that massive stinger right in my side.

It went in all the way—a hand wide at the base, leaking acid all over your insides. I slammed the guard down and it snapped off in-

404

side you, which hadn't been what I wanted—the creature fell back, and I staggered and slashed blindly, and the stinger worked its way out with a *pop*. The sword I had to hold overhead in one hand as I used the other to keep everything inside you; stuff was coming out, Harrow, I don't know precisely what stuff because I'm not a god-damn necromancer. Let's call it some small intestine. Whatever it was should've stayed safely tucked away in your abdomen but was making a pretty serious bid for escape. We should have keeled over and died saying sadly, *Oops*.

We didn't. The slippery coils went in when I pressed, and I had to get your hand out of the way of the skin growing back over your fingers. I got us to the bathroom doorway and tried to narrow the field; I shattered the skull of one scuttling toward me and severed its gross black eye stalks—and they were all *different;* each one had a different skull, and one traded mandible saws for a mouth ringed entirely in poison stingers, which it pumped like darts into every surface, and after a while I didn't even bother trying to brush them off your arms. We were upright. That was the most important thing.

I'd just blinded one when the two-hander got seized in a pair of mandibles—you didn't have the strength for me to tug it clear—and more were crowding the doorway. I was swearing, and yanking, and a skull mouth snapped in close to the hilt and the guard. I didn't pull back. You weren't wearing gloves. And it bit your damn thumb off.

Again, let me say: sorry. It was not my thumb to let them bite off. I admit completely that this was my bad, but these motherfuck-ers had a hunger that only thumbs could satisfy. It didn't matter—I was yelling, and trying to grab the damn sword away anyway, and I saw it *eat your thumb*—these details are important, so keep up with me—and your thumb was back in the next half minute. I watched it grow. The gushing stump grew a full bone, and then the meat grew up around it in the next breath, and then it all closed over in fresh skin and thumbnail. I set it back around the hilt and it worked like it had not just been chewed up by a wasp ghoul.

So I braced us in the doorway and kept going. The best place to aim was at the junctures of bodies—thorax and abdomen—as the plates over their midsections were tough as steel. Some of the wasps who were all arms on the bottom liked to come at us with ramming speed: I sawed them through. Others had four legs, and they liked to jump, so I swept their feet off when they leapt. I had to kill the one that ate your thumb by staving in its skull with the butt of my pommel, over and over, until it stopped moving.

Once I thought I'd cleared out the wave coming for us in the bathroom, I left the doorframe—and we died the third time. One of the monsters had been waiting, and it reared up to try to drive that stinger into your brain, but I half-dodged and it just smashed your head against the wall.

Harrow, I heard it. It fractured your fucking skull. I was so terrified. I was undergoing the kind of shit that I had only undergone once in the happy knowledge that it was all going to be over soon. Child, that bee smashed you. A skull should not have made those sounds. The sound of it un-smashing was even worse—like an egg blowing back out again—but as it was saving your only skull, it was music to my ears. I cleaved that bee open from the thorax down, and it disgorged huge amounts of reeking guts and bones and green blood all over me and the carpet.

At the end, we were left in a sea of dead space bees, and you were impossibly okay. Your arms didn't even hurt, not anymore. You didn't have your original thumb and I'd touched your intestines, which is usually what, fourth date, but you were fine.

* * *

It was now obvious that the station was crawling with those things. You were gone, and I did not know where the fuck you were. Our only real options were to stay and fight, or go and fight: the place wasn't getting any less filled up with wasps. And it was hotter all the time, especially in that room with the steaming piles of revenant bees.

You didn't have any gloves. You didn't have any armour. When I took off your robe, which was just puke rags by then, I found you were wearing a whole bunch of bones on your skin for no apparent reason. I was sorry to take them off in case they were any use at all, but whatever necromantic noise you'd used to fix them to yourself wasn't working, and they were making it even harder to extend your arms. So I closed my eyes and I reached under your shirt and I peeled them all off, and I tied your hair back and took your sword and left. I didn't look, and I barely touched you. Don't get mad.

There were other sounds echoing down the halls by then. I know the clash of swords on bone when I hear it. There was that huge, murmurous buzzing of invading Heralds, and there were more of those baying, bleating screeches, but there was also the absolutely fucking unmistakable sound of rapier work. The alarm cawed overhead. I didn't run, but I legged it pretty quickly down the corridor, and then, beneath the alarm, I became aware of yet another sound: someone was screaming.

In a fork off the hallway, I found the source. Dead Heralds lay in an untidy semicircle around the last living, rearing member of their gang, and fighting this bee—screaming her head off—was Lemon-mouth Prime: the Lyctor you called *Mercymorn*.

She was shrieking, drunk and howling off pure fright, every so often lunging in the wrong direction as though she couldn't see straight. I came into the room, not knowing what to do, not knowing how to help her. Despite the screaming, she was holding her own—her rapier was a steel needle flashing in and out, out of the way of the snapping jaws of the Herald, thrusting into the black eye socket in a shower of jelly. There were long, shining folds of a net wrapped around her offhand arm, but the net was not in her hand. She missed a thrust, nothing but wing, and then she drove herself into the Herald and laid that bare hand on its skull. And the Herald just kind of imploded.

The skull disappeared into dust, the thorax collapsed in on itself like a pricked balloon, and the insides blew out the back almost delicately. It slumped, and when it went still the Lyctor stopped screaming. There were thin runnels of blood coming off her face and I thought she'd been hurt, but then I realised they were coming out of her eyes like tears. She stood there with her shoulders heaving and her hand pressed over her face, pinky-reddish hair coming out of her braid, looking unhurt but pretty sorry for herself.

And she looked right at us, before I could duck back into the corridor.

The Lyctor called Mercymorn stared at your face, and I have never seen anyone so totally shocked by misery. It wasn't just fear: it was this huge, grief-stricken panic, a welter of unhappy terror. It was the face of someone who had just seen their one true love drop-kicked into a meat grinder and come out the other end as a pile of sausages.

"So *now* you come to me, First," she said raggedly. "Now you come . . . at the end of everything."

She seemed to be waiting. I didn't know what to say. No way I could pretend to be you; I knew you too well. As we both waited in idiot silence, her fear changed—her eyes narrowed—her mouth hardened from its softer line of anticipatory terror, and she said, "No," and then, "No," again. And she was so *old,* Harrow, I don't know how you dealt with all these unbelievably old bastards—she was old like Cytherea was old, and her eyes were absolutely abominable. They made my skin crawl. When she looked at us, it was like she could see right through me, and she was seeing shit I hadn't even heard of.

The Lyctor said: "You haven't come, have you? You're not *her.* That freak would have gone for me already . . . she never could act human. But you stand like a human—you gawp like a human—you *are* human," she said, with a rising horrified disgust. "But I don't understand! Harrowhark was meant to be eaten by now! She wouldn't have died for hours, and the Heralds are everywhere!"

"Lady," I said, "are you telling me *you* stabbed my necromancer?"

"Yes, and she should have thanked me for it!!" said the Lyctor, thoroughly distracted. "It wasn't *horrible*—I dulled her nerves, out of a misplaced sense of affection—I put her out in the corridor specially so she would be eaten quicker, and once she started getting eaten alive, she would have been mad and not feeling a thing! But you're the soul—the soul of the cavalier that she stuffed in the back of her brain! *What happened to your eyes?*"

"Let's go to a better question," I said, and I raised my sword in your hands. "You *know* we already killed one Lyctor, right? Me and Harrow? You know we've practised?"

"Oh, shut *up*, Harrow's cavalier," she said hysterically. "I'm trying to think. You're not her—she isn't driving you—but you have her eyes. Why? When they showed me your corpse I didn't think to check the eyes. *Stupid*, Mercy. Oversight. I thought I knew what you were, though I didn't want to believe it . . ."

I said, "What the fuck are you *talking* about?"

"I am talking about the failure of the Ninth House operation," she said.

And she cocked her flower-coloured head to the side so that her sweaty hair fell over her face, in that sizzling, gulping heat, and she stared at us, and she said in tones that were almost sedate: "I thought the commander had simply been a bad girl . . . a workaholic, putting business before family. She was the type . . . but that would have been too much of a coincidence. Let me think. Let me think. I *made* her the dolls—they were *perfect*—and then she must have played *silly buggers* with—with the *emission*," she said, suddenly, impassioned. "Of course it killed her! She was always arrogant! That moron *knew* Gideon was on her tail!"

Something in your head went *spang* when we heard my name. It sounded strangely gloopy at first, unreal, as though we were underwater. But then the pain went away.

The Lyctor continued, those weird reddish-haze eyes scrunched up as though she might cry: "And then Gideon ruined everything," she said. "Then the commander ruined everything. Then *you* ruined everything. This could have been over eighteen years ago. But now it's *messy* . . . now I have to take the River *all the way home* and fight my way through Anastasia's horrid tomb cult just because the commander always thought she was so *smart*. Don't know why Gideon was so obsessed with her . . . he never cared about beauty, and she was repellent to talk to."

I did not know what the fuck to say to this incoherent spew. She said, ragged, peevish: "What? No tongue in your head, you—you *mutant*, you *mistake*, you *great big calf-eyed fuck-up*? I need to think. I need to think. Why are those eyes now in your face? Unless . . ."

And then, of all goddamn things, her voice caught in a great, shuddery sob. She paced backward and forward. At one point, she threw her head back as though she were going to yell aloud, and that weird-hued hair shivered over her back. But she said nothing, just stood in the pit of the light, and then she turned back to us.

When she spoke at last, she sounded frozen and numb. "I see. I understand. Lipochrome. Recessive. You are the evidence. He lied to us . . . and you are all the proof I needed. I don't have to breach anything. I don't have to go back." She exhaled. "Good God . . . Cytherea would have known as soon as she looked at you."

And I said: "What the fuck are you talking about? What the *hell* are you talking about? What other Gideon?"

"The Lyctor sent to kill your mother," said Mercymorn.

"But Harrow's mother—"

"I'm not talking to *Harrowhark,* you facile dead child," she said disdainfully. "I am talking to *you* . . . Nav . . . *Gideon* Nav . . . *Gideon*! What a laugh . . . you *abomination,* you *heresy,* you failed ambition nineteen years too late."

I'm sorry, Nonagesimus. I didn't know what to do. Maybe I should've turned and gotten the hell out of there, holed up somewhere to wait until you came back. But I said: "What—*about*—my *mother*?"

"Excuse me. I am wrong. I should not use that term," said the necromantic saint. She rolled both her shoulders back and wiped those thin dilute tears of blood off her cheeks. "How she would have hated the word *mother.*"

And she raised her rapier, and she slowly unwound that net from her wrist, and it fell to the floor in great billowy shining knots. Mercy said: "Now I will clean up my mistakes. Cristabel always said I was tidy."

She darted forward with her rapier close to her body, the net trailing behind—fuck, she was quick—knocked away my sluggish counter, easily a second too late, and she stabbed us neatly through the heart. An easy thrust, with enormous strength behind it, straight past the right breastbone and right to the very centre of your heart, which had been fucked up one too many times in my keeping. It was a surgical, exact thrust. Her rapier was a slender needle, and if you'd carved us open you probably would have found that the slim blade had gone right through the central mass of the aorta. Mercymorn withdrew with the same precise, swift movement and stepped backward, rapier dripping with blood. That was her mistake.

Your heart closed over the rapier as it punctured: your heart closed over the rapier as it withdrew. The slit so close to your breastbone sealed over instantaneously, just as fast as her stab, like an immunisation jab in Drearburh.

I readied my sword, and I saw her eyes widen, just a fraction.

"It's too late in the game to have learned that trick, infant," said the Lyctor.

I swung. She parried automatically. The sword knocked her rapier to the side, and I backstepped. I needed space. I tried to remember everything you'd learned about this crazy-eyed witch, but it was like thinking through mud. I knew I didn't want her to touch me, but I didn't quite know why. The heat haze was turning the room into a sweaty fog, making the red light pouring down from the alarms overhead a wavering strobe. It made her look like she was moving when she wasn't—she just stood there, perfectly still, that lovely balanced rapier still wet with your blood and that net looking like it was twitching in her hand. All I could do was circle, sword held in a guard across your chest like this time I could protect your heart. Even if I'd been in my own body, I would have been panicking; but I was in yours, and she knew the only game I had. The fuck was I going to do, regrow your thumbs at her?

The net flicked. The damn thing looked like a gossamer slip, but it was weighted; I thought she'd just use it to tangle, not like freaking bolas. It caught me by one ankle and sent you to the ground because I still didn't understand your weight—knocked all the air from your lungs and dragged us to her. With one flick of her arm we were lying prone in front of her. She flipped that rapier downward: thumb on the pommel, hilt high over her head, readied for one downward thrust that would go right between the eyes, slamming through cartilage, angled upward into your brain.

And then there was a haptic *click* and a huge blasting noise that ripped the Lyctor's chest all to fuck. She stumbled forward; I rolled us away. Mercymorn was on her knees, and she was screaming. Not in pain, but in the way we'd first heard her screaming, that warbling bellow of absolute fear, her arms and legs twitching in helpless, spasmodic wriggles. Then she tipped over in a growing pool of blood on the floor.

I was on your feet with the sword, panting; in the doorway I'd come from stood a woman. She was shouldering a huge double-barrelled gun, and the wisps of smoke from the barrel shimmered in that red heat.

She wore a little white tunic, stained with blood. Her feet were bare. Her head was bare. Her pale sugar-brown curls frizzed in that moist, smouldering air, and her face was too pale, and her eyes were dark and dull, not the incandescent blue that was like staring into radioactive water. I would've known her anywhere. We'd killed her.

I breathed, "Dulcinea," because I was a chump, and then— "Cytherea."

The dead Lyctor did something with that heavy gun again—she angled it open with a *click*, and more thin streams of smoke emerged from the other end of the barrels. She wore a bandolier of bullets, and she palmed one and slid it in the barrel and pulled the body of the gun back over it. She was incredibly quick, and I didn't quite follow her. Mercymorn was still juddering and crying out—it didn't seem like she was actually dying, but she was frothing at the mouth like a rabid animal.

Cytherea looked at me with that dead-eyed, stony expression; and then, very slowly, she pointed the nose of the gun down.

I didn't know what to say—*Thank you? Is this like round five now?* I didn't have to say anything, because her mouth opened, and the voice was Cytherea's but the gravelly, hard-as-nails tone wasn't. "Goodbye," she said.

And Cytherea's body turned around and, gun raised, slowly stomped back out into the corridor; walking heavily and painfully, like it hurt. I was too amazed to do anything. I stared at that thin back—those pronounced, painful shoulder blades, the fine bumps of the spine.

Sorry. Maybe I should've gone for her. Like, I can imagine what you'd say. All I can say is that it was complicated back in Canaan House, and sometimes a cute older girl shows you a lot of attention, because she's bored or whatever, and you sort of have this maybe-flirting maybe-not thing going on, right, and then it turns out she's an ancient warrior who's killed all your friends and she's coming for you, and then you both die and she turns up ages later in the broiling heat on a sacred space station and like, it's *complicated*. Just saying that it happens all the time.

All I could do was stand there, sword raised, as the Lyctor thrashed mindlessly on the floor next to us, and say: "What the *fuck* is going on?"

47

THEY PLACED THE CANDLES in a ring around the Sleeper's coffin. Abigail was busying herself with an immense chalk diagram, which took some time because she had to put her red, numbed fingers back in her glove every few minutes, or have her hands warmed between her husband's. Harrowhark drew wards at the apex of each candle, as instructed, squatting beside the smiling, no-longer-intubated face of Dulcie Septimus.

No snow down here. Great icicles like stalactites seemed poised to crumble; oily pink webbing was strung from spike to spike, frosted up with cold. Drifts of broken glass and stagnant puddles of frozen fluid filled each corner, greeny-greyish in the dolorous buzzing overhead lights. Ropes of tube and ice hung over the entrances to each radiating passage in that nonagonal room, swagging over the signs that had once proclaimed each passage's use. The only letters visible beneath the sluggish, pulsing viscera were a *Y*, the *PR* that had once heralded PRESERVATION, the *AR* once belonging to MORTUARY, and an almost-entirely obscured THREE. The crystal coffin in the centre of the room was misted thickly with cold that did not wipe off even when Lieutenant Dyas, a woman Harrow was beginning to grudgingly admit feared neither pain nor death after experiencing both, scrubbed at it with her sleeve. As such they could not see inside it, which was probably a relief.

The enormous old metal-rimmed whiteboard with its faded timetable and stained brown patches had been written over again. Harrowhark had startled when she first saw it:

*END OF THE LINE. FALLING. OXYGEN CAN'T LAST THE
DISTANCE AND WON'T REDIRECT POWER FROM THE
PAYLOAD. INSTEAD I WILL MAKE YOU WATCH EVERY
MOMENT AS I GET THE LAST PRIVILEGE YOU CANNOT
ENJOY YOU BYGONE SON OF A BITCH.
I HOPE YOU'RE BOTH AS SORRY AS I AM.*

She had said to Ortus, "I thought the messages were hallucinations, even though I never hallucinated like that before. It was easier to believe I was succumbing to the madness again."

"Harrow," he had said, "I have come to the conclusion that you were never *mad* . . . though who can be the judge of madness?"

It seemed so much worse to her if it wasn't madness. She'd hate if it was under her control. She found herself saying curtly: "Then what?"

"The mind can only take so much pressure before it forms indentations," he had said, meditatively. "It is strange—years and years after his death, I so often heard the sound . . . the way he pushed at the handle, the way he manipulated the haft . . . of my father, standing outside the door of my cell."

Harrow had asked, "Did you miss him?"

He had thought about it. In the darkness of the big central room in that downstairs installation—the place he had never come to before, and that she felt she had left so much of herself inside, despite the fact that she had walked its metal-panelled halls for a few weeks only—he looked like an old statue, a Ninth House cavalier carved in the rock of some deep-set tomb.

And he had said thoughtfully, "Sometimes I imagined him coming back to life so that I might watch him die myself. The fantasy was a relief."

Now Harrowhark dropped to her haunches next to the ghost of the Seventh House necromancer as she carefully fashioned wards using the blunt end of a needle. Everyone but Harrow had presented themselves to Abigail to have wards scratched on their palms: she was embarrassed by how long it had taken her to realise that they were counter-wards, and that she did not need one. They were the dead. For now, she was alive.

Dulcie mistook Harrow's expression as curiosity over the missing tube, and she tapped one nostril and said brightly, "We thought I didn't *really* need it. I'm not breathing at all badly. Abigail and I suppose that we enforce some measure of our own rules here; that's why I'm not too badly off."

Harrow said, "That would explain why you were affected by physical stimulus—why you have needed to eat, and why you experience pain."

"Yes, and I always believed that so long as I got eight hours' sleep, did some stretches, and didn't think about it, I wouldn't get any worse," said the adept, and she smiled that dimpled, wasted smile that was the only thing that Cytherea had come close to parodying with any accuracy. She said, "Pal always said I'd be the death of him. And I was . . . He and I never even got to meet. I never even really got off Rhodes. It seems like such a bastard. You *did* kill the Lyctor, didn't you?"

"Yes," said Harrowhark.

"Was it quick?"

"Quicker than she deserved," said Harrow.

"She stabbed Protesilaus before he'd finished taking his sword out the scabbard," she said, and scratched a flourish into her ward. "Then she started asking me questions. Who were my friends? Was I well enough to go out in public? Was I married? I told her a lot of hot bullshit," finished Dulcie. "I knew she was going to take my place— thought maybe Camilla, at least, would figure out something was up . . . no such luck. I don't even remember dying—I suppose that was nice of her."

There was no resentment in that face, worn out before its time, heavily lined with the marks of pain and care. With her close-cropped curls and soft eyes, Dulcie Septimus in some lights looked like a child; in others, older than Magnus. She had a tip-tilted grin that showed little white teeth, and nowhere in that smile was a hint of pity, nor of condescension.

"I don't understand why you're here," said Harrow, throwing her House's caution to the wind. She said honestly: "I do not know you. I barely avenged you. You owe me no allegiance, and nor does your cavalier."

"Oh, Protesilaus is here because he wouldn't be able to help it," Dulcie said dismissively, putting one of the candles down and, with a total lack of shame, wriggling her hands up into her shirt so that she could warm them on her abdomen. "I love him, but he's *such* a pest. I wish he hadn't even come with me to Canaan House. I feel horrible. He should've stayed home with his wife and his sons—his wife does *tapestries* and he breeds *flowers* for a *hobby*. I stayed on their farm right after my pneumonia because they thought the sitting temperature would be better for me, and if I ever see another rose I shall scream . . . No chance of that now. Don't worry about Protesilaus. He can't help being so fantastically, dorkily noble."

"But you—"

Dulcie's smile became ferocious; her lips curled to show that some of the very white teeth were a little pointed, and her pallid eyes seemed to turn up at the corners. She was no longer languid, but breathless, alive, and resembling nothing quite so much as a malign fairy. Harrow remembered that Palamedes Sextus had made a war of his whole life in order to prosecute his desire to marry this woman.

"The only thing that ever stopped me being exactly who I wanted," she said, "was the worry that I would soon be dead . . . and now I am dead, Reverend Daughter, and I am sick of roses, and I am *horny for revenge*."

Then she took her hands away from her middle and went back to happily fixing the ward.

It did not take long to complete the circle. They worked swiftly and quietly. When they finished the coffin was cocooned in an enormous circle of enmeshed ward and candle anchorage, although Abigail looked discontented. "I hate doing anything to spirits without something to feed them," she said, "and there's no real blood here . . . there's nothing to tempt it. I wish we knew what it was anchoring itself to—what's the thanergetic link, and why has it been able to follow it to *you*? Harrowhark, you really don't have any insight into who might be haunting you? Do any of its signifiers mean anything? The suit? The blood? The gun?"

Harrow's brain, though still a jumble, was no longer a mess in a darkened room. Memory had gifted her a small torch she could light the disarray with. She remembered the clipped Cohort accents:

A standard-issue infantry sword. A two-hander.

"The sword," she said. "It's Gideon's. But none of the other signifiers match."

"Did the sword belong to anyone before her?"

"Not that I know of. Aiglamene petitioned to give it to Griddle from the Drearburh stock. I signed the order. The box was still wrapped." The light was not proving helpful enough: she was, in desperation, kicking over piles of the rubble in her own brain. "I hated that damned sword for years. I don't know why; it just felt strange— rancorous. I cannot deny that I often assumed its edge would be the last thing I saw. I don't know," she finished, frustrated.

"Never mind. I'm sure I've done worse with more," said Abigail bracingly. "Get to the perimeter. You're on point with Dulcie, and I'm pairing Magnus with Protesilaus—and then there's Ortus."

"Ortus shouldn't be fighting."

"He very much wants to. I hope there won't *be* any fighting. Are you ready?"

Harrow's lips were sore; everyone's lips were a little cracked and bleeding, and on her and Ortus bloody lips and cracking paint blended in a pinkish-grey mosaic. She found the tip of her tongue worrying the little scabby plates that now lived on her bottom lip. She looked up into the kind face of Abigail Pent, who was dead; and she said: "I owe you a great debt. You have given me much, in return for very little."

"Oh, Harrow, bless you, I always was a busybody," she said smilingly. "Don't thank me for sticking my oar in. You asked me to come, and I came. I understand you didn't ask on purpose, but I like to think that there was a grain in your soul that saw yourself in need, and perhaps thought to itself, *I wish I had Abigail Pent*. It takes a great deal of ego to be a psychopomp. Thank you for letting me be yours."

And she curtseyed to Harrowhark, with enormous grace. Harrowhark bowed in return, and found herself saying, "The body of the Locked Tomb preserve you and yours, Pent," and meaning it.

"Do you know what's in there?" asked Abigail, eyes sparkling.

Harrowhark cleared her throat and said, "Yes."

"Is it intensely mysterious?"

"Yes."

"*God*, I love tombs," said the Fifth House necromancer. "Right-o. The curtain lifts . . . Places, people."

In that echoing metal silence, they all moved to make their perimeter around the diagram. Harrowhark had dug big handfuls from Ortus's panniers, and stood shod in a crunchy, perfectly pulverized pile of bone. She watched Abigail and Magnus cross on tiptoe, nimbly dodging any line that their shoes might scuff, and in passing turn and kiss each other gravely. She was not embarrassed to see this intimacy; in fact, she found that it was vaguely interesting to see a marriage play out in front of her. There were many strictures against a necromancer marrying their own cavalier, and whatever road Abigail and Magnus had chosen to walk had been a difficult one: she knew that the marriage had preceded the cavaliership, which perhaps had made it less grotesque for both. They kissed as chastely and briefly as children; Magnus touched her cheek and said quietly, "Godspeed, my darling," and she said, "You too." That was all. No more, and no less.

It was still entirely uncertain whether her skeletons could handle this freezing, wretched cold. If she was bound by the rules of her pre-Lyctor state, it was going to be difficult. The candles wheezed and flickered but kept burning gamely on. Protesilaus stood opposite his necromancer. Ortus was there beside Harrowhark, a big black-wrapped bulk in her peripheral vision, trembling a little from cold and probable fear.

Lieutenant Dyas was her opposite. Harrow had told her back in the laboratory that Judith Deuteros was alive, and she'd gotten a rather curt "Thought so" in reply. Dyas had begun to turn away, then surprised Harrow by turning back and suddenly saying, "She'll give them hell," in tones that were scarcely less blank; but with an expression that was far from it.

Now Magnus stood at the head of the circle facing the frozen-over coffin. His necromancer did not put herself at any particular point. She had taken a jug in her hands, one of a set that Protesilaus had carried with care down the long facility ladder, and Harrow did not know what had been put inside it.

"Here is the libation, for what good it may do," said Abigail.

She carefully poured a measure of the jug's contents at the foot of the coffin. A brief spill of thin, milky, whitish liquid pooled at the base, sluggish in the cold.

"You come to conquer," she said, and spilt another runnel.

"You come in fury," she said, and spilt another.

"You come bearing ancient weapons," she said, and another.

"You come with a sword of the Ninth House," she said, and one more.

"You come to claim a body," she said, and upended the jug, and shook out the last pale drops. "This is all we know. You helpless ghost, this is not supplication . . . We came at invitation; whither did *you*? I am a spirit-caller of the House of the Fifth. I am Abigail for my mothers, Pent for my people. I who died am come in the fullness of my power, at the bidding of the Lyctor you seek to supplant. I will sever the thanergetic link you have to this woman, and I bid you—get the *hell* out."

Abigail withdrew her hand from the fat glove and laid it bravely, bare, on the icy front of the glass-covered coffin. She did not wince from the cold. A chill blue light emanated from beneath that hand, as though somebody were shining a light from beneath the necromancer's fingers. Harrow was struck by a thirst for her rightful power—to understand the theorem through a Lyctor's eyes. All she could do was watch with her senses dulled.

After a moment, the adept said: "The ties lead outside this place, Harrowhark. The spirit is linked to some physical object."

Harrow said, "Then—what?"

"Oh, we can get the spirit out of *you*," said Abigail. "But we can't kick it out of its other anchor. In other words, just because we banish it *here* doesn't mean we'll necessarily banish it *there*, outside the River . . . but let's give a good, hard pull and see what emerges."

The candles flared. Where before they had burned with a meek yellow flame, now they burned as strong and blue as the spirit-magic emanation from Abigail's hands.

Abigail asked: "Who *are* you?"

And with a sodium flare sparking from Abigail's fingers, the lid of the coffin swung open so wide that it wrenched itself off and crashed to the floor. One of the ice-fogged glass panels that had withstood all of Lieutenant Dyas's violence burst into a shower of fragments. Abigail stumbled backward, then regained her footing.

There was nothing inside.

From the passageway just behind Harrow—the corridor that ought to have led to the mortuary—a voice crackled through its haz mask: "Nice try."

A dry, unassuming *click;* an enormous blast that rattled around Harrowhark's ears, and a *crunch* as the projectile meant for her cracked into the sheet of solid bone she flung upward from behind her feet. The sheet exploded with the impact, sending chips flying through the air and knocking her forward onto that freezing cold floor and its carefully wrought diagram. A familiar spike of pain went through her head, and her temples prickled with blood sweat. Had raising a simple shield really cost her so much? Had her reserves ever truly been so shallow, even in childhood?

She rolled to the side, and someone grabbed her arm and hauled her behind the monument: Ortus. Those assembled had run for what cover they could, mainly to the entranceways of SANITISER—PRESSURE ROOM—PRESERVATION. All except Protesilaus—he had unsheathed his rapier and was the last man standing, his cape a greenish-blue in the light of those blazing candles. He had slung the end of his etched metal chain, tied with a faded green ribbon, over the back of his neck; now the dead cavalier of the Seventh neatly flipped it off one shoulder and whipped the chain into a slow circle next to him, the links making a high-pitched noise as they cut the air.

"Don't engage!" cried Abigail.

The Sleeper stood opposite, in its own doorway: haz mask gleaming dully in the candlelight, that enormous, wooden-stock gun cradled in its arms, the orange of the safety suit screamingly vivid. The Sleeper was not, in the end, of any great height or breadth, and the voice that had emerged from that mask was not inhuman. In fact, it was a woman's voice.

"You wizards never learn," said the Sleeper.

The nose of the gun jerked up with an ear-splitting bang. Protesilaus had already exploded into motion—with a great deal of grace for such a big man, he leapt to the side, and launched the whirring end of his chain out at the orange monster. It looped twice around the barrel and cinched tight. The Sleeper simply threw the gun away, and as Protesilaus tried to shake his chain free, there was another in her hands: this one so much smaller that it took Harrow a moment even to realise it was a gun.

The Sleeper walked forward, firing with each step, the hand gripping the gun supported on her other palm. These shots sounded higher and sharper, like whip cracks. The Seventh cavalier spun his chain in front of him, a blurred wheel in the air, and one of the ceiling lights shattered in a rain of sparks. The Sleeper tossed this gun to the side, broke suddenly into a run, and threw her haz-suited body into a diving handspring, jackknifing feet-first off the ground with a fluid agility that would have made even Camilla Hect erupt in a wild "Okay." Protesilaus had braced his stance for an attack and had not expected his enemy to move *past* him; by the time he shifted and started to turn, the Sleeper was on her feet again, and yet another gun was in her hand. She pivoted lightly and shot him in the small of the back.

A pop. A wet spatter emerged from his abdomen. Protesilaus dropped. Next to Harrow, Ortus moaned in terror. The Sleeper turned back toward them, handgun raised, trying to draw a bead, a wisp of smoke trickling from the muzzle. When she found no head or limb sticking out to put a bullet in, she stepped back, pointed the gun at Protesilaus's prone form, and—without looking—fired two more shots. The body jerked, then was still. Dulcie screamed.

There was silence, except for Dulcinea's panicked, wheezing breaths, punctuated by a ripping cough. Protesilaus's body lay heavy and unmoving on the cold metal of the facility floor, somehow still more animated in *this* death than he had been as the empty puppet of the seventh saint.

"Listen to your leader," said the Sleeper. "Don't engage. I'm not here for you, but don't think you can't die again. Just give me the girl, and the rest of you are free to go back to whatever hell you came from."

Abigail said, from somewhere in cover, "You must be joking."

The orange-suited figure raised the gun and fired it into the ceiling. Ortus cringed at the noise; Harrow dug her fingers into his arm, though what comfort that could provide she did not know.

"Harrowhark," called out the Sleeper.

The Sleeper said it slowly, as though she had never said it before—*Har-row-hark*, as though the syllables were strange. That was not the most arresting thing about the monster calling her name. It was the untrammelled contempt with which it was said, as though her name itself were a curse.

The Sleeper said, "You can't hurt me here. If you give yourself up to me, the ghosts can leave. If not, I end all of you. This is the only bargain. I'm giving you to the count of ten, then the offer expires. Ten."

Harrowhark said, "Who *are* you?"

"Doesn't matter to you. Nine."

"I don't negotiate with strangers."

"Doesn't matter to me. Eight."

Septimus broke cover. She stayed low, darting from the doorway where she had hidden herself toward the shelter of a bank of instruments, her shadow huge and jumping in the light of the flickering candles. She was only in the open for a second, but the Sleeper pointed the little black gun as casually as Harrow might point a finger, and fired. Her orange-wrapped arm flexed with the recoil. Dulcie cried out and fell, her leg knocked out from beneath her. Harrow closed her eyes briefly; then she began scrabbling through Ortus's panniers, winnowing for the best pieces, her fingertips slick with sweat as Ortus breathed through his teeth.

"Seven," said the Sleeper. "Six. Five—"

"My cue, I think," said Magnus Quinn.

Harrow had lost track of him entirely when the shooting started, and had assumed he was with Abigail, who seemed from her voice to be somewhere near Dulcinea. Now he emerged from the doorway immediately to the right of the one through which the Sleeper had entered. He flung himself at the Sleeper from behind, before she could turn to meet him, and grabbed her in his arms, locking them tight round her midriff, so her elbows were pinned against her sides.

From the other side of the room, Marta Dyas burst out of her own doorway, bent at the waist. The Sleeper managed to wrench her arm far enough to fire from the hip, but the shot pinged into the metal wall with a bright, hot snap. Dyas fell into a sideways roll—a much less beautiful movement than the Sleeper's impossible handspring, but one that bore the spare efficiency of long practice—and came up holding the big gun with the wooden stock that the Sleeper had tossed away. She braced it against her shoulder, looking like a drawing of some ancient soldier on a far-off battlefield, her Cohort whites gleaming pale blue in that sea of unearthly candles, and fired.

Dyas flinched back with the recoil, and a hole split open in the Sleeper's orange suit, high in the middle of the chest. But no mist of blood sprayed forth; the Sleeper twitched in Magnus's grip, but kept her footing. Dyas fired again, and again, and two more holes appeared, clustered close with the first. Harrow caught a glimpse of black beneath the bright fabric, but nothing wet or red, and the Sleeper was still struggling hard against Magnus's arm-hold.

Dyas dropped the gun and ran forward instead, hand flashing to the hilt of the dagger she wore at her side. The Sleeper jerked her head back; she was about Magnus's height, so this had the effect of smashing the back of her skull—whatever skull she had under that shapeless hood—into his face. He grunted but kept his arms locked tight. Dyas had almost closed the gap, dagger drawn and eyes narrowed, when the Sleeper lifted both legs off the ground, drew her knees up to her chest, and slammed her feet out hard.

Her boots struck Dyas in the chest as she came charging in. Magnus, unexpectedly left holding her whole weight, staggered and fell backward. All three of them went down together. Dyas and the

Sleeper came back up again with almost equal speed, Dyas perhaps a fraction faster, the dagger still in her left hand. She slashed diagonally upward; the Sleeper blocked her arm with a bent elbow, then stepped in and kneed her in the gut. Harrow heard her wheeze out a surprised breath. The Sleeper stepped through, grabbed Dyas's knife-arm in some complicated hold, and twisted. The dagger dropped to the chilly metal tiles with a musical clatter. Magnus was struggling to his feet, his mouth and chin scarlet with blood from his nose, reaching for his own rapier; the Sleeper dropped Dyas in a heap on the floor, flung out one arm, and shot him in the stomach. Harrow hadn't even seen the gun appear in her hand.

Magnus crumpled; Abigail screamed. Dyas had hauled herself up onto hands and knees, but the Sleeper kicked her hard in the ribs, rolling her onto her back. She pointed the gun down at her face.

"Four," she said.

The fallen bulk of Protesilaus the Seventh heaved itself abruptly off the ground, crashing bodily into the Sleeper as he rose, knocking her away from Dyas. She swung the gun up, but he was already too close. He smashed his bunched-up chain into the side of her head with enough force to shatter bone. It whipped the Sleeper's face mask to the side, and she stumbled, the gun slipping from her fingers. Protesilaus loosed the chain and lunged with both arms, and at first Harrow thought he had tried to grab her the same way Magnus had. Then she understood: he had wrapped the chain around her throat from behind, like a garotte, and drawn it tight. Against his muscle, even the Sleeper's bulky suit looked small. Blood was pouring freely from three dark, ragged holes in his back, running down his thighs and calves and dripping onto the floor.

"I have known one death," he said hoarsely, "and I swear that I will not know its like again."

"Smart boy," rasped the Sleeper, her voice still strangely fuzzy, as if she were speaking through a communicator. "Figuring out the limits, are we? Doesn't matter. My rules."

Dyas was back on her feet now and had drawn her rapier, but she was hesitating: it looked as though she was waiting to see whether the Seventh's garotte would have any more effect than her bullets had. The Sleeper flicked out her arms as though trying to straighten the cuffs of an invisible robe, and a gun appeared in each of her gloved hands. She reached back, tucked the snub-nosed barrel of the left-hand gun against the outside of Protesilaus's knee, and fired. There was a dull pop; he roared in pain and collapsed to one side as though someone had kicked out a stick he'd been using to lean on. As his chain went slack, Dyas lunged, in a beautifully clean strike at the Sleeper's heart. Her rapier's point drove into the haz suit and bounced, juddering to the side as though she'd stabbed a solid iron pillar. The Sleeper knocked the blade clear with her arm and smashed the butt of her other gun into the cavalier's jaw, dropping her to the floor like a sack of snow leeks dumped from the arms of a tottering Drearburh drone. Then she placed her steel-toed boot on Dyas's throat.

Harrow seized her moment, stood up, and made a long, underhand throw—

And the Sleeper *shot* the clump of bone she was forming out of midair. The Sleeper's arm moved faster than an arm could move; the bullet more accurate, perhaps, than a bullet could be. As the bone burst into powder, no shapes sprang forth. Harrow felt it become inert at the moment of impact, as though the Saint of Duty had touched it and sucked it dry. A chill settled on her heart.

"Three," said the Sleeper. "This is easy mode. Do you get it? No magic. No tricks. None of your foul bullshit. I've been doing this for years. The moment I want it to be over, it's all over."

Harrow could hear Dulcinea swearing weakly. At least she was alive. She pressed up against the icy side of the coffin and called out over it, "What happens? What happens if you take me?"

Ortus said urgently, "Lady, no."

The Sleeper said, "You'll die. It doesn't have to hurt. I'm not here to torture anyone."

"And?"

"I get your body."

"And?"

"I finish it."

"Finish *what*?"

"This isn't a conversation. Two."

Harrow peered over the coffin. Magnus and Protesilaus were both sprawled on the tiles in puddles of blood; both were moving, but neither showed any signs of getting up. Dyas was flat on her back, eyes closed as the pressure from the Sleeper's booted foot increased—she made a tight, choking noise, and when one hand frantically patted around for her sword, the Sleeper stepped from her neck to her hand with a *crunch*.

"One," said the Sleeper.

Next to Harrow, hidden behind the coffin, Ortus cleared his throat.

48

HARROW, IF I'D BEEN thinking straight, I would have finished off the Lyctor; she was totally incapacitated, and she'd tried to kill you once already. Instead I took us out into the steaming corridor—the place was filling up with smoke or steam, and the alarms were going off like crazy, and I couldn't see any sign of wherever Cytherea had gone. I picked a direction, and I set off down another hallway. The one I went down had a trail of dead bees, their skulls staring upward, green goo sprayed in big webs along the hallways—took out one living bee myself, but it was pulling itself down the corridor with a couple of skewer holes in its abdomen already, so I couldn't really add it to my count. I came to a big dim open room: high ceilings, a huge table pushed to one side and wrapped up in tarps.

There were dead Heralds everywhere. It was a fuckshow of curled-in toes and creepy human hands. The floor was seething with slime and bones. Completely gross and bad. You would've loved it.

Past the huge field of revenant space wasps, in the stinking dark, there was a kitchen area with another few dead bees. A green-stained white robe had been discarded at the threshold, and standing on one of the countertops—

I didn't recognise her at first. The last time I'd seen her, she had been flat on her ass, screaming after an impromptu divorce between her arm and her shoulder. It looked at first like she was wearing some kind of metal glove from the right shoulder down, but the light from the hallway moved over the long, dark-gold skin of the humerus, joint sliding soundlessly as the twin forearm bones moved, the rapier grasped in bony fingers closing over an ugly wad of fat where the palm should have been. Her hair and skin were colourless; that pallid face brightened to see me.

"Harry," she said. Harrow, she was genuinely delighted to see you. The smile on that thin white face was real. "Harry, you're—"

I moved closer and totally fucking ruined her day.

"Alive, bitch," I said.

That expression hardened like it had been dropped in quick-set concrete. In the gloom, her face was a pale floating blotch with shadowed features: I couldn't imagine the eyes, but I knew they wouldn't be hers. She had long since ascended to the rank of double douchebag. Ianthe flicked a lock of goo-stained hair over her shoulder, leaned against the kitchen wall, and said: "Oh—*you.*"

Nonagesimus, I'm sorry. I was averagely good all my life. At least not criminally bad. I did a bunch of shit I'm not proud of—some of it I regret, some of it I don't. I absolutely regret not kicking Crux down a flight of stairs and watching him go *Oof, ow, my bones* down each step, which now that I think about it does not help the case I am making here—I wasn't *absolute* garbage. Maybe you'd agree.

But when I saw that tall hot glass of skank and heard her diffident *Oh, you*—like she'd never *faked to your fucking face* like she couldn't see a corpse that was *obviously there*—like she'd never messed you up or messed around with you, like she'd never seen you vulnerable and smacked her pallid mummified lips—like she'd never put her hands on you, never made you want her, and never imagined there'd ever be a reckoning.

There would be a goddamn reckoning. Nonagesimus, I was going to *reck* her.

I said: "Do you want your ass kicked now, or do you want your ass kicked later, or both?"

"Please, let's address this like gentlewomen," said Ianthe, without much hope.

"Hell, no! I'm going to pull your whole ass off," I said. "You want that? You want Harrow to grow you a new bone ass where I pulled off the old one? Let's *dance*, Tridentarius."

"This can't be happening."

"She's not even into you, okay? It's just the bones. She's into *bones*."

"One of the many aspects I possess that you now tragically lack."

"Get down here," I insisted. "Fight me."

"Perhaps I should have guessed that the moment your footstep cursed this universe again, you would issue me these comedy challenges," she said wearily. "What *was* your name again? Goblin? Gonad? Help me out here."

"Your cavalier knew my name," I said. "Corona knew my name. You know my name."

She fell silent.

I said: "*Gonad* was pretty good. Mildly amusing."

"Thanks."

"*Goblin* wasn't."

"I haven't had a good day. I'm very stressed right now. Give me a break."

"You have three minutes of me being reasonable, and then I'm going to beat you so badly that you look like a Fourth House flag," I said, and lowered my sword. "Is it over? Did you do the thing, you know, fight the whatever?"

"The Resurrection Beast?" she said. "No, if you must know. We engaged it for a while. *Mercymorn* went AWOL—nobody expected that. Then Harrowhark dropped. We had expected that, though I'd hoped . . . Things got difficult. After Augustine dropped out I was *not* about to stay down there with a two-person team. That creature is . . . large. I surfaced. And here I am. And here you are."

"If you're talking about the sour-faced donkey's ass with the net," I said ("Yes, Mercy," said Ianthe instantly), "she put a sword through Nonagesimus's back. Last I saw, she was thrashing around in a puddle."

That white face in the darkness sharpened. I heard her indrawn breath. "You're certain that *Mercy* tried to kill Harrow?" she said, after a moment.

"Yeah."

"But that doesn't— Why would she—?"

"Do not fucking ask me for information. I could *not* be more lost right now."

"Help me down, Ninth," she demanded. "I cannot walk on these things without succumbing to a strong desire to scream and loose my bladder, and we have to talk, you and I."

I kicked a path for her—rolling some of the bees clear with your arms, shouldering them out the way until a thin aisle was cleared for Ianthe to walk through, shuddering all the while. When we made it out into the hallway, she took a few moments, leaning against the wall, framed against the unbelievably tacky bone decor—all the skeletons in their little outfits, and the mummified busts in niches, and the fanned-out rings of arms holding jewels or swords or whatever. That place was like a party where everyone was dead. She froze when we heard that infernal buzzing, from down the corridor. It was followed by a shout.

"Stay here," I said.

"Get fucked," she said thickly. "I absolutely did not become the eighth saint to serve the King Undying so *Gideon Nav* could play hero for me."

"Why *did* you ascend to be a Lyctor?"

"Ultimate power—and posters of my face."

Fair.

The end of the corridor opened into a wider hallway, obviously meant to showcase that same King Undying's every grotty little trophy. The hall was lined with pillars of bone sweating in the heat—runnels of moisture trickled down the pale carvings—and I readied my sword, but I was too late. The bees were already dead. They were strung up neatly from the ceilings in strangling nets of tendon, squeezed to death, thick streams of green slime dripping from their bodies all over the black-and-white tiles. Some of the lamps had been smashed in the chaos, and even now swung dangerously from the ceiling, strobing over these hideous parcels.

A figure stood in the hallway, breathing hard into the crook of his elbow. He hadn't even drawn his rapier, though somebody obviously had at some point, as piles of dead bees lay in the corner segmented neatly. It was the Lyctor you called the Saint of Patience, alive and unhurt, apart from a gleam of sweat and blood on those snobby, aristocratic features. I was struck again by how almost-unreal Lyctors always looked—or like they were *more* real than anyone else was, more present, painted in more saturated colours. He kept running one hand over his flat combed-back cap of fair, greyish hair, and looked as though he was thinking seriously about power-chundering. When he saw us standing in the doorway, he approached and snapped: "Chick, we have to get back in there. Gideon hasn't surfaced, so he's fighting the damn thing alone. Help me find your elder sister—wait, *Harrow*?" His surprise shifted almost immediately to distracted annoyance: "For the Emperor's sake, Harrowhark, if you *lived* could you not, at least, have dropped in to assist—"

But he had stopped dead, and he was looking at us.

At your face. He looked at my eyes in your face in the same way the other Lyctor had, and any colour in his own drained straight away.

I've seen a lot of things in my time—swords, pictures of ladies who lost their clothes in an accident, a bunch of corpses—eclectic, maybe, though now I think about it maybe not the widest variety—but I have never seen anyone look at anything the way those Lyctors looked at us. Mercymorn looked at us like we were the picture in the dictionary next to *unhappiness.* Augustine looked at us like we were the last thing he'd ever see.

"John," he breathed. And: "Joy." And then—he fucking *legged it.*

When I turned us around to look at her, Ianthe was watching us with cautious, half-suspicious curiosity. She never did show all her cards. It was pretty shitty the way she towered over you—over a head above your height, a bleached and charmless reed of a human. She'd never seemed *that* tall back at Canaan House, but I wasn't used to your eyeline.

"Mystery on mystery," was all she said. And then: "How I hate seeing you in her face."

"You've got two short minutes left before I punch you right in the butthole," I said.

"Follow me. We haven't got much time—quite apart from your

hurtful threats of sexual violence," she said. "Why, your fist is so big, and my butthole is so small."

"Just *move*, Tridentarius! I'm not ready to laugh at your goddamn jokes!"

She took us—gagging every time we got too close to an oozing, sagging space bee corpse, which was a much more comfortable way to laugh at her than watching her mocking mouth form the word *butthole*—to her amazing gold-and-white room. I was almost too stressed and distracted to appreciate that awe-inspiring painting of the bangin' cavalier holding a melon, with her necromancer friend standing on a plinth while the wind blew leaves to hide his junk. That was art. Completely worth dying for, just to see for myself.

"Hurry up. I have a letter for you," said Ianthe.

Harrow, it was in your handwriting. She handed me a fat, bulging envelope with your handwriting, and it said *To be given to Gideon Nav*, and I felt—strange. Time softened as I held it, and I didn't even care about the barely repressed mirthful scorn on the other girl's face. It was your curt, aggravated handwriting, curter and more aggravated than ever, like you'd written it in a hurry. I'd gotten so many letters in that handwriting, calling me names or bossing me around. You'd touched that letter, and I—you know it was killing me twice that you weren't there, right? You must know it was destroying me to be there in your body, trying to keep your thumbs on, and I couldn't even hear your damn voice?

I peeled open the envelope—you'd sealed it up tight, though I was pretty sure that Tridentarius had busted it open in between, she was just that type—and found a little piece of flimsy with the edges still ragged from where you'd torn it. The letter was wrapped around a black, folded-up bunch of angles: smoked glass, thin black frames, mirrored lenses. A little bend in one arm, but otherwise—you'd kept my sunglasses.

I slid them on your face immediately. They were a little too big for you. They kept sliding down your nose. I had to bend the hooks behind your ears to make them stay. With my eyes safely hidden, I opened the paper, and it just said one thing—four stupid goddamn words. No dry Nonagesimus explanation. No instructions. No commandments. In a way, I would've killed for one of your lists of rules about exactly how to treat your body, how I was going to have to take showers with all your clothes on, which, by the way, I'd already planned on doing.

But I almost knew what you'd written already, so I don't know why I was surprised.

ONE FLESH, ONE END.

Which did *not* make me happy, Harrow. It did not fill my heart with soft and sentimental yearning. You set me up. You set all of it up. I gave you one damn job. And instead you rolled a rock over me and turned your back. I spent all that time drowning and surfacing in you, over and over and over, and all because in the end you could not bear to do the one thing I asked you to do.

I wanted you to *use* me, you malign, double-crossing, corpse-obsessed bag of bones, you broken, used-up shithead! I wanted you to live and *not die*, you imaginary-girlfriend-having asshole! Fuck *one flesh, one end*, Harrow. I already gave my flesh to you, and I already gave you my end. I gave you my sword. I gave you myself. I did it while knowing I'd do it all again, without hesitation, because all I ever wanted you to do was eat me.

Which is, coincidentally, what your mother said to me last night.

"She is such a romantic," drawled Ianthe.

I crumpled the flimsy and crammed it in your pocket.

"Tridentarius," I said, and I had to take a breath to stop myself from hewing her in half. Then I said:

"If you keep acting like you know her—not even like you care about her, but like you *know the first thing about her*—I will end you here and now. Everything you did to her, you did because she was alone. You thought nobody gave a shit about Harrowhark Nonagesimus. You played with her because you thought it was funny. But she never gave you anything. You never got anywhere."

Naberius's eyes narrowed. I hated those eyes in that face; I kept expecting to smell hair gel. Ianthe sat down on the bed with her long skinny legs crossed at the knee, that waxen face just one more memorial on this goddamned floating funeral, and she remarked: "Did *you*?"

"What are you talking about?"

"I am talking about *forgetting*, you big-mouthed warrior nunlet," she said, and examined her fingernails, and levered a glob of dried-up green from her thumb with a brief flash of nausea. "Good God! Try taking Coronabeth's memories from me . . . I'd kill you myself. Love—don't make that face, child, I have loved plenty—true love is acquisitive. You keep anything . . . strands of hair . . . an envelope they might've licked . . . a note saying, *Good morning*, simply because they wrote it to you. Love is a revenant, Gideon Nav, and it accumulates love-stuff to itself, because it is homeless otherwise. I'm not saying she didn't care about you. One does care about one's cavalier, it can't be helped . . . but I watched Harry rearrange her brain so that she could empty herself of you."

I laughed right in her face.

"Oh, shit," I said, once I'd stopped, because it was weird to hear you giggle that much. Sorry. It was pretty funny. "You think you can make me jealous? You think *anything I did* has been to make her love me? You don't know. She didn't even tell you."

Her face didn't flicker. The wan features were schooled into a look bright and interested, but those oily brown-pebbled eyes were like a snake's.

"Enlighten me," she said.

"Hang on, I don't want to let this pass by—*Harry*?"

"I thought it was cute. *Elucidate*, Gideon, we really don't have all day."

"Like I said before. She's just not into you. She's into *bones*. She gave her heart to a corpse when she was *ten years old*," I said. "She's in love with the refrigerated museum piece in the Locked Tomb. You should've seen the look she had on when she told me about this ice-lolly bimbo. I knew the moment I saw it. I never made her look like that . . . She *can't* love me, even if I'd wanted her to. She can't love you. She can't even try."

She said, way too carefully: "Oh, please, as though—" but I cut her off.

"Don't start the *I was toying with her, mwah ha ha* noise, because I won't believe it. Your plan backfired, Tridentarius. You've got the sickness. I know the signs of Nonagesimitis. You were all lined up for a big hot injection of Vitamin H."

Ianthe scrubbed at her forehead briefly with her bone hand.

"*Really* a corpse?" she said, with not totally believable carelessness.

"She wants the D," I said. And: "The D stands for *dead.*" And: "Sorry."

"I think I need a drink," said Ianthe, and she murmured to herself: "All that fuss about the Saint of Duty. What a little hypocrite."

"Don't think this means you get more than the teeny-weeniest smidge of pity from me," I added. "If you think anything I did, I did to make her love me, then you don't know anything about her and me. I'm her cavalier, dipshit! I'd kill for her! I'd die for her. I *did* die for her. I'd do anything she needed, anything at all, before she even knew she needed it. I'm her *sword,* you pasty-faced Coronabeth-looking knock-off."

Always your sword, my umbral sovereign; in life, in death, in anything beyond life or death that they want to throw at thee and me. I died knowing you'd hate me for dying; but Nonagesimus, you hating me always meant more than anyone else in this hot and stupid universe loving me. At least I'd had your full attention.

Ianthe was chewing pettishly on a lock of that bone-yellow hair. I added, "I need *you* to lay off. I was already the worst thing that ever happened to her, and she doesn't need you trying to one-up that, like, *Bet I can make this double shit.*"

I watched her recross her legs slowly at the knee. She was no longer examining her nails. She looked at me with a searching, almost studious expression, pale lashes down over her dead-man's eyes. Her biceps weren't bad, actually, there was definite muscle in her remaining skim-milk arm. Nothing to write home about, but she didn't have to be completely ashamed. Unlike you.

"You're wrong, you know," she said calmly. "It's an interesting revelation. Perhaps it even gives some context. But my . . . attachment . . . to Harry isn't remotely what you think it is. I'm not her cavalier, her servant or thrall. I am a *Lyctor* . . . Harrow is a Lyctor . . . and the centuries will entangle us whether she wants them to or— Nav, if you persist in making jack-off motions when I am talking, I will show you what Harrow's kidneys look like."

"That! That's what I'm talking about," I said. "Don't show me her kidneys. Don't think about her kidneys. Don't do *anything* with her goddamn kidneys. Get a grip. Don't look at her blood, or lick her bones, or do any of the shit necromancers lie and say they don't do the moment two of them get nasty."

She shrugged that gold-skinned shoulder.

"What can I say," she said. "I love a little gall on gall."

"Reverse everything I just told you," I said. "Let's get married."

"Ah, the romance I have been awaiting all my life," she said pleasantly. "Babs always said it would come along . . . or at least, he once said I would *go to hell and get fucked,* which I took as a roundabout way of expressing the same thing. That's all I had to give you, Gideon: now we are going to get out of my bedroom, and I am going to take you to Teacher."

The Emperor of the Nine Houses. The Necrolord Prime.

I said, "No, thanks. I'm good."

"He needs to know. He can help you."

"I might lie down and see if this fixes itself," I suggested.

"Do you want Harrowhark to reclaim rightful ownership of her body, or not?" she asked reasonably.

She knew I couldn't argue with that, and when she looked at my face, she added: "This is your chance, Gideon. If you want to help her, this is the only way." And, for the third stab: "I will remind you that a Resurrection Beast is descending on us, on her, as we speak."

If you'd come back, maybe I wouldn't have ended up following Ianthe Tridentarius to see God. But you didn't; you were gone. Might've been a good thing in this instance, honestly. I still didn't know if you were going to kick my ass for that conversation, or if you would be sorry for me. I knew which one would have been worse.

49

"I am the Emperor's Hand; do not thou persist in this
combat; matchless am I with the long blade—"

Ortus Nigenad's voice reverberated around that ice-rimed, organ-swagged facility like one of the Sleeper's gunshots. The great body, the one that Harrowhark had in her crueller youth assumed would look best once the man was dead and his bones settled in the family monument, proved to possess a pair of lungs that could declaim to wake the dead.

Abigail's voice rose with his, though hers was desperate and somewhat wild: "Nigenad, you think too much of me!"

"Never, lady!—*Matchless alike in my magecraft. Fall to your knees and be glad that I spare thee; thy courage is mighty:*"

Book Five. Harrowhark's least favourite.

"Oh, God," she heard Abigail say. "God, please help me."

Heavy, booted steps approached the coffin. Harrow dared not poke her head around its bulk, and anyway she knew what she would see. Instead, she scattered a fistful of crushed ash in a wide half-circle around herself and Ortus and raised it into a jagged wall of calvarial bone, six feet high and an inch thick: the toughest and thickest posterior parietal she could manage in her pre-Lyctoral state. The shell absorbed some of the force of Ortus's declamation, rendering it flatter and less thunderous, but it was still impressively resonant as he continued: *"'Mightier yet is thy folly if thou think'st yet to oppose me.' The Lyctor spoke, and was silent—"*

The bone fence shattered. It was impossible. Harrow now clearly remembered the wall of bone she had summoned up around herself, Gideon, and Camilla Hect, in those dreadful final moments on the garden terrace. She had been almost spent, and yet her barrier had held off a determined onslaught by one of the Emperor's fists and gestures for at least a minute. Cytherea had been ten thousand years old and heir to limitless necromantic power. The Sleeper had a baggy orange suit and a gun collection. Yet now she shouldered her way through Harrow's wall with irritable, disgusted motions, as if it were an unexpected curtain of cobweb in a catacomb archway. The bone barely even seemed to break; it simply flaked away in chunks, like old plaster from a ceiling. The Sleeper forced her upper body through the crumbling wreckage, gun thrust out before her, and shot Ortus in the belly.

Ortus reflexively clutched at the wound, and everything went very still. He took his bloody hand away and stared at it as though awed. Harrow looked from the hole in his abdomen—small and neat, as though drilled there—to his face, and then to the Sleeper, still wedged halfway through that absurd torn rift in what should have been solid bone. The gun sent up a curl of smoke, and that haz-covered face revealed nothing.

Her cavalier cleared his throat again, and said, faltering, working that huge resonant bellow: *"Nonius, woun . . ."* He had to swallow. *"Nonius, wounded . . ."* But he managed no more.

Harrowhark's heart crumpled like foil. She latched on to the ripped edges of her wall and drove outward, hard, hurling the Sleeper backward off her feet and through the air. The shattered lumps of debris she spun upward into constructs—so easy even now, easy since she'd been a child—one, two, three, four clattering skeletons flinging themselves onto the attacker to rip and wrench with fleshless hands. The Sleeper was on her feet to meet them. She shot the first through the skull and the whole body resolved into ash, which was not how it worked—did the same to the second—the third managed to lay hold of her free arm before it got a bullet through its spinal column and crumbled into garbage. Harrow's ears pounded and her head throbbed and her skin felt wet, and she dragged up four more to follow them. She did not know why Ortus had to go mad *now*, but when the Ninth House advanced, its Reverend Daughter would advance with it.

She roared, her voice not so much a ringing trumpet as it was a howling alarm:

"Nonius, wounded full sore, spat blood and gave him a grim smile; nor did the sword in his hand shake–"

From behind her, Ortus said weakly, "Harrow—"

"Boldly he answered the saint: "Tis true that—"" and there she hesitated. Nonius's responses were generally where she began to think about anything else in the whole universe.

She became aware that Abigail was chanting: her voice did not betray any fear, nor sense of desperation. The words melted together like wax beading on an edge of a candle, sublimating into pale liquid, resolving into beads that stuck midway down the taper. Harrow caught her plea, distracted: "—when I come into my homeland, my family will sacrifice in their halls for you: the best of all our blood, the freshest; the best of all our blood, the oldest—"

As Harrow floundered, Ortus whispered—

"'Your power is great...'"

She continued hastily, "*—'your power is great, o servant of masterful Canaan; nor may I hope to be counted your equal in skill, nor in craft, nor even in bodily vigour...'*"

The Sleeper smashed a last skeleton into powder with a blow from her gloved fist that looked almost dismissive. "It's over," she said, and aimed the gun at Harrow's head.

The candles burst forth in chrysanthemum flames of blue, fully six feet high. Time seemed to gel, and Harrow, hands outflung, watched the bones she had scattered pause in midair, like falling white stars. The fire wailed upward. She swept her gaze across the room—there lay Magnus and Dyas and Protesilaus, still where they had been felled; there was Dulcie Septimus, propping herself up in a doorway with wide and violent eyes; and there was—

Abigail Pent blazed like a flare from a blue and alien sun. Long prominences of light trailed from her fingers: it seemed as though she held in her hands a book, with all the pages fleshed from that same azure radiation. Amid that frantic cold, Harrow saw that Abigail was soaking wet, wreathed in hot mistlike shimmers by spirit magic—she had thrust off her jackets and her mittens and stood there in just a dress, and her robe, and bare arms. A reek hit Harrow like a faceful of snow: water, brine, blood. A multitude of voices lifted up in Abigail's, and screamed.

Glutinous time unglued. There was a *crack* as the Sleeper fired, and a sharp metal *spang,* and nothing hit Harrow in the head. A shadow rose before her, and it was all the shadows of the room. The candles were no longer columns of great blue light, but had sunk to billowing black flames. She was frozen by the sound of a great bell: *BLA-BLANG . . . BLA-BLANG . . . BLA-BLANG.*

The First Bell of Drearburh, of the House of the Ninth, sounded loudly in that laboratory atrium. And a figure stood between Harrow and the Sleeper.

The figure wore a cuirass of black laminate that had not been favoured by the Cohort for years and years. Fibre armour, matte and unpolished, shadowy, rather than shining obsidian, with small overlapping plates layered across its surface. The rest of the armour was more timeless: black canvas breeches tucked into black greaves of leather and plex, and the stiff, unpretentious frieze hood of Drearburh, not worn up, but loose on the neck. Worn-out black polymer mitts, no more sophisticated than Griddle's.

In one of those gloved hands was a rapier of lightless black metal with a plain guard and hilt; though from that hilt clanked delicate rows of knucklebone prayer beads, terminating in what was unmistakably, even by candlelight, a carving of the Jawless Skull. In the other hand was a simple black metal dagger, its blade thrust out horizontally a few feet in front of Harrow's face, where it had blocked the Sleeper's bullet midflight.

The new arrival turned its head to look from the Sleeper to Harrow. In those black and spitting flames, what she could see of the face was—quite ordinary. Dark Drearburh hair, cut fairly short but not sacramentally shorn. The skull paint was cursory in the extreme: a

few lines painted along the bottom jaw and chin, the merest suggestion of teeth and mandible.

The flames guttered around Abigail Pent. She looked terrified,
uplifted, and openly astonished; she looked faraway, as though she
were no longer even truly with them. Her spectacles had slipped off
her nose, and in that blazing blue corona her eyes were dark and
liquid and—feral. The House of the Fifth always skinned itself over
with such airs of civilisation, with so many manners and niceties,
but they were spirit-talkers, and speakers to the dead. And the dead
were savage.

The Sleeper stepped away and lowered her gun.

"Ninth was my name," said the new arrival. "Ninth was my hearth,
and my homeland. Here have I come at your calling. None may return
from the River unless he be bidden by blood-rite; tell me, why have
I been drawn here?"

And Abigail said: "I speak your name, Matthias Nonius, cavalier
of the Ninth House. I charge you to protect the Reverend Daughter
of Drearburh, and to slay her enemies."

"Waste not your breath," said the ghost of Matthias Nonius. "Such
was my task when I lived; why now in my death would I need a reminder?"

Harrowhark said, mostly to herself: "Oh, *God.*"

As the newcomer spoke, he had circled very slightly to the right,
away from Harrow. The Sleeper had kept her gun trained on him the
whole time, cautiously, as though waiting to see what he would do. Now
she fired, and Nonius *moved.* In one long liquid evolution, he seemed
to flatten and extend himself; his whole body became a single smooth
device for deploying his rapier's blade, like a needle flicking out of a
spring housing. The point bit into one orange flank, and the Sleeper
stumbled backward. From this new tear, Harrow saw dark liquid trickle.

Nonius's body folded back into place somehow, his rapier held
with the hilt low and the tip pointing up at his opponent's face. He
resumed his slow circular drift.

"A tool for a killer of beasts," he said. "What warrior wields such
a weapon in honourable service of combat? Has dignity wholly de-

parted the Houses since I saw the starlight, or are you some raider or cutthroat?"

"You're just a ghost like the rest of them," said the Sleeper, but this time the flat voice that emanated from the haz mask carried a tinge of disbelief. "You don't get special rules."

"In life I was only a man," the ghost agreed. "But the Ninth House granted me honour, and made me, unworthy, its servant. I speak with the voice of the Tomb, and my strength is the strength of the Black Gate—why am I talking in meter?"

The Sleeper fired twice, but the sword flicked up diagonally across Nonius's body, hilt at his face, before Harrow had even heard the shots. One bullet ricocheted off into the darkness; the other seemed to hit the armour, and Nonius jerked slightly with the impact, but again the blade shot out so fast and sure that the movement hardly made sense to the eye. The Sleeper sounded a muffled curse through the face mask and dropped her weapon, which clattered on the tiles. Then she snatched back her hand and brought it out from behind her back holding a significantly longer and fatter gun. This one had a blunt, squat barrel that even to Harrow's untrained eye looked like bad news. The Sleeper braced it in both hands against her shoulder, pointed at Nonius's face.

"Go back to Hell," she said, and pulled the trigger.

There was a flat metallic snap, and nothing happened. She pulled again: nothing. She threw the gun to the side, and before it had even hit the floor it had been replaced with a long, elegant rifle. This yielded a hollow *clunk,* and a distinct lack of anything else.

The Sleeper backed away a few more steps, her plex mask as impassive as ever. Nonius followed, not closing the distance but matching it, echoing her movements.

"You ought to look after them better," he suggested.

"I killed wizard's filth like you all my life," snarled the Sleeper. This time the object that appeared in her hand was not a gun: it was some sort of fat cylinder. She flicked it downward and a slim black baton, perhaps three feet in length, telescoped suddenly outward with a noise like a bolt going home. "I killed them with guns, and bombs, and knives, and gas, and when I didn't have any of those I just got in real close and put my thumbs through their fucking eyes. You can flick that little skewer around all you like, boy. I'll choke you with it."

"I certainly hope you're a fighter," said Nonius, and raised his dagger-hand. "God knows you're not a debater."

They both lunged forward at once. As the first crack of plex on metal sounded, Harrow dropped next to Ortus. She grasped him with her hands and with a pair of skeletal arms for good measure, and started to haul him to safety.

He did not help. He was too busy watching. Much like Abigail, he was transported; not to some kind of ancestral state of primaeval ghost worship, but to a wide-eyed heaven only he understood. She had never seen Ortus look triumphant. She had never seen Ortus in the eye of any storm of his own making.

She said urgently, "What did you *do*?"

"Oh, I did *nothing*," he said breathlessly. "Pent . . . Pent is a marvel. I will write songs for Pent."

"Write them later, and hurry up now—"

"If I die my final death here," he said, "I will die knowing the only happiness that I have ever known."

"Oh, shut up and *move*," she said desperately. If all of her cavaliers were this excited for death, she was definitely the problem.

He did not move. He was smiling. "You were party to the miracle, Harrowhark. Your emphasis was almost perfect."

"He *smiles grimly* at least twenty times in that act alone, Nigenad," she snapped. "Find a new collocation."

It turned out that a relatively small amount of thanergy was all she needed to stanch the blood from his wound. His major organ function was stable enough—whatever that meant, exactly, where a ghost was concerned—and she didn't want to mess around with complex tissue repair in these circumstances. Harrow's early training had taken place in freezing, poorly lit crypts, and still this particular crypt seemed unhelpfully dark and unmanageably cold. Having propped Ortus against a wall a safe distance from the action, she turned to see what had happened to the others.

The surviving necromancers and cavaliers, whom she had to remind herself were here precisely because they had not survived, were arranged silently around the room's perimeter. Abigail was sitting on the floor, still a coruscating blue flame, and her husband had his arm around her and was leaning heavily into her with a face taut with pain: neither of them watched with any particular joy, but with a hungry intent, a cold anticipation. Dulcinea and Protesilaus had crawled to each other, leaving long snail trails of blood behind them, to meet exhausted at a point in the middle. Only the lieutenant had managed to stand, with the stiff-backed and impassive precision of a woman on a parade ground watching a drill. She looked as though at any moment she might blow a whistle for halt.

Harrow suspected a whistle would not be enough to halt this particular duel. It was like nothing she had ever seen at Canaan House, nor even like the practice bouts on the Mithraeum, which had been inhumanly fast and skilful but somehow bloodless, more dances than fights. These were two people who had spent their lives doing nothing but fighting, now freed from the shackles of flesh and time, focusing their entire selves on the business of murdering each other.

If Gideon had been there—no, if Gideon had been there, Harrow still couldn't have hoped for a running commentary. Griddle didn't know how to *do* running commentary. She would suck her breath through her teeth, or mutter in ecstasy words that meant nothing to anyone who wasn't her, things like, "right *foot*," in tones that suggested that if she died on the spot, that right foot would have somehow been the apex of her existence. Nor could she ever explain a fight after the fact in terms that Harrow could understand. But if her cavalier had been there, Harrow was fairly sure that she would have sucked her molars out of their sockets from sheer intensity of feeling.

Gideon, watching this single combat, might have better appreciated the anonymous monster called the Sleeper for what she truly was. In life she must have had few, if any, equals. Her people—whoever they had been—must have cherished her as their finest champion. She was a prodigious fighter: fast, brutal, ruthless in exploiting advantages, terrifying in her force and aggression. She had gained a wicked-looking knife with a serrated edge in her left hand, balancing the baton in her right, and she struck with it at eyes, groin, or anywhere else she could reach. The heavy haz suit did not seem to slow her at all, and she had a catlike agility in keeping with her earlier handspring; she kept swerving her body away from strikes and mixing elbow jabs, knee strikes, and even kicks into her overall assault. There was no trace in her of the beribboned show fighter: she fought like she wanted to kill you and she hoped it would hurt.

And her opponent was Matthias Nonius.

A thousand years ago, Drearburh had produced Matthias Nonius. He had not become cavalier primary until very late—more correctly he should have been *Matthias the Ninth,* but Harrowhark had never heard anyone refer to him that way. He had never been described to her as anything other than *the greatest swordsman of our House.* He was rather short of stature—arms averagely long—neither of those was correct, surely. Ortus had always given the impression he was perhaps seven feet tall and three feet wide. Nonius's ghost had emerged from the fog of legend looking more like a meek priest than a warrior.

But with the sword in his hand—a black prayer-wreathed blade of her House—and his offhand knife in the other—the type of simple black blade carried by chaplains, or nuns—he was a poem. He was absurdly still, which she thought was against the rules of all rapier swordplay; he stood lightly in place, feet positioned hip's width apart, and the Sleeper would pummel at him—take that black cosh and whip it cruelly at his ribs, gouge that long knife upward toward his inner thigh—and no blow would land. Nonius calmly parried them away as though he'd studied a list of the moves to come. It did not even seem to take him effort to block the lightning action of the knife, or of the club, or of the kick: he just stood there with the black candleflame gleaming off ebony steel and made himself a barricade.

And *then* he would move. He had lift Harrowhark had never seen in a human being: as though gravity changed its rules for him. His movements were never hasty or choppy. He would give all he had to one beautiful fall of the sword, and the Sleeper would begin to bleed.

There were fully half a dozen slits torn in her suit now, and all of them were smeared with red.

But she neither stopped nor slowed, and gradually it was wearing him down. Nonius always *did* wear down, in long fights. From Books One to Four he was matchless—his enemies died if he looked at them—but later Ortus had seen fit to add long specific duels between his god and a few named and honourable rivals. If a foe got a hit in on Nonius, it was a good indicator that they would be present for at least the next ten pages, even if half of that was talking.

The Sleeper smashed her baton down at Nonius's skull with enough force to stave it in. Nonius stepped clear and kicked her in the outside of the knee, sending her stumbling for balance, and took the opportunity to lash a clean line down her thigh with his rapier's tip. Blood spattered the floor. As he slid back into guard, Harrow saw that her clothes had changed. The bright orange haz suit had somehow become a suit of fibre duelling armour much like Nonius's own, with a padded cuirass sporting several bloodstained gashes and a set of plex-amalgam greaves. The ensemble was still the same warning orange colour, which produced a very strange effect. The blank hood with its face plate was now a peculiar curved mask of what looked like deep gold, wrought in stylised likeness of a proud face with a beaked nose and slitted holes for eyes. Only the knife and baton remained unaltered.

Bewildered, she looked up to the find the room was changing too. The nine-sided structure was the same—doorways in every wall and the great coffin at the centre—but the doorways were now arched and ceremonial, rather than squared off and industrial. The dark metal panels had become dark stone blocks of a familiar type—although the floor, with its ring of candles and the remains of its diagram, was still of metal tile patched with frost. Some of the fleshy webbing clung on the walls, but in places it had vanished along with the signs it had covered. In the corner between two arches there now hung a single ragged black banner, emblazoned in white with the Jawless Skull. It was no specific hall on Drearburh that Harrow had ever set foot in, but it was unmistakably a room of the Ninth House.

By our very presence in the River, we briefly exert space on non-space.

The struggle for control backstage is leaking over into the action out front . . .

She had been, once again, so slow. The Sleeper had found herself unable to use her firearms because there weren't any firearms in the *Noniad*. Ortus disdained them: even the nameless enemy soldiers Nonius faced were always described as wielding spears or clubs. Just as the force of the Sleeper's hatred had translated into unreasonable strength against Harrow's necromancy—the power to smash through solid walls and turn constructs into dust with her bare hands—now the force of Nonius's devotion to the Ninth, refracted through the prism of Ortus's accursed poem, was overwriting the Sleeper's rules. Even the wounds, she realised with a start, were correct. Whenever Nonius faced a serious opponent, both parties always ended up running with blood from a series of largely cosmetic wounds. In one pivotal duel in Book Nine, Nonius and a rival cavalier fought for a full hour, both bleeding heavily the entire time, and at the end simply shook hands and exchanged epigrams on valour rather than jointly passing out from hypovolemic shock.

The Sleeper had seized control of Harrow's staged memory, the story her brain was telling itself about Canaan House, and used it to prosecute her guerrilla war against the Nine Houses. Now Matthias Nonius—or at least, Ortus Nigenad's version of Matthias Nonius—was trying to turn it into an epic poem.

He was not altogether succeeding. The space was in flux. As Harrow watched, the floor beneath her feet began shimmering into close-set slabs of black lacquered stone, but the slabs faded like mist almost as soon as they appeared, and the metal tiles returned. The Sleeper whipped her baton into the side of Nonius's face, sending him staggering, and followed up with a vicious knife thrust to his belly; he turned it with the thick part of his blade, but awkwardly, and the Sleeper managed to knee him in the flank and score the knife's point down his sword arm for good measure before he shoved her away and fell back into guard.

They paused, breathing hard. Blood showed plainly on the bizarre orange armour, blooming in startling curls and petals; less so on the black Drearburh leathers, but the floor around Nonius's feet was spattered red. The Sleeper's golden mask remained smooth and perfect, whereas Nonius had gained a gash down his cheek and a split lip.

"Few have I fought so ferocious. To match you in arms is to stand against fully a hundred unworthy," he said, which was exactly the kind of thing he was supposed to say.

"You're good, but you're just another fucking zombie," she said, which wasn't. The voice still sounded husky and blurred, even without the haz suit mouthpiece.

"Who was your master in life? Whose banner and blade did you bear?" he asked. Nonius always displayed an unhealthy curiosity about the people trying to kill him. "What mission compels you to face me?"

"My master in life was revenge," said the Sleeper. "My mission is one of— Goddamn it, I'm not going to start talking like this."

"Enter the River with pride," he said, and there was something genuinely sad in his voice. "Go back to its turbulent waters . . . Fain would I spare such a fighter."

She rushed him, low and fast. The baton rang against his sword, and she struck upward with her knife, as if to impale his throat—but she flipped the blade somehow in her hand as it came, so his parry with the dagger caught empty air. The butt of her knife struck him under the chin, snapping his head back. A long, slender filigree of blood sprayed from his mouth and hung in the air for what seemed like half a second too long. Even as he fell back, his failed parry flexed in the space between them and flicked past her ribs, the dagger's tip trailing a thin and perfect arc of red.

Across the room, beyond the duel, Harrow saw Dulcie Septimus trying to limp out the doorway. Her cavalier, who had propped himself upright against its frame, shot out an arm and pulled her back, sparking indignant outrage on her face. He glanced at Ortus, and they gave each other a grim, soldierly little nod of understanding.

Harrow murmured: "Septimus has the right idea. If I raise a construct now—close in on the Sleeper from behind—Dyas wasn't badly hurt, and she still has her sword . . ."

"Nonius doesn't fight in a crowd," Ortus said tightly.

"Nigenad, you do realise this is not literally a poem."

"You saw what happened to the guns," he said. "Rules are every-thing here, Harrowhark; if we break them, I am certain we are lost."

Harrow gnawed her lip. The more ragged and brutal the fight be-came, the more it seemed to favour the Sleeper. Nonius could not get the space to bring his rapier properly to bear; he was increasingly hold-ing it against his body, using it more like a shield than the scalpel she knew it was meant to be. The floor between the fighters was one great smear of blood in which their feet skidded for purchase. As Harrow watched, Nonius did something clever with his dagger and one of the Sleeper's strikes flew wide; she lost her footing for a moment and he took the opportunity to step back, free the sword, turn it for a thrust—

She brought the baton down on the inside of his elbow with all the graceless force of a butcher chopping meat. Nonius cried out, and the black rapier of Drearburh fell from nerveless fingers and clanged to the floor. She stepped in close, drew her head back, and smashed her golden mask into his unprotected face with a dreadful crunch. He reeled backward and half-fell against the empty coffin, his newly free hand coming up to his eyes. The Sleeper advanced, her mask's impassive gaze twisted into a sneer by fresh blood.

"Fancy footwork, shitbird," she said, and raised the knife.

Matthias Nonius came off the coffin like the Emperor's wrath. He crashed into her bodily, driving her back, and then swung his knife at her exposed side. She blocked it with the baton and he kneed her in the gut, grabbed the back of her head in his empty hand, and kneed her again in the throat. They grappled—Harrow could hear her coughing wetly through the mask—and she managed to shoulder him away, but he came straight back in with a knife slash that nearly unstitched her guts. Harrow caught a glimpse of his face, now mostly blood: his nose was broken, and his lips and chin were wet with gore. There was blood in his eyes and under his hair, and his expression was one of cold and perfect murder. It was as though losing the rapier had snapped some invisible shackle. He didn't even look angry; he looked like an ending given human form.

The Sleeper struck out with the baton. He grabbed her arm, twisted, and brought his elbow's point down hard. The arm snapped wetly. Then he caught her by the back of the neck like he was pulling her in for a kiss, and jammed his dagger into her belly.

She dropped her knife, which joined her baton on the tiles, and seized his throat with both hands. He drove her all the way back against the wall, and they wrestled there for a second. Then he broke free of her hold and stumbled clear, leaving the black dagger's hilt protruding obscenely from the orange fabric at her gut.

As she grasped it with her hand and tried to pull it free, Protesilaus the Seventh left his doorway and came forward a few steps; he had detached his sheathed sword from its belt, and he flung out his arm and sailed the whole thing through the air. Nonius caught the exquisitely patterned scabbard in one bloodied hand. He drew the lovely sword of the Rose Unblown, and as the Sleeper dragged herself off the wall, brandishing the dagger, which steamed with her blood, he ran his blade through her heart.

He skewered the Sleeper up to the hilt; and as she fell, jerking, he slid down to the ground with her, supporting her with his other arm. Only when the Sleeper stopped moving did he withdraw the sword with a silken wet whisper.

The candles flared with a last burst of black flame, and then sank to a glimmer. All around them, there were sounds like sausages flung from a height as the draped tubes and ligaments fell to the ground, bouncing damply before dissolving into pinkish powder. The icicles fell, one by one, slush before they hit the tiles. There was a humming noise and a *plink*, and the electric lights in the ceiling came suddenly on, pouring down blank white light: the unkindness of hot filament. Harrowhark crossed over and crouched down next to the ghost swordsman of her House as he gently prised the mask from the Sleeper's face.

The features were slack now. They were smeared with blood from nose and mouth, but not otherwise obscured by damage. A bound-back mass of hair had been tucked into the collar, but some strands and wisps had escaped and plastered themselves in red whorls on the forehead and cheeks. That dead, proud, unforgiving face beheld them all until Nonius closed the sightless eyes, and Harrowhark was bewildered; she did not understand.

The blue flames no longer licked at Abigail's palms and skirts. She kneeled on the hard metal grille, careless of discomfort, and she asked: "Harrow, do you know her?"

The Sleeper had the unmistakable face of the portrait in the shuttle, on the planet she had killed. The woman plastered behind Corona and Judith—the familiar woman with the pitiless eyes—had fought to usurp Harrowhark's soul.

"Not at all," she said.

Nonius pushed himself to stand. He wiped the borrowed sword on his thigh, turning the blade this way and that, then presented it to Protesilaus, who was either supporting Dulcie or being supported by her; it wasn't clear, and it was ridiculous either way.

"'Tis dirtier than it deserves," he said. "Such a blade would I sooner return with better than blood and my best thanks."

Protesilaus said, "I wish that my whole House knew of my privilege. If I lived again, I would advise all the Seventh to travel to Drearburh if they sought instruction in the art. If I had but five minutes of life again, I would spend them praising you. I would speak of nothing but my reverence for you, and the Ninth House, and its nonpareil swordplay."

"I'd call that a waste of five minutes," muttered his necromancer, sotto voce. Harrowhark's cavalier was smirking with barely concealed glee.

"My lady," Nonius said.

He had turned toward her; he neatly bowed. She bowed back, and said, "I hope that your bones are blessed in the Anastasian, for your service."

"My bones fell far from home," said the cavalier, with a faint smile. "Never, I think, will a wanderer happen upon where they now lie, far though he travel. 'Tis blessing enough that I see such a Reverend Daughter and know that my House stands stalwart and dauntless, proud in the face of its foes. But I still don't know why I'm talking in meter."

Ortus was saying to Abigail, "Lady, it's *you* who should be praised. Your act of necromancy should reverberate through the Nine Houses like—like the dying refrain of a song. I would that I were still alive, so that I could complete my great work and begin the next one afresh— and call it *The Pentiad*, and perhaps alternate between five-foot and nine-foot verses—a total departure from my first work, but reflective of it—I would make you the poem, Lady Abigail, that you already are."

"I did ask you to stop flirting with my wife," said Magnus, and at Ortus's face, said instantly: "Joke, man! Joke! Do they not *have* them on the Ninth? That would explain a lot—"

"Ortus," Abigail said gravely. This was the first time Harrow had ever seen her even slightly disarrayed. Her hair, normally brushed to mirror smoothness, looked as though she had been dragged backward through the oss. She was wet with sweat. She kept rubbing her hands discreetly, and Harrow saw that they were singed. "Ortus, it should not have worked. We had no right to call the soul of Matthias Nonius. Your sword had no viable link to him—we had no thanergetic connection—we had nothing but the manuscript you gave me, in which I took the liberty of correcting a few spellings, I hope you don't mind." (Harrowhark was certain Pent had no idea how terribly she had just wounded Ortus's gratitude to her; looking at the brief, stricken expression that crossed his face, it would perhaps have been kinder to make him eat the book.) "I find myself in the astonishing position of having created a revenant link through—well—sheer passion."

That revenant turned to Ortus now. Standing together, Ortus towered head and shoulders above him. Harrow expected that same stricken horror to show on her cavalier's face; but as Ortus looked at the ghost he had spent his whole life worshipping—yet another thing she and he had in common—he flushed deeply.

"I am unworthy," he said simply.

"Clearly, that cannot be true," said Matthias Nonius. "If the Fifth speaks aright—if your art was the anchor that rendered me whole here, and gave me a body and blade for the battle—your art, not my strength, was the ultimate source of our victory."

Harrow looked away. From far off in the facility, there were more sounds: of melting ice, of snapping viscera. She found her layered robes heavy; so were the others, and they shed coats and gloves even as she watched. The air felt lighter. That reeking fog had gone. As she unwound lengths of fabric from around her neck, she found herself drawn back to the dead face of the Sleeper.

The woman had not died tranquil; her features had settled into an expression closer to determination than the peace of the grave. When rigor mortis developed—would it develop, in this parody of a world?—the whole might harden further into despair. The chin was firm; the jaw stubborn in its lines, the nasofrontal angle of the nose barely present, with flared nostrils like a large cat's. It was the jaw, and something about the eyes and brows, that kept distracting Harrow.

Something grey protruded from beneath a flap of the orange collar, against the dead skin of the Sleeper's throat. She crouched down and used one finger to hook it. It was a loop of thin chain. She tugged, carefully, and the rest emerged: plain metal links, unadorned except for a flat steel tag about the length of her thumb. She turned the tag over. The other side had been neatly etched with a single word:

AWAKE.

"Reverend Daughter," Nonius said courteously.

She stood and turned back to him. The long-dead ghost of her House still looked a mess; he had returned his rapier and dagger to their respective sheaths, but his face and throat were ghastly with drying blood streaked here and there with sweat. His dark eyes were bloodshot, his hair was matted, and his split lip was swelling up. He left sticky red footprints wherever he walked.

He said, "Does aught of the foe yet remain? Are there enemies still who would hasten to harm you?"

"If there are, I don't know about them," she said. "Pent, can you sense anything left of the invasive presence?"

"Your soul is your own again, but the ghost will still, I suspect, have a corporeal foothold on the other side. Defeating it here will not have destroyed it there. The only sure way to banish a revenant is to destroy the physical anchor it inhabits before it can escape the shell. Inanimate objects can be destroyed; corpses too, if you remove the brain. But, Harrow, we have other problems on our hands," said Abigail.

The sounds of the flesh strings hitting the floor had resolved into background noise. But now, Canaan House rumbled again: not with any great ferociousness, but with a sort of timid, rattling unease, as though more of its facade was falling away. A sheet of dust fell from the ceiling, glittering softly in the white lights that winked off and on. The others looked up at the tumbling dust with varying shades of alarm, except for Abigail, who looked grimly expectant.

"Everyone, listen. We don't have much time. The bubble is deforming," she said swiftly. "After multiple separate evolutions there are too many places where it doesn't agree with itself."

Magnus said, "Another rearrangement? Will it cause a new scenario?"

"No," said his wife. "The memories have squared themselves away, and the intruder is gone. There is no more grit for the clam to worry into a pearl. And depending on what's happening outside with— All those external factors are driving the bubble to its natural end. We ghosts must head back to the River, or risk getting absorbed or expelled by Harrow's soul."

Another low rumble from somewhere else. The far-off, musical crash of some wall or partition slowly crumbling in on itself, a great particle mass sliding to a heap.

Nonius said instantly: "If I have discharged my duty to you and my House, I am bound by another; a debt from of old that I would repay, if I can. May I leave these halls with your blessing, my lady?"

Ortus said intently: "A *debt*?"

"A dread beast haunts this course of the River, a king among monsters," he said. "A rival and ally is fighting against it, alone, and I grudge him the glory of such an impossible combat. Free me to aid him."

A terrible conviction seized Harrowhark's heart. She had been here for what seemed like such a long time that she had put to one side the pressing issues of *now:* the reality that was out there still, and the fact that she was still alive, despite her last coherent moments. A king among monsters in the River. And, perhaps worse, the realisation that she had lost a cherished and decade-long fight.

"You mean a Lyctor," said Harrow. "You actually fought a Lyctor."

"The third of the saints who serve as the Hands of the Emperor Undying," he confirmed. And then, in case she'd missed the point, "The saint who is titled for duty."

"Why is he fighting *alone*?" she demanded. A rising panic, strangely detached, was moving up the base of her spine. "Where are Augustine and Mercy? Where's Ianthe?"

"I do not know these names. Even his own is beyond me. We met long ago, and I fought him," said Nonius. She very specifically did not look at Ortus. He was being good enough not to say anything; but if he looked at her with anything close to smugness, she was going to kick his ankle.

Another rumble from above, sounding much more insistent. Harrow said, "But you're half-dead already—the Resurrection Beast terrifies ghosts—"

"I am not half-dead," he said. "I am *dead,* nothing more; but I am not afraid. This fight has sharpened my edge and awoken my senses. I am, if you like, warmed up—which in context, I realise, is not the best word choice."

Ortus said, "I will go with you," and instantly, Protesilaus said: "So will I."

"Ortus," said Harrowhark, "no. You have no idea what you're speaking of. The Beast in the River is the soul of a dead planet, come to destroy the Emperor. If there's only one Lyctor standing against it—he's dead, Nigenad."

She could not have said anything worse. His eyes shone as he said, "I have lived so much of my life in fear, my Lady Harrowhark. I will not waste my death in it. I now find that I am no longer afraid of anything . . . of death . . . of laws . . . of monsters. I will advance before I can change my mind and become, again, a coward. Even if I cannot do anything more than watch, let me go." In the face of her stupefaction, he added gently: "What else is there for me, Harrow?"

And she knew that it was useless to hold him. Fearful, Ortus had proved enormously stubborn; it was inevitable that he would be even worse in bravery. She did not know what to say. Should she thank him? Thank him *now*? Cordially request he not go and waste his ghostly adrenaline on a creature he could not hope to understand?

But Pent, more tactfully, was already speaking: "I genuinely believe the River can be crossed, Nigenad. Come with me and Magnus. We could use your help in finding Jeannemary and Isaac . . ."

"If there is a way through, you will undoubtedly find it," he said calmly. "I am relieved that, in my unworthy death, I was able to meet you. I will still write *The Pentiad*. It may just have to be a shorter poem . . . very short, if what Harrow says is right. My heart is set to go with the hero of my own House and the hero of the Seventh."

"I shall be glad to stand beside you, Ortus Nigenad; never again will I doubt the will of the Ninth," said the unbelievably tedious hero of the Seventh, who then cleared his throat and said:

> *"In the storm, the tree is glad of the root,*
> *Not of the branch."*

"Well expressed," said Ortus.

"It's from a longer work of my own," admitted Protesilaus.

From behind them, Lieutenant Dyas said, "I'm going too."

They all turned to look at her. Her injured hand was stoically clutching her rapier; Harrow noticed that she had tied the hilt to her glove with a length of wire, so that it could not fall out of her grip. She was bloody, smeared, and untidy, but perfectly calm. "I'm going," she repeated. And she shrugged. "Cohort rules."

"*What* Cohort rule, Marta?" Abigail asked, bewildered.

"'Chickenshits don't get beer,'" Dyas said. And, after a pause: "Might not be the official wording, but that's how I've always heard it."

Magnus said, more than slightly delighted, "I have *never* heard that one."

"As it happens, I have," said Matthias Nonius.

They all looked to Harrow, as though on fatal cue: legends, soldiers, poets, Magnus.

"Nonius. Nigenad. I cannot in good faith hold you," she said, finally. "You have both served your House ably, and I thank you both.

Nonius, if you owe something to the Saint of Duty, he could probably use your help. Go now. I have to get back as soon as possible myself."

He stepped back and bowed to her. It was an unpretentious, entirely modest movement. In *The Noniad* it might have taken half a page. There was no time for him to make any kind of speech, but despite over twelve books of Ortus celebrating his verbosity, he did not seem the type of man to make one; all he said was, "Many thanks, and farewell. Spirit-guide of the Fifth, can you send us four to the shore's edge?"

"Easily," Abigail said. She stepped forward and put one hand on Protesilaus's and Ortus's shoulders, and she peered through her thick glasses at them, and said quickly: "Are you—"

"For the Seventh," said Protesilaus.

"For the Second," said Marta.

"For the Ninth," said Ortus.

The candles flared up again, that black flame threatening to scorch the ceiling, and Canaan House seemed to rock again as though with some earthquake—the electric lights overhead flickered and died briefly—and all four cavaliers were gone, back into the River. Harrow found herself imagining them in her mind's eye: rising out of those turbid waters before the Saint of Duty with his spear and his sword, something looming behind him, bigger than the eye could comprehend. Bluer than death; unimaginable, advancing to greet the four dead swordsmen and the Lyctor.

She had not said goodbye. Harrow so rarely got to say goodbye.

* * *

The lights flickered again. A fine haze was rising from the grille beneath their feet, carrying a thin suggestion of smoke. The candles had gone out entirely, and their thin satiny souls were rising to heaven in the metal rafters. There was a pervasive, clinging smell of burning dust, and the continuous rumbling of softly piling rock and bending metal. They stared at each other with a left-behind, exhausted bemusement: Harrowhark and the ghosts of Dulcinea Septimus, Magnus Quinn, and Abigail Pent.

With rising agitation that she could not quite quell, Harrow found herself asking curtly: "What's my role in this exodus, Pent?"

"If you stay, there's no question of you absorbing yourself or expelling yourself," said Abigail, and there was something quite careful in the way she said it. "You're the host soul, and can only be displaced willingly—or with the kind of violence the Sleeper attempted. Spirits always wish to return to their bodies, and pine without them. The only exits for you now are the River, leaving your body completely—or you can simply go home, and wake up."

Gideon.

It had bewildered her, back at Canaan House, how the whole of her always seemed to come back to Gideon. For one brief and beautiful space of time, she had welcomed it: that microcosm of eternity between forgiveness and the slow, uncomprehending agony of the fall. Gideon rolling up her shirt sleeves. Gideon dappled in shadow, breaking promises. One idiot with a sword and an asymmetrical smile had proved to be Harrow's end: her apocalypse swifter than the death of the Emperor and the sun with him.

She could let herself go, or she could go back to her body, and let *her* go.

Nav had made it her decision, when it came to imminent death either way. The free will to say *Harrow dies* or *Harrow lives*. And she had said, albeit fuck her for saying it: *Harrow lives*, which required its opposite balance: *Gideon dies*. Now here she was back again with what she had always wanted—the choice to say *Yes*, and the choice to say *No*, with the needle of *No* sliding fatally back toward *Yes*.

She said: "If I go back, it will finally destroy her soul."

It was Magnus who stepped forward and looked at Harrow face-to-face. And perhaps she felt that more keenly: that he was the man who had, in Gideon's own words a lifetime ago, been nice to her cavalier. His mouth was hard now, but his eyes were as kind as they had ever been. And kindness was a knife.

"This whole thing happened because you wouldn't face up to Gideon dying," he said, which was a stab as precise as any Nonius had managed. "I don't blame you. But where would you be, right now, if you'd said: *She is dead*? You're keeping her things like a lover keeping old notes, but with her death, the stuff that made her *Gideon* was destroyed. That's how Lyctorhood works, isn't it? She died. She can't come back, even if you keep her stuffed away in a drawer you can't look at. You're not waiting for her resurrection; you've made yourself her mausoleum."

His wife looked at Harrow's face and murmured, "Magnus, you've made your point," but he uncharacteristically ignored her.

"D'you know, Abigail broke up with me when we were seventeen? I kept a ripped-up corner of her dance card for *three years*. It didn't even have any writing on it, or her initials, or mine. Just a ripped-up corner of card."

One of the lights detached from the ceiling above them with a trailing shower of sparks and shattered on the grille beneath. To Harrow, it sounded like a tolling bell.

"This is your ripped-up corner of card," said Magnus. "You're a smart girl, Harrowhark. You might turn some of that brain to the toughest lesson: that of grief."

The drizzling dust had become a blizzard, and something buckled against the whiteboard wall. If the destruction of Canaan House kept progressing at this rate, even if it was some kind of metaphorical shift, it would, in a very unmetaphorical sense, squash everyone flat. Rules were rules. If a chunk of her psychological landscape fell on Abigail, or Dulcie, or Magnus, it would be a second death. Their spirits would be erased from existence, never able even to enter the River. They clustered closer toward her, like plants sensing sunlight: as though she were the eye of the storm, the destruction seemed to revolve around her, and the ground beneath their feet was still.

Harrowhark found herself studying Dulcie's face: there was a strange, tucked-in stillness that made her old again, those fine sigil wrinkles on either side of the mouth that told her own lesson of suffering. Harrow said, "Then there is the River."

"The River means madness," said Abigail immediately. "You've never been there as an unanchored soul. You don't know what it's like. I haven't the faintest idea of what would happen to the secondary soul in a Lyctoral bond if the host soul abandons the body . . . You are alive, Harrowhark—that does mean something where souls are concerned. Your soul longs for your body, and without something else to inhabit, I could not even promise that in your madness you wouldn't somehow find your way back, rendering all this moot."

Even with her feelings schooled, Harrow's voice sounded feeble and childlike and plaintive. "Is there nothing I can do before entering the River that might mean I stay put?"

"No," said Abigail. "It's the River. It moves. You'd have to pick the revenant's path and travel along a thanergetic link, and that's just madness again: sitting inside—I don't know—a teapot, clinging on without sense or understanding, going slowly insane. And as I said, your soul longs for your body. What if you lose yourself to eventual madness and are reabsorbed, leading to some kind of melange—you know what Teacher was—a patchwork fusion between your soul and fragments of Gideon's? Harrowhark, you stand before a known quantity and hideous unknowns. *Don't* walk back toward the unknown."

"If it were me," Magnus said, "I'd go home, and live, and live for her."

There was a terrific crash from out in the corridor, followed by a hideous creaking as, close by, a girder came down. The noise was awesome. It was as though the world were screaming and bending all about them. The Fifth House spirit-caller lost her reserve, and took Harrow's hands in her own, and said: "I'm so sorry, Harrow. I wish it were different. I am so tremendously *sorry.*"

The ceiling above them buckled and shuddered, but held. Harrow looked at the stricken faces before her: at the now-sombre lines of the cavalier of the Fifth, his jolly face achieving a certain supernatural dignity; his historian wife, a woman whom she now knew could never be properly avenged. The tragedy of the genius and the useless death. The irreparable loss to the universe.

As though the universe could withstand more holes; as though the fabric of the universe had not become a series of lacework cut-outs linked by the thin, snappable joins of those who remained. Could the pattern sustain itself, with such absences? Could she, who had once thought herself well-versed in absence, endure alone? The answer was so obviously *no;* she was not even ready to have the question put to her.

And yet—and yet—

Harrowhark said, "You've got to go before the roof comes down on you."

Abigail gave a weary, rueful half smile. A very Fifth House embarrassment. "Not until you tell me what you're doing. *In loco parentis,* you see. I'm afraid I feel responsible for you, and need you to promise me you'll live."

"Gideon decided that for me," said Harrow. She was not really afraid; it was only that her hands were, and were shaking independent of her feelings.

The first falling chunk of ceiling landed with heavy, balletic stillness, causing them all to stumble from the shockwave. Abigail, Dulcie, and Harrow momentarily cowered beneath the automatic and totally useless arm Magnus had thrown over them, a sort of optimistic human umbrella. Harrowhark said briskly, "Pent; Quinn; Septimus. I'm poor with thanks and worse at goodbyes. Therefore, I won't bother with them."

Magnus said, "Have you—"

"Someday I'll die and get buried in the ground and you can take it up with me then," said Harrow, and found, after all, that she was not really speaking to them. "Until then—I am afraid that I have to live."

"Then this is not goodbye," said Abigail, and she reached forward to brush a stray lock of hair behind Harrowhark's ear, which was an instinct Harrow could not find it within herself to feel humiliated by. "I believe that we will see each other again."

Magnus said quickly: "Jeanne said to tell Gideon *hi.* If you see her before we do—"

"Though try not to with any great hurry," said the Fifth spirit-caller.

And then that same blue shimmer, and they were gone, without fanfare, leaving her alone—with Dulcinea Septimus.

The soft ripples within the bubble had not claimed the Seventh. She stood there amid the falling dust and the noises of shrieking steel, her skin like thin awful gossamer and her short sugar-brown curls stuck to her scalp with the ghost of sweat and blood. Harrow-hark, bewildered and stricken, drew closer to her as the world fell all around them.

"Oops! It's me again, never doing what I'm told," said Dulcie. "One more moment, please."

Harrow said, curt with bemusement, "Hurry up and go. If I ever stand before Palamedes Sextus again, I have *no* desire to explain to him why I put Dulcinea Septimus back in danger."

"I'm going to risk staying here for a moment and getting squashed into nothingness instead, actually," she said. "The Seventh says noth-ingness is the only truly beautiful thing anyway, so *nyah.*"

"Septimus, if this is about ensuring I get back into my body safely, you can trust me not to change my mind."

Dulcinea, with that strange face that was at once the twin to Cyth-erea's and yet nothing like it, smiled an extraordinarily rueful little smile that never would have fit the Lyctor's face. She reached up and clasped one of Harrow's hands between her own as one of the cor-ridors to their left came down completely.

"Actually, I've got something to tell you," she said.

50

THIRTY MINUTES BEFORE THE EMPEROR'S MURDER

THE WHOLE TIME IANTHE was leading me down those creepy, rainbow-swagged corridors, Harrow, I was wondering what the fuck had happened to you. I'd been pretty convinced that at any moment I'd find myself floating back down in the water, and there you'd be, ready to save my ass from shaking hands with the Emperor of the Nine Houses. I'd never wanted to meet God. Nobody ever met the Emperor in any of the comic books. God only ever appeared as a letter to somebody getting written out of the story, because they had to go serve the Prince Undying. I was irrationally convinced that the act of seeing God—that was the end of the story. Space was being cleared for a new character.

We stopped before a totally nondescript door, halfway open—and I mean *nondescript,* the doors to the rooms of the Emperor could've been mistaken for broom cupboards—and Ianthe stopped dead.

I cottoned on; that door wasn't meant to be open. Ianthe pressed a finger to her lips and noiselessly pushed that door further open; we crept into a dimly lit and equally boring little foyer, with another half-open door on our left into a weirdly familiar sitting room. It nagged at the back of my brain: I knew you'd been there, but it was strange how some memories were like my own and some memories were whispers through a hole in the wall. Tridentarius pressed herself up against the wall next to the sitting room, so she could see through the gap, and I did the same because yes, okay, pretty curious.

In the room was Cytherea. Cytherea's body, her back to us. She

464

had been neatly tied to a chair with a band of angry-looking tendon. I couldn't see whoever was talking to her.

"—not a difficult question," someone said, without any particular concern. "It's not as though you have anything to hide. I just want to know—how? Seriously, I'm more impressed than angry."

The voice was still gravel. "I charge you with acts committed with intent to destroy, in whole or in part, the human race—"

"Commander."

"—for which the only sentence is death; repeated mass killings, the utter disintegration of institutions political and social, languages, cultures, religions, all niceties and personal liberties of the nations, by use of—"

"Commander Wake," he said. It sounded like he scrubbed a hand over his face; there was a muffled exhalation. "I've heard this all before."

"Call me by my full name, or don't name me at all. I'll be damned if I pass up the chance to hear you speak the words."

The Emperor of the Nine Houses sighed.

"Commander *Awake Remembrance of These Valiant Dead*," he said. "All of it."

"I can't believe you feel like you're in position to demand things of me."

"*All* of it, Gaius!"

There was the preparatory sound of indrawn breath.

"*Awake Remembrance of These Valiant Dead Kia Hua Ko Te Pai Snap Back to Reality Oops There Goes Gravity*," he recited, all in one breath. "Correct?"

"They're dead words—a human chain reaching back ten thousand years," said the corpse. "How did they feel?"

"Genuinely sad, bordering on very funny," said God. "Can we talk?"

There was silence in that room. The tangled dead hair was very still. He said: "You've been trying to commit suicide by cop ever since I found you, Wake. I know when someone's trying to get me to do something, and you're acting like a woman who very much wants me to end her life."

"Telepathy," she said. "Did the ten billion give you that too?"

466 / TAMSYN MUIR

466 / TAMSYN MUIR

"Wish they had," said the Emperor. "Wake, you're acting like your mission's over, and you want me to take you out of the equation." Silence. "What was the mission?" Silence. "How did it end? What were you trying to do?"

"I'm not going to talk to you."

"We both know that's not true."

A tiny ceramic *clink*. The Emperor was probably having tea. Ianthe stared into the middle distance, packing herself as tightly into the corner as possible. We shared the corner with a white robe on a hook, and she actually wormed herself *behind* the robe, like we were playing hide-and-seek. So I did too, and had to watch whatever the fuck was going on through a thin veil of robe, next to Ianthe, so please feel some sympathy for me here.

He said, "Blood of Eden died with you, Wake. Any further action is just agonal breathing."

"We both know *that's* not true."

"You never would have fired nukes into my fleet."

"Yeah, you know a hell of a lot about me," said the corpse. "Perhaps almost as much as I know about you."

"There's a lot I don't know about you," said God. There was a brief flash of him moving through the robes—he had stood. I caught an elbow, and an arm holding a mug; he was leaning against some chair a little way out of sight. "There's a lot I *want* to know. Why the Ninth House all those years ago, Wake? There's nothing there."

She was silent. The arm gestured with the mug, and he pressed: "It took Gideon"—still weird—"two whole years to track you down and kill you. Even making you his mission in life, you had plenty of time to do some damage. Why waste your shot on my smallest House? If you'd dropped in on the Third, you could've done some real damage. And it wasn't by accident. You skipped the dummy target in the atmosphere—you found the *exact* coordinates for the House." A longer silence. He suggested, "Do you want to talk about that?"

Silence.

"You've been a revenant for nearly twenty years, Wake. It's extraordinary . . . You really are everything they said you were."

Silence.

"You're not a necromancer—"

"Necromancy is a disease you released," she said. "Necromancy needs to be strategically and deliberately cleansed."

"Don't spout bigotry, Commander, I won't kill you for it and it hurts your cause," he said calmly. "I have access to any number of cute pictures of necromantic toddlers with their first bone. They don't make for fat-cheeked roly-poly babies, but they've got a certain something, and nobody likes *toddlers* juxtaposed with *cleansed*."

"How many babies died in the bomb, Gaius?"

"All of them," he said.

And after a moment, he resumed: "I'm not really interested in this particular game, Commander. Let's speed this up. You tell me the thanergy link you rode to get here, because you certainly weren't in Cytherea's body back at Canaan House, and you tell me what you were doing at the Ninth House nineteen years ago, and I'll put you back in the River where you belong— Who's there?"

I thought we were rumbled until the outer door swung open wider, damn near squashing me and Ianthe behind it. There was movement past us, a swirl of white fabric, and the little *clink* of God putting his teacup down. Stuck in the coatrack behind the door, we were left with a view of two people in stained white robes, quietly facing where God must have been. It was the Lyctor who'd tried to kill you, and the Lyctor who'd been afraid of my face.

Everyone was silent. The whole room held its breath. It must've only been a second or two before the Emperor said urgently: "Number Seven—"

"Number Seven can eat us, for all I care," said Mercymorn. Her voice was quiet: the untrembling calm of someone who had done all their trembling already. "It's over, John. It's all come out ... it took ten thousand years, but it's all come out."

No response. Everyone in the room was still as a mock-up in a doll's house.

Then he said, as though puzzled, "*What's* all come out?"

"I suppose it would be disappointing if you made a clean breast of it now," said the Lyctor called Augustine, after a brief moment. "But go on. Try. Confess, and be the man I want you to be, rather than the man you apparently are."

"Look, I hate to be flip," said God, "but—am I in trouble?"

The Saint of Joy sat down on the empty chair and burst into angry tears. She pressed her face into her hands and sobbed violently for something like four seconds—we're talking brief—and then she stood up again, having apparently gotten it out of her system.

"Because this maybe isn't the time," he said, "given that we've got—company."

Again, thought we were rumbled. But he was just gesturing to the person in the body of Cytherea, still tied to the other chair. Both the Lyctors stared at her as though they hadn't even noticed her.

"Mercymorn the First, Augustine the First, meet Commander Wake Me Up Inside, sincerest apologies if I got that wrong," said the Emperor. "Wake—Mercy—Augustine."

"Oh, we've met," said the corpse, with immense satisfaction.

Both Augustine and Mercy drew their rapiers with one long metal whisper. I couldn't see their faces. Next to me, I couldn't even hear Tridentarius breathe: being Lyctors, maybe neither of us had to. I wasn't in a hurry to experiment.

The voice from the other end of the room said, "Sheathe those."

They didn't. Neither did they go for the shackled corpse—Wake. She had turned her head to look at them. There were petals in her hair. God said quietly, "You've met, Commander? Can you tell me more about that?"

"I met the woman. I never met the man. She was the spokesperson for both."

Mercy said, "It can't be. This can't be happening. This cannot be happening," and the other Lyctor said, "It evidently can."

And God continued, "In what context?"

"They were working for me," said the dead Commander.

Mercymorn demanded, "Are you flattering yourself, or being wrong on purpose?"

The other Lyctor interrupted, "Joy—" but she was saying, wildly:

"Oh, let it happen! If this is happening, let it happen . . . We had a *deal*, Wake! Where the hell have you been hiding for nineteen years?"

"Where—you—fucking—*left*—me," she ground out. "In my bones. Then a blade. In—that—fucking—*hole*."

Augustine said, "Mercy, don't waste your time. If this really is the lady in question—then Gideon has proved, yet again, that he is unfit for any job beyond making simple gruels and stews."

The figure in the chair strained at her bonds with a sudden, animated violence that made each rapier in each Lyctoral hand flinch. The corpse said, "You double-crossing bastards, *you* sent him after me—"

"You *knew* he was coming for you, you'd spent two years dodging him—"

"You didn't say he was forty-eight hours away and knew my target!"

"If you were on schedule it wouldn't have mattered. *You* failed to kill him the first time—*you* were a whole day behind with the delivery—oh, and now I know *why*," Mercy cried out. "*You* broke with the plan, took things into your own hands . . ."

"—necromantic wizarding fuckup—"

"—so you did the *worst thing you could possibly have done*—"

"*I did what I had to do!*" bawled the figure in the chair. She sounded legitimately unhinged now. The mouth sounded gummy, as though fringed with flecks of spittle, but I was pretty sure corpses couldn't do saliva, so. "*I* did what I had to do when the dummy ones died—even though you dried-up liches didn't give me the *first fucking clue* what I was really doing! Checking for life signs? Retrieving a *sample*? If I'd known then what I know now, I would have just shelled the place!"

"Now it comes out," said Mercy. "*Now,* I am afraid it all comes out. You would have, wouldn't you? And when you swore that you'd help evacuate the Houses, you never meant that either, did you?"

"Stop," said God quietly.

And everyone stopped.

There was a flash of—I don't know what. If it was necromancy, it was of a kind I'd never felt before. It was too sudden: more taste than theorem. There was this citrus taste in your spit. Everyone shut the fuck up, which, as spells go, was probably pretty useful.

He said, "Wake?"

"Yes?" She sounded irascibly eager; breathless, to match her actual breathlessness. There were hard, fuck-you edges to her voice.

"Will you answer my question now? Why did you go to the Ninth House, nineteen years ago?"

"To break into the Tomb."

There's an emotion that isn't fear, and I wish someone would come up with a word for it, Harrow, because right then I sure as hell didn't have one—it was this sense that started in the balls of your feet and moved right up through your legs to your spine, and I felt it in your hands, I felt it on your tongue. I felt it go chattering up the back of your head. It made your scalp softly fuzz over with electricity.

Maybe there is a word: *omen.*

"But you can't get into the Tomb." God sounded genuinely interested, but in this deeply casual way, as though he were hearing the result of a competition. It was the interest of someone at a party hearing the end of an anecdote. "Not without me."

The corpse was grim. "I came armed."

"It doesn't matter what you came armed with, Commander—"

"I had the baby," said Wake. "The baby I'd had to incubate myself for nine long fucking months, when the foetal dummies these two gave me died."

"Oh, God, it was *yours,*" said Augustine, in horror. "I thought you'd used in vitro on one of Mercy's—"

"*I said they all died,*" said Wake. "The dummies died. The ova died. Only the sample was still active, no idea how considering it was twelve weeks after the fact, but I wasn't about to look a gift horse in the mouth."

"So you used it on yourself," said Augustine. "Anything for the revolution, eh, Wake?"

"Are you judging me?"

"Only your intense self-delusion."

"I always see the job through." Wake sounded bored. "You sent me out there to kill a baby and open those doors. *Whose baby* didn't matter on my end. I carried that thing under my heart . . . threw up every morning that first trimester . . . felt it kick . . . had to induce labour and give birth in a shuttle, alone, knowing by then that Gideon was catching up . . . Do you know, I gave that thing a nickname, my whole pregnancy? I used to call it Bomb."

Anything could have happened, then. One thousand futures stretched out in front of me.

"Okay. Let's get this straight," God was saying. "You brought a baby—a baby you'd made inside yourself, well done, that's the classic—so you could, what, kill it and create a huge thanergy cascade at the door? I wish Harrowhark were here; it would do her good to know there are more people in the world with an imagination like her parents'. But you're not a necromancer; you couldn't have manipulated the thanergy burst. I mean, it's appalling, but it would never have worked—"

While he was saying all this, someone else had stepped into the foyer. It was a man who looked like he had been stripped bloody by a wind machine and hadn't healed up all the way; a wiry, knuckled-up tendon of a man, with the face of someone who had been starved once and burned recently. Joining the growing line of antiques on board this place, there was a gun holstered at his hip, and at the other hip a plain rapier with a basket hilt and a piece of fraying crimson ribbon tied to the pommel. His clothes were stained with green slime, and so was the scintillating white robe he wore, hood up over his head—he closed the door behind him and turned to look at Ianthe and me, with that weird scratched-up face and those dark eyes, and I knew that we were now well and truly rumbled.

He swept aside the robes. He looked at us, Harrow. Then he made this weird, half-grimacing, *excuse me* expression, and he reached forward. I was so far fucking gone that I didn't even flinch as he slipped the sunglasses off your nose. He slid them over his face, and then he let the robes drop back over me and Ianthe, and he walked straight into the shitshow.

Augustine lifted his head, and he said hoarsely, "Gideon?"

The woman I was pretty sure was actually my mother—wearing the body of a woman I'd had a crush on, who in turn had been wearing the identity of a woman she'd murdered, until I fell on a spike so that my boss could kill her—craned her head around in her bonds.

Harrow, I will never forget the look on her face as long as I live, or as long as I die. For the first time, she smiled—a small, dusty, crooked smile that was totally alien to Cytherea's mouth, which had smiled at me often but never like that. It was the smile for your old cellmate who'd just landed back in prison, the one that told them at least you were in it together—or more correctly, the smile of someone stepping *out* of jail after serving a very long sentence, having seen someone there waiting for her. Someone whose presence meant total reprieve, someone she hadn't expected. It was a little bit mocking. It was deeply relieved. It was a smile that said: *You came back for me?*

The Lyctor who'd taken my shades pulled the gun out of his belt before anyone could stop him. He briskly closed the distance, pressed the barrel up to the base of Cytherea's skull, and he pulled the trigger. There was a wet sound. The body jerked and its head lolled out of sight.

God exploded, "*Gideon!*"

"Wake," said Gideon II—I?—as though that explained everything.

There was movement. Then God said sadly, "Damn it, Gideon, her ghost's completely gone," and Gideon said, "Good."

Augustine said urgently, "Number Seven—"

"Got away."

"What—what, it *ran*? You got it to *run*?" When this was not met with details, Augustine said, "But—you *lived*?"

Mercymorn said, "That's not important right now! I don't care about Number Seven! I want Gideon to hear this too. I want him to know what Pyrrha died for."

Now, finally, the Emperor came into view. He calmly sat down on the chair that Mercy had vacated, in front of the head-shot corpse that was still tied up, opposite. He looked like anybody. His hair was cut short, dark brown, with no different highlights in it. His face was long and square and ordinary. And his eyes were just absolutely, insanely fucked up: deep black wells, this unreflective flat black. Even from where I was, I could see the white light that circled the irises:

a cold, flickering perimeter. At the moment, he had his chin rested on his balled-together fists, his elbows set on his knees, and those whites had lighted on Mercy.

"I think you're skipping ahead in the story," said God. "I think you're glossing over a part . . . because you think it doesn't matter? Are you embarrassed? Gideon, were you *aware* that, when you let Commander Wake get as far as she did—to the House of the Ninth, to one of our *own Houses,* our *own people*—that she was *pregnant*?"

A pause. "I was aware," said Gideon Classic.

"Why the hell did you not tell me?"

"Because I thought it was—mine."

There was a rising call of dismay from that whole room—a sort of strangled *yeeeuuurgh* from Mercymorn, an exhausted—was it a laugh?—from Augustine. He *was* laughing—in this eerie, humourless way, this huge, tired, exhausted laugh, until he had to press his face into his hand. Even then, he didn't quite stop.

And Gideon Senior said, "Forgive me, John. I didn't know anything about it," which I would have thought was a weird thing to say if I hadn't been too busy staring at Cytherea.

The Emperor said, "I've made mistakes too, Gideon . . . but you could've told me."

And Gideon Prime said, "I didn't know to."

"How long had *that* been going on?"

"Nearly two years." After a moment, he added, "It was complicated."

"I'll bet. So the plan was to kill a Lyctor's baby," said God, marvelling quietly. "A Lyctor's infant child, barely born, to start a thanergy cascade. It was a hell of a plan. But both of you knew it never could have worked . . . surely you knew it couldn't have worked. Augustine, for fuck's sake have a cigarette, you're getting hysterical."

The noise Augustine was making was nearly laughter; it was nearly not laughter at all. The Saint of Patience snapped in pure agitation: "Stop *kidding* yourself, John!"

"Everyone's being very opaque today," said God.

"You *know* we know how the blood ward works," said Mercymorn. She did not sound hysterical herself; she had swapped roles with

Augustine unexpectedly, and now sounded measured and calm, nearly dreamy. "You never kept it secret from us. I always thought it was a little over the top, Teacher . . . you were always so fussy about never bleeding . . . but Cassiopeia told me a very interesting thing about blood wards, once. She always said that they should really be called *cell* wards, because they work off thalergetic enzymes . . . which can be spoofed with a substantial thanergy burst and the blood of a close relative. A parent. A child."

The Emperor said, as though speaking to a kid: "And how would you *ever*—" and stopped.

And he said, "Mercy." And he said, "Augustine." And he said, "Mercy—" and then, "Augustine—"

"I wouldn't think about the practicalities, if I were you," said Augustine, extracting a cigarette. He tucked it into the side of his mouth. He was pretty good. His hands weren't even really shaking. "It's not worth it."

"But it was only—"

"The once? Yes, one evening planned down to the ground for five hundred years," said the Saint of Patience. He lit the end of the cigarette. "*Dios apate,* major. We needed your, ahem, genetic material, and it was the only way. It was the first time Joy and I had been in the same place for ten years. You were so damned careful, John. No vulnerabilities, no lapses. You'd have become paranoid if we'd—gone a second round. Good Lord, it all sounds so coarse. I imagine I might be hurting your feelings. God, I hope so. Right now, I find I hope so tremendously."

"It's impossible. I won't believe this. How could you even—"

"Mercymorn," said Augustine matter-of-factly.

"I didn't even—"

"Mercymorn," repeated Augustine. He took a drag from his cigarette and said, "Sorry, Gid, didn't actually want you to know all the scummy details . . . Cig?"

"I'd kill for one," said Gideon, original flavour.

There was more silence in that room as the Saint of Patience lit another cigarette and passed it to the Saint of Duty. Cytherea's empty corpse lay still and silent in its chair. The Emperor was staring at the crown of her head, probably where the bullet had exited, which I could not see. The other Lyctor leaned against the wall, staring into a shuttered window.

"So what," said the Emperor, "Gideon—you tossed Wake out the airlock—she and the baby died en route?"

"No," said Mercymorn thinly. "It didn't."

I pushed out of the robes. Ianthe tried to reach for me; I slapped her hand away. It was seven steps out of that little foyer to the centre of the room where the Emperor sat. I stood, breathing hard, my battered two-hander clutched in your hands, not knowing what to do with your arms, and not knowing what to do with your face. There was this huge, insane roaring in your ears, like close-up electrical static, and it was like I was watching us move from outside—as though we were both out of the driver's seat, Nonagesimus, and someone else was in there.

But nobody else had their hands on the controls. It was just me.

Everyone turned to look at us. Nobody said a word. I stood behind the chair with the dead body in it, a dark hole at the back of its neck. The cigarettes made thin grey ghosts curl up toward the light.

"I'm—" I said.

The world revolved.

"I'm not fucking dead," I said, which wasn't even true, and I was choking up; everything I'd ever done, everything I'd ever been through, and I was choking up.

And the Emperor of the Nine Houses, the Necrolord Prime, stood from his chair to look at you—at me; looked at my face, looked at your face, looked at my eyes in your face. It took, maybe, a million myriads. The static in your ears resolved into wordless screaming. His expression was just—gently quizzical; mildly awed.

"Hi, Not Fucking Dead," he said. "I'm Dad."

51

WHEN I WAS, LIKE, six years old, I used to play a game trying to pick out my mum's skeleton from the crowd—I'd choose a skeleton that I thought was her and hang out in the snow-leek fields, watching them endlessly breaking rocks into gravel, watching them winnow through the mulch. I used to pretend that whatever construct I'd picked knew I was watching, and would send me subtle messages. Hoe thrust into the ground three times in a row with a pause after, that was *hello*, because that wouldn't happen so often that it would beggar belief. When I was seven the captain broke it to me that my mother wasn't even in rotation yet. She only got boiled and sent out when I was eight.

Do you remember the time when we were little and I told you to stop fucking picking on me, because what if my other mum or dad was, like, *important*? I remember. You said, what's the evidence, and I said what's the . . . *not* evidence, and you said why would it matter anyway, and I said why would it *not* matter anyway, and you said I was an idiot, and we whaled on each other for a while. Then I said, what if someone came looking for me and said, *"It's me, the most important guy in the world, here's the long-lost baby I was looking for, everyone will stop treating her like shit henceforth, also I am going to murder everyone in here for what they have done and Crux goes first,"* and you told me that if anyone came looking for me you would get your parents to lock me in a closet and say that I had died of "brain malfunction," which I now know isn't a real disease, so I bet you feel stupid now?

You were furious. You said, *It doesn't matter who they are—they're not important, and they're not coming for you.*

476

I used to sit by my mother's niche and catch her up on everything. Things like: *Aiglamene says I've fixed my hand placement when I block and pivot from the lower left.* Things like: *Harrowhark was a giant bitch today.* (Told her that on the reg.) Things like: *I can do ninety-six sit-ups in two minutes now.* Absolute fourteen-year-old bullshit. Serious A-grade drivel.

It was worse when I was a kid. I remember the time you caught me telling her, *I love you,* and I can't even remember what you said, but I remember that I had you on your back—I put you straight on the fucking ground. I was always so much bigger and so much stronger. I got on top of you and choked you till your eyes bugged out. I told you that my mother had probably loved me a lot more than yours loved you. You clawed my face so bad that my blood ran down your hands; my face was under your fucking fingernails. When I let you go you couldn't even stand, you just crawled away and threw up. Were you ten, Harrow? Was I eleven?

Was that the day you decided you wanted to die?

You remember how the fuck-off great-aunts always used to say, *Suffer and learn?*

If they were right, Nonagesimus, how much more can we take until you and me achieve omniscience?

* * *

"And now we come to the heart of the matter," said the Lyctor you called Mercymorn.

She had stood up next to us—and God looked at me, and at her, and at me, and held my gaze. It was this that pinned us in place. When those white rings hovered on someone else, the blood rushed back to your brain; when they flickered back to me, I went white and blank again, mute and stupid, a floating outline.

He looked at us, and he rubbed one of his temples as though he had a headache. And he said, with an enormous sigh: "Ah. The eyes."

"Yes, *the eyes,*" she said. "*Your* child . . . Alecto's eyes."

A ripple of ice over the face. A hardening of the mouth. He said quietly, "Don't call her—"

"*Alecto! Alecto! Alecto!*" repeated Mercy shrilly. The other Lyctors flinched each time she said it, as though it were an aural stab. "John, you are trying to start a fight with me to get out of the fight I am trying to have with you, which is a painfully domestic tactic. Those are A.L.'s eyes, Lord . . . right there in *your* genetic code."

"There could be any number of explanations," said God calmly.

"Yes," said Augustine. He tapped his cigarette out into the emptied cup of tea. "There could be. You've offered us explanations for everything over the years. But—some of them didn't hold up on examination . . . It was the *power* I could never get my head around, you know? I follow power back to its source, John. It's the skill you asked me to perfect. And the longer I looked at yours, the less things added up."

"This has been troubling you for a very long time, then," God said finally. "A.L. always did bother you two the most . . . If I'm such a liar, why didn't I lie to you about her? I told you the truth about Annabel's resurrection, and in the end you killed her for it."

"My lord," said Augustine formally, "you told us the truth about Annabel—about Alecto—because *she* knew the truth about it too, and you never could control her. Even after two centuries, I'm not sure she ever managed to lie. That was what stayed my hand for such a long time. How would *you* have asked Alecto the First to lie—how would you have persuaded that mad monster into even an unsophisticated con?"

God said, "Don't call her that."

"A *monster*, John!" Augustine barked. "She was a bloody monster in a human suit! She was a monster the moment you resurrected her, and *you* went and made her *worse!*"

There was silence in that room. The air had cooled, somewhat, but it was still hot and sticky and it smelled like everyone's sweat. It smelled like hot perfume, and cigarettes, and fear.

After a moment in that silence, the Saint of Patience said: "Raised my voice. Apologies."

"Don't worry about it," said God quietly.

Mercymorn was grinding her back molars, making a sound like ball bearings fed into an industrial mincer. She stopped, and said pensively: "But you see, we all thought you were just sentimental over that horrible thing—even though she was bad in every single way, we all hated her—"

"I didn't," said Gideon Zero.

"Oh, do shut *up*, Gideon—Lord, you and she went through all the early days together; it made sense that you didn't want to kill her. We came to you, back then, we came to you and *begged* you to get rid of her. We said she was too dangerous . . . We knew the Beasts were coming, and we knew they were partly coming for *her*. She was going to get us all eaten alive." Mercy's eyes had gone almost distant, as though she was living the argument over again. "So eventually you gave way. You killed her, for us. But we never knew how you did it."

"Annabel Lee . . . was not the dying kind," said the Emperor. "It might be more accurate to say that I switched her off."

"You came to us and we asked, *Is she dead?*" said Mercy. "And you said, *As dead as I can make her* . . . I remember, Lord, that you wept."

"Well, I was very sad," said God reasonably.

"Yes! You were!" cried Mercy, like this was welcome confirmation. "You were very sad . . . but you didn't *blame* us. You said you understood. You said you'd do what was right by your Lyctors. But you wanted to honour her, so you made her a tomb, and set Anastasia to guard it . . . It all made such perfect sense, for us. What didn't make sense was *you*."

God propped his chin in his hands again. "What *about* me?" he said.

Mercy and Augustine both barked out hollow little sounds that were not in the same universe as laughs.

"You don't get your power from Dominicus," said Augustine. "It gets its power from you. There's no exchange involved, no symbiosis. You draw nothing from the system. It relies on you entirely, as we all know. You're God, John. But—as the Edenites are fond of pointing out—you were once a man. So whither that transition? Where does your power come from? Even if the Resurrection had been the greatest thanergy bloom ever triggered, it would drain away over time. And then Mercy said to me—in a moment of true Mercy vileness—she said, *What is God afraid of?*"

Those white-ringed eyes closed, and your heart almost relaxed in your chest.

He said a little irrelevantly, "Did you two just pretend to hate each other?"

"No," they said, in dreary chorus. And Augustine said, "But we have never loathed each other so intensely that we couldn't work together. It kept us honest. I never wanted to believe anything Joy was saying . . . I never wanted to believe it when she said, *What if he didn't really put down A.L.?* And then—*What if he couldn't put down A.L.?*"

The eyes opened. They opened up on you and me. Those white rings, like a migraine; those black, iridescent insides, like tar or a butterfly or obsidian glass.

And he said, "Summarise, please. You both do tend to go overboard on the foreplay."

Augustine said, "You didn't kill Alecto. And she wasn't just your bodyguard."

Mercymorn said, "Alecto was your *cavalier*."

The Emperor didn't move.

Augustine said, "The eyes have it, John. Those damn golden eyes she always had, like a cat's. When I saw young Harrowhark over there—" He jerked his thumb in our direction, which still somehow had the ability to startle me, I guess because I thought he'd forgotten we were even in the room. "—sporting those exact same lights, I freely admit my first thought was *Fuck me backward, she woke up.*

"But it didn't make sense, of course," he continued, "because if A.L. turned up on the Mithraeum, she would have been as . . . *distinctive* as ever. So why else would Harrowhark's eyes change? For the same reason our eyes changed. The completion of the Eightfold Word. She had attained actual Lyctorhood."

"Which *meant*," said Mercy, taking up the thread, "that the infant's cavalier had somehow ended up with the eyes of your Annabel Lee. There was no possible way Alecto's genetic code—to the extent she even had one, which by the way I am not convinced she ever *did*— could have ended up in a baby in the Ninth House . . . but there very much *was* a way that *your* genetic code could have, because Augustine and I worked *extremely hard* to put it there."

"All that effort to break open the Locked Tomb," said Augustine, "only to have the answer we wanted wander up in the form of one dead teenager flaunting your genes. They were never Alecto's eyes at all. They were yours, John. Alecto had your eyes from the moment any of us first saw her. And those extraordinary black eyes you've always worn . . . they were always hers."

Harrow, I was not following all of this, because necromantic theory is a lot of hot bullshit even when I'm not busy having Complex Emotions, but that last bit pinged even me as weird. I'd seen Ianthe wearing Tern's eyes, like a funeral in her face. I'd looked in the mirror and seen your face with my much more attractive and cooler eyes, and that was—weird. I'd figured out that the eye-change is what happens when two people become one. It's not what happens when two people *swap places.* No one was ever going to see that ass Naberius strutting around with a pair of bad purple eyes that got left out in the rain, because the Lyctoral eye swap relied on him taking a rapier backward to the heart. There was no way a cavalier could end up with a necromancer's eyes.

Unless the cavalier failed to die.

Mercy reached out for Augustine's cigarette. He mutely handed it to her; watched as she sucked furiously on its end, as the thin wrapper flared orange around the tip, as she tapped it—distracted and frantic—into the empty tea mug. Then she handed it back to him without a word.

"You lied to us, John," she said.

And, with a sob in her voice: "There is a perfect Lyctorhood . . . a perfect Lyctor process that preserves the cavalier, and you let us think there wasn't. You let us think we'd cracked it . . . You let us think it had to be a one-way energy transfer . . . but nobody had to die. Alfred, Pyrrha, Titania, Valancy, Nigella, Samael, Loveday, Cristabel . . . You watched us kill our cavaliers in cold blood, and none of them had to die. You had already done it yourself. But *you* had done it *perfectly*!!"

The Saint of Duty was very still. Augustine stubbed out the end of his cigarette; Mercymorn held her own fingers clutched tightly in her palms. And God sat in his chair, and looked at his hands.

There was a rustle next to us. Tridentarius emerged from her hidey-hole in the robes and stood next to me. Her expression was blank, no emotion at all. Tridentarius was still holding those cards tight to her chest.

Mercymorn said, "John, if you'd lied to me about anything else, about how the planet died, about the extinction of our species . . . or if you'd just admitted everything and said your hand was forced, or that it was for the common good, and said nice-sounding nonsense—I would have forgiven you."

"You might have *said* you forgave me," said the Emperor. He was staring at his hands now. "But I think it would have rankled . . . I know it would have rankled. There is no such thing as forgiveness, Mercy. There's only bloody truth, and blessed ignorance."

She said, "Alfred, Pyrrha, Titania, Valancy, Nigella, Samael, Loveday, Cristabel."

"They were my friends," he said, simply. "I loved them too."

Augustine said, "I've got to know. Call it morbid curiosity . . . Anastasia *didn't* misapprehend the process, did she? She nearly cracked it—the right way of doing it. I knew she was working closely with Cassiopeia . . . It didn't make sense that *I* became a Lyctor under scrambling pressure and did it right, and that Anastasia screwed it up in laboratory conditions."

God stared at him.

"Yes," he said, though it sounded far-off and confused, like he was hungover. "I was the only one she allowed to watch her attempt. She'd learned the trick was to do the Eightfold slower—more methodically—and it was still more of an accident than design. But it's not as simple as her getting it right, and me stopping her. She panicked midway through. She hadn't got his soul inside her all the way—if she had, Samael dying would have killed her too . . . They were both in danger. I killed him for her benefit, and she knew that at the time."

"Is that the truth, or the truth you tell yourself?" asked Augustine.

"What is the difference?" said God.

And then he said, with that same far-off, graveyard chill: "How am I meant to attain absolution? What's left for me to do?"

And Augustine said: "Stop your mission, John. Give up on the thing I know you've been looking for since the very beginning. Stop expanding. Stop assembling this bewildering cartography, this invasion force. I've puzzled over it for five thousand years, and I don't believe I truly understand it now. But let it go. Let them go. Nobody has to be punished anymore for what happened to humanity."

The Emperor of the Nine Houses turned to look at him.

"Augustine," he said, "if the man you were—the man you were before you died, before the Resurrection—could hear what you just said to me, he'd tear your throat out."

Augustine said, "Thanks for confirming that." And he was silent.

It was Mercy who said, "John," in a tremulous prayer—all the metal gone from her voice, replaced with a shameless tenderness. "John, you're wrong."

"Don't I know it," said the Emperor, but those scalding white-ringed eyes raised to Mercy's face.

"I *will* forgive you," she said bravely, and she swallowed three times in quick succession. Augustine looked at her with an expression of growing bewilderment. "There's one thing left—one last chance. If you can do this for me . . . if you make me believe you . . . I'll forgive everything. Rinse my memory, if you want to. That idiot infant Harrowhark did it. I'll work out how you can do it to me. I'll let you rip out my brain if you want to. But I will forgive you, if you do *just—one—thing*."

Augustine said blankly, "Mercy, don't do this."

"You never loved him as much as I did," she said, without taking her eyes from John. "This is the moment. This is the chance for un-lovable Mercymorn—critical Mercymorn—to show she is the most capable of her name . . . Every time you've said that I did not understand the human heart, that I was unfeeling, that I only knew worship without adoration . . . Watch me, Augustine. I am the second saint to serve the King Undying. I will teach you a lesson in forgiveness."

484 / TAMSYN MUIR

"You don't even know the meaning of the word," said Augustine.

God watched this exchange. Then he rose to his feet, and he worried one temple with his thumb, his gaze on Mercymorn: her eyes were like soft bloody dust, some brownish, greyish, reddish substance, all stirred together.

"Mercy," he said raggedly, "tell me what to do and I'll do it. I'll do anything. I would go to the ends of the universe, if you told me that I could suffer enough—withstand enough—learn enough—to be truly forgiven. Tell me."

Thick tears pooled in those bloody, stormy eyes. Augustine looked at her, and then he quite abruptly pressed his back to the wall and slid down until he was sitting; a posture of absolute defeat.

"Look at me and tell me you loved Cristabel," she said raggedly. "Look at me—look right in my eyes—tell me that you never wanted any harm to come to her."

God took her hands in his own.

"I loved Cristabel," he said.

"Tell me you never wanted any harm to come to her," she said.

"I loved Cristabel," he said. "I never wanted any harm to come to Cristabel. I'm so sorry. Mercy—I'm so sorry." She was in an absolute storm of tears now; she pressed her face into his chest and gave way, as though struck with a rock from behind. He held her close and said, "I'm so sorry. I loved you all—I adored you all—I thought I was doing the right thing."

She was a crumple of misery. "Tell me that you're sorry you *lied,* you bastard!"

"I lied to you," he said. "They're dead because of me—I let them die because I thought that was easier . . . and I have regretted it for nearly ten thousand years. I love you so much, Mercy; I will love you three until the end of time, until there is nothing left of me but the remnant atoms of the God and man who loved you."

"I forgive you everything, Lord," she whispered.

And she slid her hands inside him.

The Emperor of the Nine Houses came apart, layer by layer. It was instantaneous, but so simultaneously slow—so unbelievably fucking slow—that it was like we saw every moment, you and I. He *flew* apart. The body of God separated from every divine part of itself. There was a brief flare of that sinus-panicking magic, which fizzled as Mercymorn somehow disconnected all his wires at once. It was as though he were suddenly nine million particles of magnet, repelling one another. That necromancer deity in the human frame—wasn't it just, after all, a human frame?—exploded. He split into parts, and then the parts split, and the room drowned in red mist. The mist became powder, and the powder dwindled into nothingness, until Mercymorn was left standing alone, wet with sweat, and some other liquid, but clean.

Mercy turned around, to Augustine. She was not weeping now.

"It is finished," she said.

Leaving me an orphan again, though your brain didn't let me linger on that one.

52

THE SAINT OF PATIENCE stood up and crossed to her. She reached forward and took big, clawed fistfuls of his shirt.

"I wanted it to be me," she said, in this weird, unearthly calm. "I didn't want it to be you. I didn't want it to be you, Augustine, after all . . . the sin needed to be mine."

"There's hours," he said unsteadily. "If we drop through the River now—"

"We can watch our people die from close up," she said. "The dead planets could have sunk out of orbit already . . . we just don't know. We don't know how long it takes to undo the Resurrection. Millions of people . . . all those millions of our people . . . No, I had to do it. I am not very nice, Augustine, and I was never very good."

And for the first time, Ianthe's voice, which was sunk in a whisper: "Eldest sister, what have you *done*?"

"I killed Dominicus," said Mercymorn. "Killed the Second, the Third, the Fourth, the Fifth, the Sixth, the Seventh, the Eighth, the Ninth . . . and the First, though who cares about that? He is dead. He is gone. What he held together must now come apart. The sun must have died immediately, and those grey librarians will be the first to know about it—then the Seventh, and Rhodes . . . but every system that John ever put into place will cease. Every House may hear the dying cries of their life support . . . even as I speak."

Somehow I managed to say: "We have to go get everyone out. Now."

"There is no way," said Mercy, cool as death.

It was Ianthe of all people who said, "How can you say that? Will you not even try?"

"Dominicus will collapse in a few minutes, chick," said the other Lyctor. He too had the calm of a dying man. I only met that calm once, and it wasn't on a living human being: it was the calm on a dead girl's face, speared and mangled in a bed I'd told her to lie down in. "It's going to form a black hole that nobody in that system will escape. The Nine Houses are over."

"The Nine Houses are gone," echoed Mercy. "It is over . . . it is done. We always planned for a mass evacuation . . . but I had my moment . . . and I took it. I took it, Augustine. And now I will die, and face the River."

"No," said Augustine.

"Augustine, you promised me that after we did it we would go somewhere and drop into the nearest sun—"

"That was when this was a fantasy," he said. There might as well have been no one else in the room. The Saint of Duty held burning embers in his palm, more statue than man; Ianthe was staring into space, looking like a child, for all her height. Little. Bemused. I don't even want to know what I looked like. Augustine said, "That was when the plan happened under perfect conditions. Conditions we never could have fulfilled, honestly. You took your shot, and you had to take it, and now the Houses are dead. The Resurrection Beasts are still out there."

"You cannot make me do this."

"You have a job, Joy," he said. "If you kill yourself now, you'll leave everything remarkably untidy, and that's not like you, is it?"

She said numbly, "That was not the agreement."

"Bad luck," said Augustine. "It's done—as you chose to stain your hands so mine could be clean, you're going to have to put up with the fact that you picked the wrong man to enter into a suicide pact with. I hate 'em. Cristabel might have undone all my good work with Alfred, but here comes the reckoning. We're going to go round up the ships—everyone who's left—sue for peace as best we can—get the Edenites on side. And then we'll find a place to fulfil the old promise . . . Somewhere out there exists a home not paid for with blood; it won't be for us, but it *will* be for those who have been spared. Babies always get born. Houses always get built. And flowers will die on necromancy's grave."

Her throat was working. "Augustine—"

The Lyctor took her silently in his arms: they held each other like children who'd had a nightmare and had woken in a fright. Just as silently, they detached.

She said in a low voice, "He was right. There can be no forgiveness."

"Then let us not seek out forgiveness, but forgetfulness," he said. "Bury me next to you in that unmarked grave, Joy. We knew that was the only hope we ever had—that we would live to see it through . . . and pray for our own cessation. Oh, we'll still hate each other, my dear, we have hated each other too long and too passionately to stop . . . but my bones will rest easy next to your bones."

Augustine raised his head, for the first time, to look out at his frozen audience, of which probably the most animated member was Cytherea's body, which my mum had completely abandoned.

"No retribution, Gideon?" he remarked. His face was deathly livid. His features were still, but his hands were not. "I thought you might want to burn on his pyre."

I opened my mouth to speak; I was startled when the raw-looking man wearing my sunglasses said, "No."

"I'd be lying if I said I wasn't surprised," Augustine said, "but also lying if I said I wasn't pleased. Here we three are at the end . . . *Alpha, beta,* and *gamma.*"

Gideon stared at the dead cigarette in his hand, and then he said, "Well. Augustine, there's something you should know—"

White light.

It bleached the insides of your nose and the back of your throat. It hurt coming out your ears. It bled out your eyeballs. It wasn't a *flash* of light, more . . . a suddenness; when it was gone—as though it hadn't even existed, but had been a luminous hallucination—time stopped.

That light took colour from the room—everyone was a slow-motion cavalcade of greys, of eyes caught widening, of mouths parting in stone-shaded articulations of shock. I'd tried to turn us around like there was a grenade to fall on—and then, in that thousand-shaded grey, I saw—the red.

Powdery particles were resolving in the air—they were emerging from my mouth, shaking free from Ianthe's hair. First a softly tinted pale colour like a sunrise pink, then deepening to cherry colour, then to deep scarlet. They floated in midair, hesitatingly, and then inexorably travelled to one point, like dust motes beneath a ray of sunshine. A great stripping wind blew through the room like a scourge, whipping those motes up in a crimson vortex. The powder became a grit; the grit became an aggregate; and then that hot red matter resolved into bone.

It happened in an instant. It happened over a myriad. A wet red construct knitted itself back together, and then burbling out of its centre, a hot gush of pale pink meat and nerve—a lumpen squirting of organ, deep soft violets, fat-stippled cerises, coils of intestine and gentle buff-shaded curves of bowel—white pops in each eye socket, bumps of sandy pearl stuff filling in behind—the twitch of a wet red tongue in a mandible spurting teeth. The percussive, throbbing urgency of a heart, quickly hidden with a puff of bronchiae sliding into big soft lung shapes—abruptly muscled over, then dressed with belated modesty in skin—the skin shading over with a fine coating of hair at the arms, at the chest—dark hair undulating over the eyebrows, making wrinkles and ruffles over the skull. The hot white jelly of the eyes was dyed black as though oily drops had been squeezed into it—purling over in black, shining wavelets, staining it true nitid ebony—the white rings bobbing up to the surface as though they'd been ducked into the water, each matte black pupil resting in the central point.

The Emperor of the Nine Houses—the King Undying—the Prince of Death—the Necrolord Prime—stood behind Mercymorn. He reached out with his naked hand. Her chest blew outward in a hot shower of ribs, meat, and diaphragm. Her body stumbled forward—he tapped the back of her head, something went *crack*—and the Saint of Joy fell facedown before Augustine, whose chest was decorated with the desecrated remnants of her heart.

The Emperor dropped to his haunches and eased the white robe off Mercy's dead shoulders. He shrugged his naked body into it—coyly pulling it closed—and he stretched his jaw in his mouth, and wriggled the tip of his newly grown nose.

"Right," he said, and closed his eyes briefly. Then he said, "The sun has stabilized. Hope the Sixth House didn't get cooked in the flare."

He rotated his shoulders like a prize fighter, and he said, conversationally: "I never like cleaning house all at once, but it seems as though I have to, don't I? Let's make this very simple and very clear. I am going to ask each of you a question. If you give me the correct answer, you live. If not"—he nudged Mercy's leg with his bare foot—"you know what happens. I shouldn't *have* to do this, should I? This is seriously awkward and embarrassing, isn't it?"

Augustine pressed his lips together; that was it. God said, "It was a lovely bit of work on Mercymorn's part. She must have been training for thousands of years, to bring that off. But I didn't get to where I am by being able to die, you know?"

The Lyctor said, "The Resurrection Beasts—"

"Can't kill me."

"You acted afraid—"

"*Acted* is operative. But this is not an FAQ. Let's get a move on. Gideon," he said. Then he looked at us, gave a little crooked half smile, and said, "Gideon Episode One, I mean. Gideon the First—third saint to serve me—my fingers and gestures. Mate, I'm not mad about Wake. I'm not even mad that you failed to either fix or put down Harrow. I just want your loyalty. Do I have it, or not?"

"You have my loyalty," said Gideon.

"Good. You stand on *that* side of the room—yes—just there." The Saint of Duty crossed to stand on the other side of the chair, away from Augustine, away from the two dead bodies, never even giving them a backward look. Then God said, "Okay—Ianthe the First—eighth saint to serve me—my fi—"

"You have my loyalty," Ianthe interrupted.

"Choice," he said, as she crossed the room. "Obvious enthusiasm. Great stuff. This is what I like about you, Ianthe, you don't hedge your bets. Now—can't ask Wake even if I know what she'd say. It's a real pity you killed her, Gideon, I'd been planning on keeping her around . . . She had a lot to tell me, and why be an ass to the mother of your child? Speaking of . . ."

And he looked at us.

I said, "*You* told that bastard to beat up Harrow?" That was my job, after all.

God said, "I was trying to save her."

Also my job. "Go to hell, Pops."

"This isn't a question for *you*," he said patiently. "You're my kid; yikes. I'm not going to give you an ultimatum on our first day together. Let's talk about me and you later. I can't make up for all the years where I wasn't around to buy you hot chips and go to your school gala, but killing you to escape a messy relationship is a bit beneath me. Besides, that's not your body. I'd rather not punish Harrow for *you* acting out."

We were tossed across the room, not hard. Your bones and meat came to a gentle rest next to Ianthe before I could even tighten your hands on the sword.

Then the Emperor turned to Augustine.

They faced each other without aggression. The Emperor looked like a man waiting in his bathrobe on the front step, greeting someone slinking home long hours past their curfew. Hot red heart's-blood was splattered down the Lyctor's chest, running in rivulets into his robe, and some of it was speckled lightly over his face.

"Do *I* get the opportunity?" he asked.

"Yes," said the Emperor. "You do. I didn't offer it to Mercy because Mercy really pissed me off, I'm sorry to say."

"Understandably," agreed Augustine.

"Augustine the First," said the man who was God, and the God who was man. "My first saint. My first hand, and fist, and gesture. Will you swear your loyalty to me again, clean slate, fresh start? Or not?"

He murmured, "You said there was no forgiveness."

"'I pardon him, as God shall pardon me,'" said the Emperor. "Come, swear your loyalty, my son—my brother—beloved—Lyctor—saint."

Augustine lifted his eyes to the Lord. They were the same grey as they had been in the stopping of time. He looked at the blood on his front; he looked over the assembled group across the room: me jerking in your frozen skin. Ianthe. Gideon. At Cytherea's body in the chair. The collapsed body on the floor, Mercymorn's hair tumbling close to his feet in rosy, bloodied tangles. He looked at the God of the Nine Houses.

"No, John," he said.

And Augustine raised his hand.

A nauseating plunge. Like being thrown through the air, Harrow— the sickening weightlessness at the apex of a rising fall; the jolt before getting on that rickety old elevator down to the monument, to the millionth power. A lamentation of ripping metal. There was a huge, bubbling *WHUNK*—we all tipped over to one side as the station listed. The chairs tumbled over—Cytherea's corpse tumbled too, no longer bound by the wrists to anything—and I could move your meat again, though it probably wasn't the greatest moment to move. The outside shutter ripped off the window, and I saw it. I saw the water.

God had stumbled; he was pressed against the wall. Light flooded the room—weird, unearthly, poppling light. Alarmed bubbles and rills of air flattened themselves against the plex window as the whole Mithraeum was driven into increasingly dark, brownish, bloody water.

The plex buckled, shivered, then gave. The River burst through the window in a high-pressure torrent. The Emperor was sucked out into the water, and Augustine dove after him, and Ianthe waded after *him*. Harrow, the only reason we weren't pulled out too was because I was yanked back into the muscular, lean-beef arms of the saint who shared my name. He was wrestling me out of the gush as the station listed upward, you under one of his arms, him clambering into the foyer that was quickly angling upward as I held on to my sword.

"Fuck *off*," I bawled, affrighted—

He said, "Can you do necromancy?"

"*No*, I can't do necromancy—"

"Then come with me," he said.

The water surged and roared behind us. The Saint of Duty wrested open the door to the Emperor's private rooms—slammed it shut be-hind us as we crawled out into a topsy-turvy corridor, where a wash of water was already sliding down the halls from some trickle point. An-other far-off moan of metal, a cracking, crushing noise; we scrabbled upward—ricocheted down the corridor—I followed him up a narrow passage, and then I stumbled and fell into him as the station listed another way, falling on a memorial that was now the wrong way up.

"Outer ring. More stable," he said.

"But—"

"Move. We're sitting ducks."

I moved. The station kept rocking back and forth as it was swept through the water, pressure nudging it back and forth from the sidelines. An alarm was wailing somewhere. I panted, "The hell happened—"

"Augustine's dropped the whole station in the River," he said. "We've crossed over physically—body, soul, everything." And, irrelevantly: "Wish he'd given me the packet."

"What does that *mean*—"

"This," he said.

We'd reached another ring. The plex here was solid—the shutters had peeled up with the force of the drop, but the plex hadn't given, not yet—and we were tilting so far forward that we were nearly walking on the window. The River stretched out before us: some light source from the station lit the water's gloom like a spotlight.

We were falling fast, and deeper, and deeper. Sad crunchy noises kept going off overhead, as though we were a suit of armour squeezed between enormous hands. The featureless River almost made it feel as though we were hanging still—the only thing that gave context to our movement were the little figures in free dive outside.

Augustine and the Emperor—God—the man who'd contributed half of me, unknowing—wrestled as they sank, sucked down by some invisible slipstream. The water churned around them. Maybe it was some titanic necromantic battle, but up here, falling sidelong, the River water boiling away from their bodies, it just looked like they were punching each other. I saw the slim, trailing white ghost that must've been Ianthe, diving down after.

I said: "What do we do? Abandon ship? Swim to the top?"

"No," said Gideon. "Augustine's dropped us deep. I think we're already all the way down to the barathron. That's a *long* way from the surface."

"I can hold my breath."

"Funny. Breath's not the problem . . . You don't need to breathe in the River."

"So let's goddamn swim for it, I hate this—"

"Listen to the station. Hear that creaking? There's pressure down here. It's not water pressure, it's the weight of . . . whatever the River is, we never really knew. It'll get a normal person in seconds. You and I won't last much longer. And then there's the ghosts. Number Seven's gone, so they'll be back soon."

The station listed again. I said, "Okay. You're a necromancer. Are you going to do something, or what?"

"My necromancer is dead," said Gideon.

He took my sunglasses off his craggy, blasted face, and he looked down at me with eyes that would've surprised me first thing if I'd bothered to look at your memory files. They were a deep brown, with a kind of red spark to them; the brown of fractured rock glass, all mixed in with dark pupil, eyes that gave very little away. They suited the face better than the scintillating green ones you'd last seen.

"He fought it alone for hours," said the stranger. "Then with some ragtag cavalry led by that mad sweetheart Matthias. They almost had Number Seven . . . almost. Gideon never could walk away from a losing fight." Before I could respond to this, they added, "He and your mother alike."

"*Why* does it always come back to—my *mother*?" I said, my voice rising to a squeal like an emptying balloon. "Who are you? How the hell did *you* know my mother, who seemed like a real dick, by the way?"

"My name is Pyrrha Dve," said the ghost in question. "Commander of the Second House, head of Trentham Special Intelligence, cavalier to a dead Lyctor. We compartmentalized from the Eightfold Word, just like you and your girl—though I'm an accident, and he took more from me than got taken from you. I was able to go underground, even from him. Two years before you were born, my necromancer started an affair with your mother . . . not knowing I'd also been doing the same thing, using his body."

I said, "What the fuck."

"She was the most dangerous woman I'd ever met who wasn't me," said Pyrrha Dve. "You're right, though. She *was* a real dick."

At this point I was beside myself and more or less demented, so I kind of just squawked: "But what do we *do*?!"

"No idea," they—he—she said calmly. "I'd aim to get out of here alive, but our odds don't look wonderful. If we stay put, we get squashed, or eaten. If we swim, we probably still get squashed or eaten. I heal quicker than a normal human being, but not *that* much quicker."

Before I could just fundamentally lose my shit, Pyrrha suddenly sucked her breath in through her teeth, and said: "That's your plan, Augustine?"

I pressed up to the plex. The River bumped into visual depth.

We were in a huge gyre, lit by the furious electric glow from the falling station. Outside—another kilometre down, maybe—was the pale belly of the River, studded with rocky promontories. And right at the bottom—the water was churning. The station tilted forward, and I could see clearly.

A hole had opened. It was big enough to swallow up the whole of Drearburh and have room to spare. It was a huge, hideous, dark expanse, and it had seething, weird edges; it took the lights pattering over them for me to see that the edges of the hole were enormous human *teeth*. Each one must've been six bodies high and two bodies wide, with the dainty scalloped edges of incisors. The teeth shivered and trembled, like the hole was slavering. And that hole had nothing in it; that hole was blacker than space, that hole was an eaten-away tunnel of reality.

And there—falling to its centre—wrestled the miniature figures of Augustine and the Emperor. Ianthe had separated from them somewhat, floating high above, though the nerve it must have taken to position herself above that tooth-serrated expanse forced me to reframe Ianthe Tridentarius in the wake of this absolutely galactic ballsiness.

"The stoma's opened for John," said Pyrrha, and she sounded—detached, rather than triumphant, rather than grief-stricken. "It must think he's a Resurrection Beast."

The Emperor was struggling. I would've thought he could have just dropped out of the River—done what he did to Mercy, and blown Augustine to smithereens—but some kind of current was whirling them around like dolls. It seemed like it was all he could do to keep his position. Augustine had lashed them together, somehow. He was wrestling the Emperor down, inexorably, toward that mouth. Overhead, the station crunched; the plex in front of us was making a little high-pitched squealing sound.

Over and over Augustine and God rolled in the water—and then the tongues emerged.

A blast from the hole. The water boiled upward in huge, bloody-looking bubbles. Streamerlike lingual tentacles emerged—the unassuming pink you got on normal, non-Hell-bound tongues—easily a thousand of them, jostling, questing, blindly thrusting up out of that mouth. Pyrrha flinched. They were writhing together, wild and excited—the current swirled in an agitated pandemonium—there was a massive sickening jolt, and the Mithraeum started to slide again, forward . . . tilting . . . sliding.

"We're in the current now," said Pyrrha calmly. "We'll be pulled in, if the mouth doesn't close."

I said, "Does this not *worry* you? Shouldn't we do something? Shouldn't we be, I don't know, getting the fuck *out*?"

"I have been trapped in the back of a brain for ten thousand years, and my necromancer is dead," said the other cavalier. "Emotions are difficult right now. I do have a loaded revolver."

"So what—we each swallow a bullet?"

"It's an option," said Pyrrha. And: "Joke." And: "Mostly."

In the centre of that whirlpool, the tongues had breached—the two wrestling necromancers now faced each other *and* a panicked, delighted nest of wet pink tentacles. Spires of blood rose from the water as those grotesque, infernal muscles dissolved wholesale— sheared away—destroyed. But the Emperor was thrashing—one had wound around his leg—one of his hands was wrapped around Augustine's wrist, and one of Augustine's around his, as though in a parody of saving each other. Another tongue snaked upward toward

Ianthe, and she sent a thin whiplike flicker of blood to cut through that water.

Augustine was gesturing. From this far away, it looked to me as though he were screaming, hopelessly, soundlessly—beyond speech—into the water; maybe Ianthe could understand it. A tongue jerked him downward. He kicked it away, but as they shrivelled more joined their place. As he struggled, he somehow pushed the Emperor into a waiting, frenzied bed of the things, which wrapped around his legs—and the stoma sucked down.

The Mithraeum went with it. I didn't see what happened before everything rolled—pieces of the station broke off; I could see metal bouncing along the Riverbed, then whole sections of station, then garbage—panels and mechanisms, pieces of hull—twisting down to join it. The huge, encompassing weight of the ship was slowly ploughing forward, toward the hungry stoma.

It caught on some rock face. I heard rushing water, and snapping metal. That was enough.

"Fuck this," I said.

Pyrrha said, "Bullets—water—or waiting?"

I'd had this choice before. The different deaths. The death of waiting; the death of optimism. Harrow, the last time I chose to die, I died with your face the last thing I ever looked at. Let me tell you a secret: it was easy to die thinking I wouldn't have to see you go. It was so easy to check out before you did.

Now here I was, alone, holding your body hostage, in a space station at the bottom of the River and getting sucked into some kind of heinous underworld that only opened for the undead souls of monstrous planets. I had the choice of shooting myself, being crushed by the water, or waiting to get squashed by tonnes of falling metal. Or I had the choice of living to get pulled down into Hell.

I wish I could say I was thinking about you. Harrowhark, there was so much I wanted to tell you. I wish that on the edge of an ending bigger than I understood, that I was thinking about you, that the last word on your lips would be me saying your name, taken down to the dark heart of some world beyond.

But my whole life and death had come crashing down around me. It turned out I was the child of God—hey, suck it, Marshal—but also nothing more than a stick of dynamite. I was nothing but a chess move in a thousand-year game.

I mean, yeah, I was thinking about you too; if I could've turned that off I would've turned it off years ago, but more importantly—I was *absolutely fucking out of my mind Ninth House big pissed off.*

As I dithered, Pyrrha sandblasted me with the calm, "Your mother would've picked the bullet."

"Yes, well, *jail* for Mother," I said.

And taking a leaf out of your book, I thrust my sword into the whimpering plex.

It gave. Both of us got knocked back flat on our asses by the gush of foaming, filthy, hideous water—I had to hit the deck—and that whole corridor deformed: it was like a popped balloon. The world went dark. I went under before I could take a breath. We bounced off about twenty surfaces, and as water closed up over our heads, the both of us made for the hole in the side of the ship. We squeezed through a narrowing, breaking tunnel and pushed through, and then we were out.

I couldn't swim, but never fucking mind. I couldn't even tell if Pyrrha had been right about the breathing. It was like I had Crux standing on my chest. Something hideous happened in your ears. We tumbled over and over and over in the water, and I thought for the first moment that it was really the end. I thought your eyeballs were about to burst in your head.

But they didn't, and so I saw what happened as we rose from the wrecked body of that dying space station. High above the nest of tongues, Ianthe was poised as though flying—fluttering white flimsy in the heart of that vortex—as God and Augustine thrashed together. The tongues had retracted almost to the rim of the mouth, and God was not winning. Those demoniacal tongues had him almost entirely in their grip as Augustine pinned him down. The tongues seemed more interested in the Emperor than in Augustine, though they weren't *un*interested in Augustine. God's desperation, even in your darkening eyeballs, was clear.

If Augustine wanted to free himself and get clear, he'd need to stop fighting. Or he could keep fighting, make sure the stoma took the Emperor, and be taken himself in the process. Above them both the third option floated like a panicking butterfly. Ianthe could make the difference. If Augustine gave God a last good shove down into Hell, and then Ianthe pulled him free of the tongues, they could probably both escape.

I watched, dimly, as Ianthe lifted her hands. The current parted— the water flumed around her in thick, opaque curls, red with blood— the tongues lashed out all at once.

I watched Ianthe dart down, rip the tongues from the Emperor of the Nine Houses, and wrestle him clear. The tongues entwined in a bower to bear Augustine silently down to that ravenous mouth, to the Hell where only demons went.

Which was Tridentarius all over. She got one choice, and not only did she blow it, but she blew it in such a huge fucking spectacular way that you would've been impressed had you not hated her for it. Ianthe, throwing in her lot with the guy who had lied to everyone about everything. Ianthe, backstabbing her own cavalier all over again. Ianthe, with the world in the balance, reaching her hand out and pressing down on the weight marked *BAD.* She surged out of sight, covered and hidden by a blast of water. The tongues retracted and the teeth folded up, to close that chewing great void.

Then the pressure closed its hands around your wrists, and your chest pounded inward.

* * *

Harrowhark, did you know that if you die by drowning, apparently your whole life flashes in front of your eyes? I didn't know, as I died and took you along with me—having kept you alive for what, a whole two hours?—whether it was going to show me both. Like, at the end of everything, if it was going to be you and me, layered over each other as we always were. A final blurring of the edges between us, like water spilt over ink outlines. Melted steel. Mingled blood. Harrowhark-and-Gideon, Gideon-and-Harrowhark at last.

But as everything went black and I died the second time round, I didn't see you. I didn't even see me. The final thing I saw was a great sunshiny light: a blurred figure, hazing in and out around the edges. At first it looked to me like a woman—a grey-faced, dead-eyed woman, with a face so beautiful it almost went out the other side and became repellent; a woman with my eyes, dimmed dark yellow in death, whose hair fell in wet leaden hanks. I realised with exhausted indignation that, at the end of everything—after all I had been through—after the last word, the last strike, the last drop of blood in the water—your bullshit dead girlfriend had come to claim you.

And she said in the wrong voice twice removed: "Chest compressions. I know her sternum's shattered; ignore it. We need that heart pumping. On my mark."

Hands pressed. We died.

53

HALF AN HOUR AGO

"You're *sure*," Harrowhark said.

"Of course I'm not *sure*," said Dulcie Septimus. "But I'm a necromancer of the Seventh House—or I was, when I was alive. Abigail couldn't have felt what I felt, when we both looked outside. I'm not an expert with revenant spirits, but I know a little something about *puppeting*. And your body's *not* being puppeted, Harrow—something is moving it around, and not a fragment. It's not the ghost either, because it didn't feel anything like the Sleeper."

Those blue eyes watched her very carefully as she stared, unseeing, at the facility walls: at them buckling beneath the enormous pressure from above, the whole castle doing a neat controlled demolition on itself. Folding up and changing, as though caught in the grip of a giant fist.

The rips at the side—the huge rents of wall and partition—had begun to alter in a way she had seen before. They no longer looked out into darkness; they looked out into the same white, hard absence of place and time that she had seen within another bubble. A tintless, abyssal wound; her mind's contraction; her limits within the River.

"It may mean *nothing*," said Dulcie.

Harrowhark heard herself asking distantly, "Why did you tell me?"

That rueful smile again, like the shadow of old joy.

"Because I wanted you to know all the truth," said the dead daughter of the Seventh. "The whole, unpackaged, slipshod truth. Truth unvarnished and truth unclean. Pal and I were always zealots, in that line. I got told so many lies over my life, Harrowhark, and I didn't want to go back into the River having myself committed the murder of the white lie. Please understand, I'm being selfish. But I wanted you to know."

When she looked into Harrow's face again, and how it had changed, she said simply: "I'm sorry."

"There's a difference between keeping a shred of dance card," said Harrow Nonagesimus, "and saving the last dance."

Another corridor clenched in on itself. SANITISER's entrance deformed, and the ceiling suddenly sloped downward at an arresting angle, sending things shrieking overhead. The roof opened like a cloudburst; a huge flank of tile fell down over their heads. Harrowhark backed up against the coffin, and the wasted, hot-eyed wraith before her blew her a dry-mouthed kiss and disappeared under a cloud of rubble, smashing metal, and a soft shimmer of blue.

Harrow's heart was beating as though it never had before. She thought it could not beat in truth; she was her own dream, and her heart's whirring simply another fantasy of the subconscious. But nevertheless, it hammered, hard.

She said aloud, "No. I'm getting out of here."

She stood before the coffin of the Sleeper, and gathered those white, soft, solid rips in her hands, and she popped the bubble, and the River came rushing in.

It came down around her in shreds, as light and insubstantial as drifts of spiderweb. The water sprayed through white holes, rushing in with a pounding roar: that brackish, bloodied water that only existed within the River. She was buoyed up by a spray of ice water and filth—but she wasn't; she seemed to be walking down her long black corridor again—

Then Harrow was back drowning in salt water. Gideon's arms were around her. They were in the pool of Canaan House, and she had just been ducked by her cavalier. She had held her breath instinctively, though she had been serene at the time; to drown, she thought, was softer death than she deserved, and back then to die in Gideon's arms had seemed entirely correct. She could feel Gideon's fingers digging into the small of her back, could feel her shirt billowing in the pool as they sank to the bottom in a tangle.

Harrow's head broke the water. A thin skin of ice shivered apart as she emerged, panting for air, her skin burning with the cold. Her flailing sent ripples along those black, disturbed waters, but did not interrupt their gentle tidal lapping along the jagged shore. Above her head the rocky cathedral of the cave shone with a dismal heaven of luminescent worms, blinking softly on and off. They were all undead: revenant creatures and watchers, shifting restlessly forever on the rock of the Locked Tomb. Harrow was home.

Harrow floundered, not toward the shore, but to the island in the centre—to the black mausoleum of glass and ice, sitting silently and reflectively beneath that sea of dead worms. She hauled herself to shore and lay there, skin crawling, frozen half-solid, shivering and numb in that strange heat presaging hypothermic death. And yet Harrow felt no pain; she felt nothing, in fact, but a welcome sense of homecoming—the strange, tiny, pleased familiarity of finding an old book once beloved, or some other antique of childhood.

Eager now, she hauled her freezing meat to stand. She passed beneath those pillars as she had as a child, followed the pathway she still traced in dreams. She was exhausted more than cold; her head filled with the soft, heavy tiredness of too much waking and not enough sleep, of a long day on the job without rest or break. She walked into the mausoleum, and she approached the Tomb itself.

The chains in their great holes were snapped and broken. The ice crawled up the sides of the empty altar. Within that bed of ice and glass, on the stone-shaped pillow to prop the head, that final resting place of Harrowhark's one true love, lay a sword.

It was the two-handed sword that had lain at the bottom of the Sleeper's coffin, just as Dyas had seen it.

Harrowhark had come home, and she was not afraid. She did not know why she did it, but she climbed inside that empty coffin, and she took the sword within her arms. She was filled with a drowsy, comfortable certainty, as though rather than an icy tomb she had been tucked into a bed with a pillow fluffed beneath her. Her eyelids felt as heavy as the chains that lay broken around the outside of the bier. The sword she embraced shamelessly; those six feet of steel held no fear for her now.

Something rustled at her side. She had not seen it when she climbed in; it had been tucked to one side of the coffin. When she reached out to hold it in front of her face, she found a shiny mass of magazine flimsy. The crumpled front page showed a woman in a Cohort uniform that was so far from official it did not merely strain credulity, but snapped it in two pieces: a white jacket at least three sizes too small, boots, and nothing else.

The ice felt kind and warm; the stone gave as though it were cotton. Harrow lay where the Body had lain, perfectly at her ease, perfectly comfortable, and she peered blearily at the header.

"*Frontline Titties of the Fifth,*" she read, and found she was smiling helplessly to herself. She murmured: "Nav, you ass, that's not even a real publication."

Then there was a huge, side-to-side rocking, in the manner of an explosion, or a cradle. Her eyes closed. Lying in the tomb that had claimed her heart, faraway in a land she had never travelled, Harrowhark Nonagesimus fell asleep, or dropped dead, or both.

Epilogue

SIX MONTHS AFTER THE EMPEROR'S MURDER

THE THICK FUG OF a summer evening. The curfews stalling the traffic outside to a funeral crawl, with the hot sun blistering the road into sodden clags of concrete and tar. What she liked best was the way the haze of combustion from the vehicles colonized the dying rays of the sun into deep pinks and oranges, oranges into scarlets, scarlets into purples, purples into the sweet deathly navy of the night. The antisniper striping frosted over the windowpane turned everything into feeble shapes, but the colours were just as intense even if the shapes were a mush. And the murmurous honks from the traffic below—the occasional low, lamenting *blart* of a cargo carrier—were transformed by the tall buildings into an orchestral echo. The crack of the open window let the outside air, redolent of sun-warmed plastic and fumes, ruffle the drying sweat in her hair.

This time of day was a crossbar. It blocked off the afternoon, when black cloths would be tacked up over windows and she would sit in that tight, squeezing, claustrophobic heat, and she would be given the bones by the people who lived with her. She lived with three people: the person who went to work for her, the person who taught her, and the person who looked after her. The person who taught her often gave her these bones to arrange ("just whatever feels normal"), sometimes to just hold, in the hand or in the hollow of her cheek. Then the bones could be packed away in secret—the blackout curtains could come down, and the window cracked—and once the temperature

505

dropped a few degrees, she would be at the chin-up bar, or doing press-ups, or the sword would be put in her hand by the person who looked after her—"whatever feels normal," again.

And then when it was very late, they'd climb down thirty flights of stairs to street level, picking their way through abandoned sacks of clothes, or laminate takeaway boxes, the press of other people, smelling like the day-to-day sweat of working in a sultry office, or the day-to-day sweat of being outside in the heat, or the day-to-day sweat of fear. She would be taken to the little corner store with its great barricades of snacks and pills and pamphlets and thin cheap shirts, and sit on the should-be-white chairs and smell the deep fryer going, and then pick over crispy chunks of potato, or pan-blasted sweet fruit, or sausage meat in batter, with time enough after to lick her burnt and salty fingers. She and the person who looked after her had used to go to a different haunt, where the food was cheaper and the sausages more juicy—but there the man who fried the food had once said warningly, "It's hot," only to find that she had already stuffed her mouth full of lacy fried things anyway. The man had said, laughing, "Her lips should be burnt off, eh?" But her lips had not been burnt off. It had barely hurt. For some reason, because of that, they no longer patronized that sausage man.

Out there in the outskirts, soldiers walked the city, with their guns out and their riot shields slung over their shoulders, looking grimy and cross in the heat under their helmets and great reflective visors. Some nights they heard the *pop—pop—pop—rattle* of a gunfight, and on these nights they would shut the windows and lie with most of their clothes off on the floor of the bathroom.

On nights like this, in the dark, turning her face to press hot cheeks into the cool ceramic bump of the tiles below, she would look into the face of the person who looked after her. It was a comforting face to look into; it was a resolute, keen, utterly unmoved face, which did not flinch at the angry carillon of vehicle honks, nor at the sound of someone shouting from the rooms close by through the thin walls. It felt as though she had always been fond of the face, and of the dark, sharply bobbed hair; and she loved without reserve the eyes—those great lambent eyes, the iris so skilfully and gently blent that it seemed there was no tint or shade in that clear and beautiful grey.

And she would say, idly, more as prayer than demand: "Have you worked out who I am?"

"Not yet," said Camilla.

The tomb will open in

ALECTO THE NINTH

ACKNOWLEDGMENTS

I would like to again express my very great appreciation for my agent, Jennifer Jackson, who is as indefatigable as she is kind and as funny as she is indefatigable. Jennifer is a truly remarkable being and I have not managed to stump her yet. A year on I still haven't found the right words to thank Carl Engle-Laird, editor and hero, and if I did he would just remove all the parataxis. Carl, I know this universe has meant so much to both of us. Thank you for being with me on this wild ride.

The team at Tor.com are angelic beings—Ruoxi Chen, Christine Foltzer, Irene Gallo, Giselle Gonzalez, Mordicai Knode, Caroline Perny, Renata Sweeney, Natalie Zutter, as well as Matt Johnson over at Macmillan Sales, to name but a few of the host—all of them rad goth angels with leather jackets. I know there has been even more work done on my behalf than I quite understand, and their support, enthusiasm, and kindness throughout has been incredible. I am also grateful to Tommy Arnold, for incredible cover work, and Jamie Stafford-Hill for equally incredible layouts and design.

Very special thanks to Clemency Pleming and Megan Smith, first readers always, who have married each other since my last acknowledgments. Maz, you are her cavalier; that is illegal.

To everyone who got to read *Gideon the Ninth* prepub and were so enormously kind, vocal, and supportive: thank you so much. I wish I could list all their names here, but there were so many, and they did so many things, that I am afraid of leaving someone out. The tireless work of booksellers, reviewers, bloggers, and fellow authors humbled me as much as it astonished me.

I am very thankful for the people who have broken bread with me and listened to me grumble—Lissa, Bo and Ben, the Wests, Ben Raynor, Chris Douglas. My Clarion class remains treasures, one and all. Isabel Yap is a light to many, but a bonfire to me; as dedicated,

Gideon the Ninth would in a very real way not exist without her, and *Harrow the Ninth* owes her a huge and different debt. Thanks again to my family for their unending love and support, especially Andrew, who nonetheless cannot go five minutes without telling people about the time I ate too much chocolate mousse.

Harrowhark Nonagesimus did not have anyone to put soluble banana-flavoured antipsychotics under her tongue for her condition. I do, and therefore I would like to thank every key worker in my past who had to administer me medication, because they were always nice about it and often I was not.

Ultimately, I thank Matt Hosty, who mopped more blood, brewed more tea, and without whom this book would have been an excuse note. Matt, the best of this book is you. I can't wait for you to see the next one. I don't want to shock you, but it's got . . . *bones.*